About

Carol Marinelli recen_____ her job title. Thrilled to _____ she put writer. Then _____ relaxation and she put down the truth———————— third question asked for her hobbies. Well, not wanting to look obsessed she crossed the fingers on her hand and answered swimming but, given that the chlorine in the pool does terrible things to her highlights – I'm sure you can guess the real answer.

Marion Lennox is a country girl, born on an Australian dairy farm. She moved on, because the cows just weren't interested in her stories! Married to a 'very special doctor', she has also written under the name Trisha David. She's now stepped back from her 'other' career teaching statistics. Finally, she's figured what's important and discovered the joys of baths, romance and chocolate. Preferably all at the same time! Marion is an international award winning author.

Lynne Graham lives in Northern Ireland and has been a keen romance reader since her teens. Happily married, Lynne has five children. Her eldest is her only natural child. Her other children, who are every bit as dear to her heart, are adopted. The family has a variety of pets, and Lynne loves gardening, cooking, collecting all sorts and is crazy about every aspect of Christmas.

A Cinderella Story

COLLECTION

Working with Cinderella

CAROL MARINELLI

MARION LENNOX

LYNNE GRAHAM

MILLS & BOON

First Published in Great Britain 2020
By Mills & Boon, an imprint of HarperCollins*Publishers*
1 London Bridge Street, London, SE1 9GF

WORKING WITH CINDERELLA © 2020 Harlequin Books S.A.

Beholden to the Throne © 2013 Carol Marinelli
Cinderella: Hired by the Prince © 2010 Marion Lennox.
The Dimitrakos Proposition © 2014 Lynne Graham

ISBN 978-0-263-28079-1

0220

Printed and bound in Spain
by CPI, Barcelona

BEHOLDEN TO
THE THRONE

CAROL MARINELLI

For Penny Jordan
Who made me fall in love with Sheikhs.
Rest in peace, Penny.
Loved, missed and always remembered
C xxx

CHAPTER ONE

'SHEIKH King Emir has agreed that he will speak with you.'

Amy looked up as Fatima, one of the servants, entered the nursery where Amy was feeding the young Princesses their dinner. 'Thank you for letting me know. What time—?'

'He is ready for you now,' Fatima interrupted, impatience evident in her voice at Amy's lack of haste, for Amy continued to feed the twins.

'They're just having their dinner…' Amy started, but didn't bother to continue—after all, what would the King know about his daughters' routines? Emir barely saw the twins and, quite simply, it was breaking Amy's heart.

What would he know about how clingy they had become lately and how fussy they were with their food? It was one of the reasons Amy had requested a meeting with him—tomorrow they were to be handed over to the Bedouins. First they would be immersed in the desert oasis and then they would be handed over to strangers for the night. It was a tradition that dated back centuries,

Fatima had told her, and it was a tradition that could not be challenged.

Well, Amy would see about that!

The little girls had lost their mother when they were just two weeks old, and since his wife's death Emir had hardly seen them. It was Amy they relied on. Amy who was with them day in and day out. Amy they trusted. She would not simply hand them over to strangers without a fight on their behalf.

'I will look after the twins and give them dinner,' Fatima said. 'You need to make yourself presentable for your audience with the King.' She ran disapproving eyes over Amy's pale blue robe, which was the uniform of the Royal Nanny. It had been fresh on that morning, but now it wore the telltale signs that she had been finger-painting with Clemira and Nakia this afternoon. Surely Emir should not care about the neatness of her robe? He should expect that if the nanny was doing her job properly she would be less than immaculate in appearance. But, again, what would Emir know about the goings-on in the nursery? He hadn't been in to visit his daughters for weeks.

Amy changed into a fresh robe and retied her shoulder-length blonde hair into a neat ponytail. Then she covered her hair with a length of darker blue silk, arranging the cloth around her neck and leaving the end to trail over her shoulder. She wore no make-up but, as routinely as most women might check their lipstick, Amy checked to see that the scar low on her neck was covered by the silk. She hated how, in any conversation, eyes were often drawn to it, and more than that she hated the inevitable questions that followed.

The accident and its aftermath were something she would far rather forget than discuss.

'They are too fussy with their food,' Fatima said as Amy walked back into the nursery.

Amy suppressed a smile as Clemira pulled a face and then grabbed at the spoon Fatima was offering and threw it to the floor.

'They just need to be cajoled,' Amy explained. 'They haven't eaten this before.'

'They need to know how to behave!' Fatima said. 'There will be eyes on them when they are out in public, and tomorrow they leave to go to the desert—there they must eat only fruit, and the desert people will not be impressed by two spoiled princesses spitting out their food.' She looked Amy up and down. 'Remember to bow your head when you enter, and to keep it bowed until the King speaks. And you are to thank him for any suggestions that he makes.'

Thank him!

Amy bit down on a smart retort. It would be wasted on Fatima and, after all, she might do better to save her responses for Emir. As she turned to go, Clemira, only now realising that she was being left with Fatima, called out to Amy.

'Ummi!' her little voice wailed. 'Ummi!'

She called again and Fatima stared in horror as Clemira used the Arabic word for mother.

'Is this what she calls you?'

'She doesn't mean it,' Amy said quickly, but Fatima was standing now, the twins' dinner forgotten, fury evident on her face.

'What have you been teaching her?' Fatima accused.

'I have *not* been teaching her to say it,' Amy said in panic. 'I've been trying to stop her.'

She had been. Over and over she had repeated her name these past few days, but the twins had discovered a new version. Clemira must have picked it up from the stories she had heard Amy tell, and from the small gatherings they attended with other children who naturally called out to their mothers. No matter how often she was corrected, Clemira persisted with her new word.

'It's a similar sound,' Amy explained. But just as she thought she had perhaps rectified the situation, Nakia, as always, copied her sister.

'Ummi,' Nakia joined in with the tearful protest.

'Amy!' Amy corrected, but she could feel the disgust emanating from Fatima.

'If the King ever hears of this there will be trouble!' Fatima warned. 'Serious trouble.'

'I know!' Amy bit back on tears as she left the nursery. She tried to block out the cries that followed her down the long corridor as she made her way deep into the palace.

This meeting with the King was necessary, Amy told herself, as nerves started to catch up with her. Something had to be said.

Still, even if she *had* requested this audience, she was not relishing the prospect. Sheikh King Emir of Alzan was not exactly open to conversation—at least not since the death of Hannah. The walls were lined with paintings of previous rulers, all dark and imposing men, but since the death of Emir's wife, none was more imposing than Emir—and in a moment she must face him.

Must face him, Amy told herself as she saw the guards standing outside his door. As difficult as this conversation might be, there were things that needed to be said and she wanted to say them before she headed into the desert with the King and his daughters—for this was a discussion that must take place well away from tender ears.

Amy halted at the heavy, intricately carved doors and waited until finally the guards nodded and the doors were opened. She saw an office that reminded her of a courtroom. Emir sat at a large desk, dressed in black robes and wearing a *kafeya*. He took centre stage and the aides and elders sat around him. Somehow she must find the courage to state her case.

'Head down!' she was brusquely reminded by a guard.

Amy did as she was told and stepped in. She was not allowed to look at the King yet, but could feel his dark eyes drift over her as a rapid introduction was made in Arabic by his senior aide, Patel. Amy stood with her head bowed, as instructed, until finally Emir spoke.

'You have been requesting to see me for some days now, yet I am told the twins are not unwell.'

His voice was deep and rich with accent. Amy had not heard him speak in English for so very long—his visits to the nursery were always brief, and when there he spoke just a few words in Arabic to his daughters before leaving. Standing there, hearing him speak again, Amy realised with a nervous jolt how much she had missed hearing his voice.

She remembered those precious days after the twins had been born and how approachable he'd been then. Emir had been a harried king, if there was such a thing, and like any new father to twins—especially with a sick wife. He had been grateful for any suggestion she'd made to help with the tiny babies—so much so that Amy had often forgotten that he was King and they had been on first-name terms. It was hard to imagine that he had ever been so approachable now, but she held on to that image as she lifted her head and faced him, determined to reach the father he was rather than the King.

'Clemira and Nakia are fine,' Amy started. 'Well, physically they are fine…' She watched as his haughty face moved to a frown. 'I wanted to speak to you about their progress, and also about the tradition that they—'

'Tomorrow we fly out to the desert,' Emir interrupted. 'We will be there for twenty-four hours. I am sure there will be ample time then to discuss their progress.'

'But I want to speak about this well away from the twins. It might upset them to hear what I have to say.'

'They are turning one,' Emir stated. 'It's hardly as if they can understand what we are discussing.'

'They might be able to…'

Amy felt as if she were choking—could feel the scar beneath the silk around her neck inflame. For she knew how it felt to lie silent, knew how it felt to hear and not be able to respond. She knew exactly what it was like to have your life discussed around you and not be able to partake in the conversation. She simply would not let this happen to the twins. Even if there was only a slight chance that they might understand what was being said, Amy would not take that risk. Anyway, she was here for more than simply to discuss their progress.

'Fatima told me that the twins are to spend the night with the Bedouins…'

He nodded.

'I don't think that is such a good idea,' Amy went on. 'They are very clingy at the moment. They get upset if I even leave the room.'

'Which is the whole point of the separation.' Emir was unmoved. 'All royals must spend time each year with the desert people.'

'But they are so young!'

'It is the way things have long been done. It is a rule in both Alzan and Alzirz and it is not open for discussion.'

It hurt, but she had no choice but to accept that, Amy realised, for this was a land where rules and traditions were strictly followed. All she could do was make the separation as easy as possible on the twins.

'There are other things I need to speak with you about.' Amy glanced around the room—although she was unsure how many of the guards and aides spoke English, she knew that Patel did. 'It might be better if we speak in private?' Amy suggested.

'Private?' Emir questioned. His irritation made it

clear that there was nothing Amy could possibly say that might merit clearing the room. 'There is no need for that. Just say what you came to.'

'But…'

'Just say it!'

He did not shout, but there was anger and impatience in his voice, and Emir's eyes held a challenge. Quite simply, Amy did not recognise him—or rather she did not recognise him as the man she had known a year ago. Oh, he had been a fierce king then, and a stern ruler, but he had also been a man sensitive to his sick wife's needs, a man who had put duty and protocol aside to look after his ailing wife and their new babies. But today there was no mistaking it. Amy was speaking not with the husband and father she had first met, but to the King of Alzan.

'The children so rarely see you,' Amy attempted, in front of this most critical audience. 'They *miss* seeing you.'

'They have told you this, have they?' His beautiful mouth was sullied as it moved to a smirk. 'I was not aware that they had such an advanced vocabulary.'

A small murmur of laughter came from Patel before he stepped forward. 'The King does not need to hear this,' Patel said. Aware that this was her only chance to speak with him before they set off tomorrow, Amy pushed on.

'Perhaps not, but the children do need their father. They need—'

'There is nothing to discuss.' It was Emir who terminated the conversation. Barely a minute into their

meeting he ended it with a flick of his hand and Amy
was dismissed. The guards opened the door and Patel
indicated that she should leave. But instead of following the silent order to bow her head meekly and depart,
Amy stood her ground.

'On the contrary—there's an awful lot that we need
to discuss!'

She heard the shocked gasp from the aides, felt the
rise in tension from everyone present in the room, for
no one in this land would dare argue with the King—
and certainly not a mere nanny.

'I apologise, Your Highness.' Patel came over to
where Amy stood and addressed the King in a reveren-
tial voice. That voice was only for the King—when he
spoke to Amy Patel was stern, suggesting in no uncertain terms that she leave the room this very moment.

'I need to be heard!'

'The King has finished speaking with you,' Patel
warned her.

'Well, I haven't finished speaking with *him*!' Amy's
voice rose, and as it did so, it wavered—but only slightly.
Her blue eyes blinked, perhaps a little rapidly, but she
met the King's black stare as she dared to confront him.
Yes, she was nervous—terrified, in fact—but she had
come this far and she simply could not stay quiet for a
moment longer.

'Your Highness, I really do need to speak with you
about your daughters before we go to the desert. As
you know, I have been requesting an audience with you
for days now. On my contract it states that I will meet

regularly with the parents of the twins to discuss any concerns.'

It appalled her that she even had to request an appointment with him for such a thing, and that when he finally deigned to see her he could so rapidly dismiss her. He didn't even have the courtesy to hear her out, to find out what she had to say about his children. Amy was incensed.

'When I accepted the role of Royal Nanny it was on the understanding that I was to *assist* in the raising of the twins and that when they turned four...' Her voice trailed off as once again Emir ignored her. He had turned to Patel and was speaking in Arabic. Amy stood quietly fuming as a file—presumably *her* file—was placed in front of Emir and he took a moment to read through it.

'You signed a four-year contract,' Emir stated. 'You will be here till the twins leave for London to pursue their education and then we will readdress the terms, that is what was agreed.'

'So am I expected to wait another three years before we discuss the children?' Amy forgot then that he was a king—forgot her surrounds entirely. She was so angry with him that she was at her caustic best. 'I'm expected to wait another three years before we address any issues? If you want to talk about the contract, then fine—we will! The fact is the contract we both signed isn't being adhered to from your end!' Amy flared. 'You can't just pick and choose which clauses you keep to.'

'Enough!'

It was Patel who responded. He would not let his

King be bothered with such trivialities. He summoned the guard to drag her out if required, but as the guard unceremoniously took her arm to escort her out, Amy stood firm. The veil covering her hair slithered from its position as she tried to shake the guard off.

It was Emir who halted this rather undignified exit. He did not need a guard to deal with this woman and he put up his hand to stop him, said something that was presumably an instruction to release her, because suddenly the guard let go his grip on her arm.

'Go on,' Emir challenged, his eyes narrowing as he stared over to the woman who had just dared to confront him—the woman who had dared suggest that he, Sheikh King Emir of Alzan, had broken an agreement that bore his signature. 'Tell me where I have broken my word.'

She stood before him, a little more shaken, a touch more breathless, but grateful for another chance to be heard. 'The twins need a parent…' He did not even blink. 'As I said, my role is to assist in the raising of the twins both here in the palace and on regular trips to London.' Perhaps, Amy decided, it would be safer to start with less emotive practicalities. 'I haven't been home in over a year.'

'Go on,' he replied.

Amy took a deep breath, wondering how best to broach this sensitively, for he really was listening now. 'The girls need more than I can give them—they…' She struggled to continue for a moment. The twins needed love, and she had plenty of that for them, but it was a parent that those two precious girls needed most. Somehow she had to tell him that—had to remind him what Hannah had wanted for her daughters. 'Until they turn four I'm supposed to *assist* in their raising. It was agreed that I have two evenings and two nights off a week, but instead—'

He interrupted her again and spoke in rapid Arabic to Patel. There was a brief conversation between the aides before he turned back to her. 'Very well. Fatima will help you with the care of the children. You will have your days off from now on, and my staff will look into your annual leave arrangements.'

She couldn't believe it—could not believe how he had turned things around. He had made it seem as if all she was here for was to discuss her holiday entitlements.

'That will be all.'

'No!' This time she did shout, but her voice did not waver—on behalf of the twins, Amy was determined to be heard. 'That isn't the point I was trying to make. I am to *assist*—my job is to *assist* the parents in the raising of the children, not to bring them up alone. I would never have accepted the role otherwise.' She wouldn't have. Amy knew that. She had thought she was entering a loving family—not one where children, or rather female children, were ignored. 'When Queen Hannah interviewed me...'

Emir's face paled—his dark skin literally paled in the blink of an eye—and there was a flash of pain across his haughty features at the mention of his late wife. It was as if her words were ice that he was biting down on and he flinched. But almost instantaneously the pain dispersed, anger replacing it.

He stood. He did not need to, for already she was silent, already she had realised the error of her ways. From behind his desk Emir rose to his impressive height and the whole room was still and silent. No one more so than Amy, for Emir was an imposing man and not just in title. He stood well over six foot and was broad shouldered, toned. There was the essence of a warrior to him—a man of the desert who would never be tamed. But Emir was more than a warrior, he was a ruler too—a fierce ruler—and she had dared to talk back at him, had dared to touch on a subject that was most definitely, most painfully, closed.

'Leave!'

He roared the single word and this time Amy chose to obey his command, for his black eyes glittered with fury and the scar that ran through his left eyebrow was prominent, making his features more savage. Amy knew beyond doubt that she had crossed a line. There were so many lines that you did not cross here in Alzan, so many things that could not be said while working at the palace, but to speak of the late Queen Hannah, to talk of happier times, to bring up the past with King Emir wasn't simply speaking out of turn, or merely crossing a line—it was a leap that only the foolish would take. Knowing she was beaten, Amy turned to go.

'Not you!' His voice halted her exit. 'The rest of you are to leave.'

Amy turned around slowly, met the eyes of an angry

sheikh king. She had upset him, and now she must face him alone.

'The nanny is to stay.'

CHAPTER TWO

THE *nanny*.

As Amy stood there awaiting her fate those words replayed and burnt in her ears—she was quite sure that he had forgotten her name. She was raising his children and he knew nothing about her. Not that she would address it, for she would be lucky to keep her job now. Amy's heart fluttered in wild panic because she could not bear to leave the twins, could not stand to be sent home without the chance to even say goodbye.

It was that thought that propelled her apology.

'Please...' she started. 'I apologise.' But he ignored her as the room slowly cleared.

'Patel, that means you too,' Emir said when his senior aide still hovered, despite the others having left.

When Patel reluctantly followed the rest and closed the door, for the first time in almost a year Amy was alone with him—only this time she was terrified.

'You were saying?' he challenged.

'I should not have.'

'It's a bit late for reticence,' Emir said. 'You now have

the privacy that you asked for. You have your chance to speak. So why have you suddenly lost your voice?'

'I haven't.'

'Then speak.'

Amy could not look at him. Gone now was her boldness. She drew in a deep breath and, staring down, saw that her hands were pleated together. Very deliberately she separated them and placed her arms at her sides, forced her chin up to meet his stare. He was right—she had the audience she had requested. A very private, very intimidating audience, but at least now she had a chance to speak with the King. On behalf of Clemira and Nakia she would force herself to do so while she still had the chance. Amy was well aware that he would probably fire her, but she hoped that if he listened even to a little of what she had to say things might change.

They had to.

Which was why she forced herself to speak.

'When I was hired it was on the understanding that I was to assist in the raising of the children.' Her voice was calmer now, even if her heart was not. 'Queen Hannah was very specific in her wishes for the girls and we had similar values…' She faltered then, for she should not compare herself to the late Queen. 'Rather, I admired Queen Hannah's values—I understood what she wanted for her girls, and we spoke at length about their future. It was the reason why I signed such a long contract.'

'Go on,' Emir invited.

'When I took the job I understood that her pregnancy had made the Queen unwell—that it might take some considerable time for her to recover and that she might not be able to do all she wanted to for the babies. However—'

'I am sure Queen Hannah would have preferred that you were just *assisting* her in the raising of the twins,' Emir interrupted. 'I am sure that when she hired you, Queen Hannah had no intention of dying.' His lip curled in disdain as he looked down at Amy and his words dripped sarcasm. 'I apologise for the inconvenience.'

'No!' Amy refused to let him turn things around again—refused to let him miss her point. 'If Queen Hannah were still alive I would happily get up to the twins ten times in the night if I had to. She was a wonderful woman, an amazing mother, and I would have done anything for her...' Amy meant every word she said. She had admired the Queen so much, had adored her for her forward thinking and for the choices she had made to ensure the happiness of her girls. 'I would have done anything for Queen Hannah, but I—'

'You will have assistance,' Emir said. 'I will see that Fatima—'

She could not believe that he still didn't get it. Bold again now, she interrupted the King. 'It's not another nanny that the twins need. It's *you*! I am tired of getting up at night while their father sleeps.'

'Their father is the King.' His voice was both angry and incredulous. 'Their father is busy running the country. I am trying to push through a modern maternity hospital with a cardiac ward to ensure no other woman suffers as my wife did. Today I have twenty workers trapped in the emerald mines. But instead of reaching out to my people I have to hear about *your* woes. The people I rule are nervous as to the future of their country and yet you expect me, the King, to get up at night to a crying child?'

'You used to!' Amy was instant in her response. 'You used to get up to your babies.'

And there it was again—that flash of pain across his features. Only this time it did not dissipate. This time it remained. His eyes were screwed closed, he pressed his thumb and finger to the bridge of his nose and she could hear his hard breathing. Amy realised that somewhere inside was the Emir she had known and she was desperate to contact him again, to see the loving father he had once been returned to his daughters—it was for that reason she continued.

'I would bring Queen Hannah one of the twins for feeding while you would take care of the other.'

He removed his hand from his face, and stood there as she spoke, his fists clenched, his face so rigid and taut that she could see a muscle flickering beneath his eye. And she knew that it was pain not rage that she was witnessing, Amy was quite sure of it, for as sad as those times had been still they had been precious.

'And, no, I don't honestly expect you to get up at night to your babies, but is it too much for you to come in and see them each day? Is it too much to ask that you take a more active role in their lives? They are starting to talk…'

He shook his head—a warning, perhaps, that she

should not continue—but she had to let him know all that he was missing out on, even if it cost her her job.

'Clemira is standing now. She pulls herself up on the furniture and Nakia tries to copy—she claps and smiles and...'

'Stop.' His word was a raw husk.

'No!' She would not stop. Could not stop.

Amy was too upset to register properly the plea in his voice, for she was crying now. The scarf that had slipped from her head as she made her case unravelled and fell to the floor. She wanted to grab it, retrieve it, for she felt his eyes move to her neck, to the beastly scar that was there—her permanent reminder of hell—but her hands did not fly to her neck in an attempt to cover it. She had more important things on her mind—two little girls whose births she had witnessed, two little girls who had won her heart—and her voice broke as she choked out the truth.

'You need to know that things are happening with your children. It is their first birthday in two days' time and they'll be terrified in the desert—terrified to be parted from me. And then, when they return to the Palace, they'll be dressed up and trotted out for the people to admire. You will hold them, and they will be so happy that you do, but then you will go back to ignoring them...' She was going to be fired, Amy knew it, so she carried on speaking while she still could. 'I cannot stand to see how they are being treated.'

'They are treated like the princesses they are!' Emir flared. 'They have everything—'

'They have *nothing*!' Amy shouted. 'They have the best clothes and cots and furniture and jewels, and it means nothing because they don't have *you*. Just because they're gi—' Amy stopped herself from saying it, halted her words, but it was already too late.

'Go on.' His words invited her but his tone and stance did not.

'I think that I have already said enough.' There was no point saying any more, Amy realised. Emir was not going to change at her bidding. The country was not going to embrace the girls just because she did. So she picked up her scarf and replaced it. 'Thank you for your time, Your Highness.'

She turned to go and as she did his voice halted her.

'Amy...'

So he did remember her name.

She turned to look at him, met his black gaze full on. The pain was still there, witness to the agony this year must have been for him, but even as she recognised it, it vanished. His features were hardening in anger now, and the voice he had used to call her changed in that instant.

His words were stern when they came. 'It is not your place to question our ways.'

'What *is* my place?'

'An employee.'

Oh, he'd made things brutally clear, but at least it sounded as if she still had a job—at least she would not be sent away from the twins. 'I'll remember that in future.'

'You would be very wise to,' Emir said, watching as

she bowed and then walked out, leaving him standing for once alone in his sumptuous office. But not for long. Patel walked in almost the second that Amy had gone, ready to resume, for there was still much to be taken care of even at this late stage in the day.

'I apologise, Your Highness,' Patel said as he entered. 'I should never have allowed her to speak with you directly—you should not have been troubled with such trivial things.'

But Emir put up his hand to halt him. Patel's words only exacerbated his hell. 'Leave me.'

Unlike Amy, Patel knew better than to argue with the King and did as he was told. Once alone again Emir dragged in air and walked over to the window, looking out to the desert where tomorrow he would take the twins.

He was dreading it.

For reasons he could not even hint at to another, he dreaded tomorrow and the time he would spend with his children. He dreaded not just handing them over to the desert people for the night, but the time before that—seeing them standing, clapping, laughing, trying to talk, as Amy had described.

Their confrontation had more than unsettled him. Not because she had dared to speak in such a way, more because she had stated the truth.

The truth that Emir was well aware of.

Amy was right. He *had* got up at night to them when they were born. They *had* pulled together. Although it had never been voiced, both had seemed to know that they were battling against time and had raced to give Hannah as many precious moments with her babies as they could squeeze in.

He looked to his desk, to the picture of his wife and their daughters. He seemed to be smiling in the photo but his eyes were not, for he had known just how sick his wife was. Had known the toll the twins' pregnancy had taken on her heart. Six months into the pregnancy they had found out she had a weakness. Three months later she was dead.

And while Hannah was smiling in the photo also, there was a sadness in her eyes too. Had she known then that she was dying? Emir wondered. Had it been the knowledge that she would have but a few more days with her daughters that had brought dark clouds to her eyes? Or had it been the knowledge that the kingdom of Alzan needed a male heir if it was to continue? Without a son Alzan would return to Alzirz and be under Sheikh King Rakhal's rule.

He hated the words Hannah had said on the birth of their gorgeous daughters—loathed the fact that she had apologised to him for delivering two beautiful girls. His heart thumped in his chest as if he were charging into battle as silently he stood, gave his mind rare permission to recall Hannah's last words. The blood seared as it raced through his veins, and his eyes closed as her voice spoke again to him. 'Promise you will do your best for our girls.'

How? Emir demanded to a soul that refused to rest. Any day now Rakhal's wife, Natasha, was due to give birth. The rules were different in Alzirs, for there a princess could become Queen and rule.

How Rakhal would gloat when his child was born—especially if it was a son.

Emir's face darkened at the thought of his rival. He picked up the two stones that sat on his desk and held them. Though they should be cool to the touch the rare pink sapphires seemed to burn in his palm. Rakhal had been a prince when he had given him this gift to *celebrate* the arrival of the girls—a gift that had been delivered on the morning Hannah had died.

Hannah had thought them to be rubies—had really believed that the troubles between the two kingdoms might finally be fading.

Emir had let her hold that thought, had let her think the gift was a kind gesture from Rakhal, even while fully understanding the vile message behind it—sapphires were meant to be blue.

Without a male heir the kingdom of Alzan would end.

Emir hurled the precious stones across his office, heard the clatter as they hit the wall and wished they would shatter as his brain felt it might.

He hated Rakhal, but more than that Emir hated the decision that he was slowly coming to. For it was not only Hannah who had begged for reassurance on her deathbed—he had held his dying father out in the desert. He had not been able to see the King dying because blood had been pouring from a wound above Emir's eye, but he had heard his father's plea, had given his solemn word that he would do his best for his country.

Two promises he could not meet.

Emir knew he could keep but one.

His decision could not—*must* not—be based on emotion, so he picked up the photo and took one long, last look, tracing his finger over Hannah's face and the image of his girls. And then he placed it face down in a drawer and closed it.

He could not look them.

Must not.

Somehow he had to cast emotion aside as he weighed the future—not just for his children, but for the country he led.

CHAPTER THREE

IT WAS too hot to sleep.

The fan above the bed barely moved the still night air, and the fact that Amy had been crying since she put the twins down for the night did not help. Her face was hot and red, so Amy climbed out of bed, opened the French windows and stepped out onto the balcony, wishing for cool night air to hit her cheeks. But in Alzan the nights were warm and, despite a soft breeze, there was no respite.

The desert was lit by a near full moon and Amy looked out across the pale sands in the direction of Alzirz—there, the nights were cold, she had been told. Amy wished that she were there now—not just for the cool of the night, but for other reasons too. In Alzirz a princess could rule.

There girls were not simply dismissed.

But even that didn't ring true. In many ways Alzan was progressive too—there were universities for women, and on Queen Hannah's death the King had ordered that a state-of-the-art maternity hospital be built in her name—not only with the cardiac ward he had mentioned but free obstetric care for all. Sheikh King Emir had pushed his people slowly forward, yet the royals themselves stayed grounded in the ways of old, bound by rules from the past.

The two lands had long ago been one, she had been told—Alzanirz—but they had been separated many generations ago and were now fierce rivals.

She had met King Rakhal and his wife, Natasha, on a few occasions. Natasha was always disarmingly nice and interested in the girls; Rakhal, on the other hand, despite his cool politeness, was guarded. Amy had felt the hatred simmering between the two men, had almost been able to taste the deep rivalry that existed whenever they were both in a room.

Still, it was not the rival King who troubled her tonight, nor was it the King who employed her.

It was her own soul.

She had to leave. She was too involved. Of course she was. Realising the toll her job was taking on her daughter, Amy's mother was urging her to come home. But as Amy stared out to the sands she was conflicted—she simply could not imagine abandoning the twins.

Ummi.

It hurt to hear that word from Clemira and Nakia and to know she would never be one herself.

Amy gulped in air, determined not to start crying again, but though she was dealing with things better these days—though for the most part she had come to terms with her fate—on nights like tonight sometimes the pain surfaced. Sometimes all she could do was mourn a time when happiness had seemed more certain.

Or had it?

She closed her eyes and tried to remember, tried to peer into the dark black hole that was the months and weeks leading up to her accident. Slowly, painfully slowly, she was starting to remember things—choosing her wedding dress, the invitations—but all she could see were images. She simply couldn't recall how she had felt.

Amy had always worked with children, and had been about to marry and start a family of her own when a riding accident had ruined everything. Her hopes and dreams, her relationship and even her fertility had all been taken in one cruel swoop.

Maybe it was for best, Amy pondered—perhaps it was kinder *not* to remember happier times.

It had been a relief to get away from London, to escape the sympathy and the attention. But Amy's mother had warned her about taking this job—had said it was too much and too soon, that she was running away from her problems. She hadn't been.

The thought of being involved with two babies from birth, of having a very real role in their lives, had been so tempting. Queen Hannah had been well aware of the challenges her daughters would face, and she had told Amy about the disappointment that would sweep the country if her pregnancy produced girls—especially if it proved too dangerous for Hannah to get pregnant again.

Hannah had wanted the girls to be educated in London, to live as ordinary girls there. The plan had been that for four years Amy would take care of the girls in Alzan, but that they would then be schooled in the UK. Amy was to be a huge part of their lives—not a mother, of course, but more than an aunt.

How could she leave now?

How could she walk away because she didn't like the way they were being treated?

Yet how could she stay?

Amy headed down the corridor to do a final check on the twins, her bare feet making no sound. It was a path she trod many times during the day and night, especially now that they were teething. The link from her suite to the twins' sumptuous quarters was a familiar one, but as she entered the room Amy froze—for the sight that greeted her was far from familiar.

There was Emir, his back to her, holding Clemira, who slept on his chest, her head resting on his shoulder, as if it was where she belonged.

Emir stood, silent and strong, and there was a sadness in him that he would surely not want her to witness—a weariness that had only been visible in the first few days after Hannah's death. Then he had gone into *tahir*—had taken himself to the desert for a time of ritual and deep prayer and contemplation. The man who returned to the palace had been different—a remote, aloof man who only occasionally deigned to visit the nursery.

He was far from aloof now as he cradled Clemira. He was wearing black silk lounge pants and nothing else. His top half was bare. Amy had seen him like this before, but then it had not moved her.

In the first dizzy days after the twins had been born they had grappled through the night with two tiny babies. Amy had changed one nappy and handed one fresh, clean baby to Emir, so he could take her to Hannah to feed. Things had been so different then—despite their concern for Hannah there had been love and laughter filling the palace and she missed it so, missed the man she had glimpsed then.

Tonight, for a moment, perhaps that man had returned.

He'd lost weight since then, she noted. His muscles were now a touch more defined. But there was such tenderness as he held his daughter. It was an intimate glimpse of father and daughter and again she doubted he would want it witnessed. She could sense the aching grief in his wide shoulders—so much so that for a bizarre moment Amy wanted to walk up to him, rest her hand there and offer him silent support. Yet she knew he would not want that, and given she was wearing only her nightdress it was better that she quietly slip away.

'Are you considering leaving?

He turned around just as she was about to go. Amy could not look at him. Normally her head was covered, and her body too—she wondered if she would be chastised tomorrow for being unsuitably dressed—but for now Emir did not appear to notice.

She answered his question as best she could. 'I don't know what to do.'

Clemira stirred in his arms. Gently he placed her

back in her crib and stared down at his daughter for the longest time before turning back to Amy.

'You've been crying.'

'There's an awful lot to cry about.' His black eyes did not reproach her this time. 'I never thought I'd be considering leaving, When Hannah interviewed me—I mean Sheikha Queen—'

'Hannah,' he interrupted. 'That is the name she requested you call her.'

Amy was grateful for the acknowledgement, but she could not speak of this in front of the twins—could not have this conversation without breaking down. So she wished him goodnight and headed back to her room.

'Amy!' he called out to her.

She kept on walking, determined to make it to her room before breaking down, stunned when he followed her through the door.

'You cannot leave Alzan now. I think it would be better for the twins—'

'Of *course* it would be better for the twins to have me stay!' she interrupted, although she should not. Her voice rose again, although it should not. But she was furious. 'Of *course* the twins should have somebody looking after them who loves them—except it's not my job to love them. I'm an employee.'

She watched his eyes shutter for a moment as she hurled back his choice word, but he was right—she *was* an employee, and could be fired at any moment, could be removed from the twins' lives by the flick of his hand.

She was thankful for his brutal reminder earlier. She would do well to remember her place.

She brushed past him, trying to get to the safety of the balcony, for it was stifling with him in the room, but before she could get there he halted her.

'You do *not* walk off when I'm talking to you!'

'I do when you're in *my* bedroom!' Amy turned and faced him. 'This happens to be the one place in this prison of a palace where *I* get to make the rules, where I get to speak as I choose, and if you don't like it, if you don't want to hear it, *you* can leave.'

She wanted him out of the room, she wanted him gone, and yet he stepped closer, and it was Amy who stepped back, acutely aware of his maleness, shamefully aware of her own body's conflicted response.

Anger burnt and hissed, but something else did too, for he was an impressive male, supremely beautiful, and of course she had noticed—what woman would not? But down there in his office, or in the safety of the nursery, he was the King and the twins' father, down there he was her boss, but here in this room he was something else.

Somehow she must not show it, so instead she hurled words. 'I *do* love your children, and it's tearing me apart to even think of walking away, but it's been nearly a year since Hannah died and I can't make excuses any more. If they were my children and you ignored them, then I'd have left you by now. The only difference is I'd have taken them with me...' Her face was red with fury, her blue eyes awash with fresh tears, but there was something more—something she could not tell him. It meant she had to—*had to*—consider leaving, because sometimes when she looked at Emir she wanted the man he had once been to return, and shamefully, guiltily, despite herself, she wanted *him*.

She tore her eyes from his, terrified as to what he might see, and yet he stepped towards her, deliberately stepped towards her. She fought the urge to move towards him—to feel the wrap of his arms around her, for him to shield her from this hell.

It was a hell of his own making, though, Amy remembered, moving away from him and stepping out onto the balcony, once again ruing the sultry nights.

But it was not just the night that was oppressive. He had joined her outside. She gulped in air, wished the breeze would cool, for it was not just her face that was burning. She felt as if her body was on fire.

'Soon I will marry...' He saw her shoulders tense, watched her hands grip the balcony, and as the breeze caught her nightdress it outlined her shape, detailing soft curves. In that moment Emir could not speak—was this the first time he'd noticed her as a woman?

No.

But this was the first time he allowed himself to properly acknowledge it.

He had seen her in the nursery when he had visited the children a few weeks ago. That day he had sat through a difficult meeting with his elders and advisers, hearing that Queen Natasha was due to give birth soon and being told that soon he must marry.

Emir did not like to be told to do anything, and he rarely ever was.

But in this he was powerless and it did not sit well.

He had walked into the nursery, dark thoughts chasing him. But seeing Amy sitting reading to the twins, her blue eyes looking up, smiling as he entered, he had felt his black thoughts leave him. For the first time in months he had glimpsed peace. Had wanted to stay awhile with his children, with the woman he and Hannah had entrusted to care for them.

He had wanted to hide.

But a king could not hide.

Now what he saw was not so soothing. Now her soft femininity did not bring peace. For a year his passion might as well have been buried in the sands with his wife. For a year he had not fought temptation—there had been none. But something had changed since that moment in the nursery, since that day when he had noticed not just her smile but her mouth, not just her words but her voice. At first those thoughts had been stealthy, invading dreams over which he had no control, but now they were bolder and crept in by day. The scent of her perfume in an empty corridor might suddenly reach him, telling him the path she had recently walked, reminding him of a buried dream. And the mention of her name when she had requested a meeting had hauled him from loftier thoughts to ones more basic.

And basic were his thoughts now, yet he fought them.

He tried to look at the problem, not the temptation before him, the woman standing with her back to him. He wanted to turn her around, wanted to in a way he hadn't in a long time. But he was not locked in dreams now. He had control here and he forced himself to speak on.

'I did look through your contract and you are right. It has not been adhered to.'

Still she did not turn to look at him, though her body told her to. She wished he would leave—could not deal with him here even if it was to discuss the twins.

'After their birthday things are going to get busy here,' Emir said.

'When you select your bride and marry?'

He did not answer directly. 'These are complicated times for Alzan. Perhaps it would be better if the girls spent some time in London—a holiday.'

She closed her eyes, knew what was coming. Yes, a flight on his luxury jet, a few weeks at home with the twins, time with her family, luxurious hotels... What was there to say no to? Except... She took a deep breath and turned to him. 'Without you?'

'Yes,' Emir said.

She looked at the man who had so loved his children, who was now so closed off, so remote, so able to turn from them, and she had to know why.

'Is it because they remind you of Hannah?' Amy asked. 'Is that why it hurts so much to have them around?'

'Leave it,' he said. He wished the answer was that simple, wished there was someone in whom he could confide. 'I will have the trip scheduled.'

'So you can remove them a bit more from your life?'

'You do *not* talk to me like that.'

'Here I do.'

'Once I am married the twins will have a mother figure…'

'Oh, please!'

He frowned at her inappropriate response, but that did not deter her.

'Is it a mother for the twins you are selecting or a bride to give you sons?'

'I've told you already: it is not for you to question our ways. What would you know…?'

'Plenty.' Amy retorted. 'My parents divorced when I was two and I remember going to my father's; I remember when he married his new wife—a woman who had no interest in his children, who would really have preferred that we didn't inconvenience her one Saturday in two.' She stopped her tirade. There was no point. This was about the twins, not her past.

But instead of telling her off again, instead of telling her her words were inappropriate, he asked questions.

'How did you deal with it as a child?' Emir asked—because it mattered. He did want to make things better for his girls. 'Were you unhappy? Were you…?'

'Ignored?' She finished his sentence for him and Emir nodded, making her tell him some of her truth. 'Dad bought me a dolls' house.' She gave a pale smile at the memory. 'I spent hours playing with it. There the mum and dad slept and ate together. The kids played in the garden or in the living room, not up in their room…'

There she'd been able to fix things. Her smile faded and trembled. Here she couldn't fix things.

She felt his hand on her bare arm, felt his fingers brush her skin as if to comfort.

It did not.

She felt his flesh meet hers and it was all she could think of. His dark hand making contact was *all* she could think of when her mind should surely be only on the twins.

She hauled her thoughts back to them. 'Can I ask,' she said, 'that when you consider a bride you think of them?'

'Of course.'

His voice was soft and low, his hand still warm on her arm and there was a different tension surrounding them, the certainty that she was but a second away from a kiss.

A kiss that could only spell danger.

Perhaps that was his plan? Amy thought, shrugging off his hand, turning again to the desert. Perhaps he wanted her to fall in love with him. How convenient to keep her here, to bind her a little closer to the twins, to ensure that she did not resign. For he deemed her *better* for the twins.

'Leave!' She spat the word out over her shoulder, but still he stood. 'Leave…' she said again. But there was no relief when he complied, no respite when she heard the door close. Amy choked back angry tears as she stood on the balcony, she wanted to call him back, wanted to continue their discussion….wanted…

There was the other reason she had to consider leaving.

Despite herself, despite the way he had been these

past months, when he made any brief appearance in the nursery, on the rare occasions when he deigned to appear, her heart foolishly leapt at the sight of him—and lately her dreams had allowed more intimate glimpses of him. It confused her that she could have feelings for a man who paid so little attention to his own children.

Feelings that were forbidden.

Hidden.

And they must stay that way, Amy told herself, climbing into bed and willing sleep to come. But she was nervous all the same, for when she woke it would be morning.

And tomorrow she would be alone in the desert with him.

CHAPTER FOUR

'COME in.'

Amy's smile wasn't returned as the bedroom door opened and Fatima walked in.

'I'm nearly ready.'

'What are you doing?' Fatima frowned, her serious eyes moving over the mountain of coloured paper scattered over Amy's bed.

'I'm just wrapping some presents to take for the twins. I hadn't had a chance before.' She hadn't had a chance because after a night spent tossing and turning, wondering if she'd misread things, wondering what might have happened had she not told Emir to leave, Amy had, for the first time since she'd taken the role as nanny, overslept.

Normally she was up before the twins, but this morning it had been their chatter over the intercom that had awoken her and now, having given them breakfast and got them bathed and dressed, five minutes before their departure for the desert, she had popped them in their cots so she could quickly wrap the gifts.

'Their time in the desert is to be solemn,' Fatima said.

'It's their birthday.'

'The celebrations will be here at the palace.' She stood and waited as Amy removed the gifts from her open case. 'The King is ready to leave now. I will help you board the helicopter with the twins.' She called to another servant to collect Amy's case.

'You need to take the twins' cases also,' Amy told him.

'I have taken care of that.' Fatima clearly did not want the King to be kept waiting. 'Come now.'

Perhaps she had imagined last night, for Emir barely glanced at the twins and was his usual dismissive self with Amy as they boarded the helicopter. Amy was grateful for Fatima's help to strap the twins in. The twins were used to flying, and so too was Amy, but what was different this time was the lack of aides—usually at the very least Patel travelled with them, but this trip, as she had been told many times, would be different.

Amy could almost forgive his silence and his lack of interaction with the girls during the flight, for she was well aware that this was a journey he should have been making with his wife. Perhaps he was more pensive than dismissive?

Emir was more than pensive: he looked out to the desert with loathing, and the sun glinting on the canyons made him frown as he stared into the distance. He remembered the rebels who'd used to reside there—men who had refused to wait for the predictions to come true, who'd wanted Alzan to be gone and had taken matters into their own bloody hands.

'It's beautiful,' Amy commented as they swept deeper into the desert. She'd said it more to herself, but Emir responded.

'From a distance,' Emir said. 'But the closer you get…'

He did not finish. Instead he went back to staring broodily out of the window, replaying battles of the past in his mind, hearing the pounding hooves and the cries, feeling the grit of sand rubbed in wounds, history in every grain. Yet above all that he could hear *her*, reading a book to the twins, hear his daughters laughing as they impatiently turned the pages. He wanted to turn to the sound of them, to forget the pain and suffering, to set aside the past, but as King he had sworn to remember.

The heat hit Amy as soon as she stepped out of the helicopter. Emir held Nakia, while Amy carried Clemira and even though the helicopter had landed as close as possible to the compound of tents still the walk was hard work—the shifting soft sand made each step an effort. Once inside a tent, she took off her shoes and changed into slippers as Emir instructed. She thanked the pilot, who had brought in her suitcase, and then Emir led her through a passageway and after that another, as he briefly explained what would happen.

'The girls will rest before we take them to the Bedouins. There is a room for you next to them.'

They were in what appeared to be a lounge, its sandy floor hidden beneath layer after layer of the most exquisite rugs. The different areas were all separated by coloured drapes. It was like being in the heart of a vibrant labyrinth and already she felt lost.

'There are refreshments through there,' Emir explained, 'but the twins are not to have any. Today they must eat and drink only from the desert...'

Amy had stopped listening. She spun around as she heard the sound of the helicopter taking off. 'He's forgotten to bring in their luggage!' She went to run outside, but she took a wrong turn and ran back into the lounge again, appalled that Emir wasn't helping. 'You have to stop him—we need to get the twins' bags.'

'They do not need the things you packed for them. They are here to learn the ways of the desert and to be immersed in them. Everything they need is here.'

'I didn't just pack toys for them!' She could hear the noise of the chopper fading in the distance. Well, he'd just have to summon someone to get it turned around. 'Emir—I mean, Your Highness.' Immediately Amy corrected herself, for she had addressed him as she had so long ago. 'It's not toys or fancy clothes that I'm worried about. It's their bottles, their formula.'

'Here they will drink water from a cup,' Emir said.

'You can't do that to them!' Amy could not believe what she was hearing. 'That's far too harsh.'

'Harsh?' Emir interrupted. 'This land is harsh. This land is brutal and unforgiving. Yet its people have learnt to survive in it. When you are royal, when your life is one of privilege, it is expected that at least once a year you are true to the desert.'

Where, she wondered, had the caring father gone?

Where was the man who had rocked his tiny babies in strong arms? Who even last night had picked up his sleeping child just to hold her? Maybe she really had dreamt it—maybe she had imagined last night—for he stood now unmoved as Clemira and Nakia picked up on the tension and started to cry.

'We will leave soon,' Emir said.

'It's time for their nap now,' Amy said. She was expecting another argument, but instead he nodded.

'When they wake we will leave.'

'Is there anyone to help? To show me where they rest? Where the kitchen…?'

'It's just us.'

'Just us?' Amy blinked.

'There is a groundsman to tend to the animals, but here in the tent and out in the desert we will take care of ourselves.'

Oh, she had known they would be alone in the desert, but she had thought he had meant alone by royal standards—she had been quite sure that there would be servants and maidens to help them. Not once had she imagined that it would truly be just them, and for the first time the vastness and the isolation of the desert scared her.

'What if something happens?' Amy asked. 'What if one of the girls gets ill?'

'The Bedouins trust me to make the right decisions for their land and for their survival. It is right that in turn I trust them.'

'With your children?'

'Again,' Emir said, 'I have to warn you not to question our ways. Again,' he stated, 'I have to remind you that you are an employee.'

Her cheeks burned in anger but Amy scooped up the twins and found their resting area. Maybe he was right, she thought with a black smile. Maybe *she* needed time in the desert, for she was too used to things being done for her—a bit too used to having things unpacked and put away. And, yes, she was used to ringing down to the palace kitchen to have bottles warmed and food prepared. Now she had to settle two hungry, frazzled babies in the most unfamiliar surroundings.

The wind made the tent walls billow, and the low wooden cribs that lay on the floor were nothing like what the twins were used to—neither were the cloth nappies she changed them into. Emir came in with two cups of water for the girls, but that just upset them more, and when he'd left Amy took ages rocking the cribs to get the twins to settle. Her anger towards Emir rose as she did so, and it was a less than impressed Amy who finally walked out to the sight of Emir resting on the cushions.

He looked at her tightly pressed lips, saw the anger burning in her cheeks as she walked past him, and offered a rare explanation. 'There are traditions that must be upheld. Sit.' Emir watched her fingers clench at his command and perhaps wisely rephrased it. 'Please be seated. I will explain what is to take place.'

It was awkward to sit on the low cushions, but Amy remembered to tuck her feet away from him. It was difficult facing him again after last night—not that he appeared to remember it, for his eyes did not even search her face. Really he seemed rather bored at having to explain things.

'I understand that you think this is cruel, but really it is not...'

'I never said cruel,' Amy corrected. 'I said it was harsh on the girls. Had you told me earlier what was to happen I could have better prepared them. I could have had them drinking from cups.'

He conceded with a nod, and now he did look at her—could see not just the anger but that she was upset, and on behalf of his children. 'I know the year has been a difficult one. I am grateful the girls have had you.'

She was disarmed by his sudden niceness, forgot to thank him as she ought to, but Emir did not seem to notice. 'I have not been looking forward to this. Which is why, perhaps, I did not explain things. I have been trying not to think about it. Hannah was not looking forward to this time either.' Amy blinked at the revelation. 'Hannah wanted it left till the last moment—till they were a little older. I was trying to follow her wish, I did not think about cups...' He gave a shrug.

'Of course not,' Amy conceded. 'I don't expect you to. But if there was just more communication it might make things easier.'

'If she were alive still this would be difficult.'

Amy could see the battle in his face to keep his features bland, almost hear the effort to keep sentiment from his voice.

'If she were here Hannah would not have been able to

feed them, and that would have upset her.' Amy frowned as he continued. 'This is a time when babies are…' He did not know the word. 'Separated from their mother's milk.'

'Weaned off it?'

Emir nodded. 'Tradition states that they should travel for a week living on water and fruits. The desert people do not approve that I am only giving them the girls for one night, and King Rakhal also opposed it, but I explained that my children have already been…' he paused before he used the word that was new to his vocabulary '…weaned at two weeks of age.'

'And he agreed to reduce it?'

'Not for my daughters' sake.' Emir's voice deepened in hate. 'Only, I believe, because his wife is pregnant. Only because I reminded him that the rule would apply to his infant too.' He gave a rare smile. 'Perhaps Queen Natasha found out about it.'

Amy smiled back. She looked at him and was curious—more curious than she had ever been about a man. There was just so much about him she did not know, so much she had wrongly assumed. These past weeks it had not been bottles and cups on his mind, it had been their welfare. That this proud King had gone to his enemy to ask a favour spoke volumes, but it just confused her more.

'Natasha is English, like you.' Emir broke into her thoughts. 'And would be just as opposed, I presume.' His smile was wry now. 'Poor Rakhal!'

'Poor Natasha,' was Amy's response. 'If Rakhal is as stubborn as you.'

He told her some more about what would happen— that they would set off soon and would take lunch at the oasis. 'It must be soon,' Emir said, 'for the winds are gathering and we have to make it to the oasis today, so all this can take place before their first birthday.'

He did have their best interests at heart, Amy realised, even if he did not always show it. At every turn he confused her, for when the twins woke from that nap it was Emir who went to them, who helped her wrap them in shawls. When she saw him smile down at Clemira as they headed outside he was like the Emir she had once seen.

As they turned to the right of the tent Amy felt her heart sink at the familiar sound of horses whinnying— it was a sound that had once been pleasing to her, but now it only brought terror.

'Horses?' She looked at the beasts. 'We're riding to the oasis?'

'Of course.' He handed her Clemira, oblivious to the panic in her voice.

'Your Highness…'

'Emir,' he conceded.

'Emir—I can't. I thought we'd be driving.'

'Driving?' He shot out an incredulous laugh. 'You really have no idea what this is about.'

'I honestly don't think I can ride,' Amy said.

'Walk, then.' Emir shrugged. 'Though I suggest you

walk alongside a horse, for it will only be a short time before you surely decide you're not so precious.'

'It's not that!' He was so arrogant, so difficult to speak to at times. She certainly wasn't going to tell him about her accident. She didn't want a lecture on how it was better to get back on a horse, or some withering comment, or—worse—questions. 'I'm nervous around horses,' she offered.

Emir just shrugged. 'I will travel alone, then,' he said. 'You will help me to secure the twins.'

Amy bristled. He certainly wasn't going to baby her—after all, he didn't even pander to the twins. She wondered if they would fight and struggle as she secured them, but instead the girls were delighted with this new game—giggling as he balanced each one against his chest. It was Amy who was struggling as she wrapped a sash over his shoulder and tied a knot low on his waist, for she had never been closer to him.

'That's Clemira.' She did her best to keep her voice light, hoped he would not notice her shaking fingers as she wrapped the second twin and was glad to walk around to his back so he would not see her blush. She lifted his *kafeya* a little, ran the cloth behind it. Her fingers paused as she felt dark skin. She bit on her lip as she saw the nape of his neck, resisting the urge to linger.

'Done?' he asked.

'Nearly.' She finished the knot on his shoulder. 'Are you sure you can manage them both?'

'I have carried much more.' He indicated to Raul, the groundsman, to bring over his horse. As he mounted with ease the twins started to get upset—perhaps realising that they were leaving Amy behind.

'They will be fine,' Emir said.

But wasn't it *her* job to make this transition easier for them? As painful as it would be, she wanted to be there for the girls when they were handed over to strangers—wanted this last bit of time with them.

'I'll come.' The words tumbled out. 'It will be better for the girls if I ride along beside them and give them their lunch.'

'It is up to you.' Emir's voice did not betray the fact that he was relieved. He had privately been wondering how he would manage—not the ride, but the time at the oasis.

When he saw her tentativeness as she approached her animal, saw that her fear was real, he halted their departure for a moment and called to Raul, translating for Amy. 'I have asked him to bring Layyinah. She is, as her name attests, the most gentle mare.'

Layyinah was gorgeous—white and elegant, and more beautiful than any horse Amy had seen. She had huge eyes and nostrils, her forehead was broad, and Amy ran a hand over a magnificent mane.

'She's beautiful,' Amy said. 'I mean *seriously* beautiful.'

'Pure Arabian,' Emir explained. 'That bulge between her eyes is her *jibbah*. There is more…' he did not know the word '…more room that helps with her breathing in the hot air. They are built for this land. In our horses we put a lot of trust and they return it. She will look after you.'

Amy actually wanted to get on, although she was incredibly nervous. The once familiar action took her a couple of attempts, and though her robes had enough cloth in them to allow for decency it felt strange to be climbing onto a horse wearing them. But Emir had managed, Amy told herself. As she took to the saddle she was glad he had mounted his horse first, because he was there beside her, surprisingly patient and encouraging, as she took a moment to settle. The horse moved a few steps as it became accustomed to a new rider.

'*Kef.*' Emir leant over and pulled at the rein. 'It means stop,' he explained, and waited till Amy had her breath back. 'How does it feel?'

'Good,' Amy admitted. 'It feels scary, but good.'

'We will take it slowly,' Emir said. 'There is nothing to be nervous about.'

Oh, there was—but she chose not to tell him.

As they set off, even though it felt different riding on sand, the motion was soon familiar, and Amy realised how much she had missed riding. It had been a huge part of her life but she had never considered resuming it. Had never envisiaged the day she would be brave enough to try again—unexpectedly, that day was here.

She breathed in the warm air, felt the beauty of her surrounds, and for the first time she put anger and her questions aside, just drank in the moment. She heard Emir talk to his children, heard their chatter and laughter as they set off on an adventure. It was nicer just to enjoy rather than think about where this journey would take them.

'It's gorgeous.'

Emir merely shrugged.

'So peaceful.'

'When she chooses to be,' came Emir's strange answer, and he looked over to her. 'Don't let the desert seduce you. As my father told me, she is like a beautiful woman: she dazzles and lulls you, but she is always plotting.'

'What happened to your father?'

'He was killed.' Emir pointed to the distance. 'Over there.'

Despite the heat she shivered. 'And your mother?'

He did not answer.

'Emir?'

'It is not a tale to be told on your first night in the desert.' He changed the subject. 'Soon we will be there.' He pointed ahead to a shimmer on the horizon. 'Do you see the shadows?'

'Not really,' Amy admitted, but as they rode on she started to see the shadows that were in fact huge trees and shrubs.

'What will happen?'

'We will select our lunch,' Emir said, 'and then we will wait for the desert people.' He looked over, saw her tense profile, and then he looked down at the twins, lulled by the motion of the horse, safe with their father. They had both fallen asleep and he did not want to hand them over either—hating so many of his kingdom's ways.

'They've missed you.'

He heard Amy's voice but did not respond, for he had missed then so much too, and he could not share with her the reasons why.

Or perhaps he could.

He looked over as, bolder now, she rode ahead of him, her eyes on the oasis. Her scarf kept slipping, her hair was blowing behind her, and the attraction he felt was acknowledged. What just a couple of generations ago would have been forbidden was a possibility now. After all, Rakhal had an English wife—maybe there could be a way…

Poor Rakhal?

Perhaps not.

Poor Natasha. Even if they had been said as a light joke, he recalled Amy's words, knew from their conversation she was not one who would be told what to do. She would not meekly comply to his request or be flattered that he'd asked.

She was trotting now, and Emir frowned. For someone so nervous around horses, someone who hadn't wanted to ride, she was doing incredibly well. She looked as if she had been riding for years. He had a glimpse then of a different future—riding through the Alzan desert alongside her, with Clemira and Nakia and their own children too.

He must not rush this decision—and he certainly must not rush *her*.

She pulled up her horse and turned and smiled then, her face flushed from the exertion, her eyes for once unguarded, exhilarated. Emir wanted to see more of that and, patience forgotten, kicked his horse faster to join her, his urgency building with each gallop. He wanted her wild and free in his bed. Today—tonight—he would convince her. And as he slowed to a walk beside her, as he saw the spread of colour on her cheeks darken as he looked over to her, as he registered she wanted him too, he thanked the desert that had brought him a simple solution.

Maybe his kingdom and his family could somehow remain.

CHAPTER FIVE

'*La,*' Emir scolded, frowning as Nakia spat out the fruit he'd tried to feed her. 'I mean *no!*' He was fast realising that the twins mainly understood English. 'She copies her sister.'

Amy couldn't help but laugh. They were deep in the desert, sitting by the oasis, feeding the children fresh fruit that they had collected from the lush trees—or they were *trying* to feed the children, because a moment ago Clemira had done the same thing, spitting out the fruit and screwing up her face.

'Clemira is the leader.' Amy watched his jaw tighten. It would seem she had said yet another thing of which he did not approve.

Their time at the oasis was not exactly turning out to be a stunning success. As soon as Emir had put her down Clemira had promptly tried to eat the sand, and Nakia had copied and got some in her eyes.

These were two thoroughly modern princesses, thanks to Amy. They were more used to bopping around to a DVD she'd had sent from home, or swimming in the impressive palace pool, than sitting by an oasis waiting for some elder from the Bedouins to come and offer wisdom for the life journey ahead of them.

'They know nothing of our ways,' Emir said, and though Amy was tempted to murmur that she wondered why that was, she bit her tongue. 'Hannah was worried about this. She didn't like the idea of them fasting.'

'It's not fasting.' Amy was practical; she understood now why he had put this off. 'If they're hungry, they'll eat. They have finally started to drink water.'

'They are spoilt,' Emir said as Clemira again spat out the fruit he offered.

'I know,' Amy admitted. 'And it's completely my fault—I can't help it.'

To her utter surprise, he laughed. She hadn't heard him laugh in a very long while. Even though the twins were being naughty, since they had arrived at the oasis Emir had been different. He seemed more relaxed— like a father to the twins, even—and then she looked up and saw he was watching her. She blushed a little as she looked back, for he was still looking at her.

She had no idea she was being seduced, no idea that the man lounging beside her, relaxed and calm, nurtured serious intentions.

'I was not criticising you,' Emir said. 'I am glad that you spoil them. You are right—I should have given you more notice. Perhaps you could have prepared them.'

'Now I've thought about it, I don't know how I could have,' Amy admitted. 'They're going to be terrified when the Bedouin take them.'

'They are kind people,' Emir said. 'They will do them no harm.'

But his heart wasn't in it. He tasted again the fear he had felt when he was a child—could remember his screams as the wizened old man took him. He hated the rules that bound him.

Hated Rakhal.

It was kinder to his soul to look at Amy, to visit another possible option.

'What happens tomorrow when we get back to the palace?' Amy asked, unnerved by his scrutiny and desperately trying to think of something to say. 'Will it be very grand?'

'There will be a party. My brother Hassan, the second in line, should attend.'

'Should?'

'He has a great interest in horses too…' Emir gave a wry smile. 'They take up a lot of his time.'

She had heard about Prince Hassan and his wild ways, though she had never met him, just heard the whispers. Of course some things were never discussed, so she stayed silent.

She was surprised when Emir said more. 'Though his interest in horses is something I do not condone.'

She gave a small shocked laugh at his admission.

'He needs to grow up,' Emir said.

'Maybe he's happier not.'

'Perhaps,' he admitted, and thought perhaps now he understood his brother a little.

He had confronted him many times, to no avail. Emir

did not get the thrill his brother found in winning—did not understand why Hassan would roam the globe from casino to casino. Hassan had everything and more a man needed right here in Alzan. Riches aplenty, and any woman of his choosing.

He looked over to Amy. One of her hands was idly patting the sand into a mound. For the first time with a woman Emir was not certain of the outcome, but he glimpsed the thrill of the chase, the anticipation before victory.

He understood Hassan a little better now.

'King Rakhal will also be attending.'

'With his wife?' Amy checked. She had briefly met Natasha, but she remembered who she was speaking about. 'I meant will Queen Natasha be attending?'

'No.' Emir shook his head. 'She is due to give birth soon, so it is safer that she does not travel. She seems very happy here,' he pushed gently. 'At first I am sure it was daunting, but she seems to have taken well to her new role.'

'Can I ask something?' Emir was still looking at her, still inviting conversation.

Her question was not the one he was hoping for: it did not appear as if she was envisaging herself for a moment as Queen.

'Why, if their baby is a girl, can she rule?'

'Their laws are different,' Emir said. 'Do you know that Alzan and Alzirz were once the same country?'

'Alzanirz?' Amy nodded.

'There have always been twins in our royal lineage,'

Emir explained. 'Many generations ago a ruler of the time had twin sons. They were unexpected, and were not branded, so the people were unsure who the rightful heir was. It was a troubled time for the country and the King sought a solution. It was decided that the land would be divided, that each son would rule his own kingdom. The predictors of the time said that one day they would reunite…but we were both given separate rules. As soon as one rule is broken the country must become one again, the ruler being of the lineage which survived.'

'It doesn't seem fair.' She looked to his dark eyes and blinked, for they were not stern, and instead of chastising her he nodded for her to go on. 'If a princess can rule there, why not here?'

'They have another rule that they must abide by,' Emir explained. 'In Alzirz the ruler can marry only once. Rakhal's mother died in childbirth and he was not expected to survive—the prophecy was almost fulfilled.'

'But he survived?'

Emir nodded. 'Here…' He was silent for a moment before continuing. 'Here the law states that if the ruler's partner dies he can marry again.' Still he looked into her eyes. 'As must I.'

'Must?'

'The people are unsettled—especially with an impending birth in Alzirz.'

'But if you are not ready…' Amy bit her tongue, knew that to discuss would be pointless.

'Ready?' He frowned, for who was she to question him? But then he remembered she came from a land that relied on the fickle formula of attraction. The glimmer of his idea glowed brighter still. The answer to his dilemma sat beside him now, and her voice, Emir noticed, was just a little breathy when she spoke to him.

'Perhaps a year is too soon to expect…' She licked dry lips, wished she could suddenly be busy with the twins, for this conversation was far too intimate, but the girls were sitting playing with each other. 'Marriage is a huge step.'

'And a step I must take seriously. Though…' He must not rush her, Emir was aware of that. 'I am not thinking of marriage today.'

'Oh…'

Sometimes he made her dizzy. Sometimes when he looked at her with those black eyes it was all she could do to return his gaze. Sometimes she was terrified he would see the lust that burnt inside her.

Not all the time.

But at times.

And this was one of them.

Sometimes, and this was also one of them, she held the impossible thought that he might kiss her—that the noble head might lower a fraction to hers. The sun must be making her crazy because she could almost taste his mouth… The conversation *was* too intimate.

His next words made her burn.

'You are worried about tonight?' Emir said. 'About what might happen?' He saw the dart of her eyes, saw her top teeth move to her lower lip. He could kiss her mouth *now*, could feel her want, was almost certain of it. He would confirm it now. 'They will be fine.'

'They?'

Her eyes narrowed as his words confused her and he knew then that in her mind she had been alone in the tent with him. Emir suppressed a triumphant smile.

'They will be looked after,' he assured her. And so too, Emir decided, would she.

Embarrassed, she turned away, looked to the oasis, to the clear cool water. She wished she could jump in, for her cheeks were on fire now and she was honest enough with herself to know why. Perhaps it was she who was not ready for the presence of a new sheikha queen?

How foolish had she been to think he might have been about to kiss her? That Emir might even see her in that way?

'I have thought about what you said—about the girls needing someone...' He should be patient and yet he could not. 'You love my daughters.'

He said it as a fact.

It *was* a fact.

She stared deeper into the water, wondered if she was crazy with the thoughts she was entertaining—that Emir might be considering her as his lover, a mistress, a proxy mother for his girls. Then she felt his hand on her cheek and she could not breathe. She felt his finger trace down to her throat and caress the piece of flesh she truly loathed.

'What is this from?' His strong fingers were surprisingly gentle, his skin cool against her warm throat, and his questions, his touch, were both gentle and probing.

'Please, Emir...'

The Bedouin caravan was travelling towards them, the moment they were both dreading nearing. A kiss would have to wait. He stood and watched them approach—a line of camels and their riders. He listened to his daughters laughing, knowing in a short while there would be the sound of tears, and he wanted to bury his head in Amy's hair. He wanted the escape of her mouth. And yet now there was duty.

He stood and picked up both daughters, looked into their eyes so dark and trusting. He could not stand to hand them over, for he remembered being ripped from his own parents' arms, his own screams and pleas, and then the campfire and the strange faces and he remembered his own fear. Right now he hated the land that he ruled—hated the ways of old and the laws that could not be changed without both Kings' agreement.

He had survived it, Emir told himself as the wizened old man approached. The twins shrieked in terror as he held out his arms to them.

Emir walked over and spoke with the man, though Amy could not understand what was said.

'They are upset—you need to be kind with them,' Emir explained.

'It is your fear that scares them.' The black eyes were young in his wizened old face. 'You do not wish to come and speak with me?'

'I have decisions I must make alone.'

'Then make them!' the old man said.

'They are difficult ones.'

'Difficult if made from the palace, perhaps,' the old man said. 'But here the only king is the desert—it always brings solutions if you ask for them.'

Emir walked back to Amy, who should be standing in silence as the old man prepared the sand. But of course she was not.

'Who is he?' Amy asked.

'He's an elder of the Bedouins,' Emir explained. 'He is supposed to be more than one hundred and twenty years old.'

'That's impossible.'

'Not out here,' Emir said, without looking over. 'He gives wisdom to those who choose to ask for it.'

'Do *you*?' Amy asked, and then stammered an apology, for it was not her place to ask such things.

But Emir deigned a response. 'I have consulted him a few times,' he admitted, 'but not lately.' He gave a shrug. 'His answers are never straightforward...'

The old man filled two small vials with the sand he had blessed and Emir knew what was to come.

Amy felt her heart squeezing as he took the sobbing babies, and her pain turned to horror as he walked with them towards the water.

'What's happening?'

'They are to be immersed in the water and then they will be taken to the camp.'

'Emir—*no*!'

'You have rituals for your babies, do you not?' Emir snapped. 'Do babies in England not cry?'

He was right, but in that moment Amy felt as if she were bleeding, hearing their shrieks and not having the chance to kiss them goodbye. Listening to them sob as they were taken, she was not just upset; she was furious too—with herself for the part she was playing in this and with Emir.

'Ummi!' both twins screamed in the distance, and worse than her fear of his anger was resisting her urge to run to them. 'Ummi!'

She heard the fading cry and then she heard her own ones—stood there and sobbed. She didn't care if he was angry about what they called her. Right now she just ached for the babies.

And as he stood watching her weep for his children, as he heard them cry out for her, Emir knew his decision was the right one.

'They will be okay,' he tried to comfort her. 'These are the rules.'

'I thought kings made the rules,' she retorted angrily.

'This is the way of our land.' He should be angry, should reprimand her, silence her, but instead he sought to comfort her. 'They will be taken care of. They will be sung to and taught their history.' His hand was on her cheek. 'And each year that passes they will understand more...'

'I can't do this again.' So upset was Amy she did not focus on his touch, just on the thought of next year and the next, of watching the babies she loved lost to strange laws. 'I can't do this, Emir,' she was frantic. 'I have to leave.'

'No,' Emir said, for he could not lose her now. 'You can be here for them—comfort them and explain to them.'

She could. He knew that. The answer to his prayers was here and he bent his mouth and tasted her, tasted the salty tears on her cheeks, and then his lips moved to her mouth and her fear for the girls was replaced, but only with terror.

She was kissing a king. And she *was* kissing him. Her mouth was seeking an escape from her agony and for a moment she found it. She let her mind hush to the skill of his lips and his arms wrapped around her, drew her closer to him. His tongue did not prise open her lips because they opened readily, and she knew where this was leading—knew the plans he had in mind.

He wanted her to be here for his daughters—wanted to ensure she would stay. She pulled back, as her head told her to, because for Amy this was a dangerous game. With this kiss came her heart.

'No.' She wanted to get away, wanted this moment never to have happened. She could not be his lover—especially when soon he would take a bride. 'We can't…'

'We *can.*' He was insistent. His lips found hers again and her second taste was her downfall, for it made her suddenly weak.

His hands were on her hips and he pulled her firmly in, his mouth making clear his intent, and she had never felt more wanted, more feminine. His passion was her pleasure, his desire was what she had been missing, but she could not be his plaything, could not confuse things further.

'Emir, no.'

'Yes.' He could see it so clearly now—wondered why it had taken so long. 'We go now to the tent and make love.'

Again he kissed her. His mind had been busy seeking a solution, but it stilled when he tasted her lips. The pleasure he had forgone was now remembered, except with a different slant—for he tasted not any woman, but Amy. And she was more than simply pleasing. He liked the stilling of her breath as his mouth shocked her, liked the fight for control beneath his hands. Her mouth was still but her body was succumbing; he felt her momentary pause and then her mouth gave in to him, and for Emir there was something unexpected—an emotion he had never tasted in a woman. All the anger she had held in check was delivered in her response. It was a savage kiss that met him now, a different kiss, and he was hard in response. The gentle lovemaking he had intended, the tender seduction he had pictured, changed as she kissed him back.

He was surprised by the intensity of her passion, by the bundle of emotion in his arms, for though she fought him still her mouth was kissing him.

It was Emir who withdrew. He looked down at her flushed, angry face.

'Why the temper, Amy?'

'Because I didn't want you to *know*!'

'Know?' And he looked down and saw the lust she had kept hidden, felt the burn of her arousal beneath him. It consumed him, endeared her to him, told him his decision was the right one. 'Why would you not want me to know?'

'Because…' His mouth was at her ear, his breath making her shiver. She turned her face away at the admission, but it did not stop his pursuit, more stealthy now, and more delicious. 'It can come to nothing.'

'It can…' Emir said. She loathed her own weakness, but now she had tasted him she wanted him so.

'Please…' The word spilled from her lips; it sounded as if she was begging. 'Take me back to the tent.'

Except he wanted her *now*. His hands were at the buttons of her robe, pulling it down over her shoulders. Their kisses were frantic, their want building. She grappled with his robe, felt the leather that held his sword and the power of the man who was about to make love to her. She was kissing a king and it terrified her, but still it was delicious, still it inflamed her as his words attempted to soothe her.

'The people will come to accept it…'

He was kissing her neck now, moving down to her exposed breast. She ached for his mouth there, ached to give in to his mastery, but her mind struggled to understand his words. 'The people…?'

'When I take you as my bride.'

'Bride!' He might as well have pushed her into the water. She felt the plunge into confusion and struggled to come up for air, felt the horror as history repeated it-self. It was happening again.

'Emir—no!'

'Yes.' He thought she was overwhelmed by his offer—did not recognise she was dying in his arms, as his mouth moved back to take her again, to calm her. But when she spoke he froze.

'I can't have children.'

She watched the words paralyse him, saw his pupils constrict, and then watched him make an attempt to right his features. To his credit he did not drop her, but his arms stilled at her sides and then his forehead rested on hers as the enormity of her words set in.

'I had a riding accident and it left me unable to have children.' Somehow she managed to speak; somehow, before she broke down, she managed to find her voice.

'I'm sorry.'

'My fiancé was too.'

With a sob she turned from him, pulled her robe over her naked breasts and did up the buttons as she ran to where the horses were tethered. She didn't possess any fear as she untied her mare and mounted it, because fear was nothing compared to grief. She kicked her into a canter and when that did not help she galloped. She could hear the sound of Emir's beast rapidly gaining on her, could hear his shouts for her to halt, and finally she did, turning her pained eyes to him.

'I lay for five days on a machine that made me breathe and I heard my fiancé speaking with his mother. That was how I found out I couldn't have children. That was how I heard him say there really was no point marrying me…' She was breathless from riding, from anger, yet still she shouted. 'Of course that's not what he told me when I came round—he said the accident had made him realise that, though he cared, he didn't love me, that life was too short and he wasn't ready for commitment.' Emir said nothing. 'But I knew the reason he really left.'

'He's a fool, then.'

'So what does that make you?'

'I am King,' Emir answered, and it was the only answer he could give.

As soon as the tent was in sight, it was Emir who kicked his horse on, Emir who raced through the desert, and she was grateful to be left alone, to gallop, to sob, to think…

To remember.

The black hole of the accident was filling painfully—each stride from Layyinah was taking her back there again. She was a troubled bride-to-be, a young woman wondering if she wasn't making the most appalling mistake. The sand and the dunes changed to countryside; she could hear hooves pounding mud and feel the cool of spring as she came to an appalling conclusion.

She had to call the wedding off.

CHAPTER SIX

'I HAVE run you a bath.'

Emir looked up as Amy walked into the tent. He had told Raul to watch her from a distance and, after showering, had run the first bath of his life.

And it was for another.

As he had done so his gut had churned with loathing towards her fiancé—loathing that was immediately reflected in a mirror that shone back to him, for wasn't he now doing the same?

Yet he was a king.

Again that thought brought no solace.

'Thank you.'

Her pale smile as she walked into the tent confused him. He had expected anger, bitterness to enter the tent with her, but if anything she seemed calm.

Amy *was* calm.

Calmer than she had been since the accident.

She unzipped her robe and looked around the bathing area. It was lit by candles in hurricane jars—not, she realised, a romantic gesture from Emir, it was how the whole tent was lit. Yet she was touched all the same.

Amy slid into the fragrant water and closed her eyes, trying and failing not to think of the twins and how they would be coping. Doing her best not to think of Emir and what he had proposed.

Instead she looked at her past—at a time she could now clearly remember. It felt good to have it back.

She washed her hair and climbed out of the water, drying herself with the towel and then wrapping it around her. Aware she was dressed rather inappropriately, she hoped Emir would be in his sleeping area, but he was sitting on cushions as she walked quietly past him, heading to her sleeping area to put on something rather more suitable, before she faced a conversation with him.

He looked up. 'Better?'

'Much.' Amy nodded.

'You should eat.'

She stared at the food spread before him and shook her head. 'I'm not hungry,' she lied.

'You do not decline when a king invites you to dine at his table.'

'Oh, but you do when that king has just declined *you*,' Amy responded. 'My rule.' And the strangest thing was she even managed a small smile as she said it—another smile that caught Emir by surprise.

'I thought you would be...' He did not really know. Emir had expected more hurt, but instead there was an air of peace around her that he had never noticed before.

'I really am fine,' Amy said. She was aware there was a new fracture he had delivered to her heart, but it was too painful for examination just yet, so instead she explored past hurts. 'In fact I remembered something when I was riding,' Amy explained. 'Something I'd forgotten. I've been struggling with my memory—I couldn't remember the weeks before the accident.' She shook her head. 'It doesn't matter.'

She went again to head to her room, but again he called her back. 'You need to eat.' He held up a plate of *lokum* and Amy frowned at the pastry, at the selection of food in front of him.

'I thought it was just fruit that we could eat?'

'It is the twins who can eat only fruit and drink only water. I thought it better for them if we all did it.'

She saw the tension in his jaw as he spoke of the twins. Sometimes he sounded like a father—sometimes this dark, brooding King was the man she had once known.

'They will be okay.' He said it as if he was trying to convince himself.

'I'm sure they'll be fine,' Amy said. Tonight he was worried about his children. Tonight neither of them really wanted to be alone. 'I'll get changed and then I'll have something to eat.'

Was there relief in his eyes when he nodded?

There was not much to choose from—it was either her nightdress and dressing gown or yet another pale blue robe. Amy settled for the latter, brushed her damp hair and tied it back, and then headed out to him.

He was tired of seeing her in that robe. He wanted to see her in other colours—wanted to see her draped in red or emerald, wanted to see her hair loose around her shoulders and those full lips rouged. Or rather, Emir conceded as he caught the fresh, feminine scent of her as she sat down, he wanted to see the shoulders he had glimpsed moments earlier, wanted only the colour of her skin and her naked on the bed beneath him. But her revelation had denied them that chance.

'I apologise.' He came right out and said it. 'To have it happen to you twice...'

'Honestly...' Amy ate sweet pastry between words—she really was hungry. Perhaps for the first time in a year she knew what starving was. She'd been numb for so long and now it felt as if all her senses were returning. 'I'm okay.' She wondered how she might best explain what she was only just discovering herself. 'Since the accident I've felt like a victim.' It was terribly hard to express it! 'I didn't like feeling that way. It didn't feel like me. I didn't like my anger towards him.'

'You had every reason to be angry.'

'No,' Amy said. 'As it turns out, I didn't.'

'I don't understand.'

'There were a few days before I fully came round when I could hear conversations. I couldn't speak because I was on a machine.'

Emir watched her fingers go instinctively to her throat.

'That was when I heard the doctors discussing the surgery I'd had.' She was uncomfortable explaining things to him, so she kept it very brief. 'The horse had trampled me. They took me to surgery and they had to remove my ovaries. They left a small piece of one so that I didn't go into...'

'Menopause.' He said it for her, smiled because she was embarrassed, 'I do know about these things.'

'I know.' She squirmed. 'It just feels strange, speaking about it with you. Anyway, I lay there unable to speak and heard my fiancé talking to his mother—how he didn't know what to do, how he'd always wanted children. Later, after I was discharged from the hospital, he told me it was over, that he'd been having doubts for ages, that it wasn't about the accident. But I knew it was. Or rather I thought I knew it was.' She looked up at Emir's frown. 'When I was riding today I remembered the last time I rode a horse. I don't remember falling off, or being trampled, but I do remember what I was thinking. I was unhappy, Emir.' She admitted it out loud for the first time, for even back then she had kept it in. 'I felt trapped and I was wondering how I could call off the wedding. That was what I was thinking when the accident happened—he was right to end things. It wasn't working. I just didn't know it—till now.'

'You didn't love him?' Emir asked, and watched as she shook her head. As she did so a curl escaped the confines of the hair tie. He was jealous of her fingers as they caught it and twisted it as she pondered his question.

'I did love him,' she said slowly, for she was still working things out for herself, still piecing her life together. 'But it wasn't the kind of love I wanted. We'd been going out together since we were teenagers. Our engagement seemed a natural progression—we both wanted children, we both wanted the same things, or thought we did. I cared for him and, yes, I suppose I loved him. But it wasn't...' She couldn't articulate the word. 'It wasn't a passionate love,' Amy attempted. 'It was...' She still couldn't place the word.

Emir tried for her. 'Safe?'

But that wasn't the word she was looking for either.

'Logical,' Amy said. 'It was a sort of logical love. Does that make sense?'

'I think so,' Emir said. 'That is the kind of love we build on here—two people who are chosen, who are considered a suitable match, and then love grows.'

He was quiet for a moment. The conversation was so personal she felt she could ask. 'Was that the love you had with Hannah?'

'Very much so,' Emir said. 'She was a wonderful wife, and would have been an amazing mother as well as a dignified sheikha queen.'

Amy heard the love in his voice when he spoke of her and they were not jealous tears that she blinked back. 'Maybe my fiancé and I would have made it.' Amy gave a tight shrug. 'I'm quite sure we would have had a good marriage. I think I was chasing the dream—a home and children, doing things differently than my parents.'

'A grown-up dolls' house?' Emir suggested, and she smiled.

'I guess I just wanted...' She still didn't know the word for it.

'An illogical love?' Emir offered—and that was it.

'I did,' Amy said, and then she stood. 'I do.'

'Stay,' he said. 'I have not explained.'

'You don't need to explain, Emir,' Amy said. 'I know we can't go anywhere. I know it is imperative to your country's survival that you have a son.' But there was just a tiny flare of hope. 'Could you speak to King Rakhal and have the rule revoked?' Amy didn't care if she was speaking out of turn. 'It is a different time now.'

'Rakhal's mother died in childbirth,' Emir said. 'And, as I told you, for a while her baby was not expected to survive. The King of Alzirz came to my father and asked the same…' Emir shrugged his broad shoulders. 'Of course my father declined his request. He wanted the countries to be one.'

'You've thought about it, then?'

He looked at her and for the first time revealed to another person just a little of what was on his mind. 'I have more than thought about it. I approached Rakhal when my wife first became ill. His response was as you might expect.' He shook his head as he recalled that conversation. Could see again the smirk on Rakhal's face when he had broached the subject. How he had relished Emir's rare discomfort. How he had enjoyed watching a proud king reduced to plead.

Emir looked into Amy's blue eyes and somehow the chill in him thawed slightly. He revealed more of the burden that weighed heavily on his mind. 'I have thought about many things, and I am trying to make the best decision not just for my country but for my daughters.' He had said too much. Immediately Emir knew that. For no one must know everything.

She persisted. 'If you didn't have a son…'

'It would be unthinkable,' Emir said. And yet it was all he thought about. He looked to her pale blue eyes and maybe it was the wind and the sound of the desert, perhaps the dance of the shadows on the walls, but he wanted to tell her—wanted to take her to the dark place in his mind, to share it. But he halted, for he could not. 'I *will* have a son.' Which meant his bride could not be her. 'Marriage means different things for me. I am sorry if I hurt you—that was never my intention.'

'I didn't take it personally…' But at the last moment her voice broke—because her last words weren't true. She'd realised it as she said them. It was a very personal hurt, and one to be explored only in private, in the safety of her room. There she could cry at this very new loss. 'Goodnight, Emir.'

'Amy?'

She wished he would not call her back, but this time it was not to dissuade her. Instead he warned her what the night would bring.

'The wind is fierce tonight—she knows that you are new here and will play tricks with your mind.'

'You talk about the wind as if it's a person.'

'Some say she is a collection of souls.' He saw her instantly dismiss that. 'Just don't be alarmed.'

She wasn't—at first.

Amy lay in the bed and stared at the ceiling—a ceiling that rose and fell with the wind. She missed the girls more than she had ever thought possible and she missed too what might have been.

Not once had she glimpsed what Emir had been considering—not once had she thought herself a potential sheikha queen. She'd thought she might be his mistress—an occasional lover, perhaps, and a proxy mother to the twins.

Emir had been willing to marry her.

It helped that he had.

It killed that he never could.

Amy lay there and fought not to cry—not that he would be able to hear her, for the wind was whipping around the tent and had the walls and roof lifting. The flickering candles made the shadows dance as if the room were moving, so she closed her eyes and willed sleep to come. But the wind shrieked louder, and it sounded at times like the twins. She wept for them.

Later she could hear a woman screaming—the same sound she had heard the night they were born. The shouts had filled the palace a year ago this night, when the twins were being born. These screams sounded like a woman birthing—screams she would never know—and it was torture. She knew the wind played tricks, but the screams and the cries were more than she could bear.

Maybe they'd taunted Emir too, for when she opened her eyes he was standing there, still robed, his sword strapped to his hips. His *kafeya* was off. He stood watching, a dark shadow in the night, but one that did not terrify.

'When you kissed me back, when you said *please*, what did you think I meant?' he asked.

'I thought it was sex that was on offer.' If she sounded coarse she didn't care. Her hurt was too raw to smother it with lies.

'That is not our way.' Emir looked at her. 'In Alzirz they are looser with their morals. There are harems and...' He shook his head. 'I did not want that for you.'

Not for the first time, but for more shameful reasons now, she wished she were there—wished it was there that Emir was King.

'I never for a moment thought you would consider me for your bride. When we kissed—when we...' She swallowed, because it was brutal to her senses to recall it. 'When we kissed,' Amy started again, 'when we touched...' Her eyes were brave enough to meet his. 'I wasn't thinking about the future or the twins or solutions, I thought it was just me that you wanted...'

And he looked at her, and the winds were silenced. The screams and the tears seemed to halt. Surely for one night he could think like a man and not a king? Emir was honest in his response and his voice was low with passion. 'It was,' Emir said. Yes, at first he had been seducing, but later... 'When I kissed you I forgot.'

'Forgot?'

'I forgot everything but you.'

She looked over to him, saw the raw need in his eyes, saw the coffee colour of his skin and the arms that had held her, and she wanted his mouth back.

'I know we can't go anywhere. I know...' She just wanted to be a woman again—wanted one time with this astonishingly beautiful man. 'Just once…' she whispered, and Emir nodded.

'Just once,' came his reply, for that was all it must be, and with that he picked her up and carried her to his bed.

CHAPTER SEVEN

She lay on his bed and watched as he undid the leather belt and the sword fell to the floor with a gentle thud. She turned away from him then, for she was filled with terror. All too clearly she could see his braids and royal decorations and she knew what they were doing was wrong—she wanted the man, not the King, and his status was truly terrifying.

'Turn around,' Emir told her.

Slowly she did so, and saw him naked, and she feared that too—for he was more beautiful then she had even imagined and, yes, now it was safe to admit to herself that she had imagined. He hardened under her gaze. Her shy eyes took in more of him—the toned planes of his stomach, the long, solid thighs and the arms she now ached to have hold her again.

'This is wrong,' she said as he walked towards her.

'It doesn't feel wrong,' he said, and he climbed in beside her. The fact that the bodies that met were forbidden to each other only heightened their desire.

She cringed as he took off her nightgown, closed her eyes as he pushed down the bedclothes and fully exposed her. He wanted to know every piece of her skin. He kissed not her mouth but the breast that he had so nearly kissed in the desert, and she was as aroused in that instant as she had been then. She returned to that moment in the desert when he could have taken her. He kissed lower, kissed her stomach as deeply as if it were her mouth, and then he moved lower still, and she lay there writhing as he made her feel like a woman again.

Her body had craved passion for so long and he had returned it to her. She had denied herself touch, had felt untouchable, empty, and now he filled her with his tongue, touched her so intimately and not with haste.

With her moans he grew.

With her screams he lost himself more.

He had shared not an ounce of emotion since the death of his wife, but he shared it now.

There was a burden for this King that not the wisest of his council knew about. There was a decision in the making that he could only come to alone—a decision he had wrestled with for more than a year now. It was all forgotten.

He felt her fingers in his hair and the tightening of her thighs to his head. Her hips attempted to rise but he pushed her down with his mouth till she throbbed into him, and then he could wait no more.

He kneeled, looked down at all that beckoned, and she felt the roughness of his thighs part her legs further. Her body still quivered from his intimate exploration as he parted her with his thumbs. She looked with decadent, wanton fear at what would soon be deep inside her and, breathless, pleaded for it to be *now*.

He pulled back, for he must sheathe, and then he heard her whisper.

'We don't have to.'

For the first time, the fact that there could be no baby brought only relief, for neither wanted to halt things.

Now he lifted her hips, aimed himself towards her. A more deliberate lover he could not be, for he watched and manoeuvred every detail, and she let him—let him position her till he was poised at her entrance, and then he made her wait.

'Emir…'

His smile was as rare as it was wicked.

'Emir…'

He hovered closer and was cruel in his timing; that beat of space made her weep, and her mouth opened to beg him again, but her words faded as he filled her, as he drove into her with the ardour of a man ending his deprivation. He forgot his size and to be gentle, and never had she been so grateful to have a man forget.

He filled her completely, and then filled her again. He was over her, and the kiss he had first denied her was Amy's reward, for he hushed her moans with his mouth until it was Emir who could not be silent. The pleasure was now his, all pain obliterated, the shackles temporarily released. His mind soared in freedom as her body moved with his. Escape beckoned and he claimed it, groaning to hold on to it, yearning to sustain it. But the pulse of her around him was too much—the rapid tightening and flicker of intimate muscles, her hot wet cheek next to his, her breath, his name in his ear.

He lost himself to her, gave in to what was and spilled into her, called out her name as they dived into pleasure. The wind was their friend now, for it shrieked louder around them, carried their shouts and their moans and buried their secret in the sands.

CHAPTER EIGHT

OF COURSE it should never have happened.

And of course it must never be referred to again.

But it was a little before morning and they'd made love again after she'd turned and looked at him while she still could. She ran a finger across the scar above his eye about which she had often wondered and was brave enough now to ask.

'What is that from?'

'You don't ask that sort of thing.'

'Naked beside you I do.'

Maybe it was better she knew, Emir thought. Maybe then she could understand how impossible it was for them.

'Some rebels decided that they could not wait for the predictions, so they took matters into their own hands.' He did not look at her as he spoke. He felt her fingers over his scar and remembered again. 'They decided to take out one lineage.' He heard her shocked gasp. 'Of course our people had seen them approaching and they rallied. My father went out and battled, as did my brother and I…'

'And your mother?'

'She was killed in her bed.'

He removed her hand from his face, climbed out of bed, and dressed and headed to prayer. He had begged the desert for a solution and for a moment had thought one had been delivered; instead it had been a taunt. He must play by the rules, Emir realised as he remembered again that night and all he had inherited.

So he prayed for his country and his people.

He must forget about their lovemaking, the woman he had held in his arms. He had never felt closer to another, even Hannah, and he prayed for forgiveness.

He prayed for his daughters and the decision he was making and he got no comfort, for his heart still told him he was making the wrong one.

Then he remembered what his father had fought for and he knew he must honour it—so he prayed again for his country.

Amy lay silent, taking in this last time she would be in his bed, the masculine scent of him. Her hand moved to the warm area where he had slept and she yearned to wait for him to return to the bed and make love to her just one more time. But for both of them that would be unfair, so she headed to the bathing area and then to her own room.

She fixed her hair and put on the blue robe, became the nanny again.

For Emir there was both regret and relief when he returned from prayer and saw the empty bed. Regret and relief as they shared a quiet breakfast. She did not once refer to last night, but it killed him to see her in the familiar blue robe and to know what was beneath.

And when the silence deafened her, when she knew if she met his eyes just one more time, it would end in a kiss she wished him good morning and headed to her room. She lay on her bed and willed the twins to return, for sanity to come back to her life and to resume again her role.

But of course it felt different.

Her heart swelled with pride and relief when the birthday girls were returned.

Their squeals of delight as she kissed them made her eyes burn from the salt of unshed tears. She realised how close to being their mother she had come.

'What are these?' She attempted normal conversation, looked at the heart-shaped vials that now hung around their necks.

'They are filled with the sands of the desert—they must be worn till they go to bed tonight, then they are to be locked away until their wedding day.'

'They're gorgeous.' Amy held one between her finger and thumb. 'What are they for?'

'Fertility.' He almost spat the word out, his mood as dark as it had been the morning she had faced him in his office, and it didn't improve as they boarded the helicopter for their return to the palace.

The twins were crying as the helicopter took off.

'They are not to arrive with teary faces. There will be many people gathered to greet them. My people will line the streets.'

'Then comfort them!' Amy said, but his face was as hard as granite and he turned to the window. 'Emir, please.' Amy spoke when perhaps she should not, but he had been so much better with the girls yesterday, and it worried her that she had made things worse instead of better. 'Please don't let last night…'

He looked over to Amy, his eyes silencing her, warning her not to continue, and then he made things exceptionally clear. 'Do you really think what happened last night might have any bearing on the way I am with my daughters?' He mocked her with one small incredulous shake of his head. 'You are the nanny—you are in my country and you have to accept our laws and our ways. They are to be stoic. They are to be strong.'

But he did take Clemira and hold her on his knees, and when Clemira was quiet so too was Nakia.

Amy sat silent, craning her neck as the palace loomed into view, bouncing Nakia on her knee, ready to point out all the people, to tell the little girl that the waving flags were for her sister and herself.

Except the streets were empty.

She looked to Emir. His face was still set in stone and he said nothing.

He strode from the helicopter, which left Amy to struggle with the twins. He was greeted by Patel and whatever was said was clearly not good news, for Emir's already severe expression hardened even more.

Amy had no idea what was happening.

She took the twins to the nursery and waited for information, to find out what time the party would be, but with each passing hour any hope of celebration faded and again it was left to Amy to amuse the little girls on what should be the happiest of days.

Her heart was heavy in her chest and she fought back tears as she made them cupcakes in the small kitchen annexe. At supper time she sang 'Happy Birthday' to them, watched them smile in glee as they opened the presents she had wrapped for them. Amy smiled back—but her face froze when she saw Emir standing in the nursery doorway.

His eyes took in the presents, the teddies and the DVDs. He watched as Amy walked over to him, her face white with fury, and for a second he thought she might spit.

'They have everything, do they?' Her eyes challenged him. 'Some party!'

'My brother is too busy in Dubai with his horses.'

He walked over to the twins and kissed the two little dark heads. He spoke in his language to them for a few moments. 'I have their present.'

He called the servants to come in and Amy watched as the delighted twins pulled paper off a huge parcel. She bit on her lip when she saw it was a dolls' house—an exquisite one—built like the palace, with the stairs, the doors, the bedroom.

'I thought about what you said. How it helped you. I wanted the same for them.'

'How?' Even though it seemed like a lifetime ago, it had only been a couple of days. 'How on earth did you get this done so quickly?'

'There are some advantages to being King—though right now...' Emir almost smiled, almost met her eyes but did not '...I can't think of many.'

He stood from where he'd knelt with the twins and still could not look at her. He just cleared his throat and said what he had to—did what should have been done long ago.

'Fatima will be sharing in the care of the twins from now on,' Emir said, and Fatima stepped forward.

Not *assisting*, not *helping*, Amy noted.

'She speaks only a little English and she will speak none to the twins: they need to learn our ways now.'

She did not understand what had happened. For as blissful as last night had been she would give it back, would completely delete it, if it had changed things so badly for the girls.

'Emir...' She saw Fatima frown at the familiarity. 'I mean, Your Highness...'

But he didn't allow her to speak, to question, just walked from the nursery, not turning as the twins started to cry. Amy rushed to them.

'Leave them,' Fatima said.

'They're upset.' Amy stood her ground. 'It's been a long day for them.'

'It's been a long day for their country,' Fatima responded. 'It is not just the twins who will mark today—Queen Natasha gave birth to a son at sunrise.'

For a bizarre moment Amy thought of the screams she had heard last night, the cries she had thought might come from Hannah. Yet Natasha had been screaming too. She felt as if the winds were still tricking her, that the desert was always one step ahead, and watched as Fatima picked up the twins and took them to their cots. Fatima turned to go, happy to leave them to cry.

That was why there had been no celebrations, no crowds gathering in the streets. It had been a silent protest from the people—a reminder to their King that he must give them a son. Fatima confirmed it as she switched out the light.

'Unlike Alzan, the future of Alzirz is assured.'

CHAPTER NINE

'THEY won't stay quiet for that length of time unless you are holding them.'

It had been a long morning for Amy. They were practising the formalities for the new Prince's naming ceremony tomorrow, and as it was Fatima who would be travelling with the King and the Princesses, Amy had been tidying the nursery. The windows were open and she had heard their little protests, their cries to be held by their father and eventually, reluctantly, Emir had asked for Amy to be sent down.

'Fatima will be the one holding them.'

'They want you.'

'They cannot have me,' Emir said. She caught his eye then and he saw her lips tighten, because, yes, she knew how that felt. 'I will be in military uniform. I have to salute.' He stopped explaining then—not just because he'd remembered that he didn't have to, but because Nakia, who had been begging for his arms, now held her arms out to Amy. They both knew that there would be no problem if it was Amy who was travelling with him.

Not that Emir would admit it.

Not that she wanted to go.

She could not stand to be around him—could not bear to see the man she loved so cold and distant, not just with her but with the babies who craved his love.

'Can you hold *one*?' She tried to keep the exasperation from her voice as she hugged a tearful Clemira.

'I've tried that. Clemira was jealous,' he explained as Fatima sloped off with Nakia to get her a drink.

'If you can hold one then it needs to be Clemira. Keep Clemira happy and then usually Nakia is fine.' She saw him frown and she could not check her temper because he didn't know something so basic about his own daughters. 'Just hold Clemira,' she said, handing the little girl to him. 'God, it's like I'm speaking in a foreign language.'

'It is one to me!' Emir hissed, and she knew they were not talking about words.

Amy walked off, back to the palace, so she could listen to more tears from the window and do nothing, back to a role that was being eroded by the minute. She looked at the dolls' house and felt like kicking it, felt like ripping down the palace walls, but she stifled a laugh rather than turn into psycho-nanny. She polished the tables in the nursery and changed the sheets, tried to pretend she was working.

'It worked.'

She turned around at the sound of him, stood and stared. He held the twins, both asleep, their heads resting on his shoulders. She waited for Fatima to appear, except she didn't.

'Fatima is getting a headache tablet.' Emir gave a wry smile. 'I said I would bring them up.'

How sad that this was so rare, Amy reminded herself. How sad that something so normal merited an explanation—and, no, she told herself, she did *not* want him.

He went to put Clemira down and she moved to help him.

'I don't know how...' It was almost an apology.

'No.' She took one child from his arms. 'I can't put them down together now either,' she said. 'They're far too big for that.' She lowered Clemira to the mattress as Emir did the same with Nakia. 'It was easier when they were little.' She was jabbering now. 'But I've had to lower the mattress now they're standing.' She could feel him watching her mouth; she feared to look at him—just wanted Fatima to come.

'Amy...'

'They're enjoying the dolls' house.'

She kept her head down because she knew what would happen if she lifted it. She knew because it had almost happened the day before, and the day before that—moments when it had been impossible to deny, when it had almost killed not to touch, when it would have been easier to give in. But if she kissed him now this was what they would be reduced to—furtive snogs when Fatima wasn't around, a quick shag when no one was watching, perhaps? And she was better than that, Amy told herself.

But the tears were coming. She reminded herself that, even if she was crying she was strong.

It was Amy who walked out. Amy who left him watching his children as she headed to her room,

'You need to come home.'

Rather than cry she rang home, desperate for normality, for advice. Though Amy's mum didn't know all that had gone on, even if she did, Amy realised, her advice would be the same.

'Amy, you're not going to change things there. I told you that when you accepted the job.'

'But Queen Hannah…'

'Is dead.'

The harsh words hit home.

'Even Queen Hannah knew that the country would have little time for her daughters. That was why she wanted them to be educated in England.'

'I can't leave them.'

'You have no choice,' her mum said. 'Can you really stand another three years of this?'

No, Amy could not. She knew that as she hung up the phone. The last ten days had been hell. With the anniversary of Queen Hannah's death approaching the palace was subdued, but more than that, worse was to come, for there would be a wedding in a few weeks and how could she be here for that?

She couldn't.

Rather than being upset, Amy had actually been relieved that Fatima had been selected to travel with the King. She had decided that the time she would spend alone must be used wisely, but really her decision was made.

Her mother was right: she had no choice but to go home.

She had to, she told herself as she made it through another night.

By morning, she was already wavering.

She walked into the nursery where two beaming girls stood in their cots and blew kisses. They wriggled and blew bubbles as she bathed them, spat out their food and hated their new dresses, pulled out the little hair ribbons faster than Fatima could tie them.

Amy knew every new tooth in their heads, every smile was a gift for her, and she could not stand to walk away.

Except she had to.

Amy packed cases for the little girls, putting in their swimming costumes, because she knew there were several pools at the Alzirz palace.

'They won't be needing those,' Fatima said. 'I shall not be swimming with them.'

And their father certainly wouldn't, Amy thought, biting down on her lip as she struggled to maintain her composure.

She helped Fatima bring them down to wait for the King and board the helicopter.

'Be good!' Amy smiled at the girls when she wanted to kiss them and hold them. She was terribly aware that this might be the last time she would see them, that perhaps it would be kinder to all of them for her simply to leave while they were away.

As Emir strode across the palace he barely glanced at his daughters, and certainly he did not look in Amy's direction. He was dressed in military uniform as this was to be a formal event and she loathed the fact that this man still moved her. His long leather boots rang out as he walked briskly across the marble floor, only halting when Patel called out to him.

'La.' He shook his head, his reply instant, and carried on walking, but Patel called to him again and there was a brief, rather urgent discussion. Then Emir headed into his study, with Patel following closely behind.

'I'll say goodbye now!' Amy spoke to the girls, for they were getting increasingly fretful and so too was she. She must remember that they were not her babies, that they would be fine with Fatima, that they were not hers to love. But it killed her to turn around and walk up the grand staircase. It was almost impossible not to look around and respond to their tears, but she did her level best—freezing on the spot when she heard Patel's voice.

'The King wishes to speak with you.'

'Me?' Slowly Amy turned around.

'Now,' Patel informed her. 'He is busy—do not keep him waiting.'

It felt like the longest walk of her life. Amy could feel eyes on her as she walked back down the stairs, trying to quieten her mind, trying not to pre-empt what Emir wanted though her heart surely knew. She had never been summoned to speak to him before, and could only conclude that his thoughts were the same as hers—while he was gone, perhaps it was better that she leave.

It was terribly awkward to face him. Not since their night together had it been just them, for Fatima was always around, her silent criticism following Amy's every move. There was no discomfort in Emir, she noted. He looked as uninterested and as imposing as he had the last time that she had stood there, and his voice was flat.

'*You* are to accompany the children to the naming ceremony of the new Prince of Alzirz.'

'Me?' Amy swallowed. This was so not what she had been expecting. 'But I thought it was considered more suitable for Fatima to travel with them? She is more well-versed—'

'This is not a discussion,' Emir interrupted. 'You are to go now and to pack quickly. The helicopter is waiting and I have no intention of arriving late.'

'But—' She didn't understand the change of plan. She needed this time alone and was nervous about travelling with him.

'That will be all,' Emir broke in. 'As I said, I did not call you in here for a discussion.'

It was Patel who offered a brief explanation as she left the office. 'Queen Natasha wishes to discuss English nannies and has said she is looking forward to speaking with you.'

This made sense, because of course a request from Queen Natasha during the new Prince's naming ceremony must be accommodated.

It mattered not that it would break her heart.

Amy packed quickly. She selected three pale blue robes and her nightwear, and threw a few toiletries into her bag. Even if there was the helicopter, the King and his entourage waiting, still she took a moment to pack the twins' swimming costumes and her own bikini—because, unlike Fatima, she *would* swim with the girls.

Emir was at the helicopter, and she felt his air of impatience as she stepped in. He had already strapped in the girls and Fatima gave Amy a long, cool look as she left the aircraft, for it was an honour indeed to travel with the King.

It was not the easiest of journeys, though Emir did hold Nakia as they neared their destination. Again Amy watched his features harden and, looking out of the window, thought perhaps she understood why. Alzirz was celebrating as Alzan should have been on the day of the twins' birthday. The streets around the palace were lined with excited people waving flags. They all watched in excitement as dignitaries arrived for the naming of their new Prince.

How it must kill him to be so polite, Amy mused as they arrived at the palace and the two men kissed on both cheeks. She could feel the simmering hatred between them that went back generations.

Queen Natasha didn't seem to notice it. She was incredibly informal and greeted both Amy and the twins as if they were visiting relatives, rather than a nanny and two young princesses. 'They've grown!' she said.

She looked amazing, Amy noted, wearing a loose fitting white robe embroidered with flowers. She certainly didn't look like a woman who had given birth just a few days ago, and Amy felt drab beside her.

'Come through!' Natasha offered, seeing the twins were more than a little overawed by the large formal gathering. 'I'll take you to the nursery. I have to get the baby ready.' She chatted easily as they walked through the palace. 'I'll introduce you to my nanny, Kuma. She's just delightful, but I really want him to learn English.' She smiled over to Amy. 'You're not looking for a job, by any chance?' she asked shamelessly.

'I'm very happy where I am,' came Amy's appropriate response, though she was tempted to joke that Natasha might find her on the palace doorstep in a couple of days. But, no, Amy realised, even if Natasha *was* nice, even if she *was* easy to talk to, in Alzirz as in Alzan the Royal Nanny would have to be obedient to royal command. She could never put her heart through this again.

Kuma really was delightful. She was far more effusive and loving than Fatima. She smiled widely when she saw the twins, put a finger up to her lips to tell them to hush, and then beckoned them over to admire the new prince. Nakia wasn't particularly interested, but Clemira clapped her hands in delight and nearly jumped out of Amy's arms in an effort to get to the baby. She was clearly totally infatuated with the young Prince.

'He's beautiful,' Amy said. His skin was as dark as Rakhal's, but his hair was blonde like Natasha's, and Amy was suddenly filled with hopeless wonder as to what *her* babies might have been like if Emir was their father. She was consumed again with all she had lost, but then she held Clemira tighter and qualified that—all that she was losing by walking away.

'Would you like to hold him?' Natasha offered.

'He's asleep,' Amy said, because she was terrified if she did that she might break down.

'He has to get up, I'm afraid,' Natasha said. 'I want to feed him before the naming ceremony.' She scooped the sleeping infant out of his crib and, as Kuma took Clemira, handed him to Amy.

Sometimes it had hurt to hold Clemira and Nakia in those early days, to know that she would never hold her own newborn, and the pain was back now, as acute as it had been then, perhaps more so—especially when the two Kings came in. Rakhal was proud and smiling down at his son. Emir was polite as he admired the new Prince. But there was grief in his eyes and Amy could see it. She was angry on behalf of his girls, yet she understood it too—for the laws in this land, like in the desert, could be cruel.

'Come,' Emir told her, 'we should take our places.'

Her place was beside him—for the last time.

She stood where in the future she would not: holding his daughters. She held Clemira and sometimes swapped. Sometimes he held both, when he did not have to salute, so he could give Amy a rest and once, when they girls got restless, she set them on the ground, for it was a long and complicated ceremony.

'They did well,' Emir said as they walked back to the nursery with the weary twins.

'Of course they did!' Amy smiled. 'And if they'd cried

would it really have mattered? Tariq screamed the whole ceremony.'

'He did.' Emir had been thinking the same, knew he must not be so rigid. Except his country expected so little from his daughters and somehow he wanted to show them all they could be. 'Just so you know, the Alzirz nanny will be looking after the twins tonight. They are to make a brief appearance at the party, but she will dress them and take care of that.'

'Why?' Amy asked, and she watched his lips tighten as she questioned him.

'Because.' Emir answered, and he almost hissed in irritation as he felt her blue eyes still questioning him. He refused to admit that he did not know why.

'Because what?'

He wanted to turn around and tell her that he was new to this, that the intricacies of parenthood and royal protocol confused him at times too. Hannah would have been the one handling such things. It was on days like today that the duty of being a single parent was the hardest. Yet he could not say all this, so his voice was brusque when he conceded to respond. 'Sheikha Queen Natasha wants them to be close. It is how things are done. If Prince Tariq comes to stay in Alzan you will look after him for the night.'

'I thought you were rivals?'

'Of course,' Emir said. 'But Queen Natasha is new to this. She does not understand how deep the rivalry is, that though we speak and laugh and attend each other's celebrations there is no affection there.'

'None?'

'None.' His face was dark. 'The twins will be looked after by their nanny tonight. They will be brought back to you in the morning and you will all join me at the formal breakfast tomorrow.'

'But the girls will be unsettled in a new...'

He looked at her. He must have been mad to even have considered it—crazy even to think it. For she would not make a good sheikha queen. There was not one sentence he uttered that went unquestioned, not a thought in her head that she did not voice.

'You keep requesting a night off. Why then, do you complain when you get one?'

Amy reminded herself of her place.

'I'm not complaining.' She gave him a wide smile. 'I'm delighted to have a night off work. I just wasn't expecting it.'

'You can ring down for dinner to be sent to you.'

'Room service?' Amy kept that smile, remembered her place. 'And I've got my own pool... Enjoy the party.'

Of course he did not.

He was less than happy as he took his place at the gathering. He could see the changes Natasha had brought to the rather staid palace, heard laughter in the air and the hum of pleasant, relaxed conversation, and it only served to make him more tense. He held his daughters along with Kuma, and Natasha held her son. He saw Kuma being so good with them and thought perhaps Fatima was not so suitable.

Maybe a gentler nanny would suit the children best,

Emir thought. For he knew that Amy was leaving—had seen it in her eyes—and he held Clemira just a touch tighter before he handed her back to Kuma. His heart twisted again, for they should not be in this world without their mother, and a king should not be worrying about hiring a new nanny.

There was the one big decision that weighed heavily, but there were others that must be made too: their nanny, their schooling, their language, their tears, their grief, their future. He must fathom it all unshared with another who loved them. As a single father he did not know how to be.

Black was his mind as the babies were taken upstairs to the nursery, and he looked over to Rakhal, who stood with his wife by his side. Never had he felt more alone. Tonight he grieved the loss of both Hannah and Amy, and he was so distracted that he did not notice Natasha had made her way over.

'I'm sorry. This must be so difficult for you.'

He shot her a look of scorn. How dared she suggest to his face such a thing? How dared she so blatantly disrespect his girls?

But just as his mouth formed a scathing retort she continued. 'It's Hannah's anniversary soon?'

He closed his eyes for a second. Grief consumed him.

He nodded. 'She is missed.'

Natasha looked at this King with grief in his eyes, who stood apart and polite but alone. 'Where's Amy?'

'She is enjoying a night off,' he clipped, for he did

not like to think about her when he wanted her here at his side.

'I didn't mean for her to stay in her room.' Natasha laughed. 'When I said that my nanny would look after the girls I was hoping that she would join us.'

'She is the nanny,' Emir said curtly. 'She is here only to look after the children.'

'Ah, but she's English,' Natasha sighed and rolled her eyes. 'Have you any idea how nice it feels to have someone here who is from home? I was so looking forward to speaking with her—we never really got a chance earlier.'

'She will bring the twins to breakfast tomorrow,' Emir responded, uncomfortable with such overt friendliness.

When he visited Alzirz, or when duty dictated that Rakhal visit Alzan, there were firm boundaries in place, certain ways things were done, but Natasha seemed completely oblivious to them. The new Sheikha Queen did not seem to understand that it was all an act between himself and Rakhal, that there was still a deep rivalry between the two Kings, born from an innate need to protect the kingdoms, their land and their people. Natasha simply didn't understand that although they spoke politely, although they attended all necessary functions, it was only mutual hate that truly united them.

'I'll have somebody sent to get her,' Natasha persisted.

Emir could only imagine how well that would go down with Amy. She didn't like to be told what to do at the best of times, and this certainly wasn't the best of times.

'She is staff,' Emir said, and that should have ended the conversation—especially as Rakhal had now come over. At least Rakhal knew how things were done. He would terminate this conversation in an instant, would quickly realise that lines were being crossed—unlike this beaming Englishwoman.

What *was* it with them?

Natasha smiled up to her husband. 'I was just saying to Emir that I was hoping to have Amy join us tonight. I do miss having someone from home to chat to at times.'

And love must have softened Rakhal's brain, Emir thought darkly, for instead of looking to Emir, instead of gauging his response, instead of playing by the unspoken rules he looked to his wife.

'Then why don't you have someone go to the suite and see if she would care to join us?' he said. Only then did he address Emir. 'Normally Natasha's brother and his fiancée would be here tonight, to join in the celebrations, but they are in the UK for another family commitment and couldn't make it.'

Emir did not care. Emir had no desire to know why Natasha's brother and his fiancée could not be here. Had Rakhal forgotten for a moment that this was all a charade? That there was more hate in the air than the palatial ballroom could readily hold? For when he thought of his daughters, thought of his late wife and the rule Alzirz refused to revoke, Emir could happily pull his knife.

'It would be unfair to her.' Emir did his best to keep

his voice even. 'She will have only her working clothes with her.'

'I'm not that mean.' Natasha smiled. 'I wouldn't do that to her. I'll have some clothes and maidens sent to her room to help prepare her. I'll arrange it now.'

There was so much he would like to say—Emir was not used to having any decision questioned—and yet protocol dictated politeness even in this most uncomfortable of situations. He could just imagine Amy, in her present mood, if one of the servants were to knock at her door and insist that she come down and join in with the feasting and celebrations. A smile he was not expecting almost spread his lips at the very thought, but he rescued his features from expression and nodded to the waiting Queen.

'Very well, if you wish to have Amy here, I shall go now and speak to her. I will ask her to come down, though she may already have retired for the night.'

Natasha smiled back at him and Emir could not understand why she could not see the hate in his eyes as he spoke. He strode out of the grand ballroom.

As he did so Rakhal turned to his wife. 'You are meddling.'

'Of course I'm not,' Natasha lied.

But her husband knew her too well. He had had the teachings too and his wife seduced with her beauty, dazzled like the sun low in the desert. He knew his wife was plotting now.

'Natasha? You do *not* interfere in such things.'

'I'm not,' Natasha insisted. 'You have to work the

room and I would like someone to talk to in my own language. Amy seems nice.'

But of course she *was* meddling. Natasha had seen King Emir's eyes linger a little too long on Amy at times, when the nanny hadn't been aware he was watching her. She had seen the sadness behind his eyes too. And, yes, perhaps it was for selfish reasons also that she was interfering just a little, but the thought of someone from her own land to be beside her at these endless functions…

She knew that Emir must soon take a new sheikha queen, and if that queen happened to be Amy—well, who could blame her for giving Cupid a little nudge? She loved her new country—loved it so much—but the rivalry between the two nations, the bitterness between them and all the impossible rules she simply could not abide, and she was quite sure that Amy must feel the same.

Amy had not retired for the night as Emir was silently hoping as he walked through the palace to her room.

She had rung down for dinner and enjoyed a delicious feast—or tried to. She had been thinking about the girls, thinking about Emir and trying to picture her future without them. But it was too hard. So she had telephoned home, hoping for a long chat, but everybody must be at work because she had spoken to endless answering machines. And, yes, a night off was what she had asked for, and the Alzirz palace was as sumptuous as even the most luxurious hotel, but after an hour or two of reading and painting her toenails she had grown restless. Simply because it was there for the taking Amy put on her bikini and went for a long swim in her own private pool.

It was glorious—the temperature of the water perfect, the area shaded with date palms for complete privacy and protection from the fierce Alzirz sun during the day. Lying on her back, she could see the stars peeking through. But just as she started to relax, just as she had convinced herself to stop worrying about leaving Alzan, at least for tonight, she heard a bell ring from her suite.

Perhaps the maid had come to take her tray, Amy thought and, climbing out of the pool, went to answer the door. She had left her towel behind so she tied on a flimsy silk robe and called for the maid to come in. As the bell rang again Amy realised that perhaps she didn't understand English and opened the door—completely taken aback to find Emir standing there.

'It was not my intention to disturb you.' It was close to an apology, but not quite. He was a king summoning a servant, Emir reminded himself—it was a compliment in itself that he had come to her door. 'You are required downstairs.'

Amy frowned. 'Is there a problem with one of the twins?'

'Not at all.' He felt more than a little uncomfortable, especially as two damp triangles were becoming visible where her wet bikini seeped into the silk of her gown. 'Sheikha Queen Natasha has requested that you join in the celebrations.'

'No, thanks.' Amy gave a tight smile and went to

close the door, but his booted foot halted it. 'Excuse me!' was Amy's brittle response.

'You don't understand,' Emir said, but he did remove his boot. 'That is why I came personally—to explain things to you. The Queen is hosting the party. It is the Queen who has requested you to come down, not me. It would be rude…'

'Rude for who?' Amy responded—because she did not want to go down there, did not want to be Natasha's little project for the night. She particularly did not want to spend any more time with Emir than she had to—things were already difficult enough.

Now he was at her door, and she could feel the cool wetness of her gown, knew from the flick of his eyes downwards that he had seen it too—that she might just as well not be wearing it. She was frantic to have him gone.

'It's rude to give me a night off and then revoke it!' She went to close the door again, did not want to prolong this discussion.

Emir would not let things be, and unless she slammed the door in his face she'd have to stand there and listen as he spoke on.

'If the twins were awake you would be expected to bring them down.'

'The twins are not in my care tonight.'

'That is not the point.' Emir's voice was stern. He was less than impressed with Amy's behaviour—especially as a maid came into the corridor and bowed her head to him. He stood there bristling with indignation as she went in and retrieved Amy's dinner tray. 'It is not right for me to be seen standing here and arguing with...'

'An employee?' she finished for him. But she accepted it was not fitting behaviour, and once the maid had gone she held the door further open for him. 'I have nothing to wear to a party. I haven't showered. I'm not ready...'

'That is being taken care of.' He blocked her excuses as Natasha had blocked his. 'Queen Natasha is having some clothes and some maidens sent here to your room.' He turned to go. 'I expect you to be down there within half an hour.'

'Emir...'

There was a plea in her voice, a plea he had heard once before—the sound of her begging. He remembered her writhing beneath him and he hardly dared turn around.

'Don't make me do this. Go and enjoy the party on your own—make an excuse for me that is fitting. I don't know anything about...'

'Enjoy it?' He did turn around then, and he wished she were dressed—wished she looked anything other than she did now. For the gown was completely see-through. Three triangles taunted him. He could see the hard peaks of her nipples, see the flush on her neck. He should not be in this room with her for a whole set of reasons other than protocol. 'You will get dressed.'

When still she shook her head, he lost his temper. He spoke harsh angry words. It was far safer than pushing her onto the bed.

'You really think that I want to be down there? You really think that I'm enjoying making small talk, pretending that I do not hate them? If it were not for them…'

His black eyes met hers, as angry and savage as they had been the day she had first challenged him, but it did not scare her as it had then. His anger was not aimed at her, nor his words, Amy was quite sure. This would not be of his choosing, for this remote, private man to pour some of the pain out.

'Amy, please…'

Not once had he pleaded, not once that she knew of, and this came with a roar from the heart.

'I am asking you to please make this night easier for me—I am in hell down there.'

And he was. He was in hell tonight and no one knew. He could not share his burden; he carried it alone for he was King. He remembered his status and was ashamed of his words, his loss of control. But there was no smart retort from Amy. This time she stood stunned, as he was at his revelation, and he could see tears pooling in her eyes. She had glimpsed a little of his pain.

It was not that her mouth found his, nor was it his mouth which sought hers. Neither initiated the kiss. They simply joined, and he felt the bliss of oblivion. The pain ended for a moment and relief was instant. There was release and escape as her wet body pressed to his. He had craved her since that night, had wanted her each minute, and her tongue as it twisted with his, the heat of her skin through the damp gown, told him she had craved him as much.

She had.

His uniform was rough beneath her fingers, his mouth desperate on hers, his erection as fierce as his passion. She could feel him hard in her centre. It was happening again and it must not.

'Emir,' she whimpered, pulling her mouth back from his, though she did not want him to stop kissing her. Her lips ached for more as they moved from his. Regretting their departure, they returned, speaking into his mouth. 'We said just once.'

'Then get dressed,' he said, and his hands peeled off the damp robe, and his fingers worked the knot at the back of her bikini.

She moaned in his mouth as he stroked the aching peaks; his hands moved to her bottom and he pulled her up till her legs twined around him. This was way more than a kiss getting out of hand. The bed seemed an impossible distance, clothes their only barrier.

She felt the cold of brass buttons on her skin as he kissed her onto the bed, pulling at the damp bikini while his other hand moved to unbuckle his belt. And Amy realised her hands were helping his, for she was through with thinking. She could make decisions later, could work things out then. Right now she simply had to have him.

And she would have.

He would have had her.

Had the bell not rung again.

He looked down at where she lay, a breath away from

coming. Regret was in both their eyes—not just at the interruption, but at what had taken place.

'That didn't just happen,' Amy said. Except it had. And now, even more so than before, it was impossible for her to stay.

No longer could their night in the desert be put down to a one-off. The attraction between them was undeniable and yet soon he would be taking a wife.

'It won't happen again,' Emir said.

They both knew he was lying.

He buckled up his belt, took her by the hand and led her to the bathroom. He checked his appearance in the mirror and then called to open the door. He watched as maidens bought in an array of clothing. He told them that Amy was in the shower and they must quickly prepare her to be brought down, and then he called out to her where she sat, crouched and shivering on the bathroom floor.

'You will get ready quickly.' He spoke as a king would when addressing a belligerent servant. He tried to remember his place and so too must she. 'Queen Natasha is waiting for you.'

CHAPTER TEN

'TOMORROW we leave for the desert.'

Natasha was irritating. She insisted on chatting as if they were old friends. And yet, Emir conceded, he would find *any* conversation annoying now, for his mind was only on Amy and what had just taken place.

Fool, he said to himself. Fool for not resisting. Fool for being weak.

And fool because tonight he would take her, only to lose her again in the morning.

Only to have her leave.

'I'm looking forward to it.' Natasha persisted with their one-way conversation. 'After all the celebrations and pomp surrounding the birth, it will be nice to get some peace.'

Now Emir did respond—and very deliberately he chose to get things wrong. 'I'm sure that the Bedouins will take good care of him.' He saw the flare of horror in Natasha's eyes.

'Oh, it's not for that. It's way too soon to even *think* of being parted from him. That doesn't have to happen until he turns one.'

'*Before* he turns one,' Emir said, enjoying one pleasure in this night.

Two pleasures, he corrected, his mind drifting to Amy again. But he must stay focussed. He must concentrate on the conversation rather than anticipating her arrival, rather then remembering what had just happened. And perhaps it was time to give Natasha a taste of the medicine he had so recently sampled.

'I handed over the girls last week. Your husband was kind enough to grant a concession that they only stay in the desert for one night, given what happened to their mother.' He watched Natasha's lips tighten as he reminded her, none too gently, that her son would be in the desert for several nights—unless, of course, he lost his mother too. Unless he was forced to be weaned early, as Emir's daughters had been.

'How did the girls get on?' Natasha attempted to make it sound like a polite enquiry, as if she were asking after the girls rather than about what she could expect for her own son.

Emir knew that—it was the reason he didn't mollify her with his response. 'They screamed, they wept and they begged,' Emir said, watching as her face grew paler with each passing word. 'But they are the rules.' Emir shrugged. 'My daughters have been forced to be strong by circumstance, and so they survived it.'

He stopped twisting the knife then—not to save her from further distress, but because at that moment it seemed to Emir that everything simply stopped.

He had wondered far too often what Amy might look

like out of that robe—he had pictured her not just in her nightdress, or naked beneath him, but dressed as his Queen.

She stepped into that vision now and claimed it, and deep in his gut a knife twisted.

She was dressed in a dark emerald velvet gown, her lips painted red and her eyes skilfully lined with kohl. Her hair was down. But nothing, not even the work of a skilled make-up artist, could temper the glitter in her eyes and the blush of her cheeks that their kiss had evoked. A riot of ringlets framed her face.

The world was cruel, Emir decided, for it taunted him with what he could not have. It showed him exactly how good it could have been, had the rules allowed her to join him, to be at his side.

Little more than a year ago she would have been veiled and hidden. A year ago he would not have had to suffer the tease of her beauty. But there was a new Sheikha Queen in Alizirz and times were changing.

Amy was changing.

Before his eyes, as she chatted with Natasha, he witnessed the effortless seduction of her body. For even as she turned slightly away from him her gestures seemed designed for him. She threw her head back and laughed, and then, as he knew it would, her hand instinctively moved to cover the scar on her throat. She twisted her hair around her fingers and he fought his desire to snake a hand around her waist. He wanted to join in the conversation as he would with a partner, to squeeze her waist just once to remind her that soon it would be over and soon they would be alone.

He put down the glass he was gripping rather than break it.

He turned away, but her laughter filled his ears.

Emir tried to remember the shy woman who had first entered the palace. He had not noticed her—or at least not in that way. His mind had been too consumed with worry for his wife, who had been fading by the day, for him to notice Amy. He wanted that back. He wanted the invisible woman she had been then.

But she wasn't invisible now.

She was there before his eyes.

And for her he might not be King.

'Thank you so much for coming down.' Natasha kissed Amy's cheek an agonising couple of hours later. 'It was lovely to talk.'

'It was my pleasure,' Amy said. 'Thank you for the invitation.'

She meant not a word.

And neither did Emir as he too politely thanked Rakhal and headed to the stairs.

She could not do this.

She stepped out into a fragrant garden, breathed in the blossom and begged it to quell the hammering of her mind. She listened to the fountain that should soothe. Except it did not, for she understood now a little of what Emir had meant about being in hell.

To stand apart while their minds were together, to ignore the other while their bodies silently screamed, was a potent taste of what might be to come when he married.

If she stayed.

Her fury was silent as she walked to her room, but she knew what she had to do. Her eyes took in the empty bed, but the scent of him confirmed that he was there. She saw that the doors were open and looked beyond them to where he stood by the pool. His jacket was undone and his eyes met hers. She shook her head, for forbidden lovers they must not be.

'No.'

Brave in her decision, she walked towards him, her anger building as she did so, reminding herself of all she did not admire about this man. She tried to dull the passion he triggered, determined that it be over.

'I'm through with this, Emir.' She made herself say it. 'I don't even like you.'

He simply looked.

His silence let her speak.

'I could never be with a man willing to ignore his children—despite my health problems, despite the fact I can't have children. Even without that I'd never have said yes.' She was lying, she could hear it, but her mind begged for it to be true. 'How can I love a man who doesn't care about his children?'

She watched his eyes narrow. Perhaps this was not the conversation he'd been expecting. It was a mistress he wanted, Amy reminded herself, not an argument about his children. But her racing heart surely stopped for a moment when his low voice delivered a response *she* was not expecting.

'Never say that.'

She thought he might throw the drink he was holding in her face. He might just as well have, because nothing could have shocked her more than the passion in his voice when his next words were delivered.

'I love my children.'

Except his actions did not show it, even if his words sounded true.

'You say that…'

'Trust that I have my daughters' best interests at heart.'

And she looked at his pain ravaged face and into eyes that glittered with the flames of hell. Somehow she did trust him. Despite all evidence to the contrary, she did believe him.

What did this man do to her? she begged of herself.

'Please, Emir, go.'

She could not think when he was around; she lost herself when he was near.

'Go,' she said, and walked to the bedroom.

'Go.' She sobbed as still by the pool he stood.

And she knew it was hopeless. For to leave he would have to walk past her, and not to touch would be an impossible ask.

'Go.' She begged, even as she undressed for him, crying with shame at her own need.

She pulled down the zipper, slipped off the gown as he walked now towards her, her actions opposing her words as she removed her bra. Emir unbuckled his belt while entering the bedroom. Even then she shook her head. Even then she denied it as she took down her panties.

'No...' She changed her plea. She was sobbing as he kissed her down onto the bed, but she was grateful for the mattress that met her back for she got the gift of his full weight pressed into her. 'We mustn't...' She pushed at his bare chest but her fingers attempted to grip his skin, her nails wanted to dig in and leave her mark. 'Emir, you know that we mustn't...'

He took her hands and captured her wrists, held them over her head and hungrily kissed her. Then with words he fought for what they both needed tonight. 'We must.'

His words were truthful, and he was fierce. Even naked he ruled her as he told her that he would make it work.

'We *will* be together...'

'There is no way...'

'I will find a way,' he told her. 'I will make this work. I will come to you in the night-time and in later years I will visit you and the girls in London.'

'Your mistress...?'

'More than a mistress,' he said between frantic kisses. 'You will care for the twins. You will raise them.'

Was it possible to love and hate at the same time?

To be filled with both want and loathing as he bound her to him, but with a life of lies?

He offered her everything, yet gave her nothing.

A life with no voice, Amy realised, and it was then that she found hers.

'No.'

His hands released their grip but she did not push him off. Instead she wrapped her arms around his back. 'This ends tonight.'

Their bodies knew that she lied.

All night he had been wanting her, and all night she had been waiting for him. They met now and their kisses tasted of fury for the future they could not have. She felt his anger as he stabbed inside her—anger at the rules that denied him the woman he wanted by his side. But for now there was an outlet, and he was animal. He bucked inside her and she lifted her hips to him. Their eyes locked in a strange loathing of what they might make the other do so easily. So easily she came to him.

And so deeply he delivered.

He knew she would shout. He felt her lungs fill and the tension in her throat as he shot into her; he felt her scream even as it rose, for his body and his soul knew her.

She came in a way she never had before, tightened in possession as he drove her further. She was grateful for his hand that smothered her mouth, furious that the only restraint he could muster was to stifle her screams with the hand she could never take.

She told herself she hated him.

Reminded herself she did not want to be his wife.

She was relieved it was over, surely?

They lay for a suitable while, waiting for normality

to return, for the madness to subside, for him to rise from her bed and head to his own. But as he went to do so Amy's hand reached out to him and it was then that she cried, for she had proved that she lied.

Her fierce vow that it would end tonight had already been downgraded to the morning.

CHAPTER ELEVEN

MORNING came whether she wanted it to or not.

The sun did not care that it ended them.

It did what it was born to—it rose and dictated that their time was over.

She knew Emir was awake next to her. She watched the fingers of light spread across the floor and before they reached the bed she felt his hand on her hip, then her waist. She closed her eyes as he tucked her body towards him, felt his erection and wanted to wake every morning to him. She did not want to be a woman who settled for a slice of his life—didn't want to fit into allocated times. Yet had the phone not rung Amy knew that she would have.

'The twins are on their way.' Her voice was urgent as she hung up, 'Kuma is bringing them now.'

There was no time for Emir to dress and leave, but he dealt with it instantly. Picking up the uniform he had so readily discarded last night, he headed to her en suite bathroom. This time it was he who hid there.

More than a little breathless, Amy searched for something to put on. Her panic was broken by a smile as a well-manicured hand appeared from the bathroom, holding her robe.

'You need to relax,' he warned her.

It was far easier said than done, because even as she tied the knot on her robe there was a knock on the door. When she opened it, there stood Kuma holding the smiling twins, who were clearly delighted to see Amy.

'They had a wonderful night,' Kuma explained, putting them down. The twins crawled happily in. 'Clemira is really taken with the new Prince, but I think they both want someone more familiar this morning. How was your night?' Kuma beamed. 'I hear you were asked to join in the celebrations.'

'I was.' Amy nodded, nervous and trying not to show it, attempting to carry on the conversation as if she *didn't* have the King of Alzan hiding in her room.

But thankfully Kuma did not prolong things. She wanted to get back to her young charge, so she wished Amy good morning and reminded her that the twins were expected to join the royals for breakfast in hour. 'I hope that your time in Alzirz has been pleasant,' Kuma said and then she was gone.

As was their time.

Like two homing devices, or observant kittens, the twins had made a beeline for the bathroom door, their dear little hands banging, calling out to the rather big secret behind it.

'She's gone.' Amy's face was burning as the door opened and out stepped Emir. She had expected him to be wearing his uniform, but instead he was dressed in a more standard thick white towelling robe.

'I will say that I'm looking for the twins if someone sees me in the corridor.' He had already worked out how to discard all evidence. 'If you can pack my uniform…?'

'Of course.' Amy nodded, telling herself that this was what it would be like were they to continue.

The twins let out a squeal of delight as they realised the two people they loved most in the world were together in the same room. And the man who had asked her to believe that he had his daughters' best interests at heart, even if he did not always show it, the man who so often did not reveal his feelings, confused her again as he picked up the girls and greeted them tenderly.

He went to hand them to Amy, but changed his mind.

'I hear you take them swimming at the palace?'

'Every day,' Amy said. 'They love it.'

Go, her eyes begged him.

'Show me,' he said.

And so she dressed them in their little costumes, put on yesterday's red bikini, and now he wasn't a distant sheikh king who watched from the poolside. Instead he made do with his surprisingly modern black hipsters and took to the water with his daughters.

Amy was suddenly shy.

It felt wrong at first to be in the water with him— wrong to join them, wrong when he splashed her, when he caught her unguarded, when he pulled her into the trio. But after a moment she joined in.

Amy knew what was wrong—it was because it felt

right. For a little while they were a family—a family on vacation, perhaps—and they left their troubles behind.

Emir was a father to his daughters this morning, and the twins delighted at the love and affection surrounding them. Emir splashed around with Nakia, hoisted Clemira on his shoulders as she giggled in delight. And in the water with them was Amy, and he did not leave her out. They stopped for a kiss.

The pool was shaded by the palms, but the sun did not let them be. It dotted through the criss-cross of leaves and glimmered on the water. It chased and it caught up and there was nothing they could do.

'Let me get a photo,' Amy said. 'For the nursery.' She wanted the girls to have a picture with their father—a picture of the three of them together and happy.

This was how it could be, Amy realised as she looked at the image on her phone, looked at the people she felt were her family.

An almost family.

It wasn't enough.

'Get the girls ready,' Emir said as they walked back inside. 'And then bring them down to breakfast.'

She blinked at the change in him, and then she understood—in a few moments they would face each other at the breakfast table, would be expected to carry on as if nothing was between them.

Emir was back to being King.

CHAPTER TWELVE

AND so the feast continued.

The birth of the new Prince demanded an extensive celebration, and Amy could see the tiredness in Natasha's eyes as she greeted the never ending stream of guests.

It was a semi-formal breakfast. There was a long, low table groaning with all the food Amy had come to love in her time there, but she was not here to socialise or to eat, but to make sure that the twins behaved. It was assumed she would have eaten before the Princesses rose.

Of course, she was starving.

Starving, her eyes told him. He watched them linger on the *sfiha* he reached for. He was at Rakhal's table, and it would be rude not to indulge, but it tasted of guilt on his tongue.

He was weak for her. Emir knew that.

And weak kings did not make good decisions.

'Have something!' Natasha insisted, sitting next to Amy as she fed the girls. 'For goodness' sake.'

'I already ate,' Amy responded. 'But thank you.'

'I insist,' Natasha said. She saw her husband's eyes

shoot her a warning but she smiled sweetly back, for there was something that Rakhal did not know—something she had not had time to tell him.

When he had gone riding that morning she had taken tea on the balcony—had heard the sound of a family together, had felt the love in the air. She knew only too well the strain of being considered an unsuitable bride, yet things were changing here in Alzirz and they could change too in Alzan.

Amy did her best to forget she was hungry as she fed the twins. Did her best not to give in to the lure of his voice, nor turn her head when he spoke. She tried to treat him with the distant, quiet reverence that any servant would.

The twins were a little too loud, but very funny, smiling at their audience as they entertained, basking in the attention. As the breakfast started to conclude she wiped their faces, ready to take them back to their room and to pack for the journey home.

Not home, she reminded herself. She was returning to the palace.

With the evidence of last night in her case.

Just for a brief moment she lost focus, daydreamed for a second too long, considering the impossible as she recalled last night. Of course Clemira noticed her distraction.

Clemira demanded attention. 'Ummi!'

Amy snapped her eyes open, prayed for a futile second that no one had heard. But just in case they hadn't Nakia followed the leader as she always did.

'Ummi!'

'Amy!' She forced out the correction, tried to sound bright and matter of fact, but her eyes were filling with tears, her heart squeezing as still the twins insisted on using the Arabic word for mummy.

'I'll go and get them ready for the journey home.' She picked up Clemira, her hands shaking, grateful when Natasha stood and picked up Nakia.

Natasha was the perfect hostess, instantly realising the *faux pas* the little girls had made. Doing her best to smooth things over, she followed Amy out of the room with Nakia. But as Amy fled past the table she caught a brief glimpse of Emir. His face was as grey as the incoming storm—and there *would* be a storm. Amy was certain of it.

The tension chased her from the room. The realisation that continuing on was becoming increasingly impossible surrounded her now. She wished Natasha would leave when they reached the nursery, wished she would not try to make conversation, because Amy was very close to tears.

'I will go back and explain to them.' Natasha was practical. 'I know how difficult things can be at times, but once I explain how similar the words are…' She tried to make things better and, perhaps selfishly, yearned for Amy to confide in her. The only thing missing in her life was a girlfriend—someone from home to chat to, to compare the country's ways with. 'Anyway, it's surely natural that they would think of you in that way.'

'I'm not their mother.'

'I know.' Natasha misinterpreted Amy's tears as she cuddled Clemira into her—or perhaps she didn't. Her words were the truth. After all, she had heard them as a family that morning. 'It must be so hard for you—to detach, I mean, you've known them since the day they were born.'

'Why would it be hard for me to detach?' Amy met the Queen's eyes and frowned, her guard suddenly up. Natasha sounded as if she really did know how hard it was for her, and she must never know—no one must ever know. But Amy was suddenly certain that Natasha did, and her attempt to refute it was desperate. 'I'm a royal nanny—as Kuma is.'

Natasha knew she had meddled too far, but she stepped back a little too late. 'Of course you have to keep a professional detachment.' Natasha nodded. Amy was not going to confide in her, she realised, so she tried to salvage the conversation as best she could. 'After all, you will have your own babies one day.'

Amy was tired—so tired of women who assumed, who thought it was so straightforward, that parenthood was a God-given right. Maybe, too, she was tired of covering up, tired of saying the right thing, tired of putting others at ease as they stomped right over her heart.

She looked up at Natasha. 'Actually, I can't have children.' She watched the blush flood Natasha's cheeks and then fade till her skin was pale. She knew then that somehow Natasha knew about herself and Emir—perhaps they had given themselves away last night at the celebration? Perhaps they'd ignored each other just a touch too much? Or was their love simply visible to all?

Yes, love, Amy thought with a sob of bitterness—a bitterness that carried through to her words. 'So, yes, while it might have been a touch awkward for everyone at breakfast to hear the twins call me Ummi, for me it hurts like hell. Now…' She wanted her tears to fall in private, for Natasha was not her friend. 'If you'll excuse me…?'

'Amy—'

'Please!' Amy didn't care if it was the Queen she was dismissing, didn't care if this was Natasha's home. She just wanted some privacy, some space. 'Can you please just leave it?'

Had she looked up she would have seen tears in Natasha's eyes too as she nodded and left her. And Natasha's eyes filled again when she took her place back at the table and saw Emir sit tall and proud, but removed.

Natasha had seen that expression before. It was the same as it had been when he had lost Hannah. Grey and strained, his features etched in grief.

As Emir looked up, as he saw the sympathy in Natasha's expression, he knew she had been told—that Amy must have somehow confided the truth.

That it was impossible for her to be Queen.

CHAPTER THIRTEEN

HE MET the day he dreaded and rose at dawn.

His prayers were deep.

Guilt lashed like a whip to his back. He had not allowed a year to pass before he touched another woman and deep was Emir's prayer for forgiveness; yet there was nothing to forgive, his soul told him. That wasn't the prayer that she needed to hear.

He could feel Hannah reaching from the grave, desperate for him to say it, for without those words how could she rest?

'I will make the best decision.'

Still it was not what she wanted; still he was forced to look deeper. Yet he dared not.

He visited the nursery. There was Amy, curled up on the sofa, reading a book with the twins. He could not look at her. Later they rode with him in the back of a car to the edge of the desert, to visit Hannah and pay their respects.

Amy sat in the vehicle and watched the trio. When he turned to walk back to the car she watched him unseen, for the windows were heavily tinted. She ached to comfort him, to say the right thing, but it was not and could never be her place.

It had been five days since they'd returned from Alzirz.

Five days of ignoring her, Emir thought as they drove back.

Five days of denial.

And a lifetime of it to look forward to.

She could see his pain, could feel his pain as they walked back into the palace, and she proved herself a liar again.

'I'm sorry today is so hard.'

He could not look at her.

'If...' She stopped herself, but with a single word it was out there: *If it gets too tough, if things get too hard, if the night is too long...*

He turned and did not wait for the guards to open his office door; instead he strode in, saw Patel and the elders quickly shuffle some papers. But Emir knew. He did not attempt politeness, nor even ask to see what was written. He just strode to the desk and picked them up. He looked through them for a moment, a muscle flickering in his cheek as he read them.

'Sheikha Princess Jannah of Idam?' He looked to Patel—a look that demanded a rapid answer.

'She has many brothers.' Patel's voice was a touch high from fear. It was his turn to be on the receiving end of the King's anger and he did not like it one bit. 'She has many brothers. Her father too has many brothers...'

'Sheikha Noor?' Emir's voice was low, but no less ferocious.

'A strong male lineage also…' Patel's words were rapid. 'And a family of longevity.'

'Today is the anniversary of the death of Queen Hannah, and instead of being on your knees in prayer you sit and discuss the next royal intake.'

'In my defence, Your Highness, we really need to address this. The people are impatient. Today they mourn, but tomorrow they will start asking…'

'Silence!' Emir roared. It was not today that he dreaded, he realised, but tomorrow, when he must move on, and the tomorrow after that one and the next. 'You will show respect to your departed Sheikha Queen. You will give thanks for the Royal Princesses's mother.'

'Of course.'

'You do not mention the Princesses here, I note,' Emir said. 'You do not seem concerned in the least as to the new Queen's suitability for *them*.' He cursed his aide and Patel did not wait to be told to leave. Neither did the elders. Within a moment the room was cleared and he stood alone. He did not want the day over—did not want it to be tonight. For it was killing him not to go to Amy, not to draw on the comfort she would give, not to have her again and again.

He was an honourable man.

And soon he must take a wife.

He looked again to the list that had been drawn up, tried to picture himself standing with his new bride at his side while his lover, the woman he really wanted, stood next to him, holding his children as he made solemn vows.

It had never been harder to be King.

He picked up his phone. It was answered in an instant and he was grateful, for given two seconds he might have paused and changed his mind.

'Send the children's nanny to speak with me,' Emir said, and then specified, 'the English one.' He could only stand and wait to do this to her, to himself, but once, Emir needed it done this very moment. He had to bring things to a conclusion tonight—needed a clear head with which to make his decision. And with Amy in the palace it was an impossible ask. He could not get through this night with her near and yet out of reach to him.

Not an army, only distance could hold him back from her tonight.

'Are you in trouble again?' Fatima asked the minute Amy returned from her swim with the twins.

Amy was starting to warm to Fatima, and the twins were too—she was very firm, but she was also fair and kind and, perhaps more importantly, she had grown fond of the twins. They were taking over her heart, which was something they could easily do.

'Trouble?' Amy smiled, assuming the kitchen had rung again to complain about her meal choices for the twins. Or perhaps they had made too much noise when they were swimming on such a revered day. 'Probably. Why?'

'I just took a phone call and the King wishes to speak with you immediately.'

At some level she had known this was coming. Deep down she had known it was only a matter of time before it happened. She just hadn't expected it today.

She had thought they might have this night, but she could not hope for anything as Fatima suggested that she tidy herself before she met with him, because Amy's hair was still wet from the pool.

'I don't think that will be necessary,' Amy said— there seemed no point having a mini makeover when you were about to be fired.

She looked around the nursery to the twins, who were now hungrily eating the grapes Fatima was passing to them, counting them out in Arabic as she did so.

They would be okay, Amy told herself as she took the long walk through the palace.

The guards opened the door as she approached, and reminded her to bow her head until the King spoke.

She discarded that advice.

Amy walked in with her head held high, determined she would leave with grace. Except the sight of him, standing tall but so remote, made her want to be his lover again, to salvage what little they had. She opened her mouth to plead her case, but his eyes forbade her to speak and it was Emir who spoke first.

'You will leave late this afternoon. I have arranged all transport. That gives you some time to spend with the girls. I have a new nanny starting. She will assist Fatima.'

Yes, she'd wanted to do this with grace, but at the final hurdle she faltered—could not stand the thought of yet another woman taking care of *her* girls. 'No! You know the girls are better off with me—you said it your-self.'

'I did not realise then that they were learning only to speak in English, that they knew nothing of our ways…'

'They would know a whole lot more if you spent more time with them. They don't need another nanny!'

'She will be more suitable. We must hold on to the ways of old.'

'What about London? What about their education and all Queen Hannah wanted for them?'

'*This* is their land.'

She really would never see them. Amy knew this was a goodbye for ever, and she forgot to be brave and strong. 'What you said before…about me being your lover…' She could not bear to leave—would give anything, even her pride, if it meant that she could stay. Because it was three times her heart was being broken here. She was losing three of the people she most loved. 'What you said about me raising the girls in London…'

'It is the type of thing men say when they want a woman in their bed. It is the type of thing a man says when his thoughts are not clear.' Completely devoid of emotion, he threw the most hurtful words at her, a round of bullets shot rapidly straight to her heart. He didn't stop firing. 'You really think I would choose *you* for that role?' He let out an incredulous laugh at the very thought. 'Here a mistress is a man's respite—a woman he can go to to relax and not be bombarded with every-day trivialities. You would be most unsuitable.'

He was right.

Amy felt the colour flood back to her cheeks, and she felt the fire in her soul return too—a fire that had been doused by the accident, that had flared only on occasion in recent times. But it was back now, and burning even more brightly, fuelling her to stand up to him.

'I *would* be a most unsuitable mistress.' She gathered her dignity and held on to it tightly, determined that she would never let it go again. She could hardly believe the offer she had made him just a few moments before and she told him why. 'I'd be a terrible mistress, in fact. I'd bombard you with news about your daughters. Every achievement, every tear I would share with you. I would busy your distinguished brain with my voice and my opinions, and…' She walked over to him—right over to where he stood. He lifted his jaw, did not look at her as she spoke, but it did not stop her. Her words told him all he would be missing. 'And there would be *no* relaxing.'

'Go!' Emir said, and still he could not look at her.

Amy knew why. He was resisting his need for her, refusing the comfort that was within his grasp.

'Go and spend time with the twins.'

'I'm going now to pack,' Amy said. 'I'll spend the afternoon at the airport.'

There was nothing left to say to him, no point pleading with him, nothing she could do for the twins. She was an employee, that was all.

But she had been his lover.

'We both know why you need me out of here today, Emir. We both know you'd be in my bed tonight, and heaven forbid you might show emotion—might tell me what's going on in the forbidden zone of your mind. You can stop worrying about that now—I'll be gone within the hour,' Amy said. 'All temptation will be removed.'

'You flatter yourself.'

'Actually, I haven't for a while. But I will from now on.'

Amy had once read that people who had been shot sometimes didn't even know, that they could carry on, fuelled by adrenaline, without realising they had been wounded. She hadn't believed it at the time, but she knew it to be true now.

She packed her belongings and rang down to arrange a car to take her to the airport. There wasn't an awful lot to pack. She'd arrived with hardly anything and left with little more—save a heart so broken she didn't dare feel it.

And because it was a royal nanny leaving, because in this land there were certain ways that had to be adhered to, Emir came out and held Clemira while Fatima held Nakia.

Amy did the hardest thing she had ever done, but it was necessary, she realised, the right thing to do. She kissed the little girls goodbye and managed to smile and not scare them. She should probably curtsy to *him*, but Amy chose not to. Instead she climbed into the car, and after a wave to the twins she deliberately didn't look back.

Never again would she let him see her cry.

CHAPTER FOURTEEN

HE HEARD the twins wail and sob late into the night. He need not have—his suite was far from the nursery—but he walked down there several times and knew Fatima could not quieten them.

'They will cry themselves out soon,' Fatima said, putting down her sewing and standing as he approached once again. She had put a chair in the hallway while she waited for the twins to give in to sleep.

Still they refused to.

He could not comfort them. They did not seem to want his comfort, and he did not know what to do.

He walked from the nursery not towards his suite but to Amy's quarters. It was a route he took in his head perhaps a thousand times each night. It was a door he fought not to open again and again. Now that he did, it was empty—the French doors had been left open to air it, so he didn't even get the brief hit of her scent. The bed had been stripped and the wardrobes, when he looked, were bare, so too the drawers. The bathroom had been thoroughly cleaned. Like a mad man, he went through the bathroom cupboards, and then back out to the bedroom, but there was nothing of her left.

He walked back to the nursery where the babies were still screaming as Fatima sewed. When she rose as he approached he told her to sit and walked into the nursery. He turned on the lights and picked up his screaming girls.

He scanned the pinboard of photos and children's paintings. There he was, and so too Hannah, and there were hundreds of pictures of the girls. But there was not a single one of Amy—not even a handprint bore her name. Emir realised fully then that she was gone from the palace and gone from these rooms—gone from his life and from his daughters' lives too.

The twins' screams grew louder, even though he held them in his arms, and Emir envied their lack of restraint and inhibition—they could sob and beat their fists on his chest, yell with indignant rage, that she was gone.

He looked out of the window to the sky that was carrying her home now. If he called for his jet possibly he could beat her, could meet her at the airport with the girls. But she was right, Emir thought with a rueful smile—she would make a terrible mistress.

She should be his wife.

'Ummi?' Clemira begged. Now she had two mothers to grieve for. He held his babies some more until finally they were spent. He put them down in one crib, but still they would not sleep, just stared at him with angry eyes, lay hiccoughing and gulping. He ran a finger down Clemira's cheek and across her eyebrows as

Amy had shown him a year ago, but Clemira did not close her eyes. She just stared coolly back, exhausted but still defiant. Yes, she was a born leader.

As was Emir.

Except the rules did not allow him to be.

'I'm leaving for the desert,' he told Fatima as he left the nursery. 'The new nanny starts in two days.'

Fatima lowered her head as he walked off. She did not ask when he would return, did not insist that he tell her so she could tell the girls. That was how it was supposed to be, yet not as it should be, Emir realised.

He joined Amy in the sky—but in his helicopter.

Once in the desert, he had Raul ready his horse and then rode into the night. He was at the oasis for sunrise. The first year was over and now he must move on.

He prayed as he waited for counsel from the wizened old man—for he knew that he would come.

'Hannah will not rest.'

The old man nodded.

'Before she died she asked that I promise to do my best for the girls.' He looked into the man's blackcurrant eyes. 'And to do the best for me.'

'And have you?'

'First I have to do the best by my country.'

'Because you are King?'

Emir nodded. 'I made that promise to my father when he died,' he said. He remembered the loss and the pain he had suffered then. His vow had been absolute when he had sworn it. 'The best for me is to marry Amy. It is the best for the girls too. But not the best for my coun-

try.' Emir told the old man why. 'She cannot have children.' He waited for the old man to shake his head, to
tell him how impossible it was, to tell him there was no
dilemma, that it could not be; instead he sat silent, so
Emir spelt it out for him. 'She cannot give me a son.'

'And the new wife you will take can?' the old man
checked.

Emir closed his eyes.

'Perhaps your new wife will give you girls too?' the
old man said. 'As Queen Hannah did.'

'Without a son my lineage ends,' Emir hissed in frustration. 'Alzirz will swallow Alzan and the two lands
will be become one.'

'That is the prediction,' the old man said. 'You cannot fight that.'

Emir was sick of predictions, of absolutes, of a fate
that was sealed in the sand and the stars. 'It must not
happen,' Emir said. He thought of his people—the people who had rejected his daughters, was his first savage
thought. Yet they were not bad—they were scared. Emir
knew that. He loved his people and his country so much,
and they needed him as their leader. 'I cannot turn my
back on them. There are rules for Alzan...'

'And for Alzirz too,' the old man said, and Emir grew
silent. 'You are King for a reason.'

He reminded Emir of his teachings and Emir knew
again that the year had passed and it was time for Hannah to rest, time for him to face things, to come to his
decision. He stood. The old man stayed sitting.

'You will know what to do.'

He knew what to do now, and nothing could stop him.

Emir mounted his stallion and kicked him on, charged towards a land where he was not welcome uninvited. No one stopped him.

On his entering Alzirz, Rakhal's guards galloped behind and alongside him, but no one attempted to halt a king propelled by centuries of fury.

King Rakhal was alerted, and as Emir approached he saw Alzirz's King standing waiting for him outside his desert abode. His tearful wife was by his side, refusing to return to the tent; yet she would be wise to, for both men would draw swords if they had to—both men would fight to the death for what was theirs.

Emir climbed from his horse and it was he who made the first move, reaching not for his knife but deep into his robe. He took out the two precious stones that had been sent to taunt him and hurled them at Rakhal's feet. 'Never insult me again!'

Rakhal gave a black laugh. 'How did my gift insult you? They are the most precious sapphires I could find. I had my people look far and wide for them. How could they offend?'

'They arrived on the morning of Sheikh Queen Hannah's death. The insult was for her too.' He spat in the sand in the direction of the stones and then he spat again, looking to Rakhal as he told him how it would be. 'I am marrying soon.'

'I look forward to the celebrations,' Rakhal said 'Who, may I ask, is the fortunate bride?'

'You have met her,' Emir answered. 'Amy.'

'Congratulations!' Rakhal answered, and then, because of course his wife would have told him, he smiled at Emir. 'Shouldn't you also offer congratulations to me? After all, Alzan will be mine.'

'No.' Emir shook his head.

'What? Are you considering your brother as King when you step aside?' Rakhal laughed. 'That reprobate! Hassan would not stay out of the casino or be sober long enough to take the vow.' Again Rakhal laughed. 'Congratulations to me will soon be in order.'

'Not in my lifetime,' Emir said. 'And I plan to live for a very long time. I am the King and I will die the King. Alzan will cease existing when I do.' He watched the mocking smile fade from Rakhal's face. 'I pray for a long life for your son, who will inherit all that you pass on to him. I pray that the rules are kind to him and he marries a bride who gives him healthy children. I pray for a long life for her too—for your father was lonely when his wife died, was he not? But because of your rule he could not marry again. I will pray history does not repeat for your son.' He heard Natasha really weeping now, but Rakhal stood firm.

'Your people will not be happy. Your people will never accept—'

'I will deal with my people,' Emir interrupted. 'And I will continue to pray for your son. I hope that his time in the desert proves fruitful, and hardens and prepares him for all he faces. Yes, my people will be unhappy when their King has gone. They will rise and fight as their country is taken.' He watched as for the first time

Rakhal faltered when he realised the burden being placed on his newborn son, the weight both Kings carried being passed onto one. 'We are Kings, Rakhal, but without real power. For now I will rule as best I can, and do the best that I can for my children too.'

He meant it. Knew this was the right thing to do. He could no longer fight the predictions.

He rode back through the desert with rare peace in his soul. He could feel the peace in Hannah's too, for now she could rest.

Suddenly Emir halted his horse so abruptly it rose on its hind legs for a moment—or was it the shock that emanated from his master that startled the beast? Emir's realisation dawned: he had not yet discussed this with Amy. Yet surely his concern was unnecessary, he told himself. Surely no woman would refuse such a request.

But she was not from this land, and she was like no woman he knew. His last words to her had not been kind. He was back to being troubled as he realised she might not want to rule with him a people who with each passing year would grow more and more despondent. She might well prefer not to live in a land where her fertility or lack of it was a constant topic.

It dawned on him fully then—Amy might not say yes.

CHAPTER FIFTEEN

It was hell being back in England.

It was lovely to see everyone, and it was good to be home, Amy told herself. Good to be at her mother's.

For about one day, seven hours and thirty-six minutes.

But when she was told by her mother again that she'd warned her not to get too attached, as if the twins were like the hamsters she'd once brought home to care for during the school holidays, Amy knew that she had to move out.

It took her a week to find a small furnished rental while she looked around for something more permanent, something that might one day feel like home. Right now her heart still lived at the palace. At night she yearned to be next to Emir, and she still slept with one ear open for the twins. Her breasts ached as if she *were* weaning them, but she knew she had to somehow start healing—start over, start again. She'd done it once, she told herself. The next time would surely be easier. Right?

She tried to hold it together—she went out with friends, caught up with the news, bought a new London wardrobe and even went and had her hair done, in a nice layered cut with a few foils. Her friends told her she looked amazing. Those days swimming in the pool with the twins meant that she had arrived in the middle of a London winter with a deep golden tan.

She had never looked better—except her appearance didn't match the way she felt.

'You look great,' her ex fiancé told her.

If she heard it again she thought she might scream. But he'd heard she was back and wanted to catch up, and Amy was actually glad for the chance to apologise.

'For what?' he asked.

For the year of bitterness she had needlessly carried. He'd been right to end things, Amy told him.

'Are you sure about that?' he asked, before dropping her home. Fresh from a break-up with a single mum, he had revised his paternity plans and suggested that they might try again.

She *was* sure, she told him. Because it wasn't a logical love she wanted, Amy knew as she headed inside, it was an illogical one.

She knew what love was now.

Even if she did not understand it.

Even if it could never be returned.

She'd had her heart broken three times.

The accident, losing her fiancé, the aftermath—they didn't even enter the equation. They had been tiny tasters for the real grief to come.

She missed her babies, loved each little girl as fiercely as she would have loved her own. She had been there at their birth and held them every day since and she ached for them. She felt she had let Hannah down—not by sleeping with Emir, but by leaving the girls.

She was tired of being told she'd get over it—as if the love she felt didn't count, as if in a few days' times she'd wake up not missing them—but somehow she had to work out how to do just that.

She would not cry, Amy told herself. She had to keep it all together. She would look for a job next week and make some appointments—catch up on the life she'd left behind. Except as she went in her bag for her phone it was not to see if he'd called—because it had been two weeks now and still he had not—but to look at the photo of Emir and the girls that she had taken on that precious morning in Alzan.

She was horrified when she opened her bag to find that her phone was missing. Amy tipped out the contents, frantically trying to remember when she had last used her phone, positive she had taken it out with her. Perhaps she had left it at the restaurant? But, no—Amy remembered that she had sneaked a peek of the photo in the car.

It wasn't the phone that concerned her but that image of Emir, Clemira and Nakia that she could not stand to lose. It was all she had left of them.

Amy couldn't even telephone her ex to ask if he had it, because his number was in her phone. Just as she started to panic the doorbell rang. Amy ran to it, hoping he had found it, even smiling in relief as she opened the door. Her smile faded as soon as she saw who it was.

'Emir?'

There were so many questions behind that single word, but his name was all she could manage. She wasn't even sure that it was him. For a moment she even wondered if he had sent his brother, for the man standing in her doorway was the Emir she had never seen—a younger looking, more relaxed Emir—and he was smiling at her shocked expression. How dared he look so happy? How dared he look so different? For though she knew he wore suits in London, she had never seen him wear one and he truly looked breathtaking.

'Not the man you were expecting?'

'Actually, no.' She didn't have to explain herself and refused to, because even if he *had* seen her ex drop her off it was none of his business any more.

'You're a very hard person to find.'

'Am I?'

'Your mother wouldn't give me your address.'

'I wouldn't have expected her to.' Amy gave a tight shrug. 'So how *did* you find me?'

'Less than honourable ways,' he admitted.

He was powerful enough to get anything he set his mind to, and she must remember to keep her guard up around him. She could not take any more hurt, but she had to know one thing. 'Are the girls okay?'

'They're fine,' Emir said. 'Well, they miss you a lot.'

She remembered standing in his office, telling him practically the same thing, and she remembered how it had changed nothing. Yet she did ask him in—she had to know what he was here for, had to see this conversation through in the hope that she might one day move on.

'Are they here in London?'

'No.'

Emir quickly crushed that hope, but perhaps it was for the best, because she could not bear to say goodbye to them again.

'They have a new nanny. She is younger and not as rigid as Fatima. They are just starting to really settle in with her and I didn't think I should interrupt—'

'Emir, please...' She put a hand up to stop him. She really didn't need to hear how quickly and how well they were adapting to her replacement. 'I'm glad the girls are fine.'

She forced a smile and then for the first time since he'd arrived at her door remembered he was a sheikh king, she honestly forgot at times, and now that she remembered she didn't really know what to do with him.

Aware of her rather sparse furnished rental, and wondering if instant coffee would do, she remembered her manners and forced a smile for him. 'Would you like a drink?'

'I came here to talk to you.'

'You could have done that on the phone.' Except now she'd lost hers, Amy remembered. But what had seemed so devastating a few moments ago became a triviality. 'Have a seat. I'll make a drink.'

'I didn't come here for a drink.'

'Well, I'm having one.'

She headed to the fridge and opened it, grateful for the cool blast of air as she rummaged around and found some wine and then looked for glasses. She was glad for something to do—needed to have her back to him for a couple of moments as she composed herself. Amy did not want her broken heart on clear display to him, for she could be hurt so easily.

'What are you thinking?' Emir asked, the tiny kitchen area shrinking as he stepped in.

'Do you really want to know?'

'I really want to know.'

'That it's just as well this is a screwtop bottle because I don't have a corkscrew...'

'Amy!'

'And I'm wondering what happened to all the people who made the corks.' She was, and she was also wondering if the trees they came from were called cork trees, because it was safer than thinking about the man who was in her home, the man who was standing right behind her now. She knew that if she turned around it would be to a man she could not resist.

'What else are you thinking?'

'That it is cruel that you are here,' Amy said. 'That I don't want to be your mistress.' She stopped pouring the wine. She was making a mess of it anyway. Her eyes were filling with tears and she couldn't really see; she screwed her eyes closed as his hand touched her arm and swore to be strong as he turned her around. 'And I'm thinking how right I was to leave—that I don't want to be with you.'

'I don't believe that,' he said.

And his mouth was there, and already she was weakening. That in itself forced her to be strong, made her look into his eyes to speak. 'I wouldn't even want to be your wife.'

'I don't believe that either.'

'I mean it.' She reminded herself that she did. 'As I've said before, if you were my husband and they were my children I'd have left ages ago.'

'I told you that there were reasons I could not be the father I wanted to be for them, but those reasons are gone now.'

She shook her head. 'I don't want you, Emir.'

'You *do* want me.'

He was so bloody arrogant, so assured…so right.

'No.'

'That's not what your body is saying.'

He ran a hand down her arms, then removed it. She shivered, for only his touch could warm her.

'And it's not what I see in your eyes.'

So she hid them, lowered her head, and because the bench was behind her and she could not step back she lifted her hands to push him—yet she dared not touch. 'Just go, Emir,' she begged. 'I can't think straight when you're around.'

'I know,' Emir said.

She shook her head, because how could he know how it felt? After all, he was standing calm and controlled and she was a trembling mess.

'I know how impossible it is to make a wise decisions when love clouds the issue.'

She did look up then, shocked to hear him speak of love. A gasp came from her lips when he spoke next, when he said what no king should. 'I have been consid-ering abdicating.'

'*No.*' He must not think it—let alone say it. She knew from her time in Alzan the implications, knew how seri-ous this was, but Emir went on undaunted. This distant man invited her closer, and not just to his body, but to his mind; he pulled her in so her head was on his chest as he told her, shared with her his hell.

'Whenever I saw the twins laughing and happy, or crying and sad, I wanted them to come first—I did not want to rule a country that is disappointed by my daugh-ters, that does not celebrate in their birthday, that will only be appeased by a son. When I am with my daugh-ters all I want to do is step down...'

'You can't.'

'I am not sure that I want to rule a country where I cannot change the rules. I'm not sure I want to give the people the son they want just to pass the burden on to him.' He shook his head. 'No, I will not do that to my son.' He lifted her chin and looked into the eyes of the woman he loved and was completely sure. 'I love you, and I cannot lose the woman I love again.'

And it was right, Amy thought, that he acknowledged Hannah—even right that the love he felt should be com-pared to the love he had had for the Queen. And it was said so nicely that she could not help but cry.

'And neither can I put Clemira and Nakia through it again,' he went on. 'You have made my daughters so happy. They call you their mother—which is how it will be.' He watched her shake her head at the impossibility of it all. 'As soon as you left I wanted to get on a plane, but I knew I had to think this through. I will rule Alzan as best as I can in my lifetime, and if the people grow hostile, if things get too hard for you there, then the country will see less of their leader—for I will divide my time between there and here.'

'No…' Amy said, but he was close, and she was weak whenever Emir was around.

'Yes,' he said, and held her tight. 'Anyway, we will have time to work things out.' He could not help but tease, watching the colour spread up her cheeks as he spoke. 'No one needs to find out for a while yet that you cannot have children.'

'I told Natasha.' She thought his features would darken with surprise, but instead he smiled.

'I know you did.'

'I was just tired of everyone assuming…'

'I know.' And he was smiling no longer. 'I confronted Rakhal. I have told him my position.'

'What did he say?'

'That Alzan will be his.' Emir shrugged. 'I pointed out that if he does outlive me and inherit, one day it will be his son's too.' His voice was forboding, but the loathing was not aimed at her. She knew that. 'If Rakhal takes it upon himself to inform my people that you cannot have a child…' his features were dark, and now he was not smiling '…he will have *me* to deal with.'

'I can't marry you, Emir,' Amy said. 'I can't stand knowing that I'm going to disappoint your people.' That he loved her so much brought her both comfort and fear.

That he would leave his country's future in darkness for
her was almost more than she could take.

'It is not your burden to carry,' Emir said. 'I was coming to this decision even before the twins were born. I
was already considering this. For Hannah's heart was so
weak I could never have asked her to be pregnant again.
This is not of your making. We have time before the
people know—time to work out how best to tell them.'

He was doing his best to reassure her, but even if his
decision was right, she knew the pain behind it.

'I can't do it, Emir.'

'You can with me by your side. I will shield you as I
will shield the twins. You will be a wonderful queen,'
Emir said. 'The people could not have better.'

'They could.'

'No.'

He meant it.

Every word of it.

His heart was at peace with the decision he had made.
He would do everything he could for his people, but his
heart belonged to his girls and he was strong enough to
end the impossible burden, to cease the madness. He
would not place that burden on a child of his.

And here it was—the illogical love that she wanted.
Love was a strange thing: it made you both strong and
weak. Strong enough to stand by your convictions…
Weak enough maybe to give in.

Except this was Emir, and even if she forgot at times
he was King this was her life and it would be in the
spotlight.

As she wrestled with indecision the doorbell rang. She opened it to the man she had once thought she loved, and blinked at the phone he held out in his hand.

'Thank you.'

She saw him look over her shoulder to where Emir was standing, saw the raising of his eyebrows, and then without a word he turned and Amy closed the door. She was nervous to turn around and face the man she knew she loved and would love for ever. But she had to be strong, had to say no, and that slight pause had given her a moment to regroup.

'I left my phone…' She felt his black eyes on hers and couldn't quite meet them. 'We went out before…'

'I saw you return,' Emir said. 'I was waiting in my car for you. Now, we were talking about—'

'Nothing happened,' Amy broke in. 'He just wanted…'

'I do not care.' She frowned, because surely he *should* care. 'We were discussing our marriage—'

'Emir!' she interrupted him. 'My ex-fiancé just came to the door, you know we've been out together tonight, and you don't *care*?' She couldn't believe what she was hearing. 'You don't have questions?'

'None,' Emir said.

She was less than flattered. A bit of jealousy wouldn't go amiss—after all, she *had* just been out with her ex.

'Am I supposed to take it as a compliment that you trust me so much? For all you know—'

'You could take a thousand lovers, Amy.' It was Emir who interrupted now. Emir who walked to where she stood. 'But each one would leave you empty. Each one would compare poorly to me.'

'You're so sure?'

'Completely,' Emir said. 'And you could sit through a hundred dinners and dates and your mind would wander even as the first course was served.' He stood right in front of her, looked down at her, and spoke the absolute truth. 'Your mind would wander straight back to me,' he said.

And, damn him, he was right. Because tonight all she had thought of was Emir, her efforts to concentrate and to listen had been half-hearted at best.

'And when you were kissed,' he said, and put his mouth right up to hers, 'you would crave what another man could not deliver. Because my mouth knows best what to do.'

She closed her eyes, opened her mouth to deny him. For there must be no future for them. She was going to say that she would find love again—except his tongue slid into her protesting mouth and he gave her a taste, and then he drew his head back, warned her again of the life she would lead if she did not say yes.

'You would miss me for ever.'

'No,' she begged, though she knew he spoke the truth.

'You would regret the decision for the rest of your days.'

'No,' Amy insisted, though she knew he was right.

'We will be married,' he concluded, through with talking. It had taken what felt like a lifetime to come to his decision, and now that he had he wanted it sealed.

He pulled her tighter to him, so close she could hear his heart—not galloping, but steady, for he knew he was right.

His hand lifted her chin and he looked down at her mouth. 'There are so many kisses we have not had.'

He lowered his mouth and tender were the lips that met hers in an unhurried kiss that reminded her of nothing—for this side of him she had not met.

'This is the kiss I wanted to give you one morning when I saw you walking in the gardens.' His mouth claimed her for another brief moment. He ran his hands down to her waist and his lips tasted of possession and promise for later. Then he he let her go. 'That was the kiss I wanted to greet you with when you joined the party.'

'What is this?' She would not cry in front of him. She had promised herself. Yet she was failing. 'Guess the kiss?'

'Yes,' he said, and she started to cry.

He held her again and his mouth drank her tears. He held her as he had wanted to, comforted her as he had wanted to after the breakfast, when Clemira had said *Ummi* and her heart had ached for a baby of her own. He held her as had wanted to that day.

'You will never face it alone again,' he promised, for he knew his kiss had taken her back to that day.

Then he kissed her again, both hands on her face, and it tasted of regret. She was leaving him again. They were back at the palace and he was letting her go. His arms were around hers and his tongue met hers. He was ferocious as he rewrote that moment—he kissed her back to his world. Then he kissed her hard and with intent, and *this* was a kiss she recognised. His tongue was lavish in its suggestion and he pulled her into him, to let her feel his want. His hands moved over her body. This was a kiss that could lead only to one thing.

Except he stopped.

He looked down to her mouth, which was wet and wanting. He did not believe in negotiation—not when he knew that he was right. He *would* get his way. 'You will return to Alzan and we will be married.'

'You don't just *tell* me!' Amy said. 'And that's hardly a proposal. You're supposed to get down on one knee.'

'Not where I come from,' Emir said.

He took her hand and held it over his erection. She kept her palm flat, but that did not deter him. He moved her hand up and down, till her fingers ached from not holding him, till all she wanted was to slide down his zipper and free him.

Free *them*.

'You can say yes,' Emir said, 'or you can kiss it goodbye if you care to.'

She could not help but smile as his usually excellent English wavered.

'You mean, kiss it *all* goodbye.'

'No,' Emir said. 'I mean exactly what I said.' And he pulled her into him. His mouth found her ear. 'Either way I bring you to your knees.'

And he would, because she could not be without him.

'Say yes, Amy.'

'I can't.'

'Then you can't have me.'

He confused her, because he kissed her again.

He kissed her mouth when still she questioned. He kissed her eyes closed when she tried to look at all that lay ahead. He kissed her until she was in the moment—kissed her all the way to her unmade bed. He did not bring her to her knees; instead he lay her down and removed every piece of her clothing.

First he took off her shoes, and when she sat with her arms by her sides he raised them.

'Emir...'

'Tell me to stop and I will.'

Her hands stayed in the air as he took off her top.

'Tell me we should not be together,' Emir said as he unhooked her bra, 'and I will go.'

And she felt his eyes on her breasts and she wanted his mouth to be there, but still she stayed silent, so he unzipped her skirt and pushed her back on the bed. When he pulled at the hem she did not lift her hips to help him. He stared down at her and it did not deter him. Instead he undressed himself.

He took off his jacket and placed it over a chair, took ages with each shoe, and as he pulled off his socks Amy found her toes curling.

'You do not get me till you say yes.' With a cruel lack of haste he removed his tie and unbuttoned his shirt. He gave her plenty of time to halt things but still she did not and he slid off his trousers and hipsters and stood over her, naked. 'I can't hear you, Amy.'

'Because I haven't said anything,' came her response, but this time when he tugged at her skirt she did lift her hips. How could she not say yes to him? How could she not be his wife? She tried to look to the future, when she would surely regret this decision, but *yes* waited to spill from her mouth.

He took off her panties so she was naked, and still she would not give in.

Emir kneeled between her legs, kissed up one thigh and then back down, and then he turned his attention to the other one till she writhed beneath him, wanting him there at her centre. He didn't play fair. He played mean. He lifted his head and focussed instead on himself, and she watched, fascinated, desperate. He stroked himself right there at her entrance and she watched, wanted. He would make her comply.

'I can't wait for ever,' he warned.

And he was right. There would never be a better lover. Always her mind would return to him. She heard his breath quicken. She wanted him more than she wanted her sanity and she hated this game he was playing.

'You can't seduce me into saying yes.'

'I can.'

He could.

He actually could.

'Yes,' she begged, for she wanted it to be ended.

'Manners?' How cruel was his teasing.

'I've forgotten them!' she screamed, and then screamed again as he drove into her.

Fierce was the passion that filled her. He did not stop

for a second to let her think, did not let her draw breath to reconsider. He had her and he would keep her. Each buck inside Amy told her that. Each pounding thrust confirmed she was his and Amy knew that was what she wanted.

'Please…' she sobbed, her legs coiling around him, possessing him, locking him in while ensuring his release.

She gave in as he did—gave in to the ultimate pleasure, lost in the throes of an orgasm that sealed their union as they pulsed together in time, lost with the other and returned together, lying with each other as they would now every night.

And Emir slept as he never had, in an untroubled sleep, for he knew that this was right.

Except Amy could not rest beside him. She heard every car that passed and listened to the rain battering the window in the early hours of the morning. She was petrified about what she'd agreed to.

She was going to be Queen.

CHAPTER SIXTEEN

'You need to come home,' was his answer when she told him her fears, and she knew that he was right—knew that Alzan was where she wanted to be.

They did not stay long in London. Just long enough to sort out her things and for Amy to try and convince her mum, who would fly to Alzan for the wedding, that she knew what she was doing, that it would all be okay.

And how could they not be okay? she asked herself. For it felt so right to have Emir by her side.

The journey home was a blur—the luxurious plane a mere mode of transport that allowed her to follow her heart. Even the people cheering the arrival of their King and soon to be new Sheikha Queen did not really register. But for all it was a blur, for all her mind was too busy to take in every detail, Amy would never forget her return to the palace.

He held her hand as they walked through the foyer where he had *not* kissed her goodbye, as they walked up the stairs—together this time—and then to the nursery. Emir let go of her hand, stepped in first, and she walked in quietly behind and smiled at the delighted reaction when the twins saw him. They were playing with their dolls' house, making everything right in a world where they could, but their beloved toy was instantly forgotten. Their father was back and that was all the girls needed to know—and then they saw her.

'Ummi!' It was Nakia who squealed it first and Clemira frowned, glanced at her sister and chastised her, for she had learnt that word was bad.

And then Clemira looked over to where her little sister was pointing and when she saw who was there she forgot to be the leader; she just burst into tears and took first steps towards Amy.

'It's okay.' Amy realised how much she had been hurting because her pain was gone the second she picked up Clemira. Poor Nakia stood too, but her legs didn't know how to walk yet, so she burst out crying too, and cried some more when Amy picked her up. Overwhelmed, the twins cried till they were smiling, kissing her face because Amy was crying too. She looked to Emir and it was the closest to tears she had ever seen him.

He had lost so much—his parents, his wife and almost Amy. That he could trust in love again was a feat in itself, and his decision was the right one, Amy told herself as she held his new family.

How could this be wrong?

Yet Amy awoke on the morning of her wedding with dread in her heart. She understood why Emir had been unable to make his decision when love was around, for when he was close, when he was near, it felt so *right* that they marry, that love was the solution. But Emir had spent the eve of his wedding in the desert, and without him it was far more than pre-wedding jitters Amy was struggling with. This morning she didn't even have the twins to keep her busy, for they were being readied for the wedding by the new nanny.

She felt as if she were cheating the people.

The maid came in and opened the window and the room was filled with humid desert air. Amy felt as if it was smothering her as she tried to swallow the ripe fruit that had been picked at dawn in the desert and prepared and served to her.

As was the tradition for the future Queen of Alzan.

The maids watched as she drank fertility potions from huge goblets and with every mouthful Amy felt sicker. Each taste of bridal tradition choked her and reminded her of the cheat and liar she was.

She bathed and had her make-up and hair done. Her eyes were lined with kohl and her cheeks and lips rouged. But she could see the pallor in her face and the guilt in her eyes as blossom was pinned into her hair— 'For innocence,' the maiden explained. Amy closed her eyes on another lie as she remembered the love they had already made.

A dress of pale gold slithered over her head and she thought of her mother who, though there for the wedding, was stressed. She had done all she could to dissuade Amy. As late as last night she had warned her daughter of the mistake she was making, had offered to take her home; she had told Amy that she was taking on too much, that though the country was cheering at the union now it would soon turn against her, and maybe in time her husband would too.

'No.' Amy was adamant. 'He loves me.'

Yet she felt guilty accepting that love. What should be the happiest day of her life was blighted by the knowledge that she could never be the Queen the people really wanted.

And now the final touches. She could hear the excitement and anticipation building in the streets outside, for the wedding was to take place in the gardens and the people had gathered around the palace.

'The people are happy,' the maiden said as a loud cheer went up.

'It is King Rakhal and Queen Natasha, arriving,' a younger maiden informed the busy room, watching the proceedings from the window. 'They have the young Prince with them.' She looked to Amy and smiled. 'They won't be able to gloat over us for much longer.'

And now the maiden tied a necklace around her throat which had a small vial at the end of it. Amy knew even before the maiden told her that it was for fertility, for Clemira and Nakia had received a similar necklace in the desert. Emir's response then had been brusque, but the maiden was more effusive as she arranged it around Amy's throat.

'It is to ensure that the sands remain as Alzan.' She placed it over the scar on Amy's throat and Amy could feel her rapid pulse beating there against the vial, could hear the cheers from the people of Alzan building outside, she could feel the sweat removing her carefully applied make-up as the humid desert air made it impossible to breathe.

'Amy?'

She heard the concern in the young maiden's voice, and the shocked gasps from the others as they saw how much she was struggling.

'I can't do this,' was all Amy remembered saying as she slid to the ground.

CHAPTER SEVENTEEN

'SHE is late.'

Emir heard the whispers in the crowd and stared fixedly ahead. Though outwardly calm and in control, he was kicking himself, for he should not have left her alone last night. He knew the reason Amy was late was because she was reconsidering the union. He realised that perhaps, for her, it was too much too soon—after all, his decision had been more than a year in the making. But Emir knew he could not lose his love to a prediction, knew he was right, and he would go now and tell her the same.

'That is not necessary,' Patel informed him. 'She is better now, apparently. They have given her salts to smell and some fluids to drink and she will soon be on her way.'

As Amy approached she reminded Emir of the first time he had met her—pale and quiet but somehow strong. She had helped him so much at that heartbreaking time and he wanted to help *her* now, wanted to take her away from the gathered crowd, to talk to her, soothe and reassure her, but of course it was impossible.

'You are okay?' Emir checked as she joined him at his side, and his hand found hers.

She was touched at the gesture, for he had told her that today was duty, that feelings would not be on display—for in Alzan love usually came later.

Not today.

'Nervous,' Amy admitted, which was perhaps the understatement of the century.

The magnitude of what was about to take place had hit her again as she'd walked through the fragrant gardens and seen the crowd, and she had thought she might pass out again. There was Hassan, the reprobate brother, standing tall and silent by his brother's side. King Rakhal and Natasha were there too, regal and splendid, but she'd barely glanced at them. First she had looked to the twins, dressed in pale lemon and sitting on the grass holding flowers, but though she'd melted at the sight of them today it was Emir who won her heart a thousand times over.

His robe was pale gold too, as was the *kafeya* on his head, and she was overwhelmed by such male beauty, by the curve of his lips that barely smiled as they greeted her but that would caress her mouth tonight. She ached for tonight, to be in the desert with him, but of course there were formalities first.

For a country so steeped in tradition, the wedding was surprisingly simple.

'He asks,' Emir translated, 'if you agree to this union.'

'Yes,' Amy said, and then remembered and answered for the judge. *'Na'am.'*

'He asks that you will obey me.'

He saw the slight pursing of her lips, for they had discussed this a few times.

She pressed her thumb into his palm, to remind him of the million subclauses to her agreement, and then she answered, *'Na'am.'*

'He asks will you nurture the fruits of our union?' Emir saw the tears fill her eyes and he wanted to hold her, but all he could do was press his own thumb to her palm to remind her that this was right.

She could not look beyond his shoulder to where King Rakhal stood, and beside him Natasha, so she looked to her soon to be husband and answered him. The press of his thumb was a reminder of just how much this man loved her. *'Na'am.'*

The judge spoke for a few moments and she waited, then Emir's hand was in the small of her back, telling her to turn around.

'What happens now?' Amy asked.

'We go back to the palace.'

'Back?' Amy asked. 'But the wedding…?'

'We are married,' Emir said, and then he broke with tradition.

Even if it was brief she felt his arms around her, and the soft warmth of his mouth as Emir kissed his bride. It was not the cough of the elders that halted them but the two little girls who protested at the lack of attention.

Back to the palace they walked, holding one twin each, and she watched as Emir glanced up to the sky.

She knew he was telling Hannah she could rest now, that the girls would be looked after as she had wanted.

And they would be.

Amy wanted to be alone with him, wanted their night in the desert, but first came more formalities—a sumptuous meal and endless speeches. Finally it was Rakhal's turn to speak, and Amy felt her hand tighten on the glass she was holding. She wondered what barb was about to be delivered—not that she would know it when it came, for the speeches were in Arabic. Emir would translate for her.

She took a deep breath as Rakhal addressed the room, realised her fingers were suddenly tight around Emir's for he squeezed her hand back.

'My wife predicted this.' Rakhal spoke in English and Amy's head jerked up. 'She said she knew on the day she met you,' he said. 'It was the day of my father's passing.'

Amy blinked, because that was a long time ago—long before she had had feelings for Emir. Or had she? She remembered that time. Emir had gone to offer his farewell and she had spoken briefly with Natasha. She had been so confused and bitter then, so angry with Emir for the distance he put between himself and his daughters.

'I said she was wrong.' Rakhal looked at the new Queen of Alzan. 'And I said she was wrong again at my son's naming ceremony. But this is one prediction that has been proved right.' Rakhal looked to Emir. 'Your Highness, I congratulate you on your wedding.' He spoke in Arabic, some words she recognised—long life, good health—and then again he spoke in English. 'The Kingdom of Alzirz celebrates with you today.'

How hard it was to smile as he raised a glass to them.

Hard too, to make small talk with Natasha a while later, for she was so determined to be friendly.

'You look wonderful.' Natasha smiled, but Amy could not help but be cool in her responses—could not so easily manage the feigned politeness between the rivals. 'Rakhal tells me you are honeymooning in London?'

'That's right.'

'With the girls?'

'Of course,' Amy said through gritted teeth.

'When you return we must get the children together, Clemira is so taken with Tariq, and…'

'We'll see.' Amy gave a tight smile. 'Now, if you'll excuse me…'

She turned straight into the chest of Emir and he rescued her with a dance. 'You will be polite,' Emir warned her. 'You will be pleasant.'

'I *am* being.'

'No.' He had seen the ice behind her smile as she spoke with Queen Natasha. 'When a queen speaks to you…'

'I'm a queen now too.'

He smiled down at her angry eyes. 'I will speak with you later. For now I will tell you to be polite.'

'I don't get it, Emir,' she bristled.

It annoyed her how well Emir and Rakhal were getting on tonight—oh, she knew it was all for show, but still it riled her. She put it aside, for it seemed impossible to hold a grudge on this night. The whole palace was alive with celebration, there were parties in the streets outside, and though she ached to be alone in the desert with Emir, to be with her new husband, it was the best night of her life.

Amy allowed herself simply to enjoy it right up to the end, when she accepted a kiss to her hand from Rakhal and, as instructed, smiled and chatted briefly to Natasha as they prepared to leave for the desert. Then it was time to say goodbye to the twins.

God, but she loved them. Nakia was now literally following in her big sister's footsteps, toddling too, and both loved calling out 'Ummi'. They would always know about their real mother, but it was bliss not to correct them, just to scoop them into her arms. She did it now, kissed their little faces and told them she would see them tomorrow.

She feared the wedding night in the desert more than a little—always felt as if the desert knew something she didn't, as if somehow it was a step ahead of them.

'It's dark.'

The last time she had been there the sands had been lit by a huge moon, and there had been stars, but tonight the desert was clouded—not that Emir seemed concerned.

'There will be rain, which is good,' he said. 'After rain comes new growth.'

The rain met them as they landed—a driving rain that had the helicopter flounder for a moment, a pelting rain that soaked through her gown. As she stepped into the tent maidens were waiting, wrapping her in shawls, and a feast was laid out for them. There were a thousand things to get through when all she wanted was to be alone with him, to speak with him. Emir must have sensed that, for he dismissed the maidens and took her into his arms.

'Should I be offended,' Emir asked, 'that my wife did not enjoy her wedding day?'

'I loved it, Emir.' She looked up to him. 'Every moment of it.'

'Every moment?'

'I struggle to be polite to Natasha and Rakhal. I understand that I have to be, that without communication...' She did not want to talk about them on her wedding night but, yes, she might have been a little rude. 'I struggle sometimes to stay quiet when I believe there is injustice.'

'I *had* worked that out,' Emir said. 'I know there is much on your mind. All day I have wanted to speak with you. There is something you need to know, but there has not been a suitable moment.'

'Oh!' Amy had been about to say the same thing. 'Emir, there is something—'

'Amy,' he interrupted, for his news was too important not to share. 'You know I spent last night in the desert? Usually the night before the King marries is a time for feasting and celebrating; instead I spent that time speaking with Rakhal.'

'And you didn't pull your swords?'

He heard the teasing in her voice. 'Rakhal listened

to all I said to him that day—he thought long and hard about it and though things have worked out for him, though he is happy, he does not want the burden he carried to be passed on to his son. He agrees that we are Kings without power unless we make our own rules for our own lands.' Emir picked up the vial that hung around her throat, knew the terrible pressure that had been placed on her. 'Our decision will be refuted by the elders, of course, but with both Kings in full agreement there will be no going back.'

'I don't understand?'

'The predictors are wrong,' Emir said. 'Alzan and Alzirz are two strong and proud countries. It is time for them to break free from the rules of old. Of course the people and the elders will challenge this. They believe...'

'Emir!' That whooshing sound was back in her ears, 'Emir, wait!' Anguished eyes looked up to him. 'I did enjoy today, every moment of it, and if I seemed distracted at times...' Amy took a deep breath. 'I didn't faint from nerves.' She still couldn't take the news in, had been reeling from it all day. 'Well, maybe a bit. But when the palace doctor examined me...' She'd never thought she'd hear herself say these words. 'I'm pregnant, Emir.' Amy was crying now, and not just a little bit. 'I had him retake the test and he is certain—it would seem that first night...'

'But you said it was impossible.' It was Emir who didn't understand.

'There was always a slim chance, apparently,' Amy explained. 'I just didn't hear that and neither did my fiancé. And I never went back to the doctor to properly discuss things.'

Emir held her as she cried. The news was as shocking as it was happy, and it took a moment for it to sink in.

'The rules might not need to change. I might have a son,' Amy said.

And he held the bride whom he loved, come what may, and he loved her all over again.

'Soon we will be able to find out what I'm having.'

'There is no need to find out,' Emir said. 'For whatever we are given we will love. The rules *will* change.' Emir's voice was firm. 'Clemira is a born leader, that much I know, and Nakia will be a wonderful support for her. It is right she be second in line.'

'But the predictions!'

'Are just that,' Emir said, and he looked to the woman who had healed his black and tortured heart, the woman who had swept into his office and challenged his way of thinking, and he could not believe what he had. His instinct was to kiss her, to hold her and soothe her fears, and then he paused for just a moment as the news truly started to hit him. And he told her why the predictions were surely wrong. 'They did not factor in that a king might fall in love.'

EPILOGUE

'HE is beautiful,' Emir said.

Amy could not stop looking at her newborn son—could scarcely believe that she was holding her own baby in her arms. Just feeling him there, she knew all the hurts of the past were forgotten, the pain of the last twenty-four hours simply deleted as she looked down into his dark eyes.

'Are you sure he's mine?' Amy teased, because he was completely his father's son. She looked up to Emir and he kissed her gently, and she was bathed in a happiness made richer because he loved her and his daughters, with or without the gift of a son.

He took the baby in his arms and held him for a long moment, and Amy could see the pride and also the pain on his strong, proud features, for he was surely remembering the bittersweet time when he'd last held a tiny infant.

'I don't want to miss a moment of his life,' Emir said. 'I missed way too much of the twins' first year.' He closed his eyes in regret.

'Emir, there was a reason.' She understood that now.

'Every time I saw them, every time I held them, all I wanted was to do what was best for them, and yet I had the responsibility to put the future of my country first.'

'It must have been agony.'

'I was made better knowing they were looked after by you. When you left, when it was Fatima, when the ways of old were being adhered to, I knew I could not rule a country that rendered my daughters worthless. It worked in the past, but not now,' Emir explained. 'Yet it was a decision that required distance.'

'It did,' Amy agreed. 'I wish you could have spoken with me…' Her voice trailed off, because Emir was right. It was a decision that could only have been reached alone. 'It's all worked out.' She looked at her sleeping baby. 'The rules don't even have to change.'

'They do,' Emir said. 'For I never want my son to have to make a choice like the one I was forced to make. The predictors were wrong: the two countries are better separated. I am glad I have a son for many reasons, but it will prove once and for all that we are doing this because it is right rather than necessary. The people will love him as they now love the girls—as they love you.'

The changes of the past few months had been less tumultuous than Amy had feared. The old Bedouin man had laughed when Rakhal and Emir consulted him, had shrugged and shaken his head when they'd said that the predictions were wrong. But the people in the main had accepted it, reassured that their two Kings were united and strong in their decision. And even before they'd found out that Amy was expecting a baby they

had cheered for the twins, and a newspaper had celebrated with a headline about the future Queen Clemira.

'Your mother should be here any time,' Emir said,
because as soon as Amy had gone into labour Emir had
organised a plane for her.

Amy could not wait to see her mother's face when,
after all the anguish, she got to hold her grandson.

'Shall I bring the girls in to meet their new brother?'
Emir asked, handing his son back to her outstretched
arms.

'Okay,' Amy said, excited about their reaction.

She smiled as he brought the girls in. She loved them
so much—every bit as much as the baby in her arms.
She had loved them from the moment they were born.
She watched Nakia's face light up when she saw her new
brother. She was completely entranced, smothering him
with kisses, but Clemira seemed less than impressed.
She looked at him for a moment or two and then wriggled down off the bed and toddled off. Following her
sister's lead, soon so too did Nakia. Emir called for the
nanny to take them back to the playroom.

'Do you think she is jealous?' Emir asked, taking
the now sleeping baby and placing him in his crib, then
climbing onto the bed beside her. 'She barely looked
at him.'

'It's early days,' Amy said. There was no nicer place
in the world than to be in bed next to Emir with their
baby sleeping by their side. 'I'm surprised, though. She
was so taken with Tariq. I guess it will take a bit of get-

ting used…' She did not finish her sentence because it was taken over by a yawn.

Emir pulled her in. 'You need to rest.'

'Stay.'

'Of course,' Emir said. 'But you must sleep while you have the chance. The next weeks will be busy— your family arriving and the naming ceremony… And Natasha has rung and wants to come over before then. She is so looking forward to seeing the baby.'

Amy smiled, half dozing. All was well in her world as she rested safe in his arms. She would look forward to Natasha's visit—they were firm friends now and met often. Their children delighted in playing together.

'I'd love to see her, and Clemira will be thrilled to see Tariq…' Her voice trailed off again, but for a different reason. An impossible thought formed between waking and sleep. 'Emir?'

'Rest,' he told her, his eyes closed, but Amy couldn't.

'If Clemira is still as taken with Tariq in…oh, say in twenty years or so…'

She looked up and his eyes opened. The frown that had formed faded as a smile broke onto his face. 'That would make things incredibly complicated.'

'Really?'

'Or incredibly simple.' He kissed the top of her head. 'Sleep now,' he said. 'It is not something we are going to consider or force. That is not a decision we will ever make for them.'

'But if it *did* happen?' Amy pushed. 'Then the countries would become one again?'

'Perhaps,' Emir said.

She closed her eyes and stopped thinking about the future, relished the present.

Emir was the one who broke the silence, the possibility perhaps still on his mind.

'Maybe I was wrong?' Emir said, pulling her in closer, feeling absolute peace in his once troubled heart. 'Who am I to say that when the predictions were made, they did not factor in love?'

* * * * *

CINDERELLA: HIRED BY THE PRINCE

MARION LENNOX

PROLOGUE

'RAMÓN spends his life in jeans and ancient T-shirts. He has money and he has freedom. Why would he want the Crown?'

Señor Rodriguez, legal advisor to the Crown of Cepheus, regarded the woman before him with some sympathy. The Princess Sofía had been evicted from the palace of Cepheus sixty years ago, and she didn't wish to be back here now. Her face was tear-stained and her plump hands were wringing.

'I had two brothers, Señor Rodriguez,' she told him, as if explaining her story could somehow alter the inevitable. 'But I was only permitted to know one. My younger brother and I were exiled with my mother when I was ten years old, and my father's cruelty didn't end there. And now... I haven't seen a tiara in sixty years and, as far as I know, Ramón's never seen one. The only time he's been in the palace is the night his father died. I've returned to the palace because my mother raised me with a sense of duty, but how can we demand that from Ramón? To return to the place that killed his father...'

'The Prince Ramón has no choice,' the lawyer said flatly. 'And of course he'll want the Crown.'

'There's no "of course" about it,' Sofía snapped. 'Ramón spends half of every year building houses for some charity in Bangladesh, and the rest of his life on his beautiful yacht. Why should he give that up?'

'He'll be Crown Prince.'

'You think royalty's everything?' Sofía gave up hand

wringing and stabbed at her knitting as if she'd like it to be the late, unlamented Crown Prince. 'My nephew's a lovely young man and he wants nothing to do with the throne. The palace gives him nightmares, as it gives us all.'

'He must come,' Señor Rodriguez said stiffly.

'So how will you find him?' Sofía muttered. 'When he's working in Bangladesh Ramón checks his mail, but for the rest of his life he's around the world in that yacht of his, who knows where? Since his mother and sister died he lets the wind take him where it will. And, even if you do find him, how do you think he'll react to being told he has to fix this mess?'

'There won't be a mess if he comes home. He'll come, as you have come. He must see there's no choice.'

'And what of the little boy?'

'Philippe will go into foster care. There's no choice there, either. The child is nothing to do with Prince Ramón.'

'Another child of no use to the Crown,' Sofía whispered, and she dropped two stiches without noticing. 'But Ramón has a heart. Oh, Ramón, if I were you I'd keep on sailing.'

CHAPTER ONE

'JENNY, lose your muffins. Get a life!'

Gianetta Bertin, known to the Seaport locals as Jenny, gave her best friend a withering look and kept right on spooning double choc chip muffin mixture into pans. Seaport Coffee 'n' Cakes had been crowded all morning, and her muffin tray was almost bare.

'I don't have time for lectures,' she told her friend severely. 'I'm busy.'

'You need to have time for lectures. Honest, Jen.' Cathy hitched herself up onto Jenny's prep bench and grew earnest. 'You can't stay stuck in this hole for ever.'

'There's worse holes to be stuck in, and get off my bench. If Charlie comes in he'll sack me, and I won't have a hole at all.'

'He won't,' Cathy declared. 'You're the best cook in Seaport. You hold this place up. Charlie's treating you like dirt, Jen, just because you don't have the energy to do anything about it. I know you owe him, but you could get a job and repay him some other way.'

'Like how?' Jenny shoved the tray into the oven, straightened and tucked an unruly curl behind her ear. Her cap was supposed to hold back her mass of dark curls, but they kept escaping. She knew she'd now have a streak of flour across her ear but did it matter what she looked like?

And, as if in echo, Cathy continued. 'Look at you,' she

declared. 'You're gorgeous. Twenty-nine, figure to die for, cute as a button, a woman ripe and ready for the world, and here you are, hidden in a shapeless white pinafore with flour on your nose—yes, flour on your nose, Jen—no don't wipe it, you've made it worse.'

'It doesn't matter,' Jenny said. 'Who's looking? Can I get on? There's customers out there.'

'There are,' Cathy said warmly, peering out through the hatch but refusing to let go of her theme. 'You have twenty people out there, all coming here for one of your yummy muffins and then heading off again for life. You should be out there with them. Look at that guy out there, for instance. Gorgeous or what? That's what you're missing out on, Jen, stuck in here every day.'

Jenny peered out the hatch as well, and it didn't take more than a glance to see who Cathy was referring to.

The guy looked to be in his mid-thirties. He was a yachtie—she could tell that by his gear—and he was seriously good-looking. It had been raining this morning. He was wearing battered jeans, salt-stained boating shoes and a faded black T-shirt, stretched tight over a chest that looked truly impressive. He'd shrugged a battered sou'wester onto the back of his chair.

Professional, she thought.

After years of working in Coffee 'n' Cakes she could pick the classes of boaty. Holding the place up were the hard-core fishermen. Then there were the battered old salts who ran small boats on the smell of an oily rag, often living on them. Next there was the cool set, arriving at weekends, wearing gear that came out of the designer section of the *Nautical Monthly* catalogue, and leaving when they realized Coffee 'n' Cakes didn't sell Chardonnay.

And finally there were the serious yachties. Seaport was a deep water harbour just south of Sydney, and it attracted yachts doing amazing journeys. Seaport had a great dry dock where repairs could be carried out expertly and fast, so there were often one or two of these classy yachts in port.

This guy looked as if he was from one of these. His coat looked battered but she knew the brand, even from this distance. It was the best. Like the man. The guy himself also looked a bit battered, but in a good way. Worn by the sea. His tan was deep and real, his eyes were crinkled as if he spent his life in the sun, and his black hair was only really black at the roots. The tips were sun-bleached to almost fair.

He was definitely a professional sailor, she thought, giving herself a full minute to assess him. And why not? He was well worth assessing.

She knew the yachting hierarchy. The owners of the big sea-going yachts tended to be middle-aged or older. They spent short bursts of time on their boats but left serious seafaring to paid staff. This guy looked younger, tougher, leaner than a boat-owner. He looked seriously competent. He'd be being paid to take a yacht to where its owner wanted it to be.

And for a moment—just for a moment—Jenny let herself be consumed by a wave of envy. Just to go where the wind took you... To walk away from Seaport...

No. That'd take effort and planning and hope—all the things she no longer cared about. And there was also debt, an obligation like a huge anchor chained around her waist, hauling her down.

But her friend was thinking none of these things. Cathy was prodding her, grinning, rolling her eyes at the sheer good looks of this guy, and Jenny smiled and gazed a little bit more. Cathy was right—this guy was definite eye-candy. What was more, he was munching on one of her muffins—lemon and pistachio. Her favourite, she thought in approval.

And then he looked up and saw her watching. He grinned and raised his muffin in silent toast, then chuckled as she blushed deep crimson and pushed the hatch closed.

Cathy laughed her delight. 'There,' she said in satisfaction. 'You see what's out there? He's gorgeous, Jen. Why don't you head on out and ask him if he'd like another muffin?'

'As if,' she muttered, thoroughly disconcerted. She shoved

her mixing bowl into the sink. 'Serving's Susie's job. I'm just the cook. Go away, Cathy. You're messing with my serenity.'

'Stuff your serenity,' Cathy said crudely. 'Come on, Jen. It's been two years…' Then, as she saw the pain wash across Jenny's face, she swung herself off the bench and came and hugged her. 'I know. Moving on can't ever happen completely, but you can't keep hiding.'

'Dr Matheson says I'm doing well,' Jenny said stubbornly.

'Yeah, he's prescribing serenity,' Cathy said dourly. 'Honey, you've had enough peace. You want life. Even sailing… You love the water, but now you don't go near the sea. There's so many people who'd like a weekend crew. Like the guy out there, for instance. If he offered me a sail I'd be off for more than a weekend.'

'I don't want…'

'Anything but to be left alone,' Cathy finished for her. 'Oh, enough. I won't let you keep on saying it.' And, before Jenny could stop her, she opened the hatch again. She lifted the bell Jenny used to tell Susie an order was ready and rang it like there was a shipwreck in the harbour. Jenny made a grab for it but Cathy swung away so her body protected the bell. Then, when everyone was watching…

'Attention, please,' she called to the room in general, in the booming voice she used for running the Seaport Ladies' Yoga Sessions. 'Ladies and gentlemen, I know this is unusual but I'd like to announce a fantastic offer. Back here in the kitchen is the world's best cook and the world's best sailor. Jenny's available as crew for anyone offering her excitement, adventure and a way out of this town. All she needs is a fantastic wage and a boss who appreciates her. Anyone interested, apply right here, right now.'

'Cathy!' Jenny stared at her friend in horror. She made a grab for the hatch doors and tugged them shut as Cathy collapsed into laughter. 'Are you out of your mind?'

'I love you, sweetheart,' Cathy said, still chuckling. 'I'm just trying to help.'

'Getting me sacked won't help.'

'Susie won't tell Charlie,' Cathy said. 'She agrees with me. Don't you, Susie?' she demanded as the middle-aged waitress pushed her way through the doors. 'Do we have a queue out there, Suse, all wanting to employ our Jen?'

'You shouldn't have done it,' Susie said severely, looking at Jenny in concern. 'You've embarrassed her to death.'

'There's no harm done,' Cathy said. 'They're all too busy eating muffins to care. But honest, Jen, put an ad in the paper, or at least start reading the Situations Vacant. Susie has a husband, four kids, two dogs and a farm. This place is a tiny part of her life. But for you... This place has become your life. You can't let it stay that way.'

'It's all I want,' Jenny said stubbornly. 'Serenity.'

'That's nonsense,' Susie declared.

'Of course it's nonsense,' Cathy said, jumping off the bench and heading for the door. 'Okay, Stage One of my quest is completed. If it doesn't have an effect then I'll move to Stage Two, and that could be really scary.'

Coffee 'n' Cakes was a daytime café. Charlie was supposed to lock up at five, but Charlie's life was increasingly spent in the pub, so at five Jenny locked up, as she was starting to do most nights.

At least Charlie hadn't heard of what had happened that morning. Just as well, Jenny thought as she turned towards home. For all Cathy's assurances that she wouldn't be sacked, she wasn't so sure. Charlie's temper was unpredictable and she had debts to pay. Big debts.

Once upon a time Charlie had been a decent boss. Then his wife died, and now...

Loss did ghastly things to people. It had to her. Was living in a grey fog of depression worse than spending life in an alcoholic haze? How could she blame Charlie when she wasn't much better herself?

She sighed and dug her hands deep into her jacket pockets. The rain from this morning had disappeared. It was warm enough, but she wanted the comfort of her coat. Cathy's behaviour had unsettled her.

She would've liked to take a walk along the harbour before she went home, only in this mood it might unsettle her even more.

All those boats, going somewhere.

She had debts to pay. She was going nowhere.

'Excuse me?'

The voice came from behind her. She swung around and it was him. The guy with the body, and with the smile.

Okay, that was a dumb thing to think, but she couldn't help herself. The combination of ridiculously good-looking body and a smile to die for meant it was taking everything she had not to drop her jaw.

It had been too long, she thought. No one since...

No. Don't even think about going there.

'Can I talk to you? Are you Jenny?'

He had an accent—Spanish maybe, she thought, and seriously sexy. Uh oh. Body of a god, killer smile and a voice that was deep and lilting and gorgeous. Her knees felt wobbly. Any minute now he'd have her clutching the nearest fence for support.

Hey! She was a grown woman, she reminded herself sharply. Where was a bucket of ice when she needed one? Making do as best she could, she tilted her chin, met his gaze square on and fought for composure.

'I'm Jenny.' Infuriatingly, her words came out a squeak. She turned them into a cough and tried again. 'I...sure.'

'The lady in the café said you were interested in a job,' he said. 'I'm looking for help. Can we talk about it?'

He was here to offer her a job?

His eyes were doing this assessing thing while he talked. She was wearing old jeans and an ancient duffel, built for service rather than style. Was he working out where she fitted in the social scale? Was he working out whether she cared what she wore?

Suddenly she found herself wishing she had something else on. Something with a bit of…glamour?

Now that was crazy. She was heading home to put her feet up, watch the telly and go to bed. What would she do with glamour?

He was asking her about a job. Yeah, they all needed deck-hands, she thought, trying to ground herself. Lots of big yachts came into harbour here. There'd be one guy in charge—someone like this. There'd also be a couple of deckies, but the guy in charge would be the only one paid reasonable wages by the owners. Deckies were to be found in most ports—kids looking for adventure, willing to work for cheap travel. They'd get to their destination and disappear to more adventure, to be replaced by others.

Did this man seriously think she might be interested in such a job?

'My friend was having fun at my expense,' she said, settling now she knew what he wanted. Still trying to firm up her knees, though. 'Sorry, but I'm a bit old to drop everything and head off into the unknown.'

'Are you ever too old to do that?'

'Yes,' she snapped before she could stop herself—and then caught herself. 'Sorry. Look, I need to get on.'

'So you're not interested.'

'There's a noticeboard down at the yacht club,' she told him. 'There's always a list of kids looking for work. I already have a job.'

'You do have a job.' His smile had faded. He'd ditched his coat, leaving only his jeans and T-shirt. They were faded and old and…nice. He was tall and broad-shouldered. He looked loose-limbed, casually at ease with himself and quietly confident. His eyes were blue as the sea, though they seemed to darken when he smiled, and the crinkles round his eyes said smiling was what he normally did. But suddenly he was serious.

'If you made the muffins I ate this morning you're very,

very good at your job,' he told her. 'If you're available as crew, a man'd be crazy not to take you on.'

'Well, I'm not.' He had her rattled and she'd snapped again. Why? He was a nice guy offering her a job. 'Sorry,' she said. 'But no.'

'Do you have a passport?'

'Yes, but…'

'I'm sailing for Europe just as soon as I can find some company. It's not safe to do a solo where I'm going.'

'Round the Horn?' Despite herself, she was interested.

'Round the Horn,' he agreed. 'It's fastest.'

That'd be right. The boaties in charge of the expensive yachts were usually at the call of owners. She'd met enough of them to know that. An owner fancied a sailing holiday in Australia? He'd pay a guy like this to bring his boat here and have it ready for him. Maybe he'd join the boat on the interesting bits, flying in and out at will. Now the owner would be back in Europe and it'd be up to the employed skipper—this guy?—to get the boat back there as soon as he could.

With crew. But not with her.

'Well, good luck,' she said, and started to walk away, but he wasn't letting her leave. He walked with her.

'It's a serious offer.'

'It's a serious rejection.'

'I don't take rejection kindly.'

'That's too bad,' she told him. 'The days of carting your crew on board drugged to the eyeballs is over. Press gangs are illegal.'

'They'd make my life easier,' he said morosely.

'You know I'm very sure they wouldn't.' His presence as he fell into step beside her was making her thoroughly disconcerted. 'Having a press-ganged crew waking up with hangovers a day out to sea surely wouldn't make for serene sailing.'

'I don't look for serenity,' he said, and it was so much an echo of her day's thoughts that she stopped dead.

But this was ridiculous. The idea was ridiculous. 'Serenity's important,' she managed, forcing her feet into moving again. 'So thank you, but I've said no. Is there anything else you want?'

'I pay well.'

'I know what deckies earn.'

'You don't know what I pay. Why don't you ask?'

'I'm not interested.'

'Do you really sail?' he asked curiously.

He wasn't going away. She was quickening her steps but he was keeping up with ease. She had the feeling if she broke into a run he'd keep striding beside her, effortlessly. 'Once upon a time, I sailed,' she said. 'Before life got serious.'

'Your life got serious? How?' Suddenly his eyes were creasing in concern. He paused and, before she could stop him, he lifted her left hand. She knew what he was looking for.

No ring.

'You have a partner?' he demanded.

'It's none of your business.'

'Yes, but I want to know,' he said in that gorgeous accent, excellent English but with that fabulous lilt—and there was that smile again, the smile she knew could get him anything he wanted if he tried hard enough. With these looks and that smile and that voice… Whew.

No. He couldn't get anything from her. She was impervious.

She had to be impervious.

But he was waiting for an answer. Maybe it wouldn't hurt to tell him enough to get him off her back. 'I'm happily single,' she said.

'Ah, but if you're saying life's serious then you're not so happily single. Maybe sailing away on the next tide could be just what you want.'

'Look,' she said, tugging her hand away, exasperated. 'I'm not a teenager looking for adventure. I have obligations here. So you're offering me a trip to Europe? Where would that leave me? I'd get on your boat, I'd work my butt off for passage—I know you guys get your money's worth from the kids you employ—and then I'd end up wherever it is you're going. That's it. I know how it works. I wouldn't even have the fare home. I'm not a backpacker, Mr Whoever-You-Are, and I live here. I don't know you, I don't trust you and I'm not interested in your job.'

'My name's Ramón Cavellero,' he said, sounding not in the least perturbed by her outburst. 'I'm very trustworthy.' And he smiled in a way that told her he wasn't trustworthy in the least. 'I'm sailing on the *Marquita*. You've seen her?'

Had she seen her? Every person in Seaport had seen the *Marquita*. The big yacht's photograph had been on the front of their local paper when she'd come into port four days ago. With good reason. Quite simply she was the most beautiful boat Jenny had ever seen.

And probably the most expensive.

If this guy was captaining the *Marquita* then maybe he had the funds to pay a reasonable wage. That was an insidious little whisper in her head, but she stomped on it before it had a chance to grow. There was no way she could walk away from this place. Not for years.

She had to be sensible.

'Look, Mr Cavellero, this has gone far enough,' she said, and she turned back to face him directly. 'You have the most beautiful boat in the harbour. You can have your pick of any deckie in the market—I know a dozen kids at least who would kill to be on that boat. But, as for me… My friend was making a joke but that's all it was. Thank you and goodbye.'

She reached out and took his hand, to give it a good firm handshake, as if she was a woman who knew how to transact business, as if she should be taken seriously. He took it, she shook, but, instead of pulling away after one brief shake, she found he was holding on.

Or maybe it was that she hadn't pulled back as she'd intended.

His hand was strong and warm and his grip as decisive

as hers. Or more. Two strong wills, she thought fleetingly, but more…

But then, before she could think any further, she was aware of a car sliding to a halt beside them. She glanced sideways and almost groaned.

Charlie.

She could sense his drunkenness from here. One of these days he'd be caught for drink-driving, she thought, and half of her hoped it'd be soon, but the other half knew that'd put her boss into an even more foul mood than he normally was. Once upon a time he'd been a nice guy—but that was when he was sober, and she could barely remember when he'd been sober. So she winced and braced herself for an explosion as Charlie emerged from the car and headed towards them.

Ramón kept on holding her hand. She tugged it back and he released her but he shifted in closer. Charlie's body language was aggressive. He was a big man; he'd become an alcoholic bully, and it showed.

But, whatever else Ramón might be, it was clear he knew how to protect his own. His own? That was a dumb thing to think. Even so, she was suddenly glad that he was here right now.

'Hey, I want to speak to you, you stupid cow. Lose your friend,' Charlie spat at her.

Jenny flinched. Uh oh. This could mean only one thing—that one of the patrons of the café had told Charlie of Cathy's outburst. This was too small a town for such a joke to go unreported. Charlie had become universally disliked and the idea that one of his staff was advertising for another job would be used against him.

At her expense.

And Ramón's presence here would make it worse. Protective or not, Charlie was right; she needed to lose him.

'See you later,' she said to Ramón, stepping deliberately away and turning her back on him. Expecting him to leave. 'Hello, Charlie.'

But Charlie wasn't into greetings. 'What the hell do you

think you're doing, making personal announcements in my café, in my time?' He was close to yelling, shoving right into her personal space so she was forced to step backward. 'And getting another job? You walk away from me and I foreclose before the day's end. You know what you owe me, girl. You work for me for the next three years or I'll have you bankrupt and your friend with you. I could toss you out now. Your friend'll lose her house. Great mess that'd leave her in. You'll work the next four weekends with no pay to make up for this or you're out on your ear. What do you say to that?'

She closed her eyes. Charlie was quite capable of carrying out his threats. This man was capable of anything.

Why had she ever borrowed money from him?

Because she'd been desperate, that was why. It had been right at the end of Matty's illness. She'd sold everything, but there was this treatment… There'd been a chance. It was slim, she'd known, but she'd do anything.

She'd been sobbing, late at night, in the back room of the café. She'd been working four hours a day to pay her rent. The rest of the time she'd spent with Matty. Cathy had found her there, and Charlie came in and found them both.

He'd loan her the money, he said, and the offer was so extraordinary both women had been rendered almost speechless.

Jenny could repay it over five years, he'd told them, by working for half wages at the café. Only he needed security. 'In case you decide to do a runner.'

'She'd never do a runner,' Cathy had said, incensed. 'When Matty's well she'll settle down and live happily ever after.'

'I don't believe in happy ever after,' Charlie had said. 'I need security.'

'I'll pledge my apartment that she'll repay you,' Cathy had said hotly. 'I trust her, even if you don't.'

What a disaster. They'd been so emotional they hadn't thought it through. All Jenny had wanted was to get back to the hospital, to get back to Matty, and she didn't care how. Cathy's generosity was all she could see.

So she'd hugged her and accepted and didn't see the ties.

Only ties there were. Matty died a month later and she was faced with five years bonded servitude.

Cathy's apartment had been left to her by her mother. It was pretty and neat and looked out over the harbour. Cathy was an artist. She lived hand to mouth and her apartment was all she had.

Even Cathy hadn't realised how real the danger of foreclosure was, Jenny thought dully. Cathy had barely glanced at the loan documents. She had total faith in her friend to repay her loan. Of course she had.

So now there was no choice. Jenny dug her hands deep into her pockets, she bit back angry words, as she'd bitten them back many times before, and she nodded.

'Okay. I'm sorry, Charlie. Of course I'll do the weekends.'

'Hey!' From behind them came Ramón's voice, laced with surprise and the beginnings of anger. 'What is this? Four weekends to pay for two minutes of amusement?'

'It's none of your business,' Charlie said shortly. 'Get lost.'

'If you're talking about what happened at the café, I was there. It was a joke.'

'I don't do jokes. Butt out. And she'll do the weekends. She has no choice.'

And then he smiled, a drunken smile that made her shiver. 'So there's the joke,' he jeered. 'On you, woman, not me.'

And that was that. He stared defiance at Ramón, but Ramón, it seemed, was not interested in a fight. He gazed blankly back at him, and then watched wordlessly as Charlie swung himself unsteadily back into his car and weaved off into the distance.

Leaving silence.

How to explain what had just happened? Jenny thought, and decided she couldn't. She took a few tentative steps away, hoping Ramón would leave her to her misery.

He didn't. Instead, he looked thoughtfully at the receding car, then flipped open his cellphone and spoke a few sharp words. He snapped it shut and walked after Jenny, catching up and once again falling into step beside her.

'How much do you owe him?' he asked bluntly.

She looked across at him, startled. 'Sorry?'

'You heard. How much?'

'I don't believe that it's…'

'Any of my business,' he finished for her. 'Your boss just told me that. But, as your future employer, I can make it my business.'

'You're not my future employer.'

'Just tell me, Jenny,' he said, and his voice was suddenly so concerned, so warm, so laced with caring that, to her astonishment, she found herself telling him. Just blurting out the figure, almost as if it didn't matter.

He thought about it for a moment as they kept walking. 'That's not so much,' he said cautiously.

'To you, maybe,' she retorted. 'But to me… My best friend signed over her apartment as security. If I don't pay, then she loses her home.'

'You could get another job. You don't have to be beholden to this swine-bag. You could transfer the whole loan to the bank.'

'I don't think you realise just how broke I am,' she snapped and then she shook her head, still astounded at how she was reacting to him. 'Sorry. There's no need for me to be angry with you when you're being nice. I'm tired and I'm upset and I've got myself into a financial mess. The truth is that I don't even have enough funds to miss a week's work while I look for something else, and no bank will take me on. Or Cathy either, for that matter—she's a struggling painter and has nothing but her apartment. So there you go. That's why I work for Charlie. It's also why I can't drop everything and sail away with you. If you knew how much I'd love to…'

'Would you love to?' He was studying her intently. The concern was still there but there was something more. It was as if he was trying to make her out. His brow was furrowed in concentration. 'Would you really? How good a sailor are you?'

That was a weird question but it was better than talking

about her debts. So she told him that, too. Why not? 'I was born and bred on the water,' she told him. 'My dad built a yacht and we sailed it together until he died. In the last few years of his life we lived on board. My legs are more at home at sea than on land.'

'Yet you're a cook.'

'There's nothing like spending your life in a cramped galley to make you lust after proper cooking.' She gave a wry smile, temporarily distracted from her bleakness. 'My mum died early so she couldn't teach me, but I longed to cook. When I was seventeen I got an apprenticeship with the local baker. I had to force Dad to keep the boat in port during my shifts.'

'And your boat? What was she?'

'A twenty-five footer, fibreglass, called *Wind Trader*. Flamingo, if you know that class. She wasn't anything special but we loved her.'

'Sold now to pay debts?' he asked bluntly.

'How did you know?' she said, crashing back to earth. 'And, before you ask, I have a gambling problem.'

'Now why don't I believe that?'

'Why would you believe anything I tell you?' She took a deep breath. 'Look, this is dumb. I'm wrecked and I need to go home. Can we forget we had this conversation? It was crazy to tell you my troubles and I surely don't expect you to do anything about them. But thank you for letting me talk.'

She hesitated then. For some reason, it was really hard to walk away from this man, but she had no choice. 'Goodbye, Mr Cavellero,' she managed. 'Thank you for thinking of me as a potential deckhand. It was very nice of you, and you know what? If I didn't have this debt I'd be half tempted to take it on.'

Once more she turned away. She walked about ten steps, but then his voice called her back.

'Jenny?'

She should have just kept on walking, but there was something in his voice that stopped her. It was the concern again. He sounded as if he really cared.

That was crazy, but the sensation was insidious, like a siren song forcing her to turn around.

'Yes?'

He was standing where she'd left him. Just standing. Behind him, down the end of the street, she could see the harbour. That was where he belonged, she thought. He was a man of the sea. He looked a man from the sea. Whereas she…

'Jenny, I'll pay your debts,' he said.

She didn't move. She didn't say anything.

She didn't know what to say.

'This isn't charity,' he said quickly as she felt her colour rise. 'It's a proposition.'

'I don't understand.'

'It's a very sketchy proposition,' he told her. 'I've not had time to work out the details so we may have to smooth it off round the edges. But, essentially, I'll pay your boss out if you promise to come and work with me for a year. You'll be two deckies instead of one—crew when I need it and cook for the rest of the time. Sometimes you'll be run off your feet but mostly not. I'll also add a living allowance,' he said and he mentioned a sum that made her feel winded.

'You'll be living on the boat so that should be sufficient,' he told her, seemingly ignoring her amazement. 'Then, at the end of the year, I'll organise you a flight home, from wherever *Marquita* ends up. So how about it, Jenny?' And there was that smile again, flashing out to warm parts of her she hadn't known had been cold. 'Will you stay here as Charlie's unpaid slave, or will you come with me, cook your cakes on my boat and see the world? What do you say? *Marquita*'s waiting, Jenny. Come sail away.'

'It's three years' debt,' she gasped finally. Was he mad?

'Not to me. It's one year's salary for a competent cook and sailor, and it's what I'm offering.'

'Your owner could never give the authority to pay those kind of wages.'

He hesitated for a moment—for just a moment—but then he smiled. 'My owner doesn't interfere with how I run my boat,' he told her. 'My owner knows if I…if he pays peanuts, he gets monkeys. I want good and loyal crew and with you I believe I'd be getting it.'

'You don't even know me. And you're out of your mind. Do you know how many deckies you could get with that money?'

'I don't want deckies. I want you.' And then, as she kept right on staring, he amended what had been a really forceful statement. 'If you can cook the muffins I had this morning you'll make my life—and everyone else who comes onto the boat—a lot more pleasant.'

'Who does the cooking now?' She was still fighting for breath. What an offer!

'Me or a deckie,' he said ruefully. 'Not a lot of class.'

'I'd…I'd be expected to cook for the owner?'

'Yes.'

'Dinner parties?'

'There's not a lot of dinner parties on board the *Marquita*,' he said, sounding a bit more rueful. 'The owner's pretty much like me. A retiring soul.'

'You don't look like a retiring soul,' she retorted, caught by the sudden flash of laughter in those blue eyes.

'Retiring or not, I still need a cook.'

Whoa… To be a cook on a boat… With this man…

Then she caught herself. For a moment she'd allowed herself to be sucked in. To think *what if*.

What if she sailed away?

Only she'd jumped like this once before, and where had it got her? Matty, and all the heartbreak that went with him.

Her thoughts must have shown on her face. 'What is it?' Ramón asked, and his smile suddenly faded. 'Hey, Jenny, don't look like that. There's no strings attached to this offer. I swear you won't find yourself the seventeenth member of my harem, chained up for my convenience in the hold. I can even give you character references if you want. I'm extremely honourable.'

He was trying to make her smile. She did smile, but it was a wavery smile. 'I'm sure you're honourable,' she said—despite the laughter lurking behind his amazing eyes suggesting he was nothing of the kind—'but, references or not, I still don't know you.' Deep breath. *Be sensible.* 'Sorry,' she managed. 'It's an amazing offer, but I took a loan from Charlie when I wasn't thinking straight, and look where that got me. And there have been…other times…when I haven't thought straight either, and trouble's followed. So I don't act on impulse any more. I've learned to be sensible. Thank you for your offer, Mr Cavellero…'

'Ramón.'

'Mr Cavellero,' she said stubbornly. 'With the wages you're offering, I know you'll find just the crew you're looking for, no problem at all. So thank you again and goodnight.'

Then, before she could let her treacherous heart do any more impulse urging—before she could be as stupid as she'd been in the past—she turned resolutely away.

She walked straight ahead and she didn't look back.

CHAPTER TWO

HER heart told her she was stupid all the way home. Her head told her she was right.

Her head addressed her heart with severity. This was a totally ridiculous proposition. She didn't know this man.

She'd be jumping from the frying pan into the fire, she told herself. To be indebted to a stranger, then sail away into the unknown… He *could* be a white slave trader!

She knew he wasn't. Take a risk, her heart was commanding her, but then her heart had let her down before. She wasn't going down that road again.

So, somehow, she summoned the dignity to keep on walking.

'Think about it,' Ramón called after her and she almost hesitated, she almost turned back, only she was a sensible woman now, not some dumb teenager who'd jump on the nearest boat and head off to sea.

So she walked on. Round the next corner, and the next, past where Charlie lived.

A police car was pulled up beside Charlie's front door, and Charlie hadn't made it inside. Her boss was being breathalysed. He'd be way over the alcohol limit. He'd lose his licence for sure.

She thought back and remembered Ramón lifting his cellphone. Had he…

Whoa. She scuttled past, feeling like a guilty rabbit.

Ramón had done it, not her.

Charlie would guess. Charlie would never forgive her.

Uh oh, uh oh, uh oh.

By the time she got home she felt as if she'd forgotten to breathe. She raced up the steps into her little rented apartment and she slammed the door behind her.

What had Ramón done? Charlie, without his driving licence? Charlie, thinking it was her fault?

But suddenly she wasn't thinking about Charlie. She was thinking about Ramón. Numbly, she crossed to the curtains and drew them aside. Just checking. Just in case he'd followed. He hadn't and she was aware of a weird stab of disappointment.

Well, what did you expect? she told herself. I told him press gangs don't work.

What if they did? What if he came up here in the dead of night, drugged her and carted her off to sea? What if she woke on his beautiful yacht, far away from this place?

I'd be chained to the sink down in the galley, she told herself with an attempt at humour. Nursing a hangover from the drugs he used to get me there.

But oh, to be on that boat…

He'd offered to pay all her bills. Get her away from Charlie…

What was she about, even beginning to think about such a crazy offer? If he was giving her so much money, then he'd be expecting something other than the work a deckie did.

But a man like Ramón wouldn't have to pay, she thought, her mind flashing to the nubile young backpackers she knew would jump at the chance to be crew to Ramón. They'd probably jump at the chance to be anything else. So why did he want her?

Did he have a thing for older women?

She stared into the mirror and what she saw there almost made her smile. It'd be a kinky man who'd desire her like she was. Her hair was still flour-streaked from the day. She'd been working in a hot kitchen and she'd been washing up over steaming sinks. She didn't have a spot of make-up on, and her nose was shiny. *Very* shiny.

Her clothes were ancient and nondescript and her eyes were shadowed from lack of sleep. Oh, she had plenty of time for sleep, but where was sleep when you needed it? She'd stopped taking the pills her doctor prescribed. She was trying desperately to move on, but how?

'What better way than to take a chance?' she whispered to her image. 'Charlie's going to be unbearable to work with now. And Ramón's gorgeous and he seems really nice. His boat's fabulous. He's not going to chain me to the galley, I'm sure of it.' She even managed a smile at that. 'If he does, I won't be able to help him with the sails. He'd have to unchain me a couple of times a day at least. And I'd be at sea. At sea!'

So maybe…maybe…

Her heart and head were doing battle but her heart was suddenly in the ascendancy. It was trying to convince her it could be sensible as well.

Wait, she told herself severely. She ran a bath and wallowed and let her mind drift. Pros and cons. Pros and cons.

If it didn't work, she could get off the boat at New Zealand.

He'd demand his money back.

So? She'd then owe money to Ramón instead of to Charlie, and there'd be no threat to Cathy's apartment. The debt would be hers and hers alone.

That felt okay. Sensible, even. She felt a prickle of pure excitement as she closed her eyes and sank as deep as she could into the warm water. To sail away with Ramón…

Her eyes flew open. She'd been stupid once. One gorgeous sailor, and…Matty.

So I'm not that stupid, she told herself. I can take precautions before I go.

Before she went? This wasn't turning out to be a relaxing bath. She sat bolt upright in the bath and thought, *what am I thinking?*

She was definitely thinking of going.

'You told him where to go to find deckies,' she said out loud. 'He'll have asked someone else by now.'

No!

'So get up, get dressed and go down to that boat. Right now, before you chicken out and change your mind.

'You're nuts.

'So what can happen that's worse than being stuck here?' she told herself and got out of the bath and saw her very pink body in the mirror. Pink? The sight was somehow a surprise.

For the last two years she'd been feeling grey. She'd been concentrating on simply putting one foot after another, and sometimes even that was an effort.

And now…suddenly she felt pink.

'So go down to the docks, knock on the hatch of Ramón's wonderful boat and say—yes, please, I want to come with you, even if you are a white slave trader, even if I may be doing the stupidest thing of my life. Jumping from the frying pan into the fire? Maybe, but, crazy or not, I want to jump,' she told the mirror.

And she would.

'You're a fool,' she told her reflection, and her reflection agreed.

'Yes, but you're not a grey fool. Just do it.'

What crazy impulse had him offering a woman passage on his boat? A needy woman. A woman who looked as if she might cling.

She was right, he needed a couple of deckies, kids who'd enjoy the voyage and head off into the unknown as soon as he reached the next port. Then he could find more.

But he was tired of kids. He'd been starting to think he'd prefer to sail alone, only *Marquita* wasn't a yacht to sail by himself. She was big and old-fashioned and her sails were heavy and complicated. In good weather one man might manage her, but Ramón didn't head into good weather. He didn't look for storms but he didn't shy away from them either.

The trip back around the Horn would be long and tough, and he'd hardly make it before he was due to return to Bangladesh. He'd been looking forward to the challenge, but at the same time not looking forward to the complications crew could bring.

The episode in the café this morning had made him act on impulse. The woman—Jenny—looked light years from the kids he generally employed. She looked warm and homely and mature. She also looked as if she might have a sense of humour and, what was more, she could cook.

He could make a rather stodgy form of paella. He could cook a steak. Often the kids he employed couldn't even do that.

He was ever so slightly over paella.

Which was why the taste of Jenny's muffins, the cosiness of her café, the look of her with a smudge of flour over her left ear, had him throwing caution to the winds and offering her a job. And then, when he'd realised just where that bully of a boss had her, he'd thrown in paying off her loan for good measure.

Sensible? No. She'd looked at him as if she suspected him of buying her for his harem, and he didn't blame her.

It was just as well she hadn't accepted, he told himself. Move on.

It was time to eat. Maybe he could go out to one of the dockside hotels.

He didn't feel like it. His encounter with Jenny had left him feeling strangely flat—as if he'd seen something he wanted but he couldn't have it.

That made him sound like his Uncle Iván, he thought ruefully. Iván, Crown Prince of Cepheus, arrogance personified.

Why was he thinking of Iván now? He was really off balance.

He gave himself a fast mental shake and forced himself to go back to considering dinner. Even if he didn't go out to eat he should eat fresh food while in port. He retrieved steak, a tomato and lettuce from the refrigerator. A representation of the height of his culinary skill.

Dinner. Then bed?

Or he could wander up to the yacht club and check the noticeboard for deckies. The sooner he found a crew, the sooner he could leave, and suddenly he was eager to leave.

Why had the woman disturbed him? She had nothing to do with him. He didn't need to regard Jenny's refusal as a loss.

'Hello?'

For a moment he thought he was imagining things, but his black mood lifted, just like that, as he abandoned his steak and made his way swiftly up to the deck.

He wasn't imagining things. Jenny was on the jetty, looking almost as he'd last seen her but cleaner. She was still in her battered coat and jeans, but the flour was gone and her curls were damp from washing.

She looked nervous.

'Jenny,' he said and he couldn't disguise the pleasure in his voice. Nor did he want to. Something inside him was very pleased to see her again. *Extremely* pleased.

'I just… I just came out for a walk,' she said.

'Great,' he said.

'Charlie was arrested for drink-driving.'

'Really?'

'That wouldn't have anything to do with you?'

'Who, me?' he demanded, innocence personified. 'Would you like to come on board?'

'I…yes,' she said, and stepped quickly onto the deck as if she was afraid he might rescind his invitation. And suddenly her nerves seemed to be gone. She gazed around in unmistakable awe. 'Wow!'

'Wow' was right. Ramón had no trouble agreeing with Jenny there. *Marquita* was a gracious old lady of the sea, built sixty years ago, a wooden schooner crafted by boat builders who knew their trade and loved what they were doing.

Her hull and cabins were painted white but the timbers of her deck and her trimmings were left unpainted, oiled to a warm honey sheen. Brass fittings glittered in the evening light and, above their heads, *Marquita*'s vast oak masts swayed majestically, matching the faint swell of the incoming tide.

Marquita was a hundred feet of tradition and pure unashamed luxury. Ramón had fallen in love with her the moment he'd seen her, and he watched Jenny's face now and saw exactly the same response.

'What a restoration,' she breathed. 'She's exquisite.'

Now that was different. Almost everyone who saw this boat looked at Ramón and said: 'She must have cost a fortune.'

Jenny wasn't thinking money. She was thinking beauty.

Beauty... There was a word worth lingering on. He watched the delight in Jenny's eyes as she gazed around the deck, taking in every detail, and he thought it wasn't only his boat that was beautiful.

Jenny was almost as golden-skinned as he was; indeed, she could be mistaken for having the same Mediterranean heritage. She was small and compact. Neat, he thought and then thought, no, make that cute. Exceedingly cute. And smart. Her green eyes were bright with intelligence and interest. He thought he was right about the humour as well. She looked like a woman who could smile.

But she wasn't smiling now. She was too awed.

'Can I see below?' she breathed.

'Of course,' he said, and he'd hardly got the words out before she was heading down. He smiled and followed. A man could get jealous. This was one beautiful woman, taking not the slightest interest in him. She was totally entranced by his boat.

He followed her down into the main salon, but was brought up short. She'd stopped on the bottom step, drawing breath, seemingly awed into silence.

He didn't say anything; just waited.

This was the moment for people to gush. In truth, there was much to gush about. The rich oak wainscoting, the burnished timber, the soft worn leather of the deep settees. The wonderful colours and fabrics of the furnishing, the silks and velvets of the cushions and curtains, deep crimsons and dark blues, splashed with touches of bright sunlit gold.

When Ramón had bought this boat, just after the accident that had claimed his mother and sister, she'd been little more than a hull. He'd spent time, care and love on her renovation and his Aunt Sofía had helped as well. In truth, maybe Sofía's additions were a little over the top, but he loved Sofía and he wasn't about to reject her offerings. The result was pure comfort, pure luxury. He loved the *Marquita*—and right now he loved Jenny's reaction.

She was totally entranced, moving slowly around the salon, taking in every detail. This was the main room. The bedrooms were beyond. If she was interested, he'd show her those too, but she wasn't finished here yet.

She prowled, like a small cat inspecting each tiny part of a new territory. Her fingers brushed the burnished timber, lightly, almost reverently. She crossed to the galley and examined the taps, the sink, the stove, the attachments used to hold things steady in a storm. She bent to examine the additional safety features on the stove. Gas stoves on boats could be lethal. Not his. She opened the cupboard below the sink and proceeded to check out the plumbing.

He found he was smiling, enjoying her awe. Enjoying her eye for detail. She glanced up from where she was inspecting the valves below the sink and caught him smiling. And flushed.

'I'm sorry, but it's just so interesting. Is it okay to look?'

'It's more than okay,' he assured her. 'I've never had someone gasp at my plumbing before.'

She didn't return his smile. 'This pump,' she breathed. 'I've seen one in a catalogue. You've got them all through the boat?'

'There are three bathrooms,' he told her, trying not to sound smug. 'All pumped on the same system.'

'You have three bathrooms?' She almost choked. 'My

father didn't hold with plumbing. He said real sailors used buckets. I gather your owner isn't a bucket man.'

'No,' he agreed gravely. 'My owner definitely isn't a bucket man.'

She did smile then, but she was still on the prowl. She crossed to the navigation desk, examining charts, checking the navigation instruments, looking at the radio. Still seeming awed.

Then… 'You leave your radio off?'

'I only use it for outgoing calls.'

'Your owner doesn't mind? With a boat like this, I'd imagine he'd be checking on you daily.'

Your owner…

Now was the time to say he was the owner; this was his boat. But Jenny was starting to relax, becoming companionable, friendly. Ramón had seen enough of other women's reactions when they realised the level of his wealth. For some reason, he didn't want that reaction from Jenny.

Not yet. Not now.

'My owner and I are in accord,' he said gravely. 'We keep in contact when we need to.'

'How lucky,' she said softly. 'To have a boss who doesn't spend his life breathing down your neck.' And then she went right on prowling.

He watched, growing more fascinated by the moment. He'd had boat fanatics on board before—of course he had— and most of them had checked out his equipment with care. Others had commented with envy on the luxury of his fittings and furnishings. But Jenny was seeing the whole thing. She was assessing the boat, and he knew a part of her was also assessing him. In her role as possible hired hand? *Yes*, he thought, starting to feel optimistic. She was now under the impression that his owner trusted him absolutely, and such a reference was obviously doing him no harm.

If he wanted her trust, such a reference was a great way to start.

Finally, she turned back to him, and her awe had been

replaced by a level of satisfaction. As if she'd seen a work of art that had touched a chord deep within. 'I guess now's the time to say, *Isn't she gorgeous*?' she said, and she smiled again. 'Only it's not a question. She just is.'

'I know she is,' he said. He liked her smile. It was just what it should be, lighting her face from within.

She didn't smile enough, he thought.

He thought suddenly of the women he worked with in Bangladesh. Jenny was light years away from their desperate situations, but there was still that shadow behind her smile. As if she'd learned the hard way that she couldn't trust the world.

'Would you like to see the rest of her?' he asked, suddenly unsure where to take this. A tiny niggle was starting in the back of his head. Take this further and there would be trouble…

It was too late. He'd asked. 'Yes, please. Though…it seems an intrusion.'

'It's a pleasure,' he said and he meant it. Then he thought, hey, he'd made his bed this morning. There was a bonus. His cabin practically looked neat.

He took her to the second bedroom first. The cabin where Sofía had really had her way. He'd restored *Marquita* in the months after his mother's and sister's death, and Sofía had poured all her concern into furnishings. 'You spend half your life living on the floor in mud huts in the middle of nowhere,' she'd scolded. 'Your grandmother's money means we're both rich beyond our dreams so there's no reason why you should sleep on the floor here.'

There was certainly no need now for him, or anyone else on this boat, to sleep on the floor. He'd kept a rein on his own room but in this, the second cabin, he'd let Sofía have her way. He opened the door and Jenny stared in stunned amazement— and then burst out laughing.

'It's a boudoir,' she stammered. 'It's harem country.'

'Hey,' he said, struggling to sound serious, even offended, but he found he was smiling as well. Sofía had indeed gone over the top. She'd made a special trip to Marrakesh, and she'd furnished the cabin like a sheikh's boudoir. Boudoir? Who knew? Whatever it was that sheikhs had.

The bed was massive, eight feet round, curtained with burgundy drapes and piled with quilts and pillows of purple and gold. The carpet was thick as grass, a muted pink that fitted beautifully with the furnishings of the bed. Sofía had tied in crisp, pure white linen, and matched the whites with silk hangings of sea scenes on the walls. The glass windows were open while the *Marquita* was in port and the curtains blew softly in the breeze. The room was luxurious, yet totally inviting and utterly, utterly gorgeous.

'This is where you'd sleep,' Ramón told Jenny and she turned and stared at him as if he had two heads.

'Me. The deckie!'

'There are bunkrooms below,' he said. 'But I don't see why we shouldn't be comfortable.'

'This *is* harem country.'

'You don't like it?'

'I love it,' she confessed, eyes huge. 'What's not to love? But, as for sleeping in it… The owner doesn't mind?'

'No.'

'Where do you sleep?' she demanded. 'You can't give me the best cabin.'

'This isn't the best cabin.'

'You're kidding me, right?'

He smiled and led the way back down the companionway. Opened another door. Ushered her in.

He'd decorated this room. Sofía had added a couple of touches—actually, Sofía had spoken to his plumber so the bathroom was a touch…well, a touch embarrassing—but the rest was his.

It was bigger than the stateroom he'd offered Jenny. The bed here was huge but he didn't have hangings. It was more masculine, done in muted tones of the colours through the rest of the boat. The sunlit yellows and golds of the salon had been extended here, with only faint touches of the crimson and blues. The carpet here was blue as well, but short and functional.

There were two amazing paintings on the wall. Recognizable paintings. Jenny gasped with shock. 'Please tell me they're not real.'

Okay. 'They're not real.' They were. 'You want to see the bathroom?' he asked, unable to resist, and he led her through. Then he stood back and grinned as her jaw almost hit the carpet.

While the *Marquita* was being refitted, he'd had to return to Bangladesh before the plumbing was done, and Sofía had decided to put her oar in here as well. And Sofía's oar was not known as sparse and clinical. Plus she had this vision of him in sackcloth and ashes in Bangladesh and she was determined to make the rest of his life what she termed 'comfortable'.

Plus she read romance novels.

He therefore had a massive golden bath in the shape of a Botticelli shell. It stood like a great marble carving in the middle of the room, with carved steps up on either side. Sofía had made concessions to the unsteadiness of bathing at sea by putting what appeared to be vines all around. In reality, they were hand rails but the end result looked like a tableau from the Amazon rainforest. There were gold taps, gold hand rails, splashes of crimson and blue again. *There was trompe l'oeil*—a massive painting that looked like reality—on the wall, making it appear as if the sea came right inside. She'd even added towels with the monogram of the royal family his grandmother had belonged to.

When he'd returned from Bangladesh he'd come in here and nearly had a stroke. His first reaction had been horror, but Sofía had been beside him, so anxious she was quivering.

'I so wanted to give you something special,' she'd said, and Sofía was all the family he had and there was no way he'd hurt her.

He'd hugged her and told her he loved it—and that night he'd even had a bath in the thing. She wasn't to know he usually used the shower down the way.

'You...you sleep in here?' Jenny said, her bottom lip quivering.

'Not in the bath,' he said and grinned.

'But where does the owner sleep?' she demanded, ignoring his attempt at levity. She was gazing around in stupefaction. 'There's not room on his boat for another cabin like this.'

'I... At need I use the bunkroom.' And that was a lie, but suddenly he was starting to really, really want to employ this woman. Okay, he was on morally dubious ground, but did it matter if she thought he was a hired hand? He watched as the strain eased from her face and turned to laughter, and he thought surely this woman deserved a chance at a different life. If one small lie could give it to her...

Would it make a difference if she knew the truth? If he told her he was so rich the offer to pay her debts meant nothing to him... How would she react?

With fear. He'd seen her face when he'd offered her the job. There'd been an intuitive fear that he wanted her for more than her sailing and her cooking. How much worse would it be if she knew he could buy and sell her a thousand times over?

'The owner doesn't mind?' she demanded.

He gave up and went along with it. 'The owner likes his boat to be used and enjoyed.'

'Wow,' she breathed and looked again at the bath. 'Wow!'

'I use the shower in the shared bathroom,' he confessed and she chuckled.

'What a waste.'

'You'd be welcome to use this.'

'In your dreams,' she muttered. 'This place is Harems-R-Us.'

'It's great,' he said. 'But it's still a working boat. I promise you, Jenny, there's not a hint of harem about her.'

'You swear?' she demanded and she fixed him with a look that said she was asking for a guarantee. And he knew what that guarantee was.

'I swear,' he said softly. 'I skipper this boat and she's workmanlike.'

She looked at him for a long, long moment and what she saw finally seemed to satisfy her. She gave a tiny satisfied nod and moved on. 'You have to get her back to Europe fast?'

'Three months, at the latest.' That, at least, was true. His team started work in Bangladesh then and he intended to travel with them. 'So do you want to come?'

'You're still offering?'

'I am.' He ushered her back out of the cabin and closed the door. The sight of that bath didn't make for businesslike discussions on any level.

'You're not employing anyone else?'

'Not if I have you.'

'You don't even know if I can sail,' she said, astounded all over again.

He looked at her appraisingly. The corridor here was narrow and they were too close. He'd like to be able to step back a bit, to see her face. He couldn't.

She was still nervous, he thought, like a deer caught in headlights. But caught she was. His offer seemed to have touched something in her that longed to respond, and even the sight of that crazy bath hadn't made her back off. She was just like he was, he thought, raised with a love of the sea. Aching to be out there.

So…she was caught. All he had to do was reel her in.

'So show me that you can sail,' he said. 'Show me now. The wind's getting up enough to make it interesting. Let's take her out.'

'What, tonight?'

'Tonight. Now. Dare you.'

'I can't,' she said, sounding panicked.

'Why not?'

She stared up at him as if he were a species she'd never seen.

'You just go. Whenever you feel like it.'

'The only thing holding us back is a couple of lines tied to bollards on the wharf,' he said and then, as her look of panic deepened, he grinned. 'But we will bring her back tonight, if that's what's worrying you. It's seven now. We can be back in harbour by midnight.'

'You seriously expect me to sail with you? Now?'

'There's a great moon,' he said. 'The night is ours. Why not?'

So, half an hour later, they were sailing out through the heads, heading for Europe.

Or that was what it felt like to Jenny. Ramón was at the wheel. She'd gone up to the bow to tighten a stay, to see if they could get a bit more tension in the jib. The wind was behind them, the moon was rising from the east, moonlight was shimmering on the water and she was free.

The night was warm enough for her to take off her coat, to put her bare arms out to catch a moonbeam. She could let her hair stream behind her and become a bow-sprite, she thought. An omen of good luck to sailors.

An omen of good luck to Ramón?

She turned and looked back at him. He was a dark shadow in the rear of the boat but she knew he was watching her from behind the wheel. She was being judged?

So what? The boat was as tightly tuned as she could make her. Ramón had asked her to set the sails herself. She'd needed help in this unfamiliar environment but he'd followed her instructions rather than the other way round.

This boat was far bigger than anything she'd sailed on, but she'd spent her life in a sea port, talking to sailors, watching the boats come in. She'd seen yachts like this; she'd watched them and she'd ached to be on one.

She'd brought Matty down to the harbour and she'd promised him his own boat.

'When you're big. When you're strong.'

And suddenly she was blinking back tears. That was stupid. She didn't cry for Matty any more. It was no use; he was never coming back.

'Are you okay?'

Had he seen? The moonlight wasn't that strong. She

swiped her fist angrily across her cheeks, ridding herself of the evidence of her distress, and made her way slowly aft. She had a lifeline clipped to her and she had to clip it and unclip it along the way. She was as sure-footed as a cat at sea, but it didn't hurt to show him she was safety conscious—and, besides, it gave her time to get her face in order.

'I'm fine,' she told him as she reached him.

'Take over the wheel, then,' he told her. 'I need to cook dinner.'

Was this a test, too? she wondered. Did she really have sea legs? Cooking below deck on a heavy swell was something no one with a weak stomach could do.

'I'll do it.' She could.

'You really don't get seasick?'

'I really don't get seasick.'

'A woman in a million,' he murmured and then he grinned. 'But no, it's not fair to ask you to cook. This is your night at sea and, after the day you've had, you deserve it. Take the wheel. Have you eaten?'

'Hours ago.'

'There's steak to spare.' He smiled at her and wham, there it was again, his smile that had her heart saying, *Beware, Beware, Beware*.

'I really am fine,' she said and sat and reached for the wheel and when her hand brushed his—she could swear it was accidental—the *Beware* grew so loud it was a positive roar.

But, seemingly unaware of any roaring on deck, he left her and dropped down into the galley. In minutes the smell of steak wafted up. Nothing else. Just steak.

Not my choice for a lovely night at sea, she thought, but she wasn't complaining. The rolling swell was coming in from the east. She nosed the boat into the swell and the boat steadied on course.

She was the most beautiful boat.

Could she really be crew? She was starting to feel as if, when Ramón had made the offer, she should have signed a contract on the spot. Then, as he emerged from the galley bearing two plates and smiling, she knew why she hadn't. That smile gave her so many misgivings.

'I cooked some for you, too,' he said, looking dubiously down at his plates. 'If you really aren't seasick…'

'I have to eat something to prove it?'

'It's a true test of grit,' he said. 'You eat my cooking, then I know you have a cast iron stomach.' He sat down beside her and handed her a plate.

She looked down at it. Supermarket steak, she thought, and not a good cut.

She poked it with a fork and it didn't give.

'You have to be polite,' he said. 'Otherwise my feelings will be hurt.'

'Get ready for your feelings to be hurt.'

'Taste it at least.'

She released the wheel, fought the steak for a bit and then said, 'Can we put her on automatic pilot? This is going to take some work.'

'Hey, I'm your host,' he said, sounding offended.

'And I'm a cook. How long did you fry this?'

'I don't know. Twenty minutes, maybe? I needed to check the charts to remind myself of the lights for harbour re-entry.'

'So your steak cooked away on its own while you concentrated on other things.'

'What's wrong with that?'

'I'd tell you,' she said darkly, stabbing at her steak and finally managing to saw off a piece. Manfully chewing and then swallowing. 'Only you're right; you're my host.'

'I'd like to be your employer. Will you be cook on the *Marquita*?'

Whoa. So much for concentrating on steak. This, then, was when she had to commit. To craziness or not.

To life—or not.

'You mean…you really were serious with your offer?'

'I'm always serious. It was a serious offer. It *is* a serious offer.'

'You'd only have to pay me a year's salary. I could maybe

organise something...' But she knew she couldn't, and he knew it, too. His response was immediate.

'The offer is to settle your debts and sail away with you, debt free. That or nothing.'

'That sounds like something out of a romance novel. Hero on white charger, rescuing heroine from villain. I'm no wimpy heroine.'

He grinned. 'You sound just like my Aunt Sofía. She reads them, too. But no, I never said you were wimpy. I never thought you were wimpy.'

'I'd repay...'

'No,' he said strongly and took her plate away from her and set it down. He took her hands then, strong hands gripping hers so she felt the strength of him, the sureness and the authority. Authority? This was a man used to getting his own way, she thought, suddenly breathless, and once more came the fleeting thought, *I should run.*

There was nowhere to run. If she said yes there'd be nowhere to run for a year.

'You will not repay,' he growled. 'A deal's a deal, Jenny. You will be my crew. You will be my cook. I'll ask nothing more.'

This was serious. Too serious. She didn't want to think about the implications behind those words.

And maybe she didn't want that promise. *I'll ask nothing more...*

He'd said her debt was insignificant. Maybe it was to him. To her it was an insurmountable burden. She had her pride, but maybe it was time to swallow it, stand aside and let him play hero.

'Thank you,' she said, trying to sound meek.

'Jenny?'

'Yes.'

'I'm captain,' he said. 'But I will not tolerate subordination.'

'Subordination?'

'It's my English,' he apologised, sounding suddenly very Spanish. 'As in captains say to their crew, "*I will not tolerate insubordination!*" just before they give them a hundred lashes and toss them in the brink.'

'What's the brink?'

'I have no idea,' he confessed. 'I'm sure the *Marquita* doesn't have one, which is what I'm telling you. Whereas most captains won't tolerate insubordination, I am the opposite. If you'd like to argue all the way around the Horn, it's fine by me.'

'You want me to argue?' She was too close to him, she thought, and he was still holding her hands. The sensation was worrying.

Worryingly good, though. Not worryingly bad. Arguing with this guy all the way round the Horn…

'Yes. I will also expect muffins,' he said and she almost groaned.

'Really?'

'Take it or leave it,' he said. 'Muffins and insubordination. Yes or no?'

She stared up at him in the moonlight. He stared straight back at her and she felt her heart do this strange surge, as if her fuel-lines had just been doubled.

What am I getting into, she demanded of herself, but suddenly she didn't care. The night was warm, the boat was lovely and this man was holding her hands, looking down at her in the moonlight and his hands were imparting strength and sureness and promise.

Promise? What was he promising? She was being fanciful.

But she had to be careful, she told herself fiercely. She must.

It was too late.

'Yes,' she said before she could change her mind—and she was committed.

She was heading to the other side of the world with a man she'd met less than a day ago.

Was she out of her mind?

* * *

What had he done? What was he getting himself into?

He'd be spending three months at sea with a woman called Jenny.

Jenny what? Jenny who? He knew nothing about her other than she sailed and she cooked.

He spent more time on background checks for the deckies he employed. He always ran a fast check on the kids he employed, to ensure there weren't skeletons in the closet that would come bursting out the minute he was out of sight of land.

And he didn't employ them for a year. The deal was always that they'd work for him until the next port and then make a mutual decision as to whether they wanted to go on.

He'd employed Jenny for a year.

He wasn't going to be on the boat for a year. Had he thought that through? No, so he'd better think it through now.

Be honest? Should he say, *Jenny, I made the offer because I felt sorry for you, and there was no way you'd have accepted my offer of a loan if you knew I'm only offering three months' work?*

He wasn't going to say that, because it wasn't true. He'd made the offer for far more complicated reasons than sympathy, and that was what was messing with his head now.

In three months he'd be in Bangladesh.

Did he need to go to Bangladesh?

In truth, he didn't need to go anywhere. His family inheritance had been massive, he'd invested it with care and if he wished he could spend the rest of his life in idle luxury.

Only…his family had never been like that. Excluded from the royal family, Ramón's grandmother had set about making herself useful. The royal family of Cepheus was known for indolence, mindless indulgence, even cruelty. His grandmother had left the royal palace in fear, for good reason. But then she'd started making herself a life—giving life to others.

So she and her children, Ramón's father and aunt, had set up a charity in Bangladesh. They built homes in the low lying delta regions, houses that could be raised as flood levels rose, homes that could keep a community safe and dry. Ramón had been introduced to it early and found the concept fascinating.

His father's death had made him even more determined to stay away from royalty; to make a useful life for himself, so at seventeen he'd apprenticed himself to one of Cepheus's top builders. He'd learned skills from the ground up. Now it wasn't just money he was throwing at this project—it was his hands as well as his heart.

During the wet season he couldn't build. During these months he used to stay on the island he still called home, spending time with his mother and sister. He'd also spent it planning investments so the work they were doing could go on for ever.

But then his mother and his sister died. One drunken driver and his family was wiped out. Suddenly he couldn't bear to go home. He employed a team of top people to take over his family's financial empire, and he'd bought the *Marquita*.

He still worked in Bangladesh—hands-on was great, hard manual work which drove away the demons. But for the rest of the year he pitted himself against the sea and felt better for it.

But there was a gaping hole where his family had been; a hole he could never fill. Nor did he want to, he decided after a year or so. If it hurt so much to lose…to get close to someone again seemed stupid.

So why ask Jenny onto his boat? He knew instinctively that closeness was a very real risk with this woman. But it was as if another part of him, a part he didn't know existed, had emerged and done the asking.

He'd have to explain Bangladesh to her. Or would he? When he got to Cepheus he could simply say there was no need for the boat, the owner wanted her in dry dock for six months. Jenny was free to fly back to Australia—he'd pay her fare—and she could fill the rest of her contract six months later.

That'd mean he had crew not only for now but for the future as well.

A crew of one woman.

This was danger territory. The Ramón he knew well, the Ramón he trusted, was screaming a warning.

No. He could be sensible. This was a big enough boat for him to keep his own counsel. He'd learned to do that from years of sailing with deckies. The kids found him aloof, he knew, but aloof was good. Aloof meant you didn't open yourself to gut-wrenching pain.

Aloof meant you didn't invite a woman like Jenny to sail around the world with you.

A shame that he just had.

'The *Marquita*'s reported as having left Fiji two weeks ago. We think Ramón's in Australia.'

'For heaven's sake!' Sofía pushed herself up on her cushions and stared at the lawyer, perplexed. 'What's he doing in Australia?'

'Who would know?' the lawyer said with asperity. 'He's left no travel plans.'

'He could hardly expect this awfulness,' Sofía retorted. 'There's never been a thought that Ramón could inherit.'

'Well, it makes life difficult for us,' the lawyer snapped. 'He doesn't even answer incoming radio calls.'

'Ramón's been a loner since his mother and sister died,' Sofía said, and she sighed. 'It affected me deeply, so who knows how it affected him? If he wants to be alone, who are we to stop him?'

'He can't be alone any longer,' the lawyer said. 'I'm flying out.'

'To Australia?'

'Yes.'

'Isn't Australia rather big?' Sofía said cautiously. 'I mean… I don't want to discourage you, but if you flew to Perth and he ended up at Darwin… I've read about Australia and it does sound a little larger than Cepheus.'

'I believe the smallest of its states is bigger than Cepheus,' the lawyer agreed. 'But if he's coming from Fiji he'll be heading for the east coast. We have people looking out for him at every major port. If I wait in Sydney I can be with him in hours rather than days.'

'You don't think we could wait until he makes contact?' Sofía said. 'He does email me. Eventually.'

'He needs to take the throne by the end of the month or Carlos inherits.'

'Carlos?' Sofía said, and her face crumpled in distress. 'Oh, dear.'

'So you see the hurry,' the lawyer said. 'If I'm in Australia, as soon as we locate his boat I can be there. He has to come home. Now.'

'I wish we could find him before I make a decision about Philippe,' she said. 'Oh, dear.'

'I thought you'd found foster parents for him.'

'Yes, but…it seems wrong to send him away from the palace. What would Ramón do, do you think?'

'I hardly think Prince Ramón will wish to be bothered with a child.'

'No,' Sofía said sadly. 'Maybe you're right. There are so many things Ramón will be bothered with now—how can he want a say in the future of a child he doesn't know?'

'He won't. Send the child to foster parents.'

'Yes,' Sofía said sadly. 'I don't know how to raise a child myself. He's had enough of hired nannies. I think it's best for everyone.'

CHAPTER THREE

THIS was really, really foolish. She was allowing an unknown Spaniard to pay her debts and sweep her off in his fabulous yacht to the other side of the world. She was so appalled at herself she couldn't stop grinning.

Watching Cathy's face had been a highlight. 'I can't let you do it,' she'd said in horror. 'I know I joked about it but I never dreamed you'd take me seriously. You know nothing about him. This is awful.'

And Jenny had nodded solemn agreement.

'It is awful. If I turn up in some Arabic harem on the other side of the world it's all your fault,' she told her friend. 'You pointed him out to me.'

'No. Jenny, I never would have… No!'

She'd chuckled and relented. 'Okay, I won't make you come and rescue me. I know this is a risk, my love, but honestly, he seems nice. I don't think there's a harem but even if there is…I'm a big girl and I take responsibility for my own decision. I know it's playing with fire, but honestly, Cathy, you were right. I'm out of here any way I can.'

And what a way! Sailing out of the harbour on board the *Marquita* with Ramón at the helm was like something out of a fairy tale.

Fairy tales didn't include scrubbing decks, though, she conceded ruefully. There was enough of reality to keep her grounded—or as grounded as one could be at sea. Six days

later, Jenny was on her knees swishing a scrubbing brush like
a true deck-hand. They'd been visited by a flock of terns at
dawn—possibly the last they'd see until they neared land
again. She certainly hoped so. The deck was a mess.

But making her feel a whole lot better about scrubbing was
the fact that Ramón was on his knees scrubbing as well. That
didn't fit the fairy tale either. Knight on white charger scrubbing bird droppings? She glanced over and found he was
watching her. He caught her grin and he grinned back.

'Not exactly the romantic ideal of sailing into the sunset,'
he said, and it was so much what she'd been thinking that she
laughed. She sat back on her heels, put her face up to the sun
and soaked it in. The *Marquita* was on autopilot, safe enough
in weather like this. There was a light breeze—enough to
make *Marquita* slip gracefully through the water like a skier
on a downhill run. On land it would be hot, but out here on
the ocean it was just plain fabulous. Jenny was wearing shorts
and T-shirt and nothing else. Her feet were bare, her hair was
scrunched up in a ponytail to keep it out of her eyes, her nose
was white with sunscreen—and she was perfectly, gloriously
happy.

'You're supposed to complain,' Ramón said, watching her.
'Any deckie I've ever employed would be complaining by
now.'

'What on earth would I be complaining about?'

'Scrubbing, maybe?'

'I'd scrub from here to China if I could stay on this boat,'
she said happily and then saw his expression and hastily
changed her mind. 'No. I didn't mean that. You keep right on
thinking I'm working hard for my money. But, honestly, you
have the best job in the world, Ramón Cavellero, and I have
the second best.'

'I do, don't I?' he said, but his smile faded, and something
about him said he had shadows too. Did she want to ask?

Maybe not.

She'd known Ramón for over a week now, and she'd
learned a lot in that time. She'd learned he was a wonderful

sailor, intuitive, clever and careful. He took no unnecessary risks, yet on the second night out there'd been a storm. A nervous sailor might have reefed in everything and sat it out. Ramón, however, had looked at the charts, altered his course and let the jib stay at full stretch. The *Marquita* had flown across the water with a speed Jenny found unbelievable, and when the dawn came and the storm abated they were maybe three hundred miles further towards New Zealand than they'd otherwise have been.

She'd taken a turn at the wheel that night but she knew Ramón hadn't slept. She'd been conscious of his shadowy presence below, aware of what the boat was doing, aware of how she was handling her. It wasn't that he didn't trust her, but she was new crew and to sleep in such a storm while she had such responsibility might have been dangerous.

His competence pleased her, as did the fact that he hadn't told her he was checking on her. Lots of things about him pleased her, she admitted—but Ramón kept himself to himself. Any thoughts she may have had of being an addition to his harem were quickly squashed. Once they were at sea, he was reserved to the point of being aloof.

'How long have you skippered this boat?' she asked suddenly, getting back to scrubbing, not looking up. She was learning that he responded better that way, talking easily as they worked together. Once work stopped he retreated again into silence.

'Ten years,' he said.

'Wow. You must have been at kindergarten when you were first employed.'

'I got lucky,' he said brusquely, and she thought, *don't go there*. She'd asked a couple of things about the owner, and she'd learned quickly that was the way to stop a conversation dead.

'So how many crews would you have employed in that time?' she asked. And then she frowned down at what she was scrubbing. How on earth had the birds managed to soil under the rim of the forward hatch? She tried to imagine, and couldn't.

'How long's a piece of string?' Ramón said. 'I get new people at every port.'

'But you have me for a year.'

'That's right, I have,' he said and she glanced up and caught a flash of something that might be satisfaction. She smiled and went back to scrubbing, unaccountably pleased.

'That sounds like you liked my lunch time paella.'

'I loved your lunch time paella. Where did you learn to cook something so magnificently Spanish?'

'I'm part Spanish,' she said and he stopped scrubbing and stared.

'Spanish?'

'Well, truthfully, I'm all Australian,' she said, 'but my father was Spanish. He moved to Australia when he met my mother. My mother's mother was Spanish as well. Papà came as an adventuring young man. He contacted my grandmother as a family friend and the rest is history.

'So,' Ramón said slowly, sounding dazed. '*Habla usted español?* Can you speak Spanish?'

'*Sí*,' she said, and tried not to sound smug.

'I don't believe it.'

'There's no end to my talents,' she agreed and grinned, and then peered under the hatch. 'Speaking of talent… How did these birds do this? They must have lain on their sides and aimed.'

'It's a competition between them and me,' Ramón said darkly. 'They don't like my boat looking beautiful. All I can do is sail so far out to sea they can't reach me. But…you have a Spanish background? Why didn't you tell me?'

'You never asked,' she said, and then she hesitated. 'There's lots you didn't ask, and your offer seemed so amazing I saw no reason to mess it with detail. I could have told you I play a mean game of netball, I can climb trees, I have my bronze surf lifesaving certificate and I can play *Waltzing Matilda* on a gum leaf. You didn't ask and how could I tell you? You might have thought I was skiting.'

'Skiting?'

'Making myself out to be Miss Wonderful.'

'I seem to have employed Miss Wonderful regardless,' he said. And then… 'Jenny?'

'Mmm?'

'No, I mean, what sort of Spanish parents call their daughter Jenny?'

'It's Gianetta.'

'Gianetta.' He said it with slow, lilting pleasure, and he said it the way it was supposed to sound. The way her parents had said it. She blinked and then she thought no. Actually, the way Ramón said it wasn't the way her parents had said it. He had the pronunciation right but it was much, much better. He rolled it, he almost growled it, and it sounded so sexy her toes started to curl.

'I would have found out when you signed your contract,' Ramón was saying while she attempted a bit of toe uncurling. Then he smiled. 'Speaking of which, maybe it's time you did sign up. I don't want to let anyone who can play *Waltzing Matilda* on a gum leaf get away.'

'It's a dying art,' she said, relieved to be on safer ground. In fact she'd been astounded that he hadn't yet got round to making her sign any agreement.

The day before they'd sailed he'd handed Charlie a cheque. 'How do you know you can trust me to fill my part of the bargain?' she'd asked him, stunned by what he was doing, and Ramón had looked down at her for a long moment, his face impassive, and he'd given a small decisive nod.

'I can,' he'd said, and that was that.

'Playing a gum leaf's a dying art?' he asked now, cautiously.

'It's something I need to teach my grandchildren,' she told him. And then she heard what she'd said. *Grandchildren.* The void, always threatening, was suddenly right under her. She hauled herself back with an effort.

'What is it?' Ramón said and he was looking at her with concern. The void disappeared. There went her toes again, curling, curling. Did he have any idea of what those eyes did to her? They helped, though. She was back again now, safe. She could move on. If she could focus on something other than those eyes.

'So I'm assuming you're Spanish, too?' she managed.

'No!'

'You're not Spanish?'

'Absolutely not.'

'You sound Spanish.' Then she hesitated. Here was another reason she hadn't told him about her heritage—she wasn't sure. There was something else in his accent besides Spain. France? It was a sexy mix that she couldn't quite place.

'I come from Cepheus,' he said, and all was explained.

Cepheus. She knew it. A tiny principality on the Mediterranean, fiercely independent and fiercely proud.

'My father told me about Cepheus,' she said, awed that here was an echo from her childhood. 'Papà was born not so far away from the border and he went there as a boy. He said it's the most beautiful country in the world—but he also said it belonged to Spain.'

'If he's Spanish then he would say that,' Ramón growled. 'If he was French he'd say the same thing. They've been fighting over my country for generations, like eagles over a small bird. What they've come to realize, however, is that the small bird has claws and knows how to protect itself. For now they've dropped us—they've let us be. We are Cepheus. Nothing more.'

'But you speak Spanish?'

'The French and the Spanish have both taken part of our language and made it theirs,' he said, and she couldn't help herself. She chuckled.

'What's funny?' He was suddenly practically glowering.

'Your patriotism,' she said, refusing to be deflected. 'Like Australians saying the English speak Australian with a plum in their mouths.'

'It's not the same,' he said but then he was smiling again. She smiled back—and wham.

What was it with this man?

She knew exactly what it was. Quite simply he was the most gorgeous guy she'd ever met. Tall, dark and fabulous, a voice like a god, rugged, clever…and smiling. She took a deep breath and went back to really focused scrubbing. It was imperative that she scrub.

She was alone on a boat in the middle of the ocean with a man she was so attracted to her toes were practically ringlets. And she was crew. Nothing more. She was cook and deckhand. Remember it!

'So why the debt?' he asked gently, and she forgot about being cook and deckhand. He was asking as if he cared.

Should she tell him to mind his own business? Should she back away?

Why? He'd been extraordinarily kind and if he wanted to ask… He didn't feel like her boss, and at this moment she didn't feel like a deckie.

Maybe he even had the right to know.

'I lost my baby,' she said flatly, trying to make it sound as if it was history. Only of course she couldn't. Two years on, it still pierced something inside her to say it. 'Matty was born with a congenital heart condition. He had a series of operations, each riskier than the last. Finally, there was only one procedure left to try—a procedure so new it cost the earth. It was his last chance and I had to take it, but of course I'd run out of what money I had. I was working for Charlie for four hours a day over the lunch time rush—Matty was in hospital and I hated leaving him but I had to pay the rent, so when things hit rock bottom Charlie knew. So Charlie loaned me what I needed on the basis that I keep working on for him.'

She scrubbed fiercely at a piece of deck that had already been scrubbed. Ramón didn't say anything. She scrubbed a bit more. Thought about not saying more and then decided— why not say it all?

'You need to understand…I'd been cooking on the docks

since I was seventeen and people knew my food. Charlie's café was struggling and he needed my help to keep it afloat. But the operation didn't work. Matty died when he was two years, three months and five days old. I buried him and I went back to Charlie's café and I've been there ever since.'

'I am so sorry.' Ramón was sitting back on his heels and watching her. She didn't look up—she couldn't. She kept right on scrubbing.

The boat rocked gently on the swell. The sun shone down on the back of her neck and she was acutely aware of his gaze. So aware of his silence.

'Charlie demanded that you leave your baby, for those hours in the last days of his life?' he said at last, and she swallowed at that, fighting back regret that could never fade.

'It was our deal.' She hesitated. 'You've seen the worst of Charlie. Time was when he was a decent human being. Before the drink took over. When he offered me a way out—I only saw the money. I guess I just trusted. And after I borrowed the money there was no way out.'

'So where,' he asked, in his soft, lilting accent that seemed to have warmth and sincerity built into it, 'was Matty's father?'

'On the other side of the world, as far as I know,' she said, and she blinked back self-pity and found herself smiling. 'My Kieran. Or, rather, no one's Kieran.'

'You're smiling?' He sounded incredulous, as well he might.

'Yes, that's stupid. And yes, I was really stupid.' Enough with the scrubbing—any more and she'd start taking off wood. She tossed her brush into the bucket and stood up, leaning against the rail and letting the sun comfort her. How to explain Kieran? 'My father had just died, and I was bleak and miserable. Kieran came into port and he was just…alive. I met him on the wharf one night, we went dancing and I fell in love. Only even then I knew I wasn't in love with Kieran. Not with the person. I was in love with what he represented. Happiness. Laughter. Life. At the end of a wonderful week he sailed

away and two weeks later I discovered our precautions hadn't
worked. I emailed him to tell him. He sent me a dozen roses
and a cheque for a termination. The next time I emailed, to
tell him I was keeping our baby, there was no reply. There's
been no reply since.'

'Do you mind?' he said gently.

'I mind that Kieran didn't have a chance to meet his son,'
she said. 'It was his loss. Matty was wonderful.' She pulled
herself together and managed to smile again. 'But I'd imagine
all mothers say that about their babies. Any minute now I'll
be tugging photographs out of my purse.'

'It would be my privilege to see them.'

'You don't mean that.'

'Why would I not?'

Her smile faded. She searched his face and saw only truth.

'It's okay,' she said, disconcerted. She was struggling to
understand this man. She'd accepted this job suspecting he
was another similar to Kieran, sailing the world to escape responsibility, only the more she saw of him the more she
realized there were depths she couldn't fathom.

She had armour now to protect herself against the likes of
Kieran. She knew she did—that was why she'd taken the job.
But this man's gentle sympathy and practical help were something new. She tried to imagine Kieran scrubbing a deck when
he didn't have to, and she couldn't.

'So where's your family?' she asked, too abruptly, and she
watched his face close. Which was what she was coming to
expect. He'd done this before to her, simply shutting himself
off from her questions. She thought it was a method he'd
learned from years of employing casual labour, setting boundaries and staying firmly behind them.

Maybe that was reasonable, she conceded. Just because
she'd stepped outside her personal boundaries, it didn't mean
he must.

'Sorry. I'll put the buckets away,' she said, but he didn't
move and neither did she.

'I don't like talking of my family.'

'That's okay. That's your right.'

'You didn't have to tell me about your son.'

'Yes, but I like talking about Matty,' she said. She thought about it. It wasn't absolutely true. Or was it?

She only talked about Matty to Cathy, to Susie, to those few people who'd known him. But still...

'Talking about him keeps him real,' she said, trying to figure it out as she spoke. 'Keeping silent locks him in my heart and I'm scared he'll shrivel. I want to be able to have him out there, to share him.' She shrugged. 'It makes no sense but there it is. Your family...you keep them where you need to have them. I'm sorry I intruded.'

'I don't believe you could ever intrude,' he said, so softly she could hardly hear him. 'But my story's not so peaceful. My father died when I was seven. He and my grandfather... well, let's just say they didn't get on. My grandfather was what might fairly be described as a wealthy thug. He mistreated my grandmother appallingly, and finally my father thought to put things right by instigating legal proceedings. Only when it looked like my father and grandmother might win, my grandfather's thugs bashed him—so badly he died.'

'Oh, Ramón,' she whispered, appalled.

'It's old history,' he said in a voice that told her it wasn't. It still had the power to hurt. 'Nothing could ever be proved, so we had to move on as best we could. But my grandmother never got over it. She died when I was ten, and then my mother and my sister were killed in a car accident when I was little more than a teenager. So that's my family. Or, rather, that was my family. I have an aunt I love, but that's all.'

'So you don't have a home,' she said softly.

'The sea makes a wonderful mistress.'

'She's not exactly cuddly,' Jenny retorted before she thought it through, and then she heard what she'd said and she could have kicked herself. But it seemed her tongue was determined to keep her in trouble. 'I mean... Well, the sea. A *mistress*? Wouldn't you rather have a real one?'

His lips twitched. 'You're asking why don't I have a woman?'

'I didn't mean that at all,' she said, astounded at herself. 'If you don't choose to…'

But she stopped herself there. She was getting into deeper water at every word and she was floundering.

'Would you rate yourself as cuddly?' he asked, a slight smile still playing round his mouth, and she felt herself colouring from the toes up. She'd walked straight into that one.

He thoroughly disconcerted her. It was as if there was some sort of connection between them, like an electric current that buzzed back and forth, no matter how she tried to subdue it.

She had to subdue it. Ramón was her boss. She had to maintain a working relationship with him for a year.

'No. No!' She shook her head so hard the tie came loose and her curls went flying every which way. 'Of course I'm not cuddly. I got myself in one horrible mess with Kieran, and I'm not going down that path again, thank you very much.'

'So maybe the sea is to be your partner in life, too?'

'I don't want a partner,' she said with asperity. 'I don't need one, thank you very much. You're very welcome to your sea, Mr Cavellero, but I'll stick to cooking, sailing and occasional scrubbing. What more could a woman want? It sounds like relationships, for both of us, are a thing of the past.' And then she paused. She stared out over Ramón's shoulder. 'Oh!' She put her hand up to shade her eyes. 'Oh, Ramón, look!'

Ramón wheeled to see what she was seeing, and he echoed her gasp.

They'd been too intent on each other to notice their surroundings—the sea was clear to the horizon so there was no threat, but suddenly there was a great black mound, floating closer and closer to the *Marquita*. On the far side of the mound was another, much smaller.

The smaller mound was gliding through the water, surfacing and diving, surfacing and diving. The big mound lay still, like a massive log, three-quarters submerged.

'Oh,' Jenny gasped, trying to take in what she was seeing. 'It's a whale and its calf. But why…'

Why was the larger whale so still?

They were both staring out to starboard now. Ramón narrowed his eyes, then swore and made his way swiftly aft. He retrieved a pair of field glasses, focused and swore again.

'She's wrapped in a net.' He flicked off the autopilot. 'Jenny, we're coming about.'

The boat was already swinging. Jenny dropped her buckets and moved like lightning, reefing in the main with desperate haste so the boom wouldn't slam across with the wind shift.

Even her father wouldn't have trusted her to move so fast, she thought, as she winched in the stays with a speed even she hadn't known was possible. Ramón expected the best of her and she gave it.

But Ramón wasn't focused on her. All his attention was on the whale. With the sails in place she could look again at what was in front of her. And what she saw… She drew in her breath in distress.

The massive whale—maybe fifty feet long or more—was almost completely wrapped in a damaged shark net. Jenny had seen these nets. They were set up across popular beaches to keep swimmers safe, but occasionally whales swam in too close to shore and became entangled, or swam into a net that had already been dislodged.

The net was enfolding her almost completely, with a rope as thick as Jenny's wrist tying her from head to tail, forcing her to bend. As the *Marquita* glided past, Jenny saw her massive pectoral fins were fastened uselessly to her sides. She was rolling helplessly in the swell.

Dead?

No. Just as she thought it, the creature gave a massive shudder. She was totally helpless, and by her side her calf swam free, but helpless as well in the shadow of her mother's entrapment.

'*Dios*,' she whispered. It was the age-old plea she'd learned from her mother, and she heard the echo of it from Ramón's lips.

'It's a humpback,' she said in distress. 'The net's wrapped so tight it's killing her. What can we do?'

But Ramón was already moving. 'We get the sails down and start the motor,' he said. 'The sails won't give us room to manoeuvre. Gianetta, I need your help. Fast.'

He had it. The sails were being reefed in almost before he finished speaking, as the motor hummed seamlessly into life.

He pushed it into low gear so the sound was a low hum. The last thing either of them wanted was to panic the whale. As it was, the calf was moving nervously away from them, so the mother was between it and the boat.

'If she panics there's nothing we can do,' Jenny said grimly. 'Can we get near enough to cut?'

They couldn't. Ramón edged the *Marquita* close, the big whale rolled a little, the swell separated them and Jenny knew they could never simply reach out and cut.

'Can we call someone?' she said helplessly. 'There's whale rescue organisations. Maybe they could come out.'

'We're too far from land,' Ramón said. 'It's us or no one.'

No one, Jenny thought as they tried one more pass. It was hopeless. For them to cut the net the whale had to be right beside the boat. With the lurching of the swell there was no way they could steer the boat alongside and keep her there.

How else to help? To get into the water and swim, then cling and cut was far, far too risky. Jenny was a good swimmer but…

'It's open water, the job's too big, there's no way I could count on getting back into the boat,' Ramón said, and she knew he was thinking the same.

'You would do it if you could?' she asked, incredulous.

'If I knew it'd be effective. But do you think she's going to stay still while I cut? If she rolled, if I was pushed under and caught…'

As if on cue, the whale rolled again. Her massive pectoral fins were fastened hard against her, so a sideways roll was all she could do. She blew—a spray of water misted over Jenny's face, but Jenny's face was wet anyway.

'We can't leave her like this,' she whispered. 'We have to try.'

'We do,' Ramón said. 'Jenny, are you prepared to take a risk?'

There was no question. 'Of course.'

'Okay,' he said, reaching under the seat near the wheel and hauling out life jackets. 'Here's the plan. We put these on. We unfasten the life raft in case worst comes to worst and we let the authorities know what's happening. We radio in our position, we tell them what we intend to do and if they don't hear back from us then they'll know we're sitting in a life raft in the middle of the Pacific. We're wearing positional locators anyway. We should be fine.'

'What…what are we intending to do?' Jenny asked faintly.

'Pull the boat up beside the whale,' he said. 'If you're brave enough.'

She stared at him, almost speechless. How could he get so close? And, even if he did, if the whale rolled… 'You'd risk the boat?' she gasped.

'Yes.' Unequivocal.

'Could we be sure of rescue?'

'I'll set it up so we would be,' he said. 'I'm not risking our lives here. Only our boat and the cost of marine rescue.'

'Marine rescue… It'd cost a fortune.'

'Jenny, we're wasting time. Yes or no?'

She looked out at the whale. Left alone, she'd die, dreadfully, agonisingly and, without her, her calf would slowly starve to death as well.

Ramón was asking her to risk all. She looked at him and he met her gaze, levelly and calmly.

'Gianetta, she's helpless,' he said. 'I believe at some subliminal level she'll understand we're trying to help and she won't roll towards us. But you know I can't guarantee that. There's a small chance we may end up sitting in a lifeboat for the next few hours waiting to be winched to safety. But I won't do it unless I have your agreement. It's not my risk, Gianetta. It's our risk.'

Our risk.

She thought about what he was asking—what he was doing. He'd have to explain to his owner that he'd lost his boat to save a whale. He'd lose his job at the very least. Maybe he'd be up for massive costs, for the boat and for rescue.

She looked at him and she saw it meant nothing.

He was free, she thought, with a sudden stab of something that could almost be jealousy. There was the whale to be saved. He'd do what needed to be done without thinking of the future.

Life… That was all that mattered, she thought suddenly, and with it came an unexpected lifting of the dreariness of the last couple of years. She'd fought long and hard for Matty. She'd lost but she'd had him and she'd loved him and she'd worried about the cost later.

She looked out at the whale and she knew there was only one answer to give.

'Of course,' she said. 'Just give me a couple of minutes to stick a ration pack in the life raft. If I'm going to float around for a day or so waiting for rescue flights then I want at least two bottles of champagne and some really good cheeses while I'm waiting.'

Jenny didn't have a clue what Ramón intended, but when she saw she was awed. With his safeguards in place, he stood on the highest point of the boat with a small anchor—one he presumably used in shallow waters when lowering the massive main anchor would potentially damage the sea bed.

This anchor was light enough for a man to hold. Or, rather, for Ramón to hold, Jenny corrected herself. It still looked heavy. But Ramón stood with the anchor attached by a long line and he held it as if it was no weight at all, while Jenny nosed the boat as close to the whale as she dared. Ramón swung the anchor round and round, in wider and wider circles, and then he heaved with every ounce of strength he had.

The whale was maybe fifteen feet from the boat. The anchor flew over the far side of her and slid down. As it slid,

Ramón was already striding aft, a far more secure place to ma-noeuvre, and he was starting to tug the rope back in.

'Cut the motor,' he snapped. She did, and finally she real-ized what he was doing.

The anchor had fallen on the far side of the whale. As Ramón tugged, the anchor was being hauled up the whale's far side. Its hooks caught the ropes of the net and held, and suddenly Ramón was reeling in the anchor with whale attached. Or, rather, the *Marquita* was being reeled in against the whale, and the massive creature was simply submitting.

Jenny was by Ramón's side in an instant, pulling with him. Boat and whale moved closer. Closer still.

'Okay, hold her as close as you can,' Ramón said curtly as the whale's vast body came finally within an arm's length. 'If she pulls, you let go. No heroics, Gianetta, just do it. But keep tension on the rope so I'll know as soon as I have it free.'

Ramón had a lifeline clipped on. He was leaning over the side, with a massive gutting knife in his hand. Reaching so far Jenny was sure he'd fall.

The whale could roll this way, she thought wildly, and if she did he could be crushed. He was supporting himself on the whale itself, his legs still on the boat, but leaning so far over he was holding onto the netting. Slicing. Slicing. As if the danger was nothing.

She tugged on. If the whale pulled away, she'd have to release her. They'd lose the anchor. They had this one chance. Please…

But the whale didn't move, except for the steady rise and fall of the swell, where Jenny had to let out, reel in, let out, reel in, to try and keep Ramón's base steady against her.

He was slicing and slicing and slicing, swearing and slicing some more, until suddenly the tension on Jenny's rope was no longer there. The anchor lifted free, the net around the whale's midriff dislodged. Jenny, still pulling, was suddenly reeling in a mass of netting and an anchor.

And Ramón was back in the boat, pulling with her.

One of the whale's fins was free. The whale moved it a

little, stretching, and she floated away. Not far. Twenty feet, no more.

The whale stilled again. One fin was not enough. She was still trapped.

On the far side of her, her calf nudged closer.

'Again,' Ramón said grimly as Jenny gunned the motor back into action and nosed close. He was already on top of the cabin, swinging the anchor rope once more. 'If she'll let us.'

'You'll hit the calf,' she said, almost to herself, and then bit her tongue. Of all the stupid objections. She knew what his answer must be.

'It's risk the calf having a headache, or both of them dying. No choice.'

But he didn't need to risk. As the arcs of the swinging anchor grew longer, the calf moved away again.

As if it knew.

And, once again, Ramón caught the net.

It took an hour, maybe longer, the times to catch the net getting longer as the amount of net left to cut off grew smaller. But they worked on, reeling her in, slicing, reeling her in, slicing, until the netting was a massive pile of rubbish on the deck.

Ramón was saving her, Jenny thought dazedly as she worked on. Every time he leaned out he was risking his life. She watched him work—and she fell in love.

She was magnificent. Ramón was working feverishly, slashing at the net while holding on to the rails and stretching as far as he could, but every moment he did he was aware of Jenny.

Gianetta.

She had total control of the anchor rope, somehow holding the massive whale against the side of the boat. But they both knew that to hold the boat in a fixed hold would almost certainly mean capsizing. What Jenny had to do was to work with the swells, holding the rope fast, then loosening it as the whale rose and the boat swayed, or the whale sank and the boat rose. Ramón had no room for anything but holding on to the boat and slashing but, thanks to Jenny, he had an almost stable platform to work with.

Tied together, boat and whale represented tonnage he didn't want to think about, especially as he was risking slipping between the two.

He wouldn't slip. Jenny was playing her part, reading the sea, watching the swell, focused on the whale in case she suddenly decided to roll or pull away...

She didn't. Ramón could slash at will at the rope entrapment, knowing Jenny was keeping him safe.

He slipped once and he heard her gasp. He felt her hand grip his ankle.

He righted himself—it was okay—but the memory of her touch stayed.

Gianetta was watching out for him.

Gianetta. Where had she come from, this magical Gianetta?

It was working. Jenny was scarcely breathing. Please, please...

But somehow her prayers were being answered. Piece by piece the net was being cut away. Ramón was winning. They were both winning.

The last section to be removed was the netting and the ropes trapping and tying the massive tail, but catching this section was the hardest. Ramón threw and threw, but each time the anchor slipped uselessly behind the whale and into the sea.

To have come so far and not save her... Jenny felt sick.

But Ramón would not give up. His arm must be dropping off, she thought, but just as she reached the point where despair took over, the whale rolled. She stretched and lifted her tail as far as she could within the confines of the net, and in doing so she made a channel to trap the anchor line as Ramón threw. And her massive body edged closer to the boat.

Ramón threw again, and this time the anchor held.

Once more Jenny reeled her in and once more Ramón sliced. Again. Again. One last slash—and the last piece of rope came loose into his hands.

Ramón staggered back onto the deck and Jenny was hauling the anchor in one last time. He helped her reel it in, then they stood together in the mass of tangled netting on the deck, silent, awed, stunned, as the whale finally floated free. Totally free. The net was gone.

But there were still questions. Were they too late? Had she been trapped too long?

Ramón's arm came round Jenny's waist and held, but Jenny was hardly aware of it. Or maybe she was, but it was all part of this moment. She was breathing a plea and she knew the plea was echoing in Ramón's heart as well as her own.

Please…

The whale was wallowing in the swell, rolling up and down, up and down. Her massive pectoral fins were free now. They moved stiffly outward, upward, over and over, while Jenny and Ramón held their breath and prayed.

The big tail swung lazily back and forth; she seemed to be stretching, feeling her freedom. Making sure the ropes were no longer there.

'She can't have been caught all that long,' Jenny whispered, breathless with wonder. 'Look at her tail. That rope was tied so tightly but there's hardly a cut.'

'She might have only just swum into it,' Ramón said and Jenny was aware that her awe was echoed in his voice. His arm had tightened around her and it seemed entirely natural. This was a prayer shared. 'If it was loosened from the shore by a storm it might have only hit her a day or so ago. The calf looks healthy enough.'

The calf was back at its mother's side now, nudging against her flank. Then it dived, straight down into the deep, and Jenny managed a faltering smile.

'He'll be feeding. She must still have milk. Oh, Ramón…'

'Gianetta,' Ramón murmured back, and she knew he was feeling exactly what she was feeling. Awe, hope, wonder. They might, they just might, have been incredibly, wondrously lucky.

And then the big whale moved. Her body seemed to ripple. Everything flexed at once, her tail, her fins…. She rolled away, almost onto her back, as if to say to her calf: *No feeding, not yet, I need to figure if I'm okay.*

And figure she did. She swam forward in front of the boat, speeding up, speeding up. Faster, faster she swam, with her calf speeding after her.

And then, just as they thought they'd lost sight of her, she came sweeping back, a vast majestic mass of glossy black muscle and strength and bulk. Then, not a hundred yards from the boat, she rolled again, only higher, so her body was half out of the water, stretching, arching back, her pectoral fins outstretched, then falling backward with a massive splash that reached them on the boat and soaked them to the skin.

Neither of them noticed. Neither of them cared.

The whale was sinking now, deep, so deep that only a mass of still water on the surface showed her presence. Then she burst up one more time, arched back once more—and she dived once more and they saw her print on the water above as she adjusted course and headed for the horizon, her calf tearing after her.

Two wild creatures returned to the deep.

Tears were sliding uselessly down Jenny's face. She couldn't stop them, any more than she could stop smiling. And she looked up at Ramón and saw his smile echo hers.

'We did it,' she breathed. 'Ramón, we did it.'

'We did,' he said, and he tugged her hard against him, then swung her round so he was looking into her tear-stained face. 'We did it, Gianetta, we saved our whale. And you were magnificent. Gianetta, you may be a Spanish-Australian woman in name but I believe you have your nationality wrong. A woman like you… I believe you're worthy of being a woman of Cepheus.'

And then, before she knew what he intended, before she could guess anything at all, he lifted her into his arms and he kissed her.

CHAPTER FOUR

ONE moment she was gazing out at the horizon, catching the last shimmer of the whale's wake on the translucence of the sea. The next she was being kissed as she'd never been kissed in her life.

His hands were lifting her, pulling her hard in against him so her feet barely touched the deck. His body felt rock-hard, the muscled strength he'd just displayed still at work, only now directed straight at her. Straight with her.

The emotions of the rescue were all around her. He was wet and wild and wonderful. She was soaking as well, and the dripping fabric of his shirt and hers meant their bodies seemed to cling and melt.

It felt right. It felt meant. It felt as if there was no room or sense to argue.

His mouth met hers again, his arms tightening around her so she was locked hard against him. He was so close she could feel the rapid beat of his heart. Her breasts were crushed against his chest, her face had tilted instinctively, her mouth was caught…

Caught? Merged, more like. Two parts of a whole finding their home.

He tugged her tighter, tighter still against him, moulding her lips against his. She was hard against him, closer, closer, feeling him, tasting him, wanting him…

To be a part of him seemed suddenly as natural, as right,

as breathing. To be kissed by this man was an extension of
what had just happened.

Or maybe it was more than that. Maybe it was an extension of the whole of the last week.

Maybe she'd wanted this from the moment she'd seen him.

Either way, she certainly wasn't objecting now. She heard
herself give a tiny moan, almost a whimper, which was stupid
because she didn't feel the least like whimpering. She felt like
shouting, *Yes!*

His mouth was demanding, his tongue was searching for
an entry, his arms holding her so tightly now he must surely
bruise. But he couldn't hold her tight enough. She was holding
him right back, desperate that she not be lowered, desperate
that this miraculous contact not be lost.

He felt so good. He felt as if he was meant to be right here
in her arms. That she'd been destined for this moment for ever
and it had taken this long to find him.

He hadn't shaved this morning. She could feel the stubble
on his jaw, she could almost taste it. There was salt on his
face—of course there was, he'd been practically submerged,
over and over. He smelled of salt and sea, and of pure testos-
terone.

He tasted of Ramón.

'Ramón.' She heard herself whisper his name, or maybe it
was in her heart, for how could she possibly whisper when he
was kissing as if he was a man starved for a woman, starved
of *this* woman? She knew so clearly what was happening, and
she accepted it with elation. This woman was who he wanted
and he'd take her, he wanted her, she was his and he was
claiming his own.

Like the whale rolling joyously in the sea, she thought,
dazed and almost delirious, this was nature; it was right, it was
meant.

She was in his arms and she wasn't letting go.

Ramón.

'Gianetta…' His voice was ragged with heat and desire.

Somehow he dragged himself back from her and held her at arm's length. 'Gianetta, *mia*…'

'If you're asking if I want you, then the answer's yes,' she said huskily, and almost laughed at the look of blazing heat that came straight back at her. His eyes were almost black, gleaming with tenderness and want and passion. But something else. He wouldn't take her yet. His eyes were searching.

'I'll take no woman against her will,' he growled.

'You think…you think this is against my will?' she whispered, as the blaze of desire became almost white-hot and she pressed herself against him, forcing him to see how much this was not the case.

'Gianetta,' he sighed, and there was laughter now as well as wonder and desire. Before she could respond he had her in his arms, held high, cradled against him, almost triumphant.

'You don't think maybe we should set the automatic pilot or something?' she murmured. 'We'll drift.'

'The radar will tell us if we're about to hit something big,' he said, his dark eyes gleaming. 'But it can't pick up things like jellyfish, so there's a risk. You want to risk death by jellyfish and come to my bed while we wait, my Gianetta?'

And what was a girl to say to an invitation like that?

'Yes, please,' she said simply and he kissed her and he held her tight and carried her down below.

To his bed. To his arms. To his pleasure.

'She left port six days ago, heading for New Zealand.'

The lawyer stared at the boat builder in consternation. 'You're sure? The *Marquita*?'

'That's the one. The guy skippering her—Ramón, I think he said his name was—had her in dry dock here for a couple of days, checking the hull, but she sailed out on the morning tide on Monday. Took the best cook in the bay with him, too. Half the locals are after his blood. He'd better look after our Jenny.'

But the lawyer wasn't interested in Ramón's staff. He stood

on the dock and stared out towards the harbour entrance as if he could see the *Marquita* sailing away.

'You're sure he was heading for Auckland?'

'I am. You're Spanish, right?'

'Cepheus country,' the lawyer said sharply. 'Not Spain. But no matter. How long would it take the *Marquita* to get to Auckland?'

'Coupla weeks,' the boat builder told him. 'Can't see him hurrying. I wouldn't hurry if I had a boat like the *Marquita* and Jenny aboard.'

'So if I go to Auckland…'

'I guess you'd meet him. If it's urgent.'

'It's urgent,' the lawyer said grimly. 'You have no idea how urgent.'

There was no urgency about the *Marquita*. If she took a year to reach Auckland it was too soon for Jenny.

Happiness was right now.

They could travel faster, but that would mean sitting by the wheel hour after hour, setting the sails to catch the slightest wind shift, being sailors.

Instead of being lovers.

She'd never felt like this. She'd melted against Ramón's body the morning of the whales and she felt as if she'd melted permanently. She'd shape shifted, from the Jenny she once knew to the Gianetta Ramón loved.

For that was what it felt like. Loved. For the first time in her life she felt truly beautiful, truly desirable—and it wasn't just for her body.

Yes, he made love to her, over and over, wonderful love-making that made her cry out in delight.

But more.

He wanted to know all about her.

He tugged blankets up on the deck. They lay in the sun and they solved the problems of the world. They watched dolphins surf in their wake. They fished. They compared toes to see whose little toe bent the most.

That might be ridiculous but there was serious stuff, too. Ramón now knew all about her parents, her life, her baby. She told him everything about Matty, she showed him pictures and he examined each of them with the air of a man being granted a privilege.

When Matty was smiling, Ramón smiled. She watched this big man respond to her baby's smile and she felt her heart twist in a way she'd never thought possible.

He let the boom net down off the rear deck, and they surfed behind the boat, and when the wind came up it felt as if they were flying. They worked the sails as a team, setting them so finely that they caught up on time lost when they were below, lost in each other's bodies.

He touched her and her body reacted with fire.

Don't fall in love. Don't fall in love. It was a mantra she said over and over in her head, but she knew it was hopeless. She was hopelessly lost.

It wouldn't last. Like Kieran, this man was a nomad, a sailor of no fixed address, going where the wind took him.

He talked little about himself. She knew there'd been tragedy, the sister he'd loved, parents he'd lost, pain to make him shy from emotional entanglement.

Well, maybe she'd learned that lesson, too. So savour the moment, she told herself. For now it was wonderful. Each morning she woke in Ramón's arms and she thought: Ramón had employed her for a year! When they got back to Europe conceivably the owner would join them. She could go back to being crew. But Ramón would be crew as well, and the nights were long, and owners never stayed aboard their boats for ever.

'Tell me about the guy who owns this boat,' she said, two days out of Auckland and she watched a shadow cross Ramón's face. She was starting to know him so well—she watched him when he didn't know it—his strongly boned, aquiline face, his hooded eyes, the smile lines, the weather lines from years at sea.

What had suddenly caused the shadow?

'He's rich,' he said shortly. 'He trusts me. What else do you need to know?'

'Well, whether he likes muffins, for a start,' she said, with something approaching asperity, which was a bit difficult as she happened to be entwined in Ramón's arms as she spoke and asperity was a bit hard to manage. Breathless was more like it.

'He loves muffins,' Ramón said.

'He'll be used to richer food than I can cook. Do you usually employ someone with special training?'

'He eats my cooking.'

'Really?' She frowned and sat up in bed, tugging the sheet after her. She'd seen enough of Ramón's culinary skills to know what an extraordinary statement this was. 'He's rich and he eats your cooking?'

'As I said, he'll love your muffins.'

'So when will you next see him?'

'Back in Europe,' Ramón said, and sighed. 'He'll have to surface then, but not now. Not yet. There's three months before we have to face the world. Do you think we can be happy for three months, *cariño*?' And he tugged her back down to him.

'If you keep calling me *cariño*,' she whispered. 'Are we really being paid for this?'

He chuckled but then his smile faded once more. 'You know it can't last, my love. I will need to move on.'

'Of course you will,' she whispered, but she only said it because it was the sensible, dignified thing to say. A girl had some pride.

Move on?

She never wanted to move on. If her world could stay on this boat, with this man, for ever, she wasn't arguing at all.

She slept and Ramón held her in his arms and tried to think of the future.

He didn't have to think. Not yet. It was three months before he was due to leave the boat and return to Bangladesh.

Three months before he needed to tell Jenny the truth.

She could stay with the boat, he thought, if she wanted to. He always employed someone to stay on board while he was away. She could take that role.

Only that meant Jenny would be in Cepheus while he was in Bangladesh.

He'd told her he needed to move on. It was the truth.

Maybe she could come with him.

The idea hit and stayed. His team always had volunteers to act as manual labour. Would Jenny enjoy the physical demands of construction, of helping make life bearable for those who had nothing?

Maybe she would.

What was he thinking? He'd never considered taking a woman to Bangladesh. He'd never considered that leaving a woman behind seemed unthinkable.

Gianetta…

His arms tightened their hold and she curved closer in sleep. He smiled and kissed the top of her head. Her curls were so soft.

Maybe he could sound her out about Bangladesh.

Give it time, he told himself, startled by the direction his thoughts were taking him. You've known her for less than two weeks.

Was it long enough?

There was plenty of time after Auckland. It was pretty much perfect right now, he thought. Let's not mess with perfection. He'd just hold this woman and hope that somehow the love he'd always told himself was an illusion might miraculously become real.

Anything was possible.

'How do you know he'll sail straight to Auckland?'

In the royal palace of Cepheus, Sofía was holding the telephone and staring into the middle distance, seeing not the magnificent suits of armour in the grand entrance but a vision of an elderly lawyer pacing anxiously on an unknown dock half a world away. She could understand his anxiety. Things in the palace were reaching crisis point.

The little boy had gone into foster care yesterday. Philippe needed love, Sofía thought bleakly. His neglect here—all his physical needs met, but no love, little affection, just a series of disinterested nannies—seemed tantamount to child abuse, and the country knew of it. She'd found him lovely foster parents, but his leaving the palace was sending the wrong message to the population—as if Ramón himself didn't care for the child.

Did Ramón even know about him?

'I don't know for sure where the Prince will sail,' the lawyer snapped. 'But I can hope. He'll want to restock fast to get around the Horn. It makes sense for him to come here.'

'So you'll wait.'

'Of course I'll wait. What else can I do?'

'But there's less than two weeks to go,' Sofía wailed. 'What if he's delayed?'

'Then we have catastrophe,' the lawyer said heavily. 'He has to get here. Then he has to get back to Cepheus and accept his new life.'

'And the child?'

'It doesn't matter about the child.'

Yes, it does, Sofía thought. Oh, Ramón, what are you facing?

They sailed into Auckland Harbour just after dawn. Jenny stood in the bow, ready to jump across to shore with the lines, ready to help in any way she could with berthing the *Marquita*. Ramón was at the wheel. She glanced back at him and had a pang of misgivings.

They hadn't been near land for two weeks. Why did it feel as if the world was waiting to crowd in?

How could it? Their plan was to restock and be gone again. Their idyll could continue.

But they'd booked a berth with the harbour master. Ramón

had spoken to the authorities an hour ago, and after that he'd looked worried.

'Problem?' she'd asked.

'Someone's looking for me.'

'Debt collectors?' she'd teased, but he hadn't smiled.

'I don't have debts.'

'Then who…?'

'I don't know,' he said, and his worry sounded as if it was increasing. 'No one knows where I am.'

'Conceivably the owner knows.'

'What…?' He caught himself. 'I…yes. But he won't be here. I can't think…'

That was all he'd said but she could see worry building.

She turned and looked towards the dock. She'd looked at the plan the harbour master had faxed through and from here she could see the berth that had been allocated to them.

There was someone standing on the dock, at the berth, as if waiting. A man in a suit.

It must be the owner, she thought.

She glanced back at Ramón and saw him flinch.

'Rodriguez,' he muttered, and in the calm of the early morning she heard him swear. 'Trouble.'

'Is he the boat's owner?'

'No,' he said shortly. 'He's legal counsel to the Crown of Cepheus. I've met him once or twice when he had business with my grandmother. If he's here… I hate to imagine what he wants of me.'

Señor Rodriguez was beside himself. He had ten days to save a country. He glanced at his watch as the *Marquita* sailed slowly towards her berth, fretting as if every second left was vital.

What useless display of skill was this, to sail into harbour when motoring would be faster? And why was the woman in the bow, rather than Ramón himself? He needed to talk to Ramón, now!

The boat edged nearer. 'Can you catch my line?' the

woman called, and he flinched and moved backward. He knew nothing about boats.

But it seemed she could manage without him. She jumped lightly over a gap he thought was far too wide, landing neatly on the dock, then hauled the boat into position and made her fast as Ramón tugged down the last sail.

'Good morning,' the woman said politely, casting him a curious glance. And maybe she was justified in her curiosity. He was in his customary suit, which he acknowledged looked out of place here. The woman was in the uniform of the sea—faded shorts, a T-shirt and nothing else. She looked wind-blown and free. Momentarily, he was caught by how good she looked, but only for an instant. His attention returned to Ramón.

'Señor Rodriguez,' Ramón called to him, cautious and wary.

'You remember me?'

'Yes,' Ramón said shortly. 'What's wrong?'

'Nothing's wrong,' the lawyer said, speaking in the mix of French and Spanish that formed the Cepheus language. 'As long as you come home.'

'My home's on the *Marquita*. You know that.'

'Not any more it's not,' the lawyer said. 'Your uncle and your cousin are dead. As of four weeks ago, you're the Crown Prince of Cepheus.'

There was silence. Jenny went on making all secure while Ramón stared at the man on the dock as if he'd spoken a foreign language.

Which he had, but Jenny had been raised speaking Spanish like a native, and she'd picked up French at school. There were so many similarities in form she'd slipped into it effortlessly. Now… She'd missed the odd word but she understood what the lawyer had said.

Or she thought she understood what he'd said.

Crown Prince of Cepheus. Ramón.

It might make linguistic sense. It didn't make any other sort of sense.

'My uncle's dead?' Ramón said at last, his voice without inflexion.

'In a light plane crash four weeks ago. Your uncle, your cousin and your cousin's wife, all killed. Only there's worse. It seems your cousin wasn't really married—he brought the woman he called his wife home and shocked his father and the country by declaring he was married, but now we've searched for proof, we've found none. So the child, Philippe, who stood to be heir, is illegitimate. You stand next in line. But if you're not home in ten days then Carlos inherits.'

'Carlos!' The look of flat shock left Ramón's face, replaced by anger, pure and savage. 'You're saying Carlos will inherit the throne?'

'Not if you come home. You must see that's the only way.'

'No!'

'Think about it.'

'I've thought.'

'Leave the woman to tend the boat and come with me,' Señor Rodriguez said urgently. 'We need to speak privately.'

'The woman's name is Gianetta.' Ramón's anger seemed to be building. 'I won't leave her.'

The man cast an uninterested glance at Jenny, as if she was of no import. Which, obviously, was the case. 'Regardless, you must come.'

'I can look after the boat,' Jenny said, trying really hard to keep up. *I won't leave her.* There was a declaration. But he obviously meant it for right now. Certainly not for tomorrow. *Crown Prince of Cepheus?*

'There's immigration…' Ramón said.

'I can sort my papers out,' she said. 'The harbour master's office is just over there. You do what you have to do on the way to wherever you're going. Have your discussion and then come back and tell me what's happening.'

'Jenny…'

But she was starting to add things together in her head and she wasn't liking them. *Crown Prince of Cepheus.*

'I guess the *Marquita* would be *your* boat, then?' she asked flatly, and she saw him flinch.

'Yes, but...'

She felt sick. 'There you go,' she managed, fighting for dignity. 'The owner's needs always come first. I'll stow the sails and make all neat. Then I might go for a nice long walk and let off a little steam. I'll see you later.'

And Ramón cast her a glance where frustration, anger— and maybe even a touch of envy—were combined.

'If you can...'

'Of course I can,' she said, almost cordially. 'We're on land again. I can stand on my own two feet.'

There were complications everywhere, and all he could think of was Jenny. Gianetta. His woman.

The flash of anger he'd seen when he'd confessed that he did indeed own the *Marquita*; the look of betrayal...

She'd think he'd lied to her. She wouldn't understand what else was going on, but the lie would be there, as if in flashing neon.

Yes, he'd lied.

He needed to concentrate on the lawyer.

The throne of Cepheus was his.

Up until now there'd never been a thought of him inheriting. Neither his uncle nor his cousin, Cristián, had ever invited Ramón near the palace. He knew the country had been in dread of Cristián becoming Crown Prince but there was nothing anyone could do about it. Cristián had solidified his inheritance by marrying and having a child. The boy must be what, five?

For him to be proved illegitimate...

'I can't even remember the child's name,' he said across the lawyer's stream of explanations, and the lawyer cast him a reproachful glance.

'Philippe.'

'How old?'

'Five,' he confirmed.

'So what happens to Philippe?'

'Nothing,' the lawyer said. 'He has no rights. With his parents dead, your aunt has organized foster care, and if you wish to make a financial settlement on him I imagine the country will be relieved. There's a certain amount of anger…'

'You mean my cousin didn't make provision for his own son?'

'Your cousin and your uncle spent every drop of their personal incomes on themselves, on gambling, on…on whatever they wished. The Crown itself, however, is very wealthy. You, with the fortune your grandmother left you and the Crown to take care of your every need, will be almost indecently rich. But the child has nothing.'

He felt sick. A five-year-old child. To lose everything…

He'd been not much older than Philippe when he'd lost his own father.

It couldn't matter. It shouldn't be his problem. He didn't even know the little boy…

'I'll take financial care of the child,' Ramón said shortly. 'But I can't drop everything. I have twelve more weeks at sea and then I'm due in Bangladesh.'

'Your team already knows you won't be accompanying them this year,' the lawyer told him flatly, leaving no room for argument. 'And I've found an experienced yachtsman who's prepared to sail the *Marquita* back to Cepheus for you. We can be on a flight tonight, and even that's not soon enough.' Then, as the lawyer noticed Ramón's face—and Ramón was making no effort to disguise his fury—he added quickly, 'There's mounting hysteria over the mess your uncle and cousin left, and there's massive disquiet about Carlos inheriting.'

'As well there might be,' Ramón growled, trying hard to stay calm. Ramón's distant cousin was an indolent gamester, rotund, corrupt and inept. He'd faced the court more than once, but charges had been dropped, because of bribery? He wasn't close enough to the throne to know.

'He's making noises that the throne should be his. Blustering threats against you and your aunt.'

'Threats?' And there it was again, the terror he'd been raised with. *'Don't go near the throne. Ever!'*

'If the people rise against the throne…' the lawyer was saying.

'Maybe that would be a good thing.'

'Maybe it'd be a disaster,' the man said, and proceeded to tell him why. At every word Ramón felt his world disintegrate. There was no getting around it—the country was in desperate need of a leader, of some sort of stability…of a Crown Prince.

'So you see,' the lawyer said at last, 'you have to come. Go back to the boat, tell the woman—she's your only crew?—what's happening, pack your bags and we'll head straight to the airport.'

And there was nothing left for him but to agree. To take his place in a palace that had cost his family everything.

'Tomorrow,' he said, feeling ill.

'Tonight.'

'I will spend tonight with Gianetta,' Ramón growled, and the lawyer raised his brows.

'Like that?'

'Like nothing,' Ramón snapped. 'She deserves an explanation.'

'It's not as if you're sacking her,' the lawyer said. 'I've only hired one man to replace you. She'll still be needed. She can help bring the *Marquita* home and then you can pay her off.'

'I've already paid her.'

'Then there's no problem.' The lawyer rose and so did Ramón. 'Tonight.'

'Tomorrow,' Ramón snapped and looked at the man's face and managed a grim smile. 'Consider it my first royal decree. Book the tickets for tomorrow's flights.'

'But…'

'I will not argue,' Ramón said. 'I've a mind to wash my hands of the whole business and take *Marquita* straight back out to sea.' Then, at the wash of undisguised distress on the lawyer's face, he sighed and relented. 'But, of course, I won't,' he said. 'You know I won't. I will return with you to Cepheus. I'll do what I must to resolve this mess, I'll face Carlos down, but you will give me one more night.'

CHAPTER FIVE

SHE walked for four long hours, and then she found an Internet café and did some research. By the time she returned to the boat she was tired and hungry and her anger hadn't abated one bit.

Ramón was the Crown Prince of Cepheus. What sort of dangerous mess had she walked into?

She'd slept with a prince?

Logically, it shouldn't make one whit of difference that he was royal, but it did, and she felt used and stupid and very much like a star-struck teenager. All that was needed was the paparazzi. Images of headlines flashed through her head—*Crown Prince of Cepheus Takes Stupid, Naive Australian Lover*—and as she neared the boat she couldn't help casting a furtive glance over her shoulder to check the thought had no foundation.

It didn't—of course it didn't. There was only Ramón, kneeling on the deck, calmly sealing the ends of new ropes.

He glanced up and saw her coming. He smiled a welcome, but she was too sick at heart to smile back.

For a few wonderful days she'd let herself believe this smile could be for her.

She felt besmirched.

'I've just come back to get my things,' she said flatly before he had a chance to speak.

'You're leaving?' His eyes were calmly appraising.

'Of course I'm leaving.'

'To go where?'

'I'll see if I can get a temporary job here. As soon as I can get back to Australia I'll organize some way of repaying the loan.'

'There's no need for you to repay...'

'There's every need,' she flashed, wanting to stamp her foot; wanting, quite badly, to cry. 'You think I want to be in your debt for one minute more than I must? I've read about you on the Internet now. It doesn't matter whether anyone died or not. You were a prince already.'

'Does that make a difference?' he asked, still watchful, and his very calmness added to her distress.

'Of course it does. I've been going to bed with a *prince*,' she wailed, and the couple on board their cruiser in the next berth choked on their lunch time Martinis.

But Ramón didn't notice. He had eyes only for her. 'You went to bed with me,' he said softly. 'Not with a prince.'

'You are a prince.'

'I'm just Ramón, Gianetta.'

'Don't Gianetta me,' she snapped. 'That's your bedroom we slept in. Not the owner's. Here I was thinking we were doing something illicit...'

'Weren't we?' he demanded and a glint of humour returned to his dark eyes.

'It was your bed all along,' she wailed and then, finally, she made a grab at composure. The couple on the next boat were likely to lose their eyes; they were out on stalks. Dignity, she told herself desperately. Please.

'So I own the boat,' he said. 'Yes, I'm a prince. What more do you know of me?'

'Apparently very little,' she said bitterly. 'I seem to have told you my whole life story. It appears you've only told me about two minutes of yours. Apparently you're wealthy, fabulously wealthy, and you're royal. The Internet bio was sketchy, but you spend your time either on this boat or fronting some charity organisation.'

'I do more than that.'

But she was past hearing. She was past wanting to hear. She felt humiliated to her socks, and one fact stood out above all the rest. *She'd never really known him.*

'So when you saw me you thought here's a little more charity,' she threw at him, anger making her almost incoherent. 'I'll take this poverty-stricken, flour-streaked muffin-maker and show her a nice time.'

'A flour-streaked muffin-maker?' he said and, infuriatingly, the laughter was back. 'I guess if you want to describe yourself as that… Okay, fine, I rescued the muffin-maker. And we did have a nice time. No?'

But she wasn't going there. She was not being sucked into that smile ever again. 'I'm leaving,' she said, and she swung herself down onto the deck. She was heading below, but Ramón was before her, blocking her path.

'Jenny, you're still contracted to take my boat to Cepheus.'

'You don't need me…'

'You signed a contract. Yesterday, as I remember—and it was you who wanted it signed before we came into port.' His hands were on her shoulders, forcing her to meet his gaze, and her anger was suddenly matched with his. 'So you've been on the Internet. Do you understand why I have to return?'

And she did understand. Sort of. She'd read and read and read. 'It seems your uncle and cousin are dead,' she said flatly. 'There's a huge scandal because it seems your cousin wasn't married after all, so his little son can't inherit. So you get to be Crown Prince.' Even now, she couldn't believe she was saying it. *Crown Prince.* It was like some appalling twisted fairy tale. Kiss a frog, have him turn into a prince.

She wanted her frog back.

'I don't have a choice in this,' he said harshly. 'You need to believe that.' Before she could stop him, he put the back of his hand against her cheek and ran it down to her lips, a touch so sensuous that it made a shiver run right down to her toes. But there was anger behind the touch—and there was also… Regret? 'Gianetta, for you to go…'

'Of course I'm going,' she managed.

'And I need to let you go,' he said, and there was a depth of sadness behind his words that she couldn't begin to understand. 'But still I want you to take my boat home. Selfish or not, I want to see you again.'

Where was dignity when she needed it? His touch had sucked all the anger out of her. She wanted to hold on to this man and cling.

What was she thinking? No. This man was royalty, and he'd lied to her.

She had to find sense.

'I'm grabbing my things,' she said shortly, fighting for some semblance of calm. 'I'll be in touch about the money. I swear I won't owe you for any longer than absolutely necessary.'

'There's no need to repay…'

'There is,' she snapped. 'I pay my debts, even if they're to princes.'

'Can you stop calling me…'

'A prince? It's what you are and it's not new. It's not like this title's a shock to you. Yes, you seem to have inherited the Crown, and that's surprised you, but you were born a prince and you didn't tell me.'

'You didn't ask.'

'Right,' she said, fury building again. She shoved his hands away and headed below, whether he liked it or not. Ramón followed her and stood watching as she flung her gear into her carry-all.

Dignity was nowhere. The only thing she could cling to was her anger.

'So, Jenny, you think I should have introduced myself as Prince Ramón?' he asked at last, and the anger was still there. He was angry? What did that make her? Nothing, she thought bleakly. How could he be angry at her? She felt like shrivelling into a small ball and sobbing, but she had to get away from here first.

'You know what matters most?' she demanded, trying desperately to sort her thoughts into some sort of sense. 'That you didn't tell me you owned the boat. Maybe you didn't lie outright, but you had plenty of opportunities to tell me and you didn't. That's a lie in my books.'

'Would you have got on my boat if you thought I was the owner?'

There was only one answer to that. If he'd asked her and she'd known he was wealthy enough to afford such a boat— his wealth would have terrified her. 'No,' she admitted.

'So I wanted you to come with me.'

'Bully for you. And I did.' Cling to the anger, she told herself. It was all there was. If he was angry, she should be more so. She headed into the bathroom to grab her toiletries. 'I came on board and we made love and it was all very nice,' she threw over her shoulder. 'Now you've had your fun and you can go back to your life.'

'Being a prince isn't my life.'

'No?'

'Gianetta…'

'Jenny!'

'Jenny, then,' he conceded and the underlying anger in his voice intensified. 'I want you to listen.'

'I'm listening,' she said, shoving toiletries together with venom.

'Jenny, my grandfather was the Crown Prince of Cepheus.'

'I know that.'

'What you don't know,' he snapped, 'is that he was an arrogant, cruel womanizer. Jenny, I need you to understand this. My grandfather's marriage to my grandmother was an arranged one and he treated her dreadfully. When my father was ten my grandmother fell in love with a servant, and who can blame her? But my grandfather banished her and the younger children to a tiny island off the coast of Cepheus. He kept his oldest son, my uncle, at the palace, but my grandmother, my father and my aunt were never allowed back. My grandmother was royal in her own right. She had money of her own and all her life she ached to undo some of the appalling things my grandfather did, but when she tried…well, that's when my father died. And now, to be forced to go back…'

'I'm sorry you don't like it,' she said stiffly. What was he explaining this for? It had nothing to do with her. 'But your country needs you. At least now you'll be doing something useful.'

'Is that what you think?' he demanded, sounding stunned. 'That I spend my life doing nothing?'

'Isn't that the best job in the world?' She could feel the vibrations of his anger and it fed hers. *He'd known he was a prince.* 'The Internet bio says you're aligned to some sort of charity in Bangladesh,' she said shortly. 'I guess you can't be all bad.'

'Thanks.'

'Think nothing of it,' she said, and she thought, where did she go from here?

Away, her head told her, harshly and coldly. She needed to leave right now, and she would, but there were obligations. This man had got her out of a hole. He'd paid her debts. She owed him, deception or not.

'Okay, I'll be the first to admit I know nothing of your life,' she said stiffly. 'I felt like I knew you and now I realize I don't. That hurts. But I do need to thank you for paying my debt; for getting me away from Charlie. But now I'm just…scared. So I'll just get out of your life and let you get on with it.'

'You're scared?'

'What do you think?'

'There's no threat. There'd only be a threat if you were my woman.'

That was enough to take her breath away. *If you were my woman…*

'Which…which I'm not,' she managed.

'No,' he said, and there was bleakness as well as anger there now.

She closed her eyes. So what else had she expected? These two weeks had been a fairy tale. Nothing more.

Move on.

'Jenny, I have to do this,' he said harshly. 'Understand it or not, this is what I'm faced with. If I don't take the throne, then it goes to my father's cousin's son, Carlos. Carlos is as bad as my grandfather. He'd bring the country to ruin. And then there's the child. He's five. God knows…' He raked his hair with quiet despair. 'I will accept this responsibility. I must, even if it means walking away from what I most care about.'

And then there was silence, stretching towards infinity, where only emptiness beckoned.

What he most cared about? His boat? His charity work? What?

She couldn't think of what. She couldn't think what she wanted *what* to be.

'I'm sorry, Ramón,' she whispered at last.

'I'm sorry, too,' he said. He sighed and dug his hands deep into his pockets. Seemingly moving on. 'For what's between us needs to be put aside, for the sanity of both of us. But Gianetta…Jenny… What will you do in New Zealand?'

'Make muffins.' Her fury from his perceived betrayal was oozing away now, but there was nothing in its place except an aching void. Yesterday had seemed so wonderful. Today her sailor had turned into a prince and her bubble of euphoria was gone.

'Make muffins until you can afford to go back to Australia?'

'I don't have a lot of choice.'

'There is. Señor Rodriguez, the lawyer you met this morning, has already found someone prepared to skipper the *Marquita*—to bring her to Cepheus. I've already met him. He's a Scottish Australian, Gordon, ex-merchant navy. He's competent, solid and I know I can trust him with…with my boat. But he will need crew. So I'm asking you to stay on. I'm asking you if you'll sail round the Horn with him and bring the *Marquita* home. If you do that, I'll fly you back to Australia. Debt discharged.'

'It wouldn't be discharged.'

'I believe it would,' he said heavily. 'I'm asking you to sail round the Horn with someone you don't know, and I'm asking you to trust that I'll keep my word. That's enough of a request to make paying out your debt more than reasonable.'

'I don't want to.'

'Do you want to go back to cooking muffins?' He spread his hands and he managed a smile then, his wonderful, sexy, insinuating smile that had the power to warm every last part of her. 'And at least this way you'll get to see Cepheus, even if it's only for a couple of days before you fly home. And you'll have sailed around the Horn. You wanted to see the world. Give yourself a chance to see a little of it.' He hesitated. 'And, Jenny, maybe…we can have tonight?'

That made her gasp. After all that stood between them… What was he suggesting, that she spend one more night as the royal mistress? 'Are you crazy?'

'So not tonight?' His eyes grew bleak. 'No. I'm sorry, Gianetta. You and me… I concede it's impossible. But what is possible is that you remain on board the *Marquita* as crew. You allow me to continue employing you so you'll walk away at the end of three months beholden to nobody.'

No.

The word should have been shouted at him. She should walk away right now.

But to walk away for ever? How could she do that? And if she stayed on board….maybe a sliver of hope remained.

Hope for what? A Cinderella happy ending? What a joke. Ramón himself had said it was impossible.

But to walk away, from this boat as well as from this man… Cinders had fled at midnight. Maybe Cinders had more resolution than she did.

'I'll come back to the boat in the morning,' she whispered. 'If the new skipper wants to employ me and I think he's a man I can be at sea with for three months…'

'He's nothing like me,' Ramón said gently, almost bleakly. 'He's reliable and steady.'

'And not a prince?'

He gave a wintry smile. 'No, Gianetta, he's not a prince.'

'Then it might be possible.'

'I hope it will be possible.'

'No guarantees,' she said.

'You feel betrayed?'

'Of course I do,' she whispered. 'I need to go now.'

The bleakness intensified. He nodded. 'As you say. Go, my Gianetta, before I forget myself. I've learned this day that my life's not my own. But first… '

And, before she could guess what he was about, he made two swift strides across the room, took her shoulders in a grip of iron and kissed her. And such a kiss… It was fierce, it was possessive, it held anger and passion and desire. It was no kiss of farewell. It was a kiss that was all about his need, his desire, his ache to hold her to him for this night, and for longer still.

He was hungry for her, she thought, bewildered. She didn't know how real that hunger was, but when he finally put her away from him, when she finally broke free, she thought he was hurting as much as she was.

But hunger changed nothing, she thought bleakly. There was nothing left to say.

He stood silently by as she grabbed her carry-all and walked away, her eyes shimmering with unshed tears. He didn't try to stop her.

He was her Ramón, she thought bleakly. But he wasn't her prince.

He watched her go, walking along the docks carrying her holdall, her shoulders slumped, her body language that of someone weary beyond belief.

He felt as if he'd betrayed her.

So what to do? Go after her, lift her bodily into his arms? Take her to Cepheus?

How could he?

There were threats from Carlos. The lawyer was talking of

the possibility of armed insurrection against the throne. Had it truly become so bad?

His father had died because he hadn't realized the power of royalty. How could he drag a woman into this mess? It would be hard enough keeping himself afloat, let alone supporting anyone else.

How could he be a part of it himself—a royal family that had destroyed his family?

Jenny's figure was growing smaller in the distance. She wasn't pausing—she wasn't looking back.

He felt ill.

'So can we leave tonight?' He looked back and the lawyer was standing about twenty feet from the boat, calmly watching. 'I asked them to hold seats on tonight's flight as well as tomorrow.'

'You have some nerve.'

'The country's desperate,' the lawyer said simply. 'Nothing's been heard from you. Carlos is starting to act as if he's the new Crown Prince and his actions are provocative. Delay on your part may well mean bloodshed.'

'I don't want to leave her,' he said simply and turned back—but she'd turned a corner and was gone.

'I think the lady has left you,' the lawyer said gently. 'Which leaves you free to begin to govern your country. So, the flight tonight, Your Highness?'

'Fine,' Ramón said heavily and went to pack.

But fine was the last thing he was feeling.

His flight left that evening. He looked down from the plane and saw the boats in Auckland Harbour. The *Marquita* was down there with her new skipper on board. He couldn't make her out among so many. She was already dwindling to nothing as the plane rose and turned away from land.

Would Jenny join her tomorrow, he thought bleakly. Would she come to Cepheus?

He turned from the window with a silent oath. It shouldn't

matter. What was between them was finished. Whether she broke her contract or not—there was nothing he could offer her.

Jenny was on her own, as was he.

His throne was waiting for him.

And two days later the *Marquita* slipped its moorings and sailed out of Auckland Harbour—with Jenny still on board. As she watched the harbour fade into the distance she felt all the doubts reassemble themselves. Gordon, her new skipper, seemed respectful of her silence and he let her be.

She was about to sail around the Horn. Once upon a time that prospect would have filled her with adrenalin-loaded excitement.

Now… She was simply fulfilling a contract, before she went home.

CHAPTER SIX

RAMÓN'S introduction to royal life was overwhelming. He walked into chaos. He walked into a life he knew nothing about. There were problems everywhere, but he'd been back in Cepheus for less than a day before the plight of Philippe caught him and held.

On his first meeting, the lawyer's introduction to the little boy was brief. 'This is Philippe.'

Philippe. His cousin's son. The little boy who should be Crown Prince, but for the trifling matter of a lack of wedding vows. Philippe, who'd had the royal surname until a month ago and was now not entitled to use it.

The little boy looked like the child Ramón remembered being. Philippe's pale face and huge eyes hinted that he was suffering as Ramón had suffered when his own father died, and as he met him for the first time he felt his gut wrench with remembered pain.

He'd come to see for himself what he'd been told—that the little boy was in the best care possible. Señor Rodriguez performed the introductions. Consuela and Ernesto were Philippe's foster parents, farmers who lived fifteen minutes' drive from the palace. The three were clearly nervous of what this meeting meant, but Philippe had been well trained.

'I am pleased to meet you,' the little boy said in a stilted little voice that spoke of rote learning and little else. He held out a thin little arm so his hand could be shaken, and Ramón felt him flinch as he took it in his.

Philippe's foster mother, a buxom farmer's wife exuding good-hearted friendliness, didn't seem intimidated by Ramón's title, or maybe she was, but her concern for Philippe came first. 'We've been hearing good things about you,' she told Ramón, scooping her charge into her arms so he could be on eye level with Ramón, ending the formality with this decisive gesture. 'This dumpling's been fearful of meeting you,' she told him. 'But Ernesto and I are telling him he should think of you as his big cousin. A friend. Isn't that right, Your Highness?'

She met Ramón's gaze almost defiantly, and Ramón could see immediately why Sofía had chosen Consuela as Philippe's foster mother. The image of a mother hen, prepared to battle any odds for her chick, was unmistakable. 'Philippe's homesick for the palace,' she said now, almost aggressively. 'And he misses his cat.'

'You have a cat?' Ramón asked.

'Yes,' Philippe whispered.

'There are many cats at the palace,' Señor Rodriguez said repressively from beside them, and Ramón sighed. What was it with adults? Hang on, he was an adult. Surely he could do something about this.

He must.

But he wasn't taking him back to the palace.

Memories were flooding back as he watched Philippe, memories of himself as a child. He vaguely remembered someone explaining that his grandmother wanted to return to the palace and his father would organize it—or maybe that explanation had come later. What he did remember was his father leading him into the vast grand entrance of the palace, Ramón clutching his father's hand as the splendour threatened to overwhelm him. 'There's nothing to be afraid of. It's time you met your grandfather and your uncle,' his father had told him.

His mother had said later that the decision to take him had been made, 'Because surely the Prince can't refuse his grandchild, a little boy who looks just like him.' But his mother had been wrong.

Not only had he been refused, some time in the night while Ramón lay in scared solitude, in a room far too grand for a child, somehow, some time, his father had died. He remembered not sleeping all night, and the next morning he remembered his grandfather, his icy voice laced with indifference to both his son's death and his grandson's solitary grief, snarling at the servants. 'Pack him up and get him out of here,' he'd ordered.

Pack him up and get him out of here... It was a dreadful decree, but how much worse would it have been if the Crown Prince had ordered him to stay? As he was being ordered to stay now.

Not Philippe, though. Philippe was free, if he could just be made happy with that freedom.

'Tell me about your cat,' he asked, trying a smile, and Philippe swallowed and swallowed again and made a manful effort to respond.

'He's little,' he whispered. 'The other cats fight him and he's not very strong. Something bit his ear. Papà doesn't permit me to take him inside, so he lives in the stables, but he comes when I call him. He's orange with a white nose.'

'Are there many orange cats with white noses at the palace?' Ramón asked, and for some reason the image of Jenny was with him strongly, urging him on. The little boy shook his head.

'Bebe's the only one. He's my friend.' He tilted his chin, obviously searching for courage for a confession. 'Sometimes I take a little fish from the kitchen when no one's looking. Bebe likes fish.'

'So he shouldn't be hard to find.' Ramón glanced at Consuela and Ernesto, questioningly. This place was a farm. Surely one cat...

'We like cats,' Consuela said, guessing where he was going. 'But Señor Rodriguez tells us the palace cats are wild.

They're used to keep the vermin down and he says no one can catch one, much less tame one.'

'I'm sure we could tame him.' Ernesto, a wiry, weathered farmer, spoke almost as defiantly as his wife. 'If you, sir, or your staff, could try to catch him for us…'

'I'll try,' Ramón said. 'He's called Bebe, you say? My aunt has her cat at the palace now. She understands them. Let's see what we can do.'

Jenny would approve, he thought, as he returned to the palace, but he pushed the idea away. This was *his* challenge, as was every challenge in this place. It was nothing to do with Jenny.

As soon as he returned to the palace he raided the kitchens. Then he set off to the stables with a platter of smoked salmon. He set down the saucer and waited for a little ginger cat with a torn ear to appear. It took a whole three minutes.

Bebe wasn't wild at all. He stroked his ears and Bebe purred. He then shed ginger fur everywhere while he wrapped himself around Ramón's legs and the chair legs in the palace entrance and the legs of the footman on duty. Jenny would laugh, Ramón thought, but he shoved that thought away as well. Just do what comes next. *Do not think of Jenny.*

Bebe objected—loudly—to the ride in a crate on the passenger seat of Ramón's Boxster, but he settled into life with Philippe—'as if Philippe's been sneaking him into his bed for the last couple of years,' Consuela told him, and maybe he had.

After that, Philippe regained a little colour, but he still looked haunted. He missed the palace, he confided, as Ramón tried to draw him out. In a world of adults who hadn't cared, the palace itself had become his stability.

Pack him up and get him out of here…

It made sense, Ramón thought. If the servants' reaction to Philippe was anything to go by, he'd be treated like illegitimate dirt in the palace. And then there was his main worry, or maybe it wasn't so much a worry but a cold, hard certainty.

There was so much to be done in this country that his role

as Crown Prince overwhelmed him. He had to take it on; he
had no choice, but in order to do it he must be clear-headed,
disciplined, focused.

There was no link between love and duty in this job. He'd
seen that spelled out with bleak cruelty. His grandmother had
entered the palace through love, and had left it with her
dreams and her family destroyed. His father had tried again
to enter the palace, for the love of his mother, and he'd lost
his life because of it. There were threats around him now,
veiled threats, and who knew what else besides?

And the knowledge settled on his heart like grey fog. To
stay focused on what he must do, he could put no other person
at risk. Sofia was staying until after the coronation. After that
she'd leave and no one would be at risk but him. He'd have
no distractions and without them maybe, just maybe, he could
bring this country back to the prosperity it deserved.

But Philippe... And Jenny?

They'd get over it, he told himself roughly. Or Philippe
would get over his grief and move on. Jenny must never be
allowed to know that grief.

And once again he told himself harshly, this was nothing
to do with Jenny. There'd never been a suggestion that they
take things further. Nor could there be. This was his life and
his life only, even if it was stifling.

This place was stifling. Nothing seemed to have changed
since his grandfather's reign, or maybe since long before.

Lack of change didn't mean the palace had been allowed
to fall into disrepair, though. Even though his grandfather
and uncle had overspent their personal fortunes, the Crown
itself was still wealthy, so pomp and splendour had been
maintained. Furnishings were still opulent, rich paintings still
covered the walls, the woodwork gleamed and the paintwork
shone. The staff looked magnificent, even if their uniforms
had been designed in the nineteenth century.

But the magnificence couldn't disguise the fact that every
one of the people working in this palace went about their
duties with impassive faces. Any attempt by Ramón to pene-

trate their rigid facades was met with stony silence and, as the weeks turned into a month and then two, he couldn't make inroads into that rigidity.

The servants—and the country—seemed to accept him with passive indifference. He might be better than what had gone before, the newspapers declared, but he was still royal. Soon, the press implied, he'd become just like the others.

When he officially took his place as Crown Prince, he could make things better for the people of this county. He knew that, so he'd bear the opulence of the palace, the lack of freedom. He'd bear the formality and the media attention. He'd cope also with the blustering threats of a still furious Carlos; along with the insidious sense that threats like this had killed his father. He'd face them down.

Alone.

Once Philippe had recovered from his first grief, surely he'd be happy on the farm with Consuela and Ernesto.

And also… Jenny would be happy as a muffin-maker?

Why did he even think of her? Why had he ever insisted that she come here? It would have been easier for both of them if he'd simply let her go.

For she was Jenny, he reminded himself harshly, a dozen times a day. She was not Gianetta. She was free to go wherever she willed. She was Jenny, with the world at her feet.

Yet he watched the *Marquita*'s progress with an anxiety that bordered on obsession, and he knew that when Jenny arrived he would see her one last time. He must.

Was that wise?

He knew it wasn't. There was no place for Jenny here, as there was no place for Philippe.

He'd been alone for much of his adult life. He could go on being alone.

But he'd see Jenny once again first. Sensible or not.

Please…

Eleven weeks and two days after setting sail from Auckland, the *Marquita* sailed into Cepheus harbour and found a party.

As they approached land, every boat they passed, from tiny pleasure craft to workmanlike fishing vessels, was adorned in red, gold and deep, deep blue. The flag of Cepheus hung from every mast. The harbour was ringed with flags. There were people crowded onto the docks, spilling out of harbourside restaurants. Every restaurant looked crammed to bursting. It looked like Sydney Harbour on a sunny Sunday, multiplied by about a hundred, Jenny thought, dazed, as she made the lines ready to dock.

'You reckon they're here to welcome us?' Gordon called to her, and she smiled.

She'd become very fond of Gordon. When she'd first met him, the morning after Ramón had left, she'd been ready to walk away. Only his shy smile, his assumption that she was coming with him and his pleasure that she was, had kept her on board. He reminded her of her father. Which helped.

She'd been sailing with him now for almost three months. He'd kept his own counsel and she'd kept hers, and it had taken almost all those months for her emotions to settle.

Now…approaching the dock she was so tense she could hardly speak. Normally she welcomed Gordon's reserve but his silence was only adding to her tension.

There was no need for her to be tense, she told herself. She'd had a couple of surreal weeks with royalty. In true princely fashion he'd rescued her from a life of making muffins, and now she could get on with her life.

With this experience of sailing round the Horn behind her, and with Gordon's references, maybe she could get another job on board a boat. She could keep right on sailing. While Ramón…

See, that was what she couldn't let herself think. The future and Ramón.

It had been a two-week affair. Nothing more.

'What's the occasion?' Gordon was behind the wheel, calling to people on the boat passing them. But they didn't understand English, or Gordon's broad mixed accent.

'Why the flags and decorations?' she called in Spanish and was rewarded by comprehension.

'Are you from another planet?' they called, incredulous. 'Everyone knows what's happening today.'

Their language was the mix of Spanish and French Ramón had used with the lawyer. She felt almost at home.

No. This was Ramón's home. Not hers.

'We're from Australia,' she called. 'We know nothing.'

'Well, welcome.' The people raised glasses in salutation. 'You're here just in time.'

'For what?'

'For the coronation,' they called. 'It's a public holiday. Crown Prince Ramón Cavellero of Cepheus accepts his Crown today.'

Right. She stood in the bow and let her hands automatically organize lines. Or not. She didn't know what her hands were doing.

First thought? Stupidly, it was that Ramón wouldn't be meeting her.

Had she ever believed he would? Ramón was a Prince of the Blood. He'd have moved on.

'Is that our berth?' Gordon called, and she caught herself, glanced at the sheet the harbour master had faxed through and then looked ahead to where their designated berth should be.

And drew in her breath.

Ramón wasn't there. Of course he wasn't. But there was a welcoming committee. There were four officials, three men and a woman, all in some sort of official uniform. The colours of their uniform matched the colours of the flags.

This yacht belonged to royalty, and representatives of royalty were there to meet them.

'Reckon any of them can catch a line?' Gordon called and she tried to smile.

'We're about to find out.'

Not only could they catch a line, they were efficient, courteous and they took smoothly over from the time the *Marquita* touched the dock.

'Welcome,' the senior official said gravely, in English. 'You are exactly on time.'

'You've been waiting for us?'

'His Highness has had you tracked from the moment you left Auckland. He's delighted you could be here today. He asks that you attend the ceremony this afternoon, and the official ball this evening.'

Jenny swung around to stare at Gordon—who was staring back at her. They matched. They both had their mouths wide open.

'Reckon we won't fit in,' Gordon drawled at last, sounding flabbergasted. 'Reckon there won't be a lot of folk wearing salt-crusted oilskins on your guest list.'

'That's why we're here,' the official said smoothly. 'Jorge here will complete the care of the *Marquita*, while Dalila and Rudi are instructed to care for you. If you agree, we'll escort you to the palace, you'll be fitted with clothing suitable for the occasion and you'll be His Highness's honoured guests at the ceremonies this afternoon and this evening.'

Jenny gasped. Her head was starting to explode. To see Ramón as a prince…

'We can't,' Gordon muttered.

But Jenny looked at the elderly seaman and saw her mixture of emotions reflected on his face. They'd been at sea for three months now, and she knew enough of Gordon to realize he stacked up life's events and used them to fill the long stretches at sea that he lived for.

He was staring at the officials with a mixture of awe and dread. And desire.

If she didn't go, Gordon wouldn't go.

And, a little voice inside her breathed, she'd get to see Ramón one last time.

Once upon a time Ramón had been her skipper. Once upon a time he'd been her lover. He'd moved on now. He was a Crown Prince.

She'd see him today and then she'd leave.

* * *

For the *Marquita* to berth on the same day as his coronation was a coincidence he couldn't ignore, making his resolution waver.

He'd made the decision to send his apologies when the boat berthed, for Jenny to be treated with all honour, paid handsomely and then escorted to the airport and given a first-class ticket back to Australia. That was the sensible decision. He couldn't allow himself to be diverted from his chosen path. But when he'd learned the *Marquita*'s date of arrival was today he'd given orders before he thought it through. Sensible or not, he would see Jenny this one last time.

Maybe he should see it as an omen, he decided as he dressed. Maybe he was meant to have her nearby, giving him strength to take this final step.

Servants were fussing over his uniform, making sure he looked every inch the Ruler of Cepheus, and outside there was sufficient security to defend him against a small army. Carlos's blustering threats of support from the military seemed to have no foundation. On his own he had nothing to fear, and on his own he must rule.

The last three months had cemented his determination to change this country. If he must accept the Crown then he'd do it as it was meant to be done. He could change this country for the better. He could make life easier for the population. The Crown, this ultimate position of authority, had been abused for generations. If anyone was to change it, it must be him.

Duty and desire had no place together. He knew that, and the last months' assessment of the state of the country told him that his duty was here. He had to stay focused. *He didn't need Jenny.*

But, need her or not, he wanted Jenny at the ceremony. To have her come all this way and not see her—on this of all days—*that* was more unthinkable than anything.

He would dance with her this night, he thought. Just this once, he'd touch her and then he'd move forward. Alone.

The doors were swinging open. The Master of State was waiting. Cepheus was waiting.

He'd set steps in place to bring this country into the twenty-first century, he thought with grim satisfaction. His coronation would cement those steps. Fulfilling the plans he'd set in place over the last few weeks would mean this country would thrive.

But maybe the population would never forget the family he came from, he thought as he was led in stately grandeur to the royal carriage. There were no cheers, no personal applause. Today the country was celebrating a public holiday and a continuum of history, but the populace wasn't impressed by what he personally represented. His grandfather's reputation came before him, smirching everything. Royalty was something to be endured.

The country had celebrated the birth of a new Crown Prince five years ago. That deception still rankled, souring all.

Philippe should be here, he thought. The little boy should play some part in this ceremony.

But, out at the farm, Philippe was finally starting to relax with him, learning again to be a little boy. He still missed the palace, but to bring him back seemed just as impossible as it had been three months ago.

Philippe was now an outsider. As he was himself, he thought grimly, glancing down at his uniform that made him seem almost ludicrously regal. And the threats were there, real or not.

He could protect Philippe. He *would* protect Philippe, but from a distance. Jenny was here for this day only. Sofía would be gone. He could rule as he needed to rule.

'It's time, Your Highness,' the Head of State said in stentorian tones, and Ramón knew that it was.

It was time to accept that he was a Prince of the Blood, with all the responsibility—and loss—that the title implied.

The great chorus of trumpets sounded, heralding the beginning of ceremonies and Jenny was sitting in a pew in the vast cathedral of Cepheus feeling bewildered. Feeling transformed. Feeling like Cinderella must have felt after the fairy godmother waved her wand.

For she wasn't at the back with the hired help. She and Gordon were being treated like royalty themselves.

The palace itself had been enough to take her breath away, all spirals and turrets and battlements, a medieval fantasy clinging to white stone cliffs above a sea so blue it seemed to almost merge with the sky.

The apartment she'd been taken to within the palace had taken even more of her breath away. It was as big as a small house, and Gordon had been shown into a similar one on the other side of the corridor. Corridor? It was more like a great hall. You could play a football match in the vast areas—decorated in gold, all carvings, columns and ancestral paintings—that joined the rooms. Dalila had ushered her in, put her holdall on a side table and instructed a maid to unpack.

'I'm not staying here,' Jenny had gasped.

'For tonight at least,' Dalila had said, formally polite in stilted English. 'The ball will be late. The Prince requires you to stay.'

How to fight a decree like that? How indeed to fight, when clothes were being produced that made her gasp all over again.

'I can't wear these.'

'You can,' the woman decreed. 'If you'll just stay still. Dolores is a dressmaker. It will take her only moments to adjust these for size.'

And Jenny had simply been too overwhelmed to refuse. So here she was, in a pew ten seats from the front, right on the aisle, dressed in a crimson silk ball-gown that looked as if it had been made for her. It was cut low across her breasts, with tiny capped sleeves, the bodice clinging like a second skin, curving to her hips and then flaring out to an almost full circle skirt. The fabric was so beautiful it made her feel as if she was floating.

There was a pendant round her neck that she hoped was paste but she suspected was a diamond so big she couldn't comprehend it. Her hair was pinned up in a deceptively simple knot and her make-up had been applied with a skill so great that when she looked in the mirror she saw someone she didn't recognize.

She felt like…Gianetta. For the first time in her life, her father's name seemed right for her.

'I'm just glad they can't see me back at the Sailor's Arms in Auckland,' Gordon muttered, and she glanced at the weathered seaman who looked as classy as she did, in a deep black suit that fitted him like a glove. He, too, had been transformed, like it or not. She almost chuckled, but then the music rose to a crescendo and she stopped thinking about chuckling. She stopped thinking about anything at all—anything but Ramón.

Crown Prince Ramón Cavellero of Cepheus.

For so he was.

The great doors of the cathedral had swung open. The Archbishop of Cepheus led the way in stately procession down the aisle, and Ramón trod behind, intent, his face set in lines that said this was an occasion of such great moment that lives would change because of it.

He truly was a prince, she thought, dazed beyond belief. If she'd walked past him in the street—no, if she'd seen his picture on the cover of a magazine, for this wasn't a man one passed in the street, she would never have recognized him. His uniform was black as night, skilfully cut to mould to his tall, lean frame. The leggings, the boots, the slashes of gold, the tassels, the fierce sword at his side, they only accentuated his aura of power and strength and purpose.

Or then again…maybe she would have recognized him. His eyes seemed to have lost their colour—they were dark as night. His mouth was set and grim, and it was the expression she'd seen when he'd known she was leaving.

He looked like…an eagle, she thought, a fierce bird of prey, ready to take on the world. But he was still Ramón.

He was so near her now. If she put out her hand…

He was passing her row. He was right here. And as he passed… His gaze shifted just a little from looking steadily ahead. Somehow it met hers and held, for a nano-second, for a fraction that might well be imagined. And then he was gone, swept past in the procession and the world crowded back in.

He hadn't smiled, but had his grimness lifted, just a little?

'He was looking for you,' Gordon muttered, awed. 'The guy who helped me dress said he told the aides where we were to sit. It's like we're important. Are you important to him then, lass?'

'Not in a million years,' she breathed.

She'd come.

It was the only thing holding him steady.

Gianetta. Jenny.

Her name was in his mind, like a mantra, said over and over.

'By the power vested in me…'

He was kneeling before the archbishop and the crown was being placed on his head. The weight was enormous.

She was here.

He could take this nowhere. He knew that. But still, for now, she was here on this day when he needed her most.

She was here, and his crown was the lighter for it.

The night seemed to be organized for her. As the throng emerged from the great cathedral, an aide appeared and took her arm.

'You're to come this way, miss. And you, too, sir,' he said to Gordon. 'You're official guests at the Coronation Dinner.'

'I reckon I'll slope back down to the boat,' Gordon muttered, shrinking, but Jenny clutched him as if she were drowning.

'We went round the Horn together,' she muttered. 'We face risk together.'

'This is worse than the Horn.'

'You're telling me,' Jenny said, and the aide was ushering them forward and it was too late to escape.

They sat, midway down a vast banquet table, where it

seemed half the world's dignitaries were assembled. Gordon, a seaman capable of facing down the world's worst storms, was practically shrinking under the table. Jenny was a bit braver, but not much. She was recognizing faces and names and her eyes grew rounder and rounder as she realized just who was here. There were speeches—of course—and she translated for Gordon and was glad of the task. It took her mind off what was happening.

It never took her mind off Ramón.

He was seated at the great formal table at the head of the room, gravely surveying all. He looked born to the role, she thought. He listened with gravitas and with courtesy. He paid attention to the two women on either side of him—grand dames, both of them, queens of their own countries.

'I have friends back in Australia who are never going to believe what I've done tonight,' she whispered to Gordon and her skipper nodded agreement.

Then once more the aide was beside them, bending to whisper to Jenny.

'Ma'am, I've been instructed to ask if you can waltz.'

'If I can…?'

'His Royal Highness wishes to dance with you. He doesn't wish to embarrass you, however, so if there's a problem…'

No. She wanted to scream, *no.*

But she glanced up at the head table and Ramón was watching her. Those eagle eyes were steady. 'I dare you,' his gaze was saying, and more.

'I can waltz,' she heard herself say, her eyes not leaving Ramón's.

'Excellent,' the aide said. 'I'll come to fetch you when we're ready.'

'You do that,' she said faintly.

What have I done?

The entrance to the grand ballroom was made in state. Ramón led the procession, and it was done in order of rank, which meant Jenny came in somewhere near the rear. Even that was intimidating—all the guests who hadn't been at the dinner were assembled in line to usher the dining party in.

If the ground opened up and swallowed her she'd be truly grateful. Too many people were looking at her.

Why had she agreed to dance?

Ramón was so far ahead she couldn't see him. Ramón. Prince Ramón.

She wasn't into fairy tales. Bring on midnight.

And Gordon had deserted her. As she took the aide's arm, as she joined the procession, he suddenly wasn't there. She looked wildly around and he was smiling apologetically but backing firmly away. But she was being ushered forward and there was no way she could run without causing a spectacle.

Cinderella ran, she thought wildly. At midnight.

But midnight was still a long time away.

Courage. If Cinders could face them all down, so could she. She took a deep breath and allowed herself to be led forward. The aide was ushering her into the ballroom, then into an alcove near the entrance. Before them, Ramón was making a grand sweep of the room, greeting everyone. The heads of the royal houses of Europe were his entourage, nodding, smiling, doing what royalty did best.

And suddenly she realized what was happening. Why she'd been directed to stand here. She was close to the door, where Ramón must end his circuit.

She felt frozen to the spot.

Ramón. Prince Ramón.

Ramón.

The wait was interminable. She tried to focus on anything but what was happening. A spot on the wax of the polished floor. The hem of her gown. Anything.

But finally, inevitably, the aide was beside her, ushering her forward and Ramón was right in front of her. Every eye in the room was on him. Every eye in the room was on her.

She was Jenny. She made muffins. She wanted to have hysterics, or faint.

Ramón was before her, his eyes grave and questioning.

'Gianetta,' he said softly, and every ear in the room was straining to hear. 'You've arrived for my coronation, and I thank you. You've brought my boat home and thus you've linked my old life with my new. Can I therefore ask for the honour of this dance?'

There was an audible gasp throughout the room. It wasn't said out loud but she could hear the thought regardless. *Who?*

But Ramón was holding out his hand, waiting for her to put hers in his. Smiling. It was the smile she loved with all her heart.

Was this how Cinders felt?

And then Cinders was forgotten. Everything was forgotten. She put her hand in his, she tried hard to smile back and she allowed the Crown Prince of Cepheus to lead her onto the ballroom floor.

Where had she learned to dance?

Ramón had been coached almost before he could walk. His grandmother had thought dancing at least as important as any other form of movement. He could thus waltz without thinking. He'd expected to slow his steps to Jenny's, to take care she wasn't embarrassed, but he'd been on the dance floor less than ten seconds before he realized such precautions weren't necessary. He took her into his arms in the waltz hold, and she melted into him as if she belonged.

The music swelled in an age-old, well-loved waltz and she was one with the music, one with him.

He'd almost forgotten how wonderful she felt.

He had to be formal, he told himself harshly. He needed to hold her at arm's length—which was difficult when he was not holding her at arm's length at all. He needed to be courteously friendly and he needed to thank her and say goodbye.

Only not yet. Not goodbye yet.

'Where did you learn to dance?' he managed, and it was a dumb thing to say to a woman after a three-month separation, but the tension eased a little and she almost smiled.

'Dancing's not reserved for royalty. My Papà was the best.'

This was better. There was small talk in this. 'He should have met my grandmother.'

'Yes,' she said, and seemed to decide to let herself enjoy the music, the dance, the sensation of being held for a couple more circuits of the floor while the world watched. And then… 'Ramón, why are you doing this?'

'I'm sorry?'

'Why did you ask me to dance…first?'

'I wanted to thank you.'

'You paid me, remember? It's me who should be thanking. And the world is watching. For you to ask me for the first dance…'

'I believe it's the last dance,' he said, and the leaden feeling settled back around his heart as the truth flooded back. Holding her was an illusion, a fleeting taste of what could have been, and all at once the pain was unbearable. 'I've wanted to hold you for three months,' he said simply, and it was as if the words were there and had to be said, whether he willed them or not. 'Jenny, maybe even saying it is unwise but, wise or not, I've missed you every single night.' He hesitated, then somehow struggled back to lightness, forcing the leaden ache to stay clear of his voice. He couldn't pass his regret onto her. He had to say goodbye—as friends. 'Do you realize how much work there is in being a Crown Prince?'

'I have no idea,' she said faintly. 'I guess…there's speeches to make. Ribbons to cut. That sort of thing.'

'Not so much of that sort of thing.' His hand tightened on her waist, tugging her closer. Wanting her closer. Sense decreed he had to let her go, but still not yet. 'I haven't even been official Crown Prince until today,' he said, fighting to make his voice sound normal. 'I've not even been qualified as a ribbon-cutter until now. I've been a prince in training. Nothing more. Nothing less. But I have been practising my waltzing. My Aunt Sofía's seen to that. So let's see if we can make the ghosts of your Papà and my Grand-mère proud.'

She smiled. He whirled her around in his arms and she felt like thistledown, he thought. She felt like Jenny.

He had to let her go.

He didn't feel like a prince, she thought as he held her close and their bodies moved as one. If she closed her eyes he felt like Ramón. Just Ramón, pure and simple. The man who'd stolen her heart.

It was impossible, he'd said. Of course it was. She'd known it for three months and nothing had changed.

The world was watching. She had to keep it light.

'So it's been practising speeches and waltzing,' she ventured at last. 'While we've been braving the Horn.'

'That and getting leggings to fit,' he murmured into her ear. 'Bloody things, leggings. I'd almost prefer the Horn.'

'But leggings are so sexy.'

'Sexy isn't leggings,' he said. His eyes were on her and she could see exactly what he was thinking.

'Don't,' she whispered, feeling her colour rising. Every eye in the room was on them.

'I've missed you for three long months,' he said, lightness disappearing. He sounded goaded almost past breaking point.

'Ramón, we had two weeks,' she managed. 'It didn't mean anything.'

He stopped dancing. Others had taken to the floor now, but they were on the edge of the dance floor. Ramón and Jenny had central position and they were still being watched.

'Are you saying what we had didn't mean anything to you?' he asked, his voice sounding suddenly calm, almost distant.

'Of course it did,' she said, blushing furiously. 'At the time. Ramón, please, can we keep dancing? I don't belong here.'

'Neither do I,' he said grimly, and he took her in his arms again and slipped back into the waltz. 'I should be leaving for Bangladesh right now. My team's left without me for the first time in years.'

'Speeches are important,' she said cautiously.

'They are.' The laughter and passion had completely disappeared now, leaving his voice sounding flat and defeated. 'Believe it or not, this country needs me. It's been bled dry by my grandfather and my uncle. If I walk away it'll continue to be bled dry by a government that's as corrupt as it is inept. It's not all ribbon-cutting.'

'It's your life,' she said simply. 'You're bred to it and you shouldn't be dancing with me.'

'I shouldn't be doing lots of things, and I'll not be told who I should be dancing with tonight. I know. This can only be for now *but I will dance with you tonight.*'

The music was coming to an end. The outside edge of the dance floor was crowded, but the dancers were keeping clear of the Crown Prince and his partner. A space was left so that, as soon as the dance ended, Ramón could return to his royal table.

Waiting for him were the crowned heads of Europe. Men and women who were watching Jenny as if they knew instinctively she had no place among them.

'You have danced with me,' Jenny said softly, disengaging her hands before he realized what she intended. 'I thank you for the honour.'

'There's no need to thank me.'

'Oh, but there is,' she said, breathless. 'The clothes, this moment, you. I'll remember it all my life.'

She looked up into his eyes and felt an almost overwhelming urge to reach up and kiss him, just a kiss, just a moment, to take a tiny taste of him to keep for ever. But the eyes of the world were on her. Ramón was a prince and his world was waiting.

'I believe there are women waiting to dance with the Crown Prince of Cepheus,' she murmured. 'We both need to move on, so thank you, Ramón. Thank you for the fantasy.'

'Thank you, Gianetta,' he murmured, and he raised his hand and touched her cheek, a feather touch that seemed a gesture of regret and loss and farewell. 'It's been my honour. I will see you before you leave.'

'Do you think…?'

'It's unwise? Of course it's unwise,' he finished for her. 'But it's tonight only. Tomorrow I need to be wise for the rest of my life.'

'Then maybe tomorrow needs to start now,' she said unsteadily and she managed a smile, her very best peasant to royalty smile, and turned and walked away. Leaving the Crown Prince of Cepheus looking after her.

What had he said? *'We can't take it further…'*

Of course they couldn't. What was she thinking of? But still she felt like sobbing. What was she doing here? Why had she ever come? She'd slip away like Gordon, she thought, just as soon as the next dance started, just as soon as everyone stopped watching her.

But someone was stepping into her path. Another prince? The man was dark and bold and so good-looking that if she hadn't met Ramón first she would have been stunned. As it was, she hardly saw him.

'May I request the honour of this dance?' he said, and it wasn't a question. His hand took hers before she could argue, autocratic as Ramón. Where did they learn this? Autocracy school?

It seemed no wasn't a word in these men's vocabularies. She was being led back onto the dance floor, like it or not.

'What's needed is a bit of spine,' she told herself and somehow she tilted her chin, fixed her smile and accepted partner after partner.

Most of these men were seriously good dancers. Many of these men were seriously good-looking men. She thought briefly of Cathy back in Seaport—*'Jenny, get a life!'* If Cathy could see her now…

The thought was almost enough to make her smile real. If only she wasn't so aware of the eyes watching her. If only she wasn't so aware of Ramón's presence. He was dancing with beautiful woman after beautiful woman, and a couple of truly impressive royal matriarchs as well.

He was smiling into each of his partner's eyes, and each one of them was responding exactly the same.

They melted.

Why would they not? Anyone would melt in Ramón's arms.

And suddenly, inexplicably, she was thinking of Matty, of her little son, and she wondered what she was doing here. This strange creature in fancy clothes had nothing to do with who she really was, and all at once what she was doing seemed a betrayal.

'It's okay,' she told herself, feeling suddenly desperate. 'This is simply an unbelievable moment out of my life. After tonight I'll return to being who I truly am. This is for one night only,' she promised Matty. 'One night and then I'm back where I belong.'

Her partner was holding her closer than was appropriate. Sadly for him, she was so caught up in her thoughts she hardly noticed.

Ramón was dancing so close that she could almost reach out and touch him. He whirled his partner round, his gaze caught hers and he smiled, and her partner had no chance at all.

That smile was so dangerous. That smile sucked you in.

'So who are your parents?' her partner asked, and she had to blink a few times to try and get her world moving again.

'My parents are dead,' she managed. 'And yours?'

'I beg your pardon?'

'Who are your parents?'

'My father is the King of Morotatia,' her partner said in stilted English. 'My mother was a princess in her own right before she married. And I am Prince Marcelo Pietros Cornelieus Maximus, heir to the throne of Morotatia.'

'That's wonderful,' she murmured. 'I guess you don't need to work for a living then?'

'Work?'

'I didn't think so,' she said sadly. 'But you guys must need muffins. I wonder if there's an opening around here for a kitchen maid.'

But, even as she said it, she knew even that wasn't possible. She had no place here. This was the fairy tale and she had to go home.

CHAPTER SEVEN

THE night was becoming oppressive. She was passed on to her next partner, who gently grilled her again, and then another who grilled her not so gently until she almost snapped at him. Finally supper was announced. She could escape now, she thought, but then a dumpy little lady with a truly magnificent tiara made a beeline for her, grasped her hands and introduced herself.

'I'm Ramón's Aunt Sofía. I'm so pleased to meet you.' She tucked her arm into Jenny's as if she was laying claim to her—as indeed she was, as there were those around them who were clearly waiting to start the inquisitions again.

'Aunt…'

Sofía turned to see Ramón approaching. He had one of the formidable matrons on his arm. Queen of somewhere? But Sofía was not impressed.

'Go away, Ramón,' Sofía commanded. 'I'm taking Jenny into supper. You look after Her Highness.'

'Sofía was always bossy,' the Queen of somewhere said, but she smiled, and Ramón gave his aunt a smile and gave Jenny a quick, fierce glance—one that was enough to make her toes curl—and led his queen away.

Sofía must rank pretty highly, Jenny thought, so dazed she simply allowed herself to be led. The crowd parted before them. Sofía led them to a small alcove set with a table and truly impressive tableware. She smiled at a passing servant and in two minutes there were so many delicacies before them Jenny could only gasp.

Sofía ate two bite-sized cream éclairs, then paused to demand why Jenny wasn't doing likewise.

'I'm rather in shock,' Jenny confessed.

'Me too,' Sofía confessed. 'And Ramón too, though we're making the best of it.'

'But Ramón's the Crown Prince,' Jenny managed. 'How can he be intimidated?' She could see him through the crowd. He drew every eye in the room. He looked truly magnificent—Crown Prince to the manor born.

'Because he wasn't meant to be royal,' Sofía said darkly, but then her darkness disappeared and she smiled encouragingly at Jenny. 'Just like you're not. I'm not sure what Ramón's told you so I thought maybe there's things you ought to know.'

'I know the succession was a shock,' Jenny ventured, and Sofía nodded vigorously and ate another éclair.

'Yes,' she said definitely. 'We were never expected to inherit. Ramón's grandfather—my father—sent my mother, my younger brother and I out of the palace when my brother and I were tiny. We were exiled, and kept virtual prisoners on an island just off the coast. My mother was never permitted to step back onto the mainland.'

Jenny frowned. Why was she being told this? But she could do nothing but listen as Sofía examined a meringue from all angles and decided not.

'That sounds dreadful,' Sofía continued, moving on to a delicate chocolate praline, popping it in and choosing another. 'But, in truth, the island is beautiful. It was only my mother's pain at what was happening to her country, and at losing her elder son that hurt. As we grew older my younger brother married an islander—a lovely girl. Ramón is their son. So Ramón's technically a prince, but until three months ago the only time he was at the palace was the night his father died.'

There were places here she didn't want to go. There were

places she had no right to go to. 'He…he spends his life on his yacht,' she ventured.

'No, dear, only part of it, and that's only since his mother and sister died. He trained as a builder. I think he started building things almost as soon as he could put one wooden block on top of another. He spends every dry season in Bangladesh, building houses with floating floors. Apparently they're brilliant—villagers can adjust their floor levels as flood water rises. He's passionate about it, but now, here he is, stuck as Crown Prince for ever.'

'I imagine he was trained for it,' Jenny said stiffly, still not sure where this was going.

'Only in that my mother insisted on teaching us court manners,' Sofía retorted. 'It was as if she knew that one day we'd be propelled back here. We humoured her, though none of us ever expected that we would. Finally, my brother tried to reinstate my mother's rights, to allow her to leave the island, and that's when the real tragedy started.'

'That was when Ramón's father was killed?'

'Yes, dear. By my father's thugs,' Sofía said, her plump face creasing into distress. The noise and bustle of the ballroom was nothing, ignored in her apparent need to tell Jenny this story. 'My mother ached to leave, and we couldn't believe my father's vindictiveness could last for years. But last it did, and when my brother was old enough he mounted a legal challenge. It was met with violence and with death. My father invited my brother here, to reason with him, so he came and brought Ramón with him because he thought he'd introduce his little son to his grandfather. So Ramón was here when it happened, a child, sleeping alone in this dreadful place while his father was killed. Just…alone.'

She stared down at her chocolate, but she wasn't seeing it. She was obviously still stunned at the enormity of what had happened. 'That's what royalty does,' she whispered. 'What is it they say? Absolute power corrupts absolutely. So my father had his own son killed, simply because he dared to defy him. We assume…we want to believe that it was simply his thugs going too far, meant to frighten but taking their orders past the point of reason. But still, my father must have employed them, and he must have known the consequences. This place…the whole of royalty is tainted by that murder. And now Carlos…the man who would have been Crown Prince if Ramón hadn't agreed to come home…is in the wings, threatening. He's here tonight.'

She gestured towards the supper table where a big man with more medals than Ramón was shovelling food into his mouth.

'He makes threats but so quietly we can't prove anything. He's here always, with his unfortunate wife towed in his wake, and he's just waiting for something to happen to Ramón. I can walk away—Ramón insists that I will walk away—but Ramón can't.'

Jenny was struggling to take everything in. She couldn't focus on shadows of death. She couldn't even begin to think of Carlos and his threats. She was still, in fact, struggling with genealogy. And Ramón as a little boy, alone as his father died…

'So…so the Crown Prince who's just been killed was your older brother?' she managed.

'Yes,' Sofía told her, becoming calm once more. 'Not that I ever saw him after we left the palace. And he had a son, who also had a son.' She shrugged. 'A little boy called Philippe. There's another tragedy. But it's not your tragedy, dear,' she said as she saw Jenny's face. 'Nor Ramón's. Ramón worries, but then Ramón worries about everything.' She hesitated, and then forged ahead as if this was something she'd rehearsed.

'But, my dear, Ramón's been talking about you,' she confessed. 'He says…he says you're special. Well, I can see that. I watched Ramón's face as he danced with you and it's exactly the same expression I saw on his father's face when he danced with his mother. If Ramón's found that with you…'

'He can't possibly…' Jenny started, startled, but Sofía was allowing no interruptions.

'You can't say it's impossible if it's already happened. All

I'm saying is that you don't have to be royal to be with Ramón. What I'm saying is give love a chance.'

'How could I…?' She stopped, bewildered.

'By not staying in this palace,' Sofía said, suddenly deadly serious. 'By not even thinking about it. Ramón's right when he tells me such a union is impossible, dangerous, unsuitable, and he can't be distracted from what he must do. You don't fit in and neither should you. Our real home, our lovely island, is less than fifteen minutes' helicopter ride from here. If Ramón could settle you there as his mistress, he'd have an escape.'

'An escape?' she whispered, stunned.

'From royalty,' Sofía said bluntly. 'Ramón needs to do his duty but if he could have you on the side…' She laid a hand over Jenny's. 'It could make all the difference. And he'd look after you so well. I know he would. You'd want for nothing. So, my dear, will you listen to Ramón?'

'If he asks…to have me as his some-time mistress?' she managed.

'I'm just letting you know his family would think it was a good thing,' Sofía said, refusing to be deterred by Jenny's obvious shock. 'You're not to take offence, but it's nothing less than my duty to tell you that you're totally unsuitable for this place, even if he'd have you here, which he won't. You're not who Ramón needs as a wife. He needs someone who knows what royalty is and how to handle it. That's what royal pedigree is—there's a reason for it. But, as for a partner he loves…that's a different thing. If Ramón could have you now and then…'

She paused, finally beginning to flounder. The expression on Jenny's face wasn't exactly encouraging. She was finding it impossible to contain her anger, and her humiliation.

'So you'd have him marry someone else and have me on the side,' she said dangerously.

'It's been done for generation upon generation,' Sofía said with asperity. Then she glanced up with some relief as a stranger approached, a youngish man wearing more medals than Ramón. 'But here's Lord Anthony, wanting an introduction. He's frightfully British, my dear, but he's a wonderful dancer. Ramón won't have any more time for you tonight. He'll have so little time… But I'm sure he could fit you in every now and then, if you'll agree to the island. So you go and dance with Lord Anthony, and remember what I said when you need to remember it.'

Jenny danced almost on automatic pilot. She desperately wanted to leave, but slipping away when the world was watching was impossible. As Sofía had warned her, she barely saw Ramón again. He was doing his duty, dancing with one society dame after another.

She'd been lucky to be squeezed in at all, she thought dully. What *was* she doing here?

It wasn't made better with her second 'girls' talk' of the night. Another woman grabbed her attention almost straight after Sofía. This lady was of a similar age to Sofía, but she was small and thin, she had fewer jewels and she had the air of a frightened rabbit. But she was a determined frightened rabbit. She intercepted Jenny between partners. When the next man approached she hissed, 'Go away,' and stood her ground until they were left alone.

'I'm Perpetua,' she said, and then, as Jenny looked blank, she explained. 'I'm Carlos's wife.'

Carlos. The threat.

'He's not dangerous,' Perpetua said, obviously reading her expression, and she steered her into the shadows with an air of quiet but desperate determination. 'My husband's all talk. All stupidity. It's this place. It's being royal. I just wanted to say…to say…'

She took a deep breath and out it came, as if it had been welled up for years. 'They say you're common,' she said. 'I mean…ordinary. Not royal. Like me. I was a schoolteacher, and I loved my work and then I met Carlos. For a while we were happy, but then the old Prince decided he liked my husband. He used to take him gambling. Carlos got sucked into the lifestyle, and that's where he stays. In some sort of fantasy world, where he's more royal than Ramón. He's done some really stupid things, most of them at the Prince's goading. In these last months when he thought he would inherit the throne, he's been…a little bit crazy. There's nothing I can do, but it's so painful to see the way he is, the way he's acting. And then I watched you tonight. The way you looked at Ramón when you were dancing.'

'I don't understand,' Jenny managed.

'Just get away from it,' she whispered. 'Whatever Ramón says, don't believe it. Just run. Oh, I shouldn't say anything. I'm a royal wife and a royal wife just shuts up. Do you want that? To be an appendage who just shuts up? My dear, don't do it. Just run.' And then, as yet another potential partner came to claim Jenny's hand, she gave a gasping sob, shot Jenny one last despairing glance and disappeared into the crowd.

Just run. That was truly excellent advice, Jenny thought, as she danced on, on autopilot. It was the best advice she'd had all night. If she knew where she was, if she knew how to get back to the boat in the dark in the middle of a strange city, that was just what she'd do.

She'd never felt so alone. She was Cinderella without her coach and it wasn't even midnight.

But finally the clock struck twelve. Right on cue, a cluster of officials gathered round Ramón as a formal guard of honour. Trumpets blared with a final farewell salute, and the Crown Prince Ramón of Cepheus was escorted away.

He'd be led to his harem of nubile young virgins, Jenny decided, fighting back an almost hysterical desire to laugh. Or cry. Or both. She was so weary she wanted to sink and, as if the thought had been said aloud, a footman was at her side, courteously solicitous.

'Ma'am, I'm to ask if you'd like to stay on to continue dancing, or would you like to be escorted back to your chambers?'

'I'd like to be escorted back to the yacht.'

'That's not possible, ma'am,' he said. 'The Prince's orders are that you stay in the palace.' And then, as she opened her mouth to argue, he added flatly, 'There's no transport to the docks tonight. I'm sorry, ma'am, but you'll have to stay.'

So that, it seemed, was that. She was escorted back to the palace. She lay in her ridiculously ostentatious bedchamber, in her ridiculously ostentatious bed, and she tried for sleep.

How was a girl to sleep after a night like this?

She couldn't. Her crimson ball-gown was draped on a hanger in the massive walk-in wardrobe. The diamond necklet still lay on her dresser. Her Cinderella slippers were on the floor beside her bed.

At least she'd kept both of them on, she thought ruefully. It hadn't quite been a fairy tale.

Only it had been a fairy tale. Gianetta Bertin—Jenny to her friends—had attended a royal ball. She'd been led out onto the dance floor with a prince so handsome he made her knees turn to jelly. For those few wonderful moments she'd let herself be swept away into a magic future where practicalities disappeared and there was only Ramón; only her love.

And then his aunt had told her that she was totally un-suitable to be a royal wife but she could possibly be his mistress. Only not here. How romantic.

And then someone called Perpetua had warned her against royalty, like the voice of doom in some Gothic novel. *Do not trust him, gentle maiden.*

How ridiculous.

And, as if in response to her unanswerable question, some-one knocked on the door.

Who'd knock on her bedroom door at three in the morning?

'Who is it?' she quavered, and her heart seemed to stop until there was a response.

'I can't get my boots off,' a beloved voice complained from the other side of the door. 'I was hoping someone might hang on while I pull.'

'I… I believe my contract was all about muffins and sails,' she managed, trying to make her voice not squeak, trying to

kick-start her heart again while warnings and sensible decisions went right out of the window. *Ramón.*

'I know I have no right to ask.' There was suddenly seriousness behind Ramón's words. 'I know this isn't sensible, I
know I shouldn't be here, but Jenny, if tonight is all there is
then I'm sure, if we read the contract carefully, there might
be something about boots. Something that'd give us an excuse
for…well, something about helping me for this night only.'

'Don't you have a valet?' she whispered and then wondered
how he'd hear her through the door. But it was as if he was
already in the room with her.

'Valets scare the daylights out of me,' he said. 'They're
better dressed than I am. Please, Jenny love, will you help me
off with my boots?'

'I don't think I'm brave enough.'

'You helped a trapped whale. Surely you can help a trapped
prince. For this night only.'

'Ramón…'

'Open the door, Gianetta,' he said in a different voice, a
voice that had her flinging back her bedcovers and flying to
the door and tugging it open. Despite what Sofía had said,
despite Perpetua's grim warnings, this was Ramón. Her
Ramón.

And there he was. He wasn't smiling. He was just…him.

He opened his arms and she walked right in.

For a long moment she simply stood, held against him,
feeling the strength of his heartbeat, feeling his arms around
her. He was still in his princely uniform. There were medals
digging into her cheek but she wasn't complaining. His heart
was beating right under those medals, and who cared about a
bit of metal anyway?

Who cared what two royal women had said to her? Who
cared that this was impossible?

They had this night.

He kissed the top of her head and he held her tight and she
felt protected and loved—and desperate to haul him into the
room right there and then.

But there was a footman at the top of the stairs. Just standing, staring woodenly ahead. He was wigged, powdered, almost a dummy. But he was real.

It was hard to seize a prince and haul him into her lair when a footman was on guard.

'Um…we have an audience,' she whispered at last.

He kissed her hair again and said gravely, 'Do you care?'

'If we walk into my room and shut the door we won't have an audience,' she tried.

'Ah, but the story will out,' he said gravely.

'So it should if you go creeping into strange women's bedrooms in the small hours. I should yell the house down.'

She was trying to sound indignant. She was trying to pull back so she could be at arm's length, so she could see his face. She wasn't trying hard enough. She sounded happy—and there was no way she was pulling back from this man.

'You could if you wanted and you'd have help,' he said gravely. 'The footman's on guard duty. In case the Huns invade—or strange women don't want strange men doing this creeping thing you describe. But if the woman was to welcome this strange man, then we don't need an audience. Gianetta, are you hungry?'

Hungry. The thought was so out of left field that she blinked.

'Hungry?'

'I'm starving. I was hoping you might come down to the kitchen with me.'

'After I've pulled your boots off?'

'Yup.'

'You want me to be your servant?'

'No,' he said, lightness giving way instantly to a gravity she found disconcerting. 'For this night, I want you to be my friend.'

Her friend, the prince?

Her friend, her lover?

Ramón.

Part-time mistress?

Forget Sofía, she told herself fiercely. Forget Perpetua. Tonight she'd hold on to the fairy tale.

'So…so there's no royal cook?' she managed.

'There are three, but they scare me more than my valet. They wear white hats and speak with Italian accents and say béchamel a lot.'

'Oh, Ramón…'

'And there's no security camera in the smaller kitchen,' he told her, and she looked up into his face and it was all she could do not to burst into spontaneous combustion.

'So will you come?' His eyes dared her.

'I'm coming.' Mistress or not, dangerous or not, right now she'd take whatever he wanted to give. Stupid? Who knew? She only knew that there was no way she could walk away from this man this night.

'Slippers and robe first,' he suggested and she blinked.

'Pardon?'

'Let's keep it nice past the footman.' He grinned. 'And do your belt up really tight. I like a challenge.'

'Ramón…'

'Second kitchen, no security camera,' he said and gave her a gentle push back into her bedroom. 'Slippers and gown. Respectability's the thing, my love. All the way down the stairs.'

They were respectable all the way down the stairs. The footman watched them go, his face impassive. When they reached the second kitchen another footman appeared and opened the door for them. He ushered them inside.

'Would you like the door closed?' he said deferentially and Ramón nodded.

'Absolutely. And make sure the Huns stay on that side.'

'The Huns?' the man said blankly.

'You never know what they're planning,' Ramón said darkly. 'If I were you, I'd take a walk around the perimeter of the palace. Warn the troops.'

'Your Highness…'

'Just give us a bit of privacy,' Ramón said, relenting at the look of confusion on the man's face. 'Fifty paces from the kitchen door, agreed?'

Finally there was a smile—sort of—pulled back instantly with a gasp as if the man had realized what he was doing and maybe smiling was a hanging offence. Impassive again, he snapped his heels and moved away and Ramón closed the door and leaned on it.

'This servant thing's got knobs on it. Three months and they still treat me like a prince.'

'You are a prince.'

'Not here,' he said. 'Not now. I'm me and you're you and the kitchen door is closed. And so…'

And so he took her into his arms and he held her so tight the breath was crushed from her body. He held her like a man drowning holding on to a lifeline. He held her and held her and held her, as if there was no way he could ever let her go.

He didn't kiss her. His head rested on her hair. He held her until her heart beat in synchronisation with his. Until she felt as if her body was merging with his, becoming one. Until she felt as if she was truly loved—that she'd come home.

How long they stayed there she could never afterwards tell—time disappeared. This was their moment. The world was somewhere outside that kitchen door, the servants, Sofía's words, Perpetua's warnings, tomorrow, but for now all that mattered was this, her Ramón. Her love.

The kitchen was warm. An old fire-stove sent out a gentle heat. A small grey cat slept in a basket by the hearth. All Jenny had seen of this palace was grandeur, but here in this second kitchen the palace almost seemed a home.

It did feel like home. Ramón was holding her against his heart and she was where she truly belonged.

She knew it was an illusion, and so must he. Maybe that was why he held her for so long, allowing nothing, no words, no movement, to intrude. As if, by holding her, the world could be kept at bay. As if she was something that he must lose, but he'd hold on while he still could.

Finally he kissed her as she needed to be kissed, as she ached to be kissed, and she kissed him back as if he was truly her Ramón and the royal title was nothing but a crazy fantasy locked securely on the other side of the door.

With the Huns, she thought, somewhat deliriously. Reality and the Huns were being kept at bay by powdered, wigged footmen, giving her this time of peace and love and bliss.

She loved this man with all her heart. Maybe what Sofía had said was wrong. Maybe the Perpetua thing was crazy.

The cat stirred, coiling out of her basket, stretching, then stepping daintily out to inspect her food dish. The tiny movement was enough to make them stir, to let a sliver of reality in. But only a sliver.

'She's only interested in her food,' Jenny whispered. 'Not us.'

'I don't blame her. I'm hungry, too.' Ramón's voice was husky with passion, but his words were so prosaic that she chuckled. It made it real. Her Prince of the Blood, dressed in medals and tassels and boots that shone like mirrors, was smiling down at her with a smile that spoke of devilry and pure latent sex—and he was hungry.

'For…for what?' she managed, and the devilry in his eyes darkened, gleamed, sprang into laughter.

'I'd take you on the kitchen table, my love,' he said simply. 'But I just don't trust the servants that much.'

'And we'd shock the cat,' she whispered and he chuckled.

'Absolutely.'

He was trying to make his voice normal, Jenny thought. He was trying to make their world somehow normal. In truth, if Ramón carried out his earlier threat to untie the cord of her dressing gown, if he took that to its inevitable conclusion, there was no way she'd deny him. Only sense was prevailing. Sort of.

Where he led, she'd follow, but if he was trying to be prosaic…maybe she could be, too.

'I could cook in this kitchen,' she said, eyeing the old range appraisingly, the rows of pots and pans hanging from overhead rails, the massive wooden table, worn and pitted from years of scrubbing.

'The pantry adjoins both kitchens,' Ramón said hopefully. 'I'm sure there's eggs and bacon in there.'

'Are you really hungry?'

'At dinner I had two queens, one duke and three prime ministers within talking range,' he said. 'They took turns to address me. It's very rude for a Crown Prince to eat while being addressed by a Head of State. My Aunt Sofía was watching. If I'd eaten I would have had my knuckles rapped.'

'She's a terrifying lady,' Jenny said and he grinned.

'I love her to bits,' he said simply. 'Like I love you.'

'Ramón…'

'Gianetta.'

'This is…'

'Just for tonight,' he said softly and his voice grew bleak. 'I know this is impossible. After tonight I'll ask nothing of you, but Gianetta…just for tonight can we be…us?'

His face was grim. There were vast problems here, she knew, and she saw those problems reflected in his eyes. Sofía had said the ghost of his father made this palace hateful, yet Ramón was stuck here.

Can we be us?

Maybe they could go back to where they' started.

'Do you want bacon and eggs, or do you want muffins?' she asked and tried to make her voice prosaic.

'You could cook muffins here?' Astonishment lessened the grimness.

'You have an oven warmed for a cat,' she said. 'It seems silly to waste it. It'll mean you need to wait twenty minutes instead of five minutes for eggs and bacon.'

'And the smell will go all through the palace,' he said in satisfaction. 'There's an alibi if ever I heard one. We could give a couple to Manuel and Luis.'

'Manuel and Luis?'

'Our Hun protectors. They think I'm taunting them if I use their real names, but surely a muffin couldn't be seen as a taunt.' His eyes were not leaving hers. He wanted her. He ached for her. His eyes said it all, but he was keeping himself rigidly under control.

'You think we might find the ingredients?' he asked, but she was already opening the panty door, doing a visual sweep of the shelves, then checking out the first of three massive refrigerators. As anxious as he to find some way of keeping the sizzle between them under control, and to keep the tension on his face at bay.

'There's more ingredients than you can shake a stick at.'

'Pardon?'

'Lots of ingredients,' she said in satisfaction. 'It seems a shame to abandon bacon entirely. You want bacon and cheese muffins, or double chocolate chip?'

'Both,' he said promptly. 'Especially if I get to lick the chocolate chip bowl.'

'Done,' she said and smiled at him and his smile met hers and she thought, whoa I am in such trouble. And then she thought, whatever Sofía said, or Perpetua said, no matter how impossible this is, I'm so deeply in love, there's no way I'll ever be able to climb out.

CHAPTER EIGHT

THEY made muffins. Not just half a dozen muffins because: 'If I'm helping, it's not such a huge ask to make heaps,' Ramón declared. 'We can put them on for breakfast and show the world what my Gianetta can do.'

'You'll upset the chefs,' Jenny warned.

'If there's a turf war, you win hands down.'

'A turf war…' She was pouring choc chips into her mixture but she hesitated at that. 'I'm not interested in any turf war. Frankly, this set-up leaves me terrified.'

'It leaves me terrified.'

'Yes, but…'

'But I have no choice,' he said flatly, finishing the sentence for her. 'I know that. In the good old days, as Crown Prince I could have simply had my soldiers go out with clubs and drag you to my lair.'

'And now you give me choices,' she retorted, trying desperately to keep things light, whisking her muffin mix more briskly than she needed. 'Just as well. I believe clubbing might create an International Incident.'

'I miss the good old days,' he said morosely. He was sitting on the edge of the table, swinging his gorgeous boots, taking taste tests of her mixture. So sexy the kitchen seemed to sizzle. 'What use is being a prince if I can't get my woman?'

My woman. She was dreaming, Jenny thought dreamily. She was cooking muffins for her prince.

My woman?

She started spooning her mixture into the pans and Ramón reached over and took the trays and the bowl from her. 'I can do this,' he said. 'If you do something for me.'

'What?'

'Pull my boots off. I asked you ages ago.'

'I thought you were kidding.'

'They're killing me,' he confessed. 'I've spent my life in either boat shoes, bare feet or steel-toed construction boots. These make me feel like my feet are in corsets and I can't get them off. Please, dear, kind Jenny, will you pull my boots off?'

He was sitting on the table. He was spooning muffin mixture into pans. He was holding his boots out for her to pull.

This was so ridiculous she couldn't help giggling.

She wiped her hands—it'd be a pity to get chocolate on leather like this—took position, took a boot in both hands—and pulled.

The boot didn't budge. It was like a second skin.

'See what I mean,' Ramón said morosely. 'And I really don't want to wake a valet. You think I should cut them off?'

'You can't cut them,' Jenny said, shocked, and tried again. The boot budged, just a little.

'Hey,' Ramón said, continuing to spoon. 'It's coming.'

'I'll pull you off the table if I tug any harder,' Jenny warned.

'I'm strong,' he said, too smugly, keeping on spooning. 'My balance is assured.'

'Right,' she said and glowered, reacting to his smugness. She wiped both her hands on her dressing gown, took the boot in both hands, took a deep breath—and pulled like she'd never pulled.

The boot held, gripped for a nano-second and then gave. Jenny lurched backward, boot in hand, lost her balance and fell backwards.

Ramón slid off the table, staggered—and ended up on the floor.

The half-full bowl slid off after him, tipped sideways and mixture oozed out over the floor.

Jenny stared across at him in shock. Ramón stared back at her—her lovely prince, half bootless, sprawled on the floor, surrounded by choc chip muffin mixture.

Her Ramón.

She couldn't help it. She laughed out loud, and it was a magical release of tension, a declaration of love and happiness if ever there was one, and she couldn't help what happened next either. It was as if restraint had been thrown to the wind and she could do what she liked—and there was no doubting what she'd like. She slid over the floor, she took Ramón's face in both her hands—and she kissed him.

And Ramón kissed her back—a thoroughly befuddled, laughing, wonderful kiss. He tasted of choc chip muffin. He tasted of love.

He tugged her close, hauling her backward with him so she was in his arms, and they were so close she thought she must…they must…

And then the door burst open and Sofía was standing in the doorway staring at them both as if they'd lost their minds.

Maybe they had.

The little cat was delicately licking muffin mixture from the floor. Sofía darted across and retrieved the cat as if she were saving her from poison.

'Hi, Sofía,' Ramón said innocently from somewhere underneath his woman. Jenny would have pulled away but he was having none of it. He tugged her close and held, so they were lying on the floor like two children caught out in mischief. Or more.

Sofía stared down at them as if she couldn't believe her eyes. 'What do you think you're doing?' she hissed.

'Making muffins, Ramón said, and he would have pulled Jenny closer but the mixture of confusion and distress on Sofía's face was enough to have her pulling away. The timer was buzzing. Somehow she struggled to her feet. She opened the oven and retrieved her now cooked bacon muffins. Then she thought what the heck, she might as well finish what she'd started, so she put the almost full tray of choc chip muffins in to replace them.

'Gianetta's a professional,' Ramón said proudly to his aunt, struggling up as well. 'I told you she was fabulous.'

'Are you out of your minds?'

'No, I…'

'You're just like the rest,' she hissed at him. 'They're all womanisers, all the men who've ever held power here. You have her trapped. Ramón, what on earth is it that you're planning?'

'I'm not planning anything.'

'If it's marriage… You can't. I know Philippe needs a mother but this is…'

'It's nothing to do with Philippe,' Ramón snapped. 'Why are you here?'

'Why do you think?' Sofía's anger was becoming almost apoplectic. 'Did you think the two of you were invisible? Everyone knows where you are. Ramón, think about what you're doing. You're no longer just responsible for yourself. You represent a country now! She's a nice girl, I won't let you ruin her, or trap her into this life.'

'I won't do either,' Ramón said, coldly furious. 'We're not talking marriage. We're not talking anything past this night. Jenny will be leaving…'

'Ramón, if she goes to the island now… There'll be such talk. To take her in the palace kitchen…'

'He didn't *take* me…' It was Jenny's turn to be angry now. 'My dressing gown cord's still done up.'

'No one can tell that from outside,' Sofía snapped and walked across and tugged the door wide. 'See? The harm's done,' she said, as two footmen stepped smartly away from the door.

'You can't be happy here,' she whispered. 'No one knows anyone. No one trusts.'

'I know that,' Ramón told her. 'Sofía, stop this.'

'I told her you should take her to the island. I told her. You should have waited.'

'Excuse me?' Jenny said. 'Can you include me in this?'

'It's nothing to do with you,' Sofía said and then seemed to think about it. Her anger faded and she suddenly sounded weary and defeated. 'No. I mean…even if you were suitable as a royal bride—which you aren't—you aren't tough enough. To do it with no training…'

'Sofía, don't do this,' Ramón said. Sofía's distress was clear and real. 'We aren't talking about marriage.'

'Then you're ruining her for nothing. And here's your valet, come to see what all the fuss is about.'

'I don't want my valet,' Ramón snapped. 'I don't want any valet.'

'You don't have a choice,' Sofía said with exasperation. 'None of us do. Ramón, go away. I'll stay here with Jenny until these…whatever you're making…muffins?…are cooked. We'll make the best of a bad situation but there's no way we can keep this quiet. This, with your stupid insistence on dancing with her first tonight… She'll have paparazzi in her face tomorrow, whether she leaves or not.'

'Paparazzi…' Jenny said faintly.

'Leave now, Ramón, and don't go near her again. She needs space to see what a mess this situation is.'

'She doesn't want space.'

'Yes, I do,' Jenny said. Philippe? Paparazzi? There were so many unknowns. What was she getting into?

She felt dizzy.

She felt bereft.

'Jenny,' Ramón said urgently but Sofía was before him, pushing herself between them.

'Leave it,' she told them both harshly. 'Like it or not, Ramón is Crown Prince. He needs to fit his new role. He might think he wants you but he doesn't have a choice. *You* don't belong in our world and you both know it.' She glanced along the corridor where there were now four servants waiting. 'So… There's to be no seduction tonight. We're all calmly eating muffins and going to bed. Yes?'

'Yes,' Jenny said before Ramón could reply. She didn't

want to look at him. She couldn't. Because the laughter in his eyes had gone.

The servants were waiting to take over. The palace was waiting to take over.

She lay in her opulent bed and her head spun so much she felt dizzy.

She was lying on silk sheets. When she moved, she felt as if she was being caressed.

She wasn't being caressed. She was lying in a royal bed, in a royal boudoir. Alone. Because why?

Because Ramón was a Crown Prince.

Even when she'd lain with him in his wonderful yacht, believing he was simply the skipper and not the owner, she'd felt a sense of inequality, as if this couldn't be happening to her.

But it had happened, and now it was over.

What else had she expected?

Since she'd met Ramón her ache of grief had lifted. Life had become…unreal. But here it was again, reality, hard and cold as ice, slamming her back to earth. Grief was real. Loss was real. Emptiness and heartache had been her world for years, and here they were again.

Her time with Ramón, her time tonight, had been some sort of crazy soap bubble. Even before Sofía had spelled it out, she'd known it was impossible.

Sofía said she was totally unsuitable. Of course she was.

But…but…

As the night wore on something strange was happening. Her grief for Matty had been in abeyance during the two weeks with Ramón, and again tonight. It was back with her now, but things had changed. Things were changing.

Ever since Matty was born, things had happened to Jenny. Just happened. It was as if his birth, his medical problems, his desperate need, had put her on a roller coaster of emotions that she couldn't get off. Her life was simply doing what came next.

But the chain of events today had somehow changed

things. What Sofía and then Perpetua had said had stirred something deep within. Or maybe it was how Ramón had made her feel tonight that was making her feel different.

She'd seen the defeat on Ramón's face and she recognized that defeat. It was a defeat born of bleak acceptance.

Once upon a time she'd shared it. Maybe she still should. But…but…

'Why should I run?' she whispered and she wondered if she'd really said it.

It didn't make any sense. Sofía and Perpetua were right. So was Ramón. What was between them was clearly impossible, and there'd be a million more complications she hadn't thought of yet.

Philippe? The child Sofía had talked of?

She didn't go near children. Not after Matty.

And royalty? She had no concept of what Ramón was facing. Threats? The unknown Carlos?

There were questions everywhere, unspoken shadows looming from all sides, but overriding everything was the fact that she wanted Ramón so much she could almost cry out loud for him. What she wanted right now was to pad out into the palace corridor, yell at the top of her lungs for Ramón and then sit down and demand answers.

She'd had her chance. She'd used it making muffins. And kissing her prince.

He'd kissed her back.

The memory made her smile. Ramón made her smile.

Maybe the shadows weren't so long, she thought, but she knew they were.

'I'd be happy as his lover,' she whispered to the night. 'For as long as he wanted me. Just as his lover. Just in private. Back on his boat, sailing round the world, Ramón and me.'

It wasn't going to happen. And would she be happy on his island, being paid occasional visits as Sofía had suggested?

No!

She lay back on her mound of feather pillows and she stared up at the ceiling some more.

She stared at nothing.

Jenny and Ramón, the Crown Prince of Cepheus? No and no and no.

But still there was this niggle. It wasn't anger, exactly. Not exactly.

It was more that she'd found her centre again.

She'd found something worth fighting for.

Gianetta and the Crown Prince of Cepheus? No and no and no.

The thing was, though, sense had gone out of the window.

The car crash that had killed his mother and his sister had left him with an aching void where family used to be. For years he'd carried the grief as a burden, thinking he could bear no more, and the way to avoid that was to not let people close.

He loved his work in Bangladesh—it changed people's lives—yet individual lives were not permitted to touch him.

But there was something about Jenny…Gianetta…that broke the barriers he'd built. She'd touched a chord, and the resonance was so deep and so real that to walk away from her seemed unthinkable.

For the last three months he'd tried to tell himself what he'd felt was an illusion, but the moment he'd seen her again he'd known it was real. She was his woman. He knew it with a certainty so deep it felt primeval.

But to drag her into the royal limelight, into a place where the servants greeted you with blank faces…into a place where his father had died and barely a ripple had been created…where Carlos threatened and he didn't know which servants might be loyal and which might be in Carlos's pay… here his duty lay to his people and to have his worry centred on one slip of a girl…

On Jenny.

No.

Could he love her enough to let her go?

He must.

He had a deputation from neighbouring countries meeting

him first thing in the morning to discuss border issues. Refugees. The thought did his head in.

Royalty seemed simple on the outside—what had Jenny said?—cutting ribbons and making speeches. But Cepheus was governed by royalty. He'd set moves afoot to turn it into a democracy but it would take years, and meanwhile what he did would change people's lives.

Could he do it alone? He must.

He had no right to ask Jenny to share a load he found insupportable. To put her into the royal limelight... To ask her to share the risks that had killed his father... To distract himself from a task that had to be faced alone...

There was no choice at all.

CHAPTER NINE

Jenny didn't see Ramón all the next day. She couldn't. 'Affairs of State,' Sofía told her darkly, deeply disapproving when Jenny told her she had no intention of leaving until she'd spoken to Ramón. 'There's so much business that's been waiting for Ramón to officially take charge. Señor Rodriguez tells me he's booked for weeks. Poor baby.'

Poor baby? Jenny thought of the man whose boot she'd pulled off, she thought of the power of his touch, and she thought 'poor baby' was a description just a wee bit wide of the mark.

So what was she to do? By nine she'd breakfasted, inspected the palace gardens—breathtakingly beautiful but *so* empty—got lost twice in the palace corridors, and she was starting to feel as if she was climbing walls.

She headed out to the gardens again and found Gordon, pacing by one of the lagoon-sized swimming pools. It seemed the darkness and the strange city last night had defeated even him.

'All this opulence gives me the creeps,' he said, greeting her with relief. 'I've been waiting for you. How about if we slope off down to the docks? It's not so far. A mile or so as the crow flies. We could get out the back way, avoid the paparazzi.'

'I do need to come back,' she whispered, looking at the cluster of cameramen around the main gate with dismay, and Gordon surveyed her with care.

'Are you sure? There's talk, lass, about last night.'

And there it was again, that surge of anger.

'Then maybe I need to give them something to talk about,' she snapped.

The meetings were interminable—men and women in serious suits, with serious briefcases filled with papers covered with serious concerns, not one of which he could walk away from.

This country had been in trouble for decades—was still in trouble. It would take skill and commitment to bring it back from the brink, to stop the exodus of youth leaving the country, to take advantage of the country's natural resources to bring prosperity for citizens who'd been ignored for far too long.

The last three months he'd spent researching, researching, researching. He had the knowledge now to make a difference, but so much work was before him it felt overwhelming.

He should be gearing up right now to spend the next six months supervising the construction of houses in Bangladesh, simple work but deeply satisfying. He'd had to abandon that to commit to this, a more direct and personal need.

And this morning he'd had to abandon Jenny.

Gianetta.

The two words kept interplaying in his head. Jenny. Gianetta.

Jenny was the woman who made muffins, the woman who saved whales, the woman who made him laugh.

Gianetta was the woman he took to his bed. Gianetta was the woman he would make his Princess—*if* he didn't care so much, for her and for his country.

Where was she now?

He'd been wrong last night. Sofía had spelled out their situation clearly and he could do nothing but agree.

He should be with her now, explaining why he couldn't take things further. She'd be confused and distressed. But there was simply no option for him to spend time with her today.

So… He'd left orders for her to be left to enjoy a day of leisure. The *Marquita* was a big boat; it was hard work to crew her and she'd been sailing for three months. Last night had been…stressful. She deserved to rest.

He had meetings all day and a formal dinner tonight. Tomorrow, though, he'd make time early to say goodbye. If she stayed that long.

And tomorrow he'd promised to visit Philippe.

He glanced at his watch. Tomorrow. It was twenty-two hours and thirty minutes before a scheduled visit with his woman. Wedging it in between affairs of state and his concern for a child he didn't know what to do with.

Jenny. How could he ever make sense of what he felt for her?

He knew, in his heart, that he couldn't.

The *Marquita* meant work, and in work there was respite.

The day was windless so they could unfurl the sails and let them dry. The boat was clean, but by common consensus they decided it wasn't clean enough. They scrubbed the decks, they polished brass, they gave the interior such a clean that Martha Gardener would be proud of them.

Jenny remade the bed in the great stateroom, plumped the mass of pillows, looked down at the sumptuous quilts and wondered again, what had she been thinking?

She'd slept in this bed with the man she loved. She loved him still, with all her heart, but in the distance she could see the spires of the palace, glistening white in the Mediterranean sunshine.

The Crown Prince of Cepheus. For a tiny time their two disparate worlds had collided, and they'd seemed almost equal. Now, all that was left was to find the courage to walk away.

Perhaps.

Eighteen hours and twenty-two minutes. How many suits could he talk to in that time? How many documents must he read?

He had to sign them all and there was no way he could sign without reading.

His eyes were starting to cross.

Eighteen hours and seven minutes.

Would she still be here?

Surely she wouldn't leave without a farewell.

He deserved it, he thought, but please…no.

They worked solidly until mid-afternoon. Gordon was checking the storerooms, taking inventory, making lists of what needed to be replaced. Jenny was still obsessively cleaning.

Taking away every trace of her.

But, as the afternoon wore on, even she ran out of things to do. 'Time to get back to the palace,' Gordon decreed.

'We could stay on board.'

'She's being pulled out of the water tonight so engineers can check her hull in the morning. We hardly have a choice tonight.'

'Will you stay on as Ramón's skipper?'

'I love this boat,' he said simply. 'For as long as I'm asked, I'll stay. If that means staying at the palace from time to time, I'll find the courage.'

'I don't have very much courage,' she whispered.

'Or maybe you have sense instead,' Gordon said stoutly. He stood back for her to precede him up to the deck. She stepped up—and suddenly the world was waiting for her.

Paparazzi were everywhere. Flashlights went off in her face, practically blinding her. She put her hand over her eyes in an instinctive gesture of defence, and retreated straight back down again.

Gordon slammed the hatch after her.

'Tell us about yourself,' someone called from the dock. 'You speak Spanish, right?'

'We're happy to pay for your story,' someone else called.

'You and Prince Ramón were on the boat together for two weeks, alone, right?' That was bad enough. But then…

'Is it true you had a baby out of wedlock?' someone else called while Jenny froze. 'And the baby died?'

They knew about her Matty? They knew....

She wanted to go home right now. She wanted to creep into a bunk and stay hidden while Gordon sailed her out of the harbour and away.

Serenity. Peace. That was what she'd been striving for since Matty died. Where was serenity and peace now?

How could she find it in this?

'I'll talk to them,' Gordon said, looking stunned and sick, and she looked at this big shy man and she thought why should he fight her battles? Why should anyone fight her battles?

Maybe she had to fight to achieve this so-called serenity, she thought. Maybe that was what her problem had been all along. She'd been waiting for serenity to find her, when all along it was something she needed to fight for.

Or maybe it wasn't even serenity that she wanted.

Then, before she had time to decide she'd lost her mind entirely—for maybe she had; she certainly wasn't making sense to herself and Gordon was looking really worried—she flung open the hatch again and stepped out onto the deck.

His cellphone was on mute in his pocket. He felt it vibrate, checked it and saw it was Gordon calling. Gordon wouldn't call him except in an emergency.

The documents had just been signed and the Heads of State were lining up for a photo call. These men had come for the coronation and had stayed on.

Cepheus was a small nation. These men represented far more powerful nations than his, and Cepheus had need of powerful allies. Nevertheless, he excused himself and answered.

'Paparazzi know about Jenny's baby,' Gordon barked, so loud he almost burst Ramón's eardrum. 'They're on the jetty. We're surrounded. You need to get her out of here.'

He felt sick. 'I'll have a security contingent there in two

minutes,' he said, motioning to Señor Rodriguez, who, no doubt, had heard every word. 'I need to get to the docks,' he told him. 'How long?'

'It would take us fifteen minutes, Your Highness, but we can't leave here,' Rodriguez said. The man was seriously good. He already had security on his second phone. 'Security will have dealt with it before we get there. There's no need…'

There was a need, but as he glanced back at the Heads of State he knew his lawyer was right. To leave for such a reason could cause insupportable offence. It could cause powerful allies to turn to indifference.

His sense of helplessness was increasing almost to breaking point. *He couldn't protect his woman.*

'You can see, though,' Señor Rodriguez said, obviously realising just how he was torn. He turned back to the men and women behind him. 'If you'll excuse us for a moment,' he said smoothly. 'An urgent matter of security has come up. We'll be five minutes, no more.'

'I will go,' Ramón said through gritted teeth.

'It will be dealt with before you arrive,' Señor Rodriguez said again. 'But we have security monitors on the royal berth. I can switch our cameras there to reassure you until you see our security people take over. If you'll come aside…'

So Ramón followed the lawyer into an anteroom. He stared at the monitor in the corner, and he watched in grim desperation as his woman faced the press.

They'd pull her apart, he thought grimly—and there was nothing he could do to help her.

The cameras went wild. Questions were being shouted at her from all directions.

Courage, she told herself grimly. Come on, girl, you've hidden for long enough. Now's the time to stand and fight.

She ignored the shouts. She stood still and silent, knowing she looked appalling, knowing the shots would be of her at her worst. She'd just scrubbed out a boat. She didn't look like anyone famous. She was simply Jenny the deckhand, standing waiting for the shouting to stop.

And finally it did. The journalists fell silent at last, thinking she didn't intend to respond.

'Finished?' she asked, quirking an eyebrow in what she hoped looked like sardonic amusement, and the shouting started again.

Serenity, she told herself. She tapped a bare toe on the deck and waited again for silence.

'I've called His Highness,' Gordon called up from below. 'Security's on its way. Ramón'll send them.'

It didn't matter. This wasn't Ramón's fight, she thought. Finally, silence fell again; baffled silence. The cameras were still in use but the journalists were clearly wondering what they had here. She waited and they watched. Impasse.

'You do speak English?' one asked at last, a lone question, and she nodded. A lone question, not shouted, could be attended to.

And why not all the others, in serene order? Starting now.

'Yes,' she said, speaking softly so they had to stay silent or they couldn't hear her. 'I speak English as well as Spanish and French. My parents have Spanish blood. And I did indeed act as crew for His Highness, Prince Ramón, as we sailed between Sydney and Auckland.' She thought back through the questions that had been hurled at her, mentally ticking them off. 'Yes, I'm a cook. I'm… I *was* also a single mother. My son died of a heart condition two years ago, but I don't wish to answer any more questions about Matty. His death broke my heart. As for the rest… Thank you, I enjoyed last night, and yes, rumours that I cooked for His Highness early this morning are true. I'm employed as his cook and crew. That's what I've been doing for the last three months and no, I'm not sure if I'll continue. It depends if he needs me. What else? Oh, the personal questions. I'm twenty-nine years old. I had my appendix out when I was nine, my second toes are longer than my big toes and I don't eat cabbage. I think your country is lovely and the *Marquita* is the prettiest boat in the world.

However, scrubbing the *Marquita* is what I'm paid to do and that's what I'm doing. If you have any more questions, can you direct them to my secretary?'

She grinned then, a wide, cheeky grin which only she knew how much effort it cost to produce. 'Oh, whoops, I forgot I don't have a secretary. Can one of you volunteer? I'll pay you in muffins. If one of you is willing, then the rest can siphon your questions through him. That's so much more dignified than shouting, don't you think?'

Then she gave them all a breezy wave, observed their shocked silence and then slipped below, leaving them dumbfounded.

She stood against the closed hatch, feeling winded. Gordon was staring at her in amazement. As well he might.

What was she doing?

Short answer? She didn't know.

Long answer? She didn't know either. Retiring from this situation with dignity was her best guess, though suddenly Jenny had no intention of retiring.

Not just yet.

This was a state-of-the-art security system, and sound was included. Not only did Ramón see everything, he heard every word Jenny spoke.

'It seems the lady doesn't need protecting,' Señor Rodriguez said, smiling his relief as Jenny disappeared below deck and Ramón's security guards appeared on the docks.

Ramón shook his head. 'I should have been there for her.'

'She's protected herself. She's done very well.'

'She shouldn't have been put in that position.'

'I believe the lady could have stayed below,' the lawyer said dryly. 'The lady chose to take them on. She has some courage.'

'She shouldn't…'

'She did,' the lawyer said, and then hesitated.

Señor Rodriguez had been watching on the sidelines for many years now. His father had been legal advisor to Ramón's grandmother, and Sofía had kept him on after Ramón's father died, simply to stay aware of what royalty was doing. Now he was doing the job of three men and he was thoroughly enjoying himself. 'Your Highness, if I may make so bold…'

'You've never asked permission before,' Ramón growled, and the lawyer permitted himself another small smile.

'It's just…the role you're taking on…to do it alone could well break you. You're allowing me to assist but no one else. This woman has courage and honour. If you were to…'

'I won't,' Ramón snapped harshly, guessing where the lawyer was going and cutting him off before he went any further. He flicked the screen off. There was nothing to see but the press, now being dispersed by his security guards. 'I do this alone or not at all.'

'Is that wise?'

'I don't know what's wise or not,' Ramón said and tried to sort his thoughts into some sort of sense. What was happening here? The lawyer was suggesting sharing the throne? With Jenny?

Jenny as his woman? Yes. But Jenny in the castle?

The thought left him cold. The night of his father's death was still with him, still haunting him.

Enough. 'We have work to do,' he growled and headed back to the room where the Heads of State were waiting.

'But…' the lawyer started, but Ramón was already gone.

CHAPTER TEN

HE MANAGED a few short words with her that night as he passed the supper room. It was all he had, as he moved from the evening's meetings to his briefing for tomorrow. To his surprise, Jenny seemed relaxed, even happy.

'I'm sorry about today,' he said. 'It seemed you handled things very well.'

'I talked too much,' she said, smiling. 'I need to work on my serenity.'

'Your serenity?'

'I'm not very good at it.' Her smile widened. 'But I showed promise today. Dr Matheson would be proud of me. By the way, I hope it's okay that Gordon and I are staying here tonight. The boat's up on the hard, and who wants to sleep on a boat in dry dock? Besides, staying in a palace is kind of fun.'

Kind of fun... He gazed into the opulent supper room, at the impassive staff, and he thought...*kind of fun*?

'So I can stay tonight?' she prompted.

He raked his hair. 'I should have had Señor Rodriguez organise airline tickets.'

'Señor Rodriguez has better things to do than organise my airline tickets. I'll organise them when I'm ready. Meanwhile, can I stay tonight?'

'Of course, but Jenny, I don't have time...'

'I know you don't,' she said sympathetically. 'Señor Rodriguez says these first days are crazy. It'll get better, he says, but I'll not add to your burdens tonight. I hope I never will.'

Then, before he could figure how to respond, a servant appeared to remind him he was late for his next briefing. He was forced to leave Jenny, who didn't seem the least put out. She'd started chatting cheerfully to the maid who was clearing supper.

To his surprise, the maid was responding with friendliness and animation. Well, why wouldn't she, he told himself as he immersed himself again into royal business. Jenny had no baggage of centuries of oppression. She wasn't royal.

She never could be royal. He could never ask that of her, he thought grimly. But, as the interminable briefing wore on, he thought of Jenny—not being royal. He thought of her thinking of the palace as fun, and he almost told the suits he was talking to where to go.

But he didn't. He was sensible. He had a country to run, and when he was finally free Jenny had long gone to bed.

And there was no way he was knocking on her door tonight.

He missed her at breakfast, maybe because he ate before six before commencing the first of three meetings scheduled before ten. He moved through each meeting with efficiency and speed, desperate to find time to see her, but the meetings went overtime. He had no time left. His ten o'clock diary entry was immovable.

This appointment he'd made three months ago. Four hours every Wednesday. Even Jenny would have to wait on this.

Swiftly he changed out of his formal wear into jeans, grabbed his swimmers and made his way to the palace garages. He strode round the rows of espaliered fruit trees marking the end of the palace gardens—and Jenny was sitting patiently on a garden bench.

She was wearing smart new jeans, a casual cord jacket in a pale washed apricot over a creamy lace camisole and creamy

leather ballet flats. Her curls were brushed until they shone.
She looked rested and refreshed and cheerful.

She looked beautiful.

She rose and stretched and smiled a welcome. Gianetta.

Jenny, he told himself fiercely. This was Jenny, his guest
before she left for ever.

A very lovely Jenny. Smiling and smiling.

'Do you like it?' she demanded and spun so she could be
admired from all angles. 'This is the new smart me.'

'Where on earth…?'

'I went shopping,' she said proudly. 'Yesterday, when we
finally escaped from that mob. Your security guys kindly
escorted me to some great shops and then stood guard while
I tried stuff on. Neat, yes?'

'Neat,' he said faintly and her face fell and he amended his
statement fast. 'Gorgeous.'

'No, that won't do either,' she said reprovingly. 'My borrowed ball-gown was gorgeous. But this feels good. I thought
yesterday I haven't had new clothes for years and the owner
of the boutique gave me a huge discount.'

'I'll bet she did,' he said faintly.

She grinned. 'I know, it was cheeky, but I thought if I'm
to be photographed by every cameraman in the known universe there has to be some way I can take advantage. She was
practically begging me to take clothes.'

'Gordon said you were upset.'

'Gordon was upset.'

'I should have been there.'

'Then the cameramen would have been even more persistent,' she said gently. 'But I have clothes to face them now,
and they're not so scary. So…I pinned Señor Rodriguez down
this morning and he says you're going to see Philippe. So I
was wondering…' Her tone became more diffident. 'Would
it upset you if I came along? Would it upset Philippe?'

'No, but I can't ask you…'

'You're not asking,' she said and came forward to slip her

hands into his. 'You're looking trapped. I don't want you to feel that way. Not by me.'

'You'd never make me feel trapped,' he said. 'But Jenny, I can't expect…'

'Then don't expect,' she said. 'Señor Rodriguez told me all about Philippe. No, don't look like that. The poor man never had a chance; I practically sat on him to make him explain things in detail. Philippe's your cousin's son. Everyone thought he stood to inherit, only when his parents died it turned out they weren't actually married. According to royal rules, he's illegitimate. Now he has nothing.'

'He's well cared for. He has lovely foster parents.'

'Sofía says you've been visiting him every week since you got here.'

'It's the least I can do when he's lost his home as well as his parents.'

'He can't stay here?'

'No,' he said bleakly. 'If he's here he'll be in the middle of servants who'll either treat him like royalty—and this country hates royalty—or they'll treat him as an illegitimate nothing.'

'Yet you still think he should be here,' Jenny said softly.

'No.'

'Because this is where you were when your father died?'

'What the…?'

'Sofía,' she said simply. 'I asked, she told me. Ramón, I'm so sorry. It must have been dreadful. But that was then. Now is now. Can I meet him?'

'I can't ask that of you,' he said, feeling totally winded. 'And he's the same age your little boy would have been…'

'Ramón, can we take this one step at a time?' she asked. 'Let's just go visit this little boy—who's not Matty. Let's just leave it at that.'

So they went and for the first five miles or so they didn't speak. Ramón didn't know where to take this.

There were so many things in this country that needed his

attention but over and over his thoughts kept turning to one little boy. Consuela and Ernesto were lovely but they were in their sixties. To expect them to take Philippe long-term…

He glanced across at Jenny and found she was watching him. He had the top down on his Boxster coupe. The warm breeze was blowing Jenny's curls around her face. She looked young and beautiful and free. He remembered the trapped woman he'd met over three months ago and the change seemed extraordinary.

How could he trap her again? He couldn't. Of course he couldn't. He didn't intend to.

Yet—she'd asked to come. Was she really opening herself up to be hurt again?

'I can't believe this country,' she said, smiling, and he knew she was making an attempt to keep the conversation neutral. Steering away from undertones that were everywhere. 'It's like something on a calendar.'

'There's a deep description.'

'It's true. There's a calendar in the bathroom of Seaport Coffee 'n' Cakes and it has a fairy tale palace on it. All white turrets and battlements and moats, surrounded by little stone houses with ancient tiled roofs, and mountains in the background, and just a hint of snow.'

'There's no snow here,' he said, forced to smile back. 'We're on the Mediterranean.'

'Please,' she said reprovingly. 'You're messing with my calendar. So, as I was saying…'

But then, as he turned the car onto a dirt track leading to a farmhouse, she stopped with the imagery and simply stared. 'Where are we?'

'This is where Philippe lives.'

'But it's lovely,' she whispered, gazing out over grassy meadows where a flock of alpacas grazed placidly in the morning sun. 'It's the perfect place for a child to live.'

'He's not happy.'

'I imagine that might well be because his parents are dead,' she said, suddenly sharp. 'It'll take him for ever to adjust to their loss. If ever.'

'I don't think his parents were exactly hands-on,' Ramón told her. 'My uncle and my cousin liked to gamble, and so did Maria Therese. They spent three-quarters of their lives in Monaco and they never took Philippe. They were on their way there when their plane crashed.'

'So who took care of Philippe?'

'He's had a series of nannies. The palace hasn't exactly been a happy place to work. Neither my uncle nor my cousin thought paying servants was a priority, and I gather as a mother Maria Therese was…difficult. Nannies have come and gone.'

'So Philippe's only security has been the palace itself,' Jenny ventured.

'He's getting used to these foster parents,' Ramón said, but he wasn't convincing himself. 'They're great.'

'I'm looking forward to meeting them.'

'I'll be interested to hear your judgement.' Then he paused. 'Gianetta, are you sure you want to do this? Philippe's distressed and there's little I can do about it. It won't help to make you distressed as well. Would you like to turn back?'

'Well, that'd be stupid,' Jenny said. 'Philippe will already know you're on your way. To turn back now would be cruel.'

'But what about you?'

'This isn't about me,' she said, gently but inexorably. 'Let's go meet Philippe.'

He was the quietest little boy Jenny had ever met. He looked just like Ramón.

The family resemblance was amazing, she thought. Same dark hair. Same amazing eyes. Same sense of trouble, kept under wraps.

His foster parents, Consuela and Ernesto, were voluble and friendly. They seemed honoured to have Ramón visit, but not so overawed that it kept them silent. That was just as well, as their happy small talk covered up the deathly silence emanating from Philippe.

They sat at the farmhouse table eating Consuela's amazing strawberry cake. Consuela and Ernesto chatted, Ramón answered as best he could, and Jenny watched Philippe.

He was clutching a little ginger cat as if his life depended on it. He was too thin. His eyes were too big for his face.

He was watching his big cousin as if he was hungry.

I feel like that, she thought, and recognized what she'd thought and intensified her scrutiny. She had the time and the space to do it. Consuela and Ernesto were friendly but they were totally focused on Ramón. Philippe had greeted Jenny with courtesy but now he, too, was totally focused on Ramón.

Of course. Ramón was the Crown Prince.

Only Ramón's title didn't explain things completely, Jenny decided. Ramón was here in his casual clothes. He didn't look spectacular—or any more spectacular than he usually did—and a child wouldn't respond to an adult this way unless there was a fair bit of hero worship going on.

'Does Prince Ramón really come every week?' she asked Consuela as she helped clear the table.

'Every week since he's been back in the country,' the woman said. 'We're so grateful. Ernesto and I have had many foster children—some from very troubled homes—but Philippe's so quiet we don't seem to get through to him. He never says a thing unless he must. He hardly eats unless he's forced, and he certainly doesn't know how to enjoy himself. But once a week Ramón...I mean Crown Prince Ramón... comes and takes him out in his car and it's as if he lights up. He comes home happy, he eats, he tells us what he's done and he goes to bed and sleeps all night. Then he wakes and Ramón's not here, and his parents aren't here, and it all starts again. His Highness brought him his cat from the palace and that's made things better but now...we're starting to wonder if it's His Highness himself the child pines for.'

'He can't have become attached to Ramón so fast,' Jenny

said, startled, and Consuela looked at her with eyes that had seen a lot in her lifetime, and she smiled.

'*Caro*, are you telling me that's impossible?'

Oh, help, was she so obvious? She glanced back to where Ernesto and Ramón were engaged in a deep conversation about some obscure football match, with Philippe listening to every word as if it was the meaning of life—and she found herself blushing from the toes up.

'We're hearing rumours,' Consuela said, seemingly satisfied with Jenny's reaction. 'How lovely.'

'I…there's nothing.' *How fast did rumours spread?*

'There's everything,' Consuela said. 'All our prince needs is a woman to love him.'

'I'm not his class.'

'Class? Pah!' Consuela waved an airy hand at invisible class barriers. 'Three months ago Philippe was Prince Royal. Now he's the illegitimate son of the dead Prince's mistress. If you worry about class then you worry about nothing. You make him happy. That's all anyone can ask.' Her shrewd gaze grew intent. 'You know that Prince Ramón is kind, intelligent, honourable. Our country needs him so much. But for a man to take on such a role…there must be someone filling his heart as well.'

'I can't…'

'I can see a brave young woman before me, and I'm very sure you can.'

All of this was thoroughly disconcerting. She should just shut up, she thought. She should stick with her new found serenity. But, as she wiped as Consuela washed, she pushed just a little more. 'Can I ask you something?'

'Of course.'

'You and Ernesto… You obviously love Philippe and you're doing the best you can for him. But if Philippe wants to be at the palace… Why doesn't Ramón…why doesn't His Highness simply employ you to be there for him?'

The woman turned and looked at Jenny as if she were crazy. 'Us? Go to the palace?'

'Why not?'

'We're just farmers.'

'Um…excuse me. Didn't you just say…?'

'That's for you,' Consuela said, and then she sighed and dried her hands and turned to Jenny. 'I think that for you, you're young enough and strong enough to fight it, but for us…and for Philippe…the lines of class at the palace are immovable.'

'Would you try it, though?' she asked. 'Would you stay in the palace if Ramón asked it of you?'

'Maybe, but he won't. He won't risk it, and why should he?' She sighed, as if the worries of the world were too much for her, but then she pinned on cheerfulness, smiled determinedly at Jenny and turned back to the men. Moving on. 'Philippe. His Highness, Prince Ramón, asked if you could have your swimming costume prepared. He tells me he wishes to take you to the beach.'

Football was abandoned in an instant. 'In your car?' Philippe demanded of Ramón, round-eyed.

'In my car,' Ramón said. 'With Señorina Bertin. If it's okay with you.'

The little boy turned his attention to Jenny and surveyed her with grave attention. Whatever he saw there, it seemed to be enough.

'That will be nice,' he said stiffly.

'Get your costume, poppet,' Consuela said, but Philippe was already gone.

So they headed to the beach, about five minutes' drive from the farmhouse. Philippe sat between Jenny and Ramón, absolutely silent, his eyes straight ahead. But Jenny watched his body language. He could have sat ramrod still and not touched either of them, but instead he slid slightly to Ramón's side so his small body was just touching his big cousin.

Ramón was forging something huge here, Jenny thought. Did he know?

Maybe he did. Maybe he couldn't help but know. As he

drove he kept up a stream of light-hearted banter, speaking to Jenny, but most of what he said was aimed at Philippe.

Did Gianetta know this little car was the most wonderful car in the world? Did she know he thought this was the only one of its kind that had ever been fitted with bench seats— designed so two people could have a picnic in the car if it was raining? Why, only two weeks ago he and Philippe had eaten a picnic while watching a storm over the sea, and they'd seen dolphins. And now the bench seat meant there was room for the three of them. How about that for perfect? And it was red. Didn't Jenny think red was great?

'I like pink,' Jenny said, and Ramón looked as if she'd just committed blasphemy.

'You'd have me buy a pink car?'

'No, that'd be a waste. You could spray paint this one,' she retorted, and chuckled at their combined manly horror.

Philippe didn't contribute a word but she saw him gradually relax, responding to their banter, realizing that nothing was expected of him but that he relax and enjoy himself.

And he did enjoy himself. They arrived at the beach and Ramón had him in the water in minutes.

Jenny was slower. Señor Rodriguez had told her they often went swimming so she'd worn her bikini under her jeans, but for now she was content to paddle and watch.

The beach was glorious, a tiny cove with sun-bleached sand, gentle waves and shallow turquoise water. There were no buildings, no people and the mountains rose straight from the sea like sentinels guarding their privacy.

There'd be bodyguards. She'd been vaguely aware of cars ahead and behind them all day and shadowy figures at the farmhouse, but as they'd arrived at the beach the security presence was nowhere to be seen. The guards must be under orders to give the illusion of total privacy, she thought, and that was what they had.

Ramón had set this time up for Philippe. For a little cousin he was not beholden to in any way. A little boy who'd be miserable at the palace?

She paddled on, casually kicking water out in front of her, pretending she wasn't watching.

She was definitely watching.

Ramón was teaching Philippe to float. The little boy was listening with all the seriousness in the world. He was aching to do what his big cousin was asking of him. His body language said he'd almost die for his big cousin.

'If you float with your face in the water and count to ten, then I'll lift you out of the water,' Ramón was saying. 'My hand will be under your tummy until we reach ten and I'll count aloud. Then I'll lift you high. Do you trust me to do that?'

He received a solemn nod.

'Right,' Ramón said and Philippe leaned forward, leaned further so he was floating on Ramón's hand. And put his face in the water.

'One, two three…ten!' and the little boy was lifted high and hugged.

'Did you feel my hand fall away before I lifted you up? You floated? Hey, Gianetta, Philippe floated!' Ramón was spinning Philippe around and around until he squealed. His squeal was almost the first natural sound she'd heard from him. It was a squeal of delight, of joy, of life.

Philippe was just a little bit older than Matty would be right now. Ramón had worried about it. She'd dismissed his worry but now, suddenly, the knowledge hit her so hard that she flinched. She was watching a little boy learn to swim, and her Matty never would. Everything inside her seemed to shrink. Pain surged back, as it had surged over and over since she'd lost her little son.

But something about this time made it different. Something told her it must be different. So for once, somehow, she let the pain envelop her, not trying to deflect it, simply riding it out, letting it take her where it would. Trying to see, if she allowed it to take its course, whether it would destroy her or whether finally she could come out on the other side.

She was looking at a man holding a little boy who wasn't

Matty—a little boy who against all the odds, she was starting to care about.

The heart swells to fit all comers.

It was a cliché. She'd never believed it. Back at the hospital, watching Matty fade, she'd looked at other children who'd come in ill, recovered then gone out again to face the world and she'd felt…nothing. It had been as if other children were on some parallel universe to the one she inhabited. There was no point of contact.

But suddenly, unbidden, those universes seemed to have collided. For a moment she thought the pain could make her head explode—and then she knew it wouldn't.

Matty. Philippe. Two little boys. Did loving Matty stop her feeling Philippe's pain?

Did loss preclude loving?

How could it?

She gazed out over the water, at this big man with the responsibilities of the world on his shoulders, and at this little boy whose world had been taken away from him.

She knew how many cares were pressing in on Ramón right now. He'd taken this day out, not for himself, but because he'd made a promise to Philippe. Every week, he'd come. Affairs of State were vital, but this, he'd decreed, was more so.

She thought fleetingly of the man who'd fathered Matty, who'd sailed away and missed his whole short life.

Philippe wasn't Ramón's son. He was the illegitimate child of a cousin he'd barely known and yet…and yet…

She was blinking back tears, struggling to take in the surge of emotions flooding through her, but slowly the knot of pain within was easing its grip, letting her see what lay past its vicious hold.

Ramón had lost his family and he'd been a loner ever since, but now he was being asked to take on the cares of this country and the care of this little boy. This country depended on him. Philippe depended on him. But for him to do it alone…

Class barriers were just that, she thought. Grief was another barrier—and barriers could be smashed.

Could she face them all down?

Would Ramón want her to?

And if she did face them down for Ramón's sake, and for hers, she thought, for her thoughts were flowing in all sorts of tangents that hardly made sense, could she love Philippe as well? Could the knot of pain she'd held within since Matty's death be untied, maybe used to embrace instead of to exclude?

Her vision was blurred with tears and it was growing more blurred by the second. Ramón looked across at her and waved, as if to say, *what's keeping you; come in and join us.* She waved back and turned her back on them, supposedly to walk up the beach and strip off her outer clothes. In reality it was to get her face in order—and to figure if she had the courage to put it to the test.

Maybe they didn't want her. Maybe her instinctive feelings for Philippe were wrong, and maybe what Ramón was feeling for her stemmed from nothing more than a casual affair. Her heart told her it was much more, but then her heart was a fickle thing.

No matter. If she was mistaken she could walk away—but first she could try.

And Matty…

Surely loving again could never be a betrayal.

This was crazy, she told herself as she slipped off her clothes and tried to get her thoughts in order. She was thinking way ahead of what was really happening. She was imagining things that could never be.

Should she back off?

But then she glanced back at the two males in the shallows and she felt so proprietorial that it threatened to overwhelm her. My two men, she thought mistily, or they could be. Maybe they could be.

The country can have what it needs from Ramón but I'm lining up for my share, she told herself fiercely. If I have the courage. And maybe the shadows of Matty can be settled, warmed, even honoured by another love.

She sniffed and sniffed again, found a tissue in her bag, blew her nose and decided her face was in order as much as she could make it. She wriggled her bare toes in the sand and wriggled them again. If she dived straight into the waves and swam a bit to start with, she might even look respectable before she reached them.

And if she didn't…

Warts and all, she thought. That was what she was offering.

For they all had baggage, she decided, as she headed for the water. Her grief for Matty was still raw and real. This must inevitably still hurt.

And Ramón? He was an unknown, he was Crown Prince of Cepheus to her Jenny.

She was risking rejection, and everything that went with it.

Consuela said she had courage. Maybe Consuela was wrong.

'Maybe I'm just pig-headed stubborn,' she muttered to herself, heading into the shallows. 'Maybe I'm reading this all wrong and he doesn't want me and Philippe doesn't need me and today is all I have left of the pair of them.'

'So get in the water and get on with it,' she told herself.

'And if I'm right?'

'Then maybe serenity's not the way to go,' she muttered. 'Maybe the opposite's what's needed. Oh, but to fight for a prince…'

Maybe she would. For a prince's happiness.

And for the happiness of one small boy who wasn't Matty.

They swam, they ate a palace-prepared picnic on the sand and then they took a sleepy Philippe back to the farmhouse. Once again they drove in silence. What was between them seemed too complicated for words.

Dared she?

By the time they reached the farm, Philippe was asleep but,

as Ramón lifted him from the car, he jerked awake, then sobbed and clung. Shaken, Ramón carried him into the house, while Jenny stared straight ahead and wondered whether she could be brave enough.

It was like staring into the night sky, overwhelmed by what she couldn't see as much as what she could see. The concept of serenity seemed ridiculous now. This was facing her demons, fighting for what she believed in, fighting for what she knew was right.

Dared she?

Two minutes later Ramón was back. He slid behind the wheel, still without a word, and sat, grim-faced and silent.

Now or never. Jenny took a deep breath, reached over and put her hand over his.

'He loves you,' she whispered.

He stared down at their linked hands and his mouth tightened into a grim line of denial. 'He can't. If it's going to upset him then I should stop coming.'

'Do you want to stop?'

'No.'

'Then why not take him back to the palace? Why not take him home?'

There was a moment's silence. Then, 'What, take him back to the palace and wedge him into a few moments a day between my appointments? And the rest of the time?'

'Leave him with people who love him.'

'Like…'

'Like Consuela and Ernesto.' Then, at the look on his face, she pressed his hand tighter. 'Ramón, you're taking all of this on as it is. Why not take it as it could be?'

'I don't know what you mean.'

'Just try,' she said, figuring it out as she went. 'Try for change. You say the palace is a dreadful place to live. So it is, but the servants are terrified of your title. They won't let you close because they're afraid. The place isn't a home, it's a mausoleum. Oh, it's a gorgeous mausoleum but it's a mausoleum for all that. But it could change. People like Consuela and Ernesto could change it.'

'Or be swallowed by it.'

'There's no need to be melodramatic. You could just invite them to stay for a couple of days to start with. Tell Philippe that his home is here—make that clear so he won't get distraught if...*when* he has to return. You can see how it goes. You won't be throwing him back anywhere.'

'I won't make him sleep in those rooms.'

And there it was, out in the open, raw and dreadful as it had been all those years ago. And, even worse, Jenny was looking at him as if she understood.

And maybe she did.

'You were alone,' she whispered. ' Your father brought you to the palace and he was killed and you were alone.'

'It's nothing.'

'It's everything. Of course it is. But this is now, Ramón. This is Philippe. As it's not Matty, it's also not you. Philippe won't be alone.'

'This is nonsense,' he said roughly, trying to recover some sort of footing. 'It's impossible. Sofía saw that even before I arrived. Philippe's illegitimate. The country would shun him.'

'They'd love him, given half a chance.'

'How do you know?' he snapped. 'He was there for over four years and no one cared.'

'Maybe no one had a chance. The maid I talked to this morning said no one was permitted near except the nursery staff, and Philippe's mother was constantly changing the people who worked with him. He's better off here if no one loves him at the palace, of course he is. But you could change that.' She hesitated. 'Ramón, I'm thinking you already have.'

He shook his head, shaking off demons. 'This is nonsense. I won't risk *this*.'

'This?'

'You know what I mean.' His face grew even more strained. 'Gianetta...'

'Yes?'

'I hate it,' he said explosively. 'The paparazzi almost mobbed you yesterday. The threat from Carlos… How can anyone live in that sort of environment? How could you?'

Her world stilled. Her heart seemed to forget to beat. *How could you?* They were no longer talking about Philippe, then. 'Am I…am I being invited?' she managed.

'No!' There was a long silence, loaded with so many undercurrents she couldn't begin to figure them out. Through the silence Ramón held the steering wheel, his knuckles clenched white. Fighting demons she could hardly fathom.

'We need to get back,' he said at last.

'Of course we do,' she said softly, but she knew this man now. Maybe two weeks of living together was too soon to judge someone—or maybe not. Maybe she'd judged him the first time she'd seen him. Okay, she hardly understood his demons, but demons there were and, prince or not, maybe the leap had to be hers.

'You know that I love you,' she said gently into the warm breeze, but his expression became even more grim.

'Don't.'

'Don't say what I feel?'

'You don't want this life.'

'I like tiaras,' she ventured, trying desperately for lightness. 'And caviar and French champagne. At least,' she added honestly, 'I haven't tasted caviar yet, but I'm sure I'll like it. And if I don't, I'm very good at faking.'

'Jenny, don't make this any harder than it has to be,' he snapped, refusing to be deflected by humour. 'I was a fool to bring you to Cepheus. I will not drag you into this royal life.'

'You don't have to drag me anywhere. I choose where to go. All you need to do is ask.'

'Just leave it. You don't know… The paparazzi yesterday was just a taste. Right now you're seeing the romance, the fairy tale. You'll wake in a year's time and find nothing but a cage.'

'You don't think you might be overreacting?' she ventured. 'Not everyone at the Coronation ball looked like they've been locked up all their lives. Surely caviar can't be that bad.'

But he wasn't listening. 'You're my beautiful Jenny,' he said. 'You're wild and free, and I won't mess with who you are. You'll always be my Jenny, and I'll hold you in my heart for ever. From a distance.'

'From how big a distance? From a photo in a frame?' she demanded, indignant. 'That sounds appalling. Or, better still, do you mean as your mistress on your island?'

He stared at her as if she'd grown two heads. 'What the…?'

'That's what Sofía said we should do.'

'I do not want you as my mistress,' he said through gritted teeth.

'So you don't want me?' His anger was building, and she thought *good*. An angry Ramón might just lose control, and control had gone on long enough. She wanted him to take her into his arms. In truth she wanted him to take her any way he wanted, but he was fighting his anger, hauling himself back from the brink.

'I want you more than life itself, but I will not take you.' He took a deep ragged breath. 'I could never keep you safe.'

'Well, that's nonsense. I know karate,' she retorted. 'I can duck and I can run and I can even punch and scratch and yell if I need to. Not that I'll need to. Perpetua says Carlos is all bluster.'

'Perpetua…'

'Is a very nice lady with an oaf for a husband and with very old-fashioned ideas about royal wives shutting up. Ideas that I don't believe for one minute. You'll never see me shutting up.'

'It doesn't matter,' he said, exasperated. 'I want you free.'

'Free?' She was fighting on all fronts now, knowing only that she was fully exposed and she had no defence. All she had was her love for this man. 'Like our whale?' she demanded. 'That's just perspective. Our whale's free now to swim to Antarctica, but she has to stop there and turn around.

A minnow can feel free in an aquarium if it's a beautiful aquarium.'

She hesitated then, seeing the tension on his face stretched almost to breaking point. She'd gone far enough. 'Ramón, let's not take this further,' she said gently. 'What's between us…let's leave it for now. Let's just think of Philippe. Is his room still as it was at the palace?'

'No one's touched the nursery.'

'So you could go in right now and say, *Philippe, what about coming back to the palace for a night or two?* Tell him maybe if it works out he could come for two nights every week. See how it goes.'

'Jenny…'

'Okay, maybe it is impossible,' she said. 'This is not my life and it's not my little cousin. But you know him now, Ramón, and maybe things have changed. All I know is that Philippe's breaking his heart in there, and if he returned to the palace there's no way he'd be alone. Consuela is looking out the window and I wouldn't mind betting she knows exactly what we're talking about. She's bursting to visit the palace, even if she's scared, and if you raise one finger to beckon she'll have bags packed and Bebe in his cat crate and you can still reach your three o'clock appointment. And, before you start raising quibbles like who'll look after their alpacas, you're the prince, surely you can employ half this district to look after this farm. So decide,' she said bluntly. 'You've been making life and death decisions about this country. Now it's time to make one about your family.'

'Philippe's not my family.'

'Is he not? It might have started with sympathy, Ramón Cavellero, but it's not sympathy that's tugging him to you now. Is it?'

'I don't do…love.'

'You already have. Just take the next step. All it needs is courage.' She hesitated. 'Ramón, I know how it hurts to love and to lose. You've loved and you've lost, but Philippe is going right on loving.'

'He can't,' he said but he was looking at the window where Consuela was indeed peeping through a chink in the curtains.

And then he was looking at Jenny—Gianetta—who knew which?—and she was looking back at him with faith. Faith that he could take this new step.

'*You* can,' she said.

'Gianetta,' he said and would have taken her into his arms right then, part in exasperation, part in anger—and there were a whole lot more parts in there besides, but she held up her hands in a gesture of defence.

'Not me. Not now. This is you and Philippe. Do you want him or not?'

He looked at her for a long moment. He glanced back at the farmhouse, and Philippe was at the window now, as well as Consuela.

And there was only one answer to give.

So, half an hour later—Ramón would be late for his meeting but not much—his little red Boxster finally left the farmhouse, with Philippe once again snuggled between Ramón and Jenny. There was a cat crate at Jenny's feet. The Boxster was definitely crowded.

Behind them, Consuela and Ernesto drove their farm truck, packed with enough luggage to last them for two days.

Or more, Jenny thought with satisfaction. There were four big suitcases on the back. For all she talked of class differences, Consuela seemed more than prepared to take a leap into the unknown.

If only Ramón could join her.

CHAPTER ELEVEN

THE moment he swung back into the palace grounds affairs of State took over again. Ramón couldn't stay to watch Philippe's reaction to being back at the palace. He couldn't stay to see that Consuela and Ernesto were treated right.

He couldn't stay with Jenny.

'We can do this. Go,' Jenny told him and he had no choice. He went, to meeting upon interminable meeting. Once again he was forced to work until the small hours.

Finally, exhausted beyond belief, he made his way through the palace corridors towards his personal chambers. Once again he passed Jenny's door—and he didn't knock.

But then he reached the nursery. To his surprise, Manuel was standing outside the door, at attention. The footmen were posted at the top of the stairs. Had a change been ordered? But Manuel spoke before he could ask.

'I'm not permitted to move,' the man said, and it was as if a statue had come to life. 'But the little boy and Señorina Bertin... I thought you wouldn't wish them harm so I took it upon myself to stay here.'

'Good idea.' He hesitated, taking in the full context of what the man had said. Reaching the crux. 'Señorina Bertin's in there?'

'Yes, sir,' Manuel said and he opened the nursery door before Ramón could say he hadn't meant to go in; he was only passing.

Only of course he had meant to go in. Just to check.

Manuel closed the door after him. The room was in darkness but the moon was full, the curtains weren't drawn and he could see the outline of the bed against the windows. It was a truly vast bed for a small child. A ridiculous bed.

He moved silently across the room and looked down—and there were two mounds in the bed. A child-sized one, with a cat-shaped bump over his feet, and a Jenny-shaped one, and the Jenny-shaped one spoke.

'You're not a Hun?' she whispered, and he blinked.

'Pardon?'

'Manuel's saving us from the Huns. I thought you might have overpowered him and be about to…plunder and pillage. I'm very glad you're not.'

'I'm glad I'm not a Hun either,' he said and smiled down at her, and he could feel her smile back, even if he couldn't quite see it. 'What are you doing here?'

'Shh. He's only just gone back to sleep.'

He tugged a chair forward and sat, then leaned forward so he was inches away from Jenny's face. Philippe was separated from them by Jenny's body but he could see that her arm was around him. The sight made him feel…made him feel…

No. There were no words to describe it.

'This is Consuela's job,' he managed.

'She was here until midnight. The staff put Consuela and Ernesto into one of the state apartments, and it's so grand it's made Ernesto quiver. Ernesto seems more frightened than Philippe so I said I'd stay.'

She said she'd stay. With a little boy who was the same age as her Matty. In this room that he'd once slept in. He looked at her, at the way Philippe's body was curved against hers, at the way she was holding him, and he felt things slither and change within him. Knots that had been around his heart for ever slipped away, undone, free.

'Gianetta…' he whispered and placed his fingers on her lips, wondering. If she'd found the courage to do this…

'Shh,' she said again. 'He woke and he was a little upset. I don't want him to wake again.'

'But you soothed him.'

'I told him the story of the whale. He loved it. I told him about his cousin, the hero, saviour of whales. Saviour of this country. We both thought it was pretty cool.'

'Gianetta…'

'Jenny. Your employee. And Manuel is out there.'

'Manuel can go…'

'Manuel can't go,' she said seriously. 'Neither of us is sure where to take this. You need to sleep, Ramón.'

'I want…'

'I know,' she said softly and she placed a finger on his lips in turn. 'We both want. I can feel it, and it's wonderful. But there's things to think about for both of us. For now… Give me my self-respect and go to your own bedroom tonight.' She smiled at him then and he was close enough to see a lovely loving smile that made his heart turn over. 'Besides,' she said. 'Tonight I'm sleeping with Philippe. One man a night, my love. I have my reputation to think of.'

'He's not Matty,' he said before he could stop himself.

'Philippe's not Matty, no.'

'But… Jenny, doesn't that tear you in two?'

'I thought it would,' she said on a note of wonder. 'But now… He fits exactly under my arm. He's not Matty but it's as if Matty has made a place for him. It feels right.'

'Jenny…'

'Go to bed, Ramón,' she said simply. 'We all have a lot of thinking to do this night.'

He left and she was alone in the dark with a sleeping child. She'd given her heart, she thought. She'd given it to both of them, just like that.

What if they didn't want it?

It was theirs, she thought, like it or not.

Bebe stirred and wriggled and padded his way up the bed

to check she was still breathing, that she'd still react if he kneaded his paws on the bedcover.

'Okay, I can learn to love you, too,' she told the little cat. 'As long as your claws don't get all the way through the quilt.' Satisfied, Bebe slumped down on the coverlet across her breast and went back to sleep, leaving her with her thoughts.

'They have to want me,' she whispered in the dark. 'Oh, they have to want me or I'm in such big trouble.'

And in the royal bedchamber, the apartment of the Crown Prince of Cepheus, there was no sleep at all.

Once upon a time a child had slept alone in this palace and known terror. Now the man lay alone in his palace and knew peace.

He woke and he knew, but he couldn't do a thing about it.

It'd take him a week, Señor Rodriguez told him, this signing, signing and more signing. He had to formally accept the role of Crown Prince before he could begin to delegate, so from dawn his time was not his own.

'I need two hours this afternoon,' he growled to his lawyer as he saw his packed diary. 'You've scheduled me an hour for lunch. Take fifteen minutes from each delegation; that gives me another hour, so between one and three is mine.'

'I've already started organising it,' his lawyer told him. 'We all want you to have time with the child.'

'All?'

'I believe the staff have been missing him,' the lawyer said primly. 'It seems there are undercurrents neither the Princess Sofía nor I guessed.'

He didn't say more, but they agreed a message would be sent to Jenny and to Philippe that he'd spend the early afternoon with them. Then Ramón put his head down and worked.

He finished just before one. He'd have finished earlier only someone dared ask a question. Was he aware there were up to fifty students in each class in the local schools, and didn't he agree this was so urgent it had to be remedied right now?

He did agree. How could he put his own desire to be with Jenny and Philippe before the welfare of so many other children? Señor Rodriguez disappeared, leaving Ramón to listen and think and agree to meet about the issue again tomorrow. Finally he was free to walk out, to find the where-abouts of Philippe…and of Jenny.

'They're by the pool, Your Highness.' It was the maid who normally brought in his coffee and, to his astonishment, she smiled as she bobbed her normal curtsy. 'It's so good to have him back sir. There's refreshments being served now. If you'd like to have your lunch with them…'

Bemused, he strolled out the vast palace doors into the gardens overlooking the sea.

There was a party happening by the pool, and the perfec-tion of the scene before him was marred. Or not marred, he corrected himself. Just changed.

The landscape to the sea had been moulded to create a series of rock pools and waterfalls tumbling down towards the sea. Shade umbrellas and luxurious cream beach loungers were discreetly placed among semi-tropical foliage, blending unobtrusively into the magical garden setting.

Now, however… At the biggest rock pool chairs and tables had been hauled forward to make a circle. There were balloons attached around every umbrella. This wasn't tasteful at all, he thought with wry amusement. The balloons were all colours and sizes, as though some had been blown up by men with good lungs, and some had been blown up by a five-year-old. They were attached to the umbrellas by red ribbons, with vast crimson bows under each bunch.

And there were sea dragons floating in the rock pool. Huge plastic sea dragons, red, green and pink, with sparkly tiaras. Sea dragons with tiaras? What on earth…?

Jenny was in the water, and so was Philippe and so was…Sofía? They were on a sea dragon apiece, kicking their way across the water, seemingly racing. Sofía was wearing neck to knee swimmers and she was winning, whooping her elderly lungs out with excitement.

There was more, he thought, stunned. Señor Rodriguez was sitting by the edge of the pool, wearing shorts, his skinny frame a testament to a life spent at his desk. He was cheering Sofía at full roar. As were Consuela and Ernesto, yelling their lungs out for their foster son. 'Go, Philippe, go!'

There were also servants, all in their ridiculous uniforms, but each of them was yelling as loudly as everyone else. And another woman was cheering too, a woman who looked vaguely familiar. And then he recognised her. Perpetua. Carlos's wife! What the…?

He didn't have time to take it all in. Sofía reached the wall by a full length of sea dragon. Philippe came second and Jenny fell off her dragon from laughing.

It felt crazy. It was a palace transformed into something else entirely. He watched as Philippe turned anxiously to find Jenny. She surfaced, still laughing, she hugged him and his heart twisted and he forgot about everything, everyone else.

She saw him. She waved and then staggered—holding Philippe with one arm was a skill yet to be mastered. 'Welcome to our pool party, Your Highness,' she called. 'Have you come to try our sausage rolls?'

'Sausage rolls,' he said faintly, and looked at the table where there was enough food for a small army.

'Your chefs have never heard of sausage rolls,' she said, clambering up the pool steps with Philippe in her arms and grinning as Sofía staggered out as well, still clutching her sea dragon. 'Philippe and I had to teach them. And we have fairy bread and lamingtons, and tacos and tortillas and strawberries and éclairs—and I love this place. Philippe does too, don't you Philippe? We've decided it's the best place to visit in the world.'

Visit. He stood and watched as woman and child disappeared under vast towels and he thought…*visit*.

'Oh, and we invited Perpetua,' Jenny said from under her towel, motioning in the general direction of the pallid little lady standing uncertainly under the nearest umbrella.

Perpetua gave him a shy, scared smile. 'You know Carlos's wife? And Carlos, too.'

'And Carlos, too?' he demanded. Perpetua's smile slipped. 'I told him to come,' she whispered. 'When Gianetta invited us. He said he would. He just has to…he's been making silly threats that he doesn't mean. He wants to apologise.' Her voice was almost pleading. 'He'd never hurt…'

And maybe he wouldn't, Ramón thought. For Carlos was approaching them now, escorted by palace footmen. The footmen were walking really close. Really close.

'He's not going to hurt anyone,' Perpetua whispered. 'He's just been silly. I was so pleased when Gianetta rang. He needs a chance to explain.'

'Explain what?' Ramón said and Perpetua fell silent, waiting for Carlos himself to answer.

Ramón's gaze flew to Jenny. She met his gaze full on. She'd set this up, he thought.

One of the maids had taken over rubbing Philippe dry. The maid was laughing and scolding, making Philippe smile back. She was a servant he'd thought lacked emotion.

Had the servants turned to ice through mistreatment and fear?

What else had fear done?

He looked again at Carlos, a big, stupid man who for a few short weeks, while Ramón couldn't be found, had thought the throne was his. For the dream to be snatched away must have shattered his world.

Maybe stupid threats could be treated as they deserved, Ramón thought, feeling suddenly extraordinarily light-headed. And if threats weren't there…

'We invited both Carlos and Perpetua,' Jenny was saying. 'Because of Philippe. Philippe says Perpetua's always been nice to him.'

'He's a sweetheart,' Perpetua said stoutly, becoming braver. 'I worried about him whenever I stayed here.'

'You used to stay in the palace?' Ramón asked, surprised again. What had Señor Rodriguez told him? Perpetua was a nice enough woman, intelligent, trained as a grade school teacher, but always made to feel inferior to Carlos's royal relatives.

'A lot,' Perpetua said, becoming braver. 'Carlos liked being here. Philippe and I became friends, didn't we, sweetheart. But then Carlos said some silly things.' Her gaze met her husband's. 'I used to believe…well, I'm a royal wife and a royal wife stays silent. But Gianetta says that's ridiculous. So I'm not staying silent any longer. You're sorry, aren't you, dear?'

Was he? Ramón watched Carlos, sweating slightly in a suit that was a bit too tight, struggling to come to terms with this new order, and he even felt a bit sorry for him.

'I shouldn't have said it,' Carlos managed.

'You said you'd kill…'

'You know how it is.' Carlos was almost pleading. 'I mean…heat of the moment. I was only saying…you know, wild stuff. What I'd do if you didn't look after the country… that sort of thing. It got blown up. You didn't take it seriously. Please tell me you didn't take it seriously.'

Was that it? Ramón thought, relief running through him in waves. History had created fear—not fear for himself but fear for family. His family.

A family he could now build. In time…

And with that thought came another. He wasn't alone.

Delegation. Why not start now?

'Perpetua, you used to be a grade teacher,' he said, speaking slowly but thinking fast, thinking back to the meeting he'd just attended. 'Do you know the conditions in our schools?'

'Of course I do,' Perpetua said, confused. 'I mean, I haven't taught for twenty years—Carlos doesn't like me to—but I have friends who are still teachers. They have such a hard time…'

'Tomorrow morning I'm meeting with a deputation to see what can be done about the overcrowding in our classrooms,' he said. 'Would you like to join us?'

'Me?' she gasped.

'I need help,' he said simply. 'And Carlos… How can you help?'

There was stunned silence. Even Philippe, who was wrapped in a towel and was now wrapping himself around a sausage roll stopped mid-bite and stared. This man who'd made blustering threats to kill…

How can you help?

Jenny moved then, inconspicuously slipping to his side. She stood close and she took his hand, as if she realized just how big it was. Just how important this request was.

Defusing threats to create a future.

Refusing to stand alone for one moment longer.

'I can't…' Carlos managed at last. 'There's nothing.'

'Yes, dear, there is.' Perpetua had found her voice, and she, too, slipped to stand beside her man. 'Sports. Carlos loves them, loves watching them, but there's never been enough money to train our teenagers. And the football stadium's falling down.'

'You like football?' Ramón asked.

'Football,' Philippe said, lighting up.

'I…'

'You could give me reports on sports facilities,' Ramón said, thinking fast, trying to figure out something meaningful that the man could do. 'Tell me what needs to be done. Put in your recommendations. I don't know this country. You do. I need help on the ground. So what do we have here? Assistant to the Crown for Education. Assistant to the Crown for Sport.'

'And I'll be Assistant to the Crown for New Uniforms for The Staff,' Sofía said happily. 'I'd like to help with that.'

'I can help with floating,' Philippe said gamely. 'But can I help with football, too?'

'And Gianetta?' Perpetua said, looking anxious. 'What about Jenny?'

'I need to figure that out,' Ramón said softly, holding his love close, his world suddenly settling in a way that was leaving him stunned. 'In private.'

Philippe had finished his sausage roll now, and he carried the loaded tray over to his big cousin.

'Would you like to eat one?' he asked. 'And then will you teach me to float some more?'

'Of course I will,' he said. 'On one condition.'

Philippe looked confused, as well he might.

No matter. Sometimes a prince simply had to allocate priorities, and this was definitely that time. He tugged Jenny tighter, then, audience or not, he pulled her into his arms and gave her a swift possessive kiss. It was a kiss that said he was pushed for time. He knew he couldn't take this further, not here, not now, but there was more where that came from.

'My condition to you all,' he said softly, kissing her once more, a long lingering kiss that said, pushed for time or not, this was what he wanted most in the world, 'is that Señor Rodriguez changes my diary. This night is mine.'

The car came to collect her just before sunset. She was dressed again as Gianetta, in a long diaphanous dress made of the finest layers of silk and chiffon with the diamonds at her throat. Two maids and Sofía and Consuela and Perpetua had clucked over her to distraction. Sofía had added a diamond bracelet of her own, and had wept a little.

'Oh, my dear, you're so beautiful,' she'd said mistily. 'Do you think he'll propose?'

Jenny hadn't answered. She couldn't. She was torn between laughter and tears.

Ramón's kisses had promised everything, but nothing had been said. Mistress to a Crown Prince? Wife?

Dared she think wife?

How could she think anything? After a fast floating lesson Ramón had been swept away yet again on his interminable business and she'd been left only with his demand.

'A car will come for you at seven. Be ready.'

She was ready, but she was daring to think nothing.

Finally, at seven the car came and Señor Rodriguez handed her into the limousine with care and with pride. The reverberations from this afternoon were being felt all around the country, and the lawyer couldn't stop smiling.

'Where's Ramón?' she managed.

'Waiting for you,' the lawyer said, sounding inscrutable until he added, 'How could any man not?'

So she was driven in state, alone, with only a chauffeur for company. The great white limousine was driven slowly through the city, out along the coast road, up onto a distant headland where it drew to a halt.

Two uniformed footmen met her, Manuel and Luis, trying desperately to be straight-faced. There was a footpath leading from where the car pulled in to park, winding through a narrow section of overgrown cliff. Manuel and Luis led her silently along the path, emerged into a clearing, then slipped silently back into the shadows. Leaving her to face what was before her.

And what was before her made her gasp. A headland looking out all over the moonlit Mediterranean. A table for two. Crisp white linen. Two cushioned chairs with high, high backs, draped all in white velvet, each leg fastened with crimson ties.

Silverware, crystal, a candelabrum magnificent enough to take her breath away.

Soft music coming from behind a slight rise. Real music. *There were real musicians somewhere behind the trees.*

Champagne on ice.

And then Ramón stepped from the shadows, Ramón in full ceremonial, Ramón looking more handsome than any man she'd met.

The sound of frogs came from beneath the music behind him. Her frog prince?

'If I kiss you, will you join your friends, the frogs?' she whispered before she could help herself and he laughed and came towards her and took her hands in his.

'No kissing,' he said tenderly. 'Not yet.'

'What…?' She could barely speak. 'What are we waiting for?'

'This,' he said and went down on bended knee.

She closed her eyes. This couldn't be happening.

This was happening.

'This should wait until after dinner,' he said softly, 'but it's been burning a hole in my pocket for three hours now.' And, without more words, he lifted a crimson velvet box and held it open. A diamond ring lay in solitary splendour, a diamond so wonderful…so amazing…

'Is it real?' she gasped and he chuckled.

'That's Jenny speaking. I think we need Gianetta to give us the right sense of decorum.'

Gianetta. She took a deep breath and fought for composure. She could do this.

'Sire, you do me honour.'

'That's more like it,' he said and his dark eyes gleamed with love and with laughter. 'So, Gianetta, Jenny, my love, my sailor, my cook extraordinaire, my heart…I give you my love. The past has made us solitary, but it's up to both of us to move forward. To leave solitude and pain behind. You've shown me courage, and I trust that I can match it. So Gianetta, my dearest love, if I promise to love you, cherish you, honour you, for as long as we both shall live, will you do me the honour of taking my hand in marriage?'

She looked down into his loving eyes. Then she paused for a moment, taking time to gaze around her, at the night, at the stars, the accoutrements of royalty, at the lights of Cepheus glowing around them. Knowing also there was a little boy waiting as well.

Her family. Her love, starting now.

'I believe I will,' she said gently and, before he could respond, she dropped to her own knees and she took his hands in hers.

'Yes, my love and my prince, I believe I will.'

THE DIMITRAKOS
PROPOSITION

LYNNE GRAHAM

CHAPTER ONE

'BEARING IN MIND the history of the company's expansion and success, it *is* a most unjust will,' Stevos Vannou, Ash's lawyer, declared heavily in the simmering silence, a wary eye locked to the very tall, dark and powerfully built male across the office.

Acheron Dimitrakos, known as Ash to his inner circle, and Greek billionaire founder of the global giant DT Industries, said nothing. He did not trust himself to speak. Usually his control was absolute. But not today. He had trusted his father, Angelos, as far as he trusted anyone, which was to say *not* very much, but it had never once crossed his mind that the older man would even consider threatening the company that Ash had single-handedly built with the bombshell that his last will and testament had become. If Ash didn't marry within the year, he would lose half of the company to his stepmother and her children, who were already most amply provided for by the terms of his father's will. It was unthinkable; it was a brutally unfair demand, which ran contrary to every honourable scruple and the high standards that Ash had once believed the older man held dear to his heart. It just went to show—as if Ash had ever had any doubt—you couldn't trust anybody, and your nearest and dearest were the most likely to plunge a knife into your back when you were least expecting it.

'DT is *my* company,' Ash asserted between compressed lips.

'But regretfully not on paper,' Stevos countered gravely. 'On paper you never had your father transfer his interest to you. Even though it is indisputably the company that *you* built.'

Still, Ash said nothing. Cold dark eyes fringed with ridiculously long black lashes locked on the sweeping view of the City of London skyline that his penthouse office enjoyed, his lean, darkly handsome features set in hard, forbidding lines of restraint. 'A long court case disputing the will would seriously undermine the company's ability to trade,' he said eventually.

'Picking a wife would definitely be the lesser evil,' the lawyer suggested with a cynical chuckle. 'That's all you have to do to put everything back to normal.'

'My father knew I had no intention of ever marrying. That is exactly why he did this to me,' Ash ground out between clenched teeth, his temper momentarily escaping its leash as he thought of the utterly unhinged woman his misguided father had expected him to put in the role. 'I don't want a wife. I don't want children. I don't want *any* of that messing up my life!'

Stevos Vannou cleared his throat and treated his employer to a troubled appraisal. He had never seen Acheron Dimitrakos betray anger before or, indeed, any kind of emotion. The billionaire head of DT Industries was usually as cold as ice, possibly even colder, if his discarded lovers in the many tabloid stories were to be believed. His cool, logical approach, his reserve and lack of human sentiment were the stuff of legend. According to popular repute when one of his PAs had gone into labour at a board summit, he had told her to stay and finish the meeting.

'Forgive me if I'm being obtuse but I would suggest that any number of women would line up to marry you,' Ash's companion remarked cautiously, thinking of his own wife, who threatened to swoon if she even saw Acheron's face in print. 'Choosing would be more of a challenge than actually finding a wife.'

Ash clamped his mouth shut on an acid rejoinder, well aware the portly little Greek was out of his depth and only trying to be helpful even if stating the obvious was more than a little simplistic. He knew he could snap his fingers and get a wife as quickly and easily as he could get a woman into his bed. And he understood exactly why it was *so* easy: the money was the draw. He had a fleet of private jets and homes all over the world, not to mention servants who waited on him and his guests hand and foot. He paid well for good service. He was a generous lover too but every time he saw dollar signs in a woman's eyes it turned him off hard and fast. And more and more he noticed the dollar signs *before* he noticed the beautiful body and that was taking sex off the menu more often than he liked. He needed sex as he needed air to breathe, and couldn't really comprehend why he found the greed and manipulation that went with it so profoundly repellent. Evidently somewhere down inside him, buried so deep he couldn't root it out, there lurked an oversensitive streak he despised.

It was worse that Acheron knew exactly what lay behind the will and he could only marvel at his father's inability to appreciate that the woman he had tried to push Acheron towards was anathema to him. Six months before the older man's death there had been a big scene at his father's home, and Acheron had steered clear of visiting since then, which was simply one more nail in the coffin of the proposed bride-to-be. He had tried to talk to his stepmother about the problem but nobody had been willing to listen to common sense, least of all his father, who had been sufficiently impressed by the lady's acting ability to decide that the young woman he had raised from childhood would make his only son the perfect wife.

'Of course, perhaps it is possible that you could simply ignore the will and *buy* out your stepmother's interest in the company,' the lawyer suggested glibly.

Unimpressed, Ash shot the older man a sardonic glance. 'I will not pay for what is mine by right. Thank you for your time.'

Recognising the unmistakable note of dismissal, Stevos hastily stood up to leave while resolving to inform his colleagues of the situation immediately to sort out a plan of action. 'I'll put the best business minds in the firm on this challenge.'

Jaw line clenched as hard as a rock, Ash nodded even though he had little hope of a rescue plan. Experience told him that his father would have taken legal advice as well and would never have placed such a binding clause in his will without the assurance that it was virtually foolproof.

A wife, Ash reflected grimly. He had known since childhood that he would never take a wife and never father a child. That caring, loving gene had passed him by. He had no desire for anyone to grow up in his image or follow in his footsteps, nor did he wish to pass on the darkness he kept locked up inside himself. In fact, he didn't even like children, what little contact he had had with them simply bearing out his belief that children were noisy, difficult and annoying. Why would any sane adult want something that had to be looked after twenty-four hours a day and gave you sleepless nights into the bargain? In the same way why would any man want only one woman in his bed? The *same* woman, night after night, week after week. Ash shuddered at the very suggestion of such severe sexual confinement.

He recognised that he had a decision to make and he resolved to act fast before the news of that ridiculous will hit the marketplace and damaged the company he had built his life around.

'Nobody sees Mr Dimitrakos without an appointment *and* his prior agreement,' the svelte receptionist repeated frigidly. 'If you don't leave, Miss Glover, I will be forced to call Security to have you removed from the building.'

In answer, Tabby plonked her slight body back down on the plush seating in the reception area. Across from her sat an older man studying documents from a brief-case and talking urgently in a foreign language on his cell phone. Knowing she looked like hell did nothing for her confidence in such luxurious surroundings but she hadn't had a full night's sleep for some time, she no longer owned any decent clothes and she was desperate. Nothing *less* than desperation would have brought her to DT Industries seeking an interview with the absolute seven-letter-word of a man who had summarily refused to take any responsibility for the child whom Tabby loved with all her heart. Acheron Dimitrakos was a selfish, ar-rogant pig and what she had read about his womanising exploits in one of her clients' glossy scandal-sheet mag-azines had not improved her opinion. The man who had more money than Midas had turned his back on Amber without even expressing a desire to meet with Tabby as his co-guardian, or checking out the little girl's welfare.

The call to Security by Reception was duly made in clear crystalline tones undoubtedly intended to scare

Tabby off before the guards arrived. Her small face stiff, she stayed where she was, her slight body rigid with tension while she frantically tried to think up another plan of approach because gatecrashing Acheron's office wasn't going very well. But it wasn't as if she had had a choice, although she acknowledged that the situation was very serious indeed when such a callous personality became her last hope.

And then fate took a hand she wasn't expecting and she wasted a split second simply staring when she saw the tall dark man from the magazine pictures striding across Reception with a couple of suited men following in his wake. Tabby flew to her feet and raced after him. 'Mr Didmitrakos…Mr Dimitrakos!' she launched, stumbling over the syllables of his wretchedly complicated surname.

And at the exact same moment as her very tall and commanding quarry paused by the lift wearing an expression of sheer disbelief at her approach, the security guards came at a literal run, muttering fervent apologies to the man in front of her!

'I'm Amber's other guardian, Tabby Glover!' Tabby explained in feverish haste as both her arms were suddenly grabbed by the two men with him and she was yanked back a step from her proximity to him. 'I need to see you…I tried to get an appointment but I couldn't even though it's desperately important that we talk before the weekend!'

Security really was in need of sharpening up if they allowed him to be cornered on the top floor of his own building by a crazy woman, Ash reflected in exasperation. The young woman was wearing a worn jacket, track pants and trainers, her fair hair tied up in a high ponytail, pale shadowed face bare of make-up. She was small and plain, not at all the kind of woman who would have attracted his attention…although no sooner had he decided that than he noticed her remarkable blue eyes, which were an unusual violet in shade and dominated her pinched features.

'*Please!*' Tabby gasped. 'You can't be this selfish— nobody could be! Amber's father was a member of your family—'

'I have no family,' Ash informed her drily. 'Escort her out,' he told the security officers, who took over from his bodyguards in restraining Tabby even though she hadn't put up a struggle. 'And make sure this doesn't happen again.'

Taken aback that he wouldn't even give her five minutes of his time, that he betrayed no recognition even of Amber's name, Tabby was momentarily silenced. Then she swore at him like a fishwife, angrily employing language that had never left her lips before. In response, his brilliant dark eyes glittered with a raw angry hostility that momentarily shocked her because that cool front he wore evidently concealed much murkier depths.

'Mr Dimitrakos…?' Another voice interposed, and Tabby turned her head in surprise to see the older man who had been seated near her in the waiting area.

'The child—you'll recall your late cousin's guardianship request, which you turned down a couple of months ago?' Stevos Vannou hurtled forward to remind Acheron Dimitrakos in a quiet, respectful undertone.

An inconsequential memory pinged in the back of Ash's shrewd brain and drew his straight black brows together into a frown. 'What of it?'

'You selfish bastard!' Tabby raked at him, outraged by his lack of reaction and the consequences that his indifference to Amber's fate were about to visit on the child. 'I'll go to the press with this…you don't deserve anything better. All that wretched money and you can't do anything good with it!'

'*Siopi!* Keep quiet,' Acheron told her sternly in Greek and then English.

'And you and whose army is going to make me?' Tabby snapped back, unimpressed, the fighting spirit that had carried her through many years of loss and disappointment rising to the fore again to strengthen her backbone.

'What does she want?' Acheron asked his lawyer in English as if she weren't there.

'I suggest we take this back into your office,' Stevos remarked on a loaded hint.

Savage impatience gripped Ash. Only three days earlier he had returned from his father's funeral and, without even allowing for his grief at the older man's sudden death from a heart attack, it had turned into a very frustrating week. The very last thing he was in the mood for was a drama about some child he had never met and couldn't have cared less about. Troy Valtinos, oh, yes, he could remember now, a third cousin he had also *never* met, who had unexpectedly died and, in doing so, had attempted to commit his infant daughter to Ash's care. An act of sheer inexplicable insanity, Acheron reflected in exasperation, thinking back incredulously to that brief discussion with Stevos some months earlier. He was a childless single male without family back-up and he travelled constantly. What on earth could anyone have supposed he would do with an orphaned baby girl?

'I'm sorry I swore at you,' Tabby lied valiantly in an effort to build a bridge and win a hearing. 'I shouldn't have done that—'

'Your mouth belongs in the gutter,' Acheron breathed

icily and he addressed the security guards, 'Free her. You can take her out when I'm done with her.'

Tabby gritted her teeth together, straightened her jacket and ran uncertain hands down over her slender denim-clad thighs. Ash briefly studied her oval face, his attention lingering on her full pink mouth as a rare flight of sexual fantasy took him to the brink of picturing where else that mouth might be best employed other than in the gutter. The stirring at his groin put him in an even worse mood, reminding him of how long it had been since he had indulged his healthy libido. He knew he had to be in a very bad way if he could react to such an ignorant female.

'I'll give you five minutes of my valuable time,' Acheron breathed with chilling reluctance.

'Five minutes when a child's life and happiness hang in the balance? How very generous of you,' Tabby replied sarcastically.

Roaring rancour assailed Acheron because he wasn't accustomed to such rudeness, particularly not from women. 'You're insolent as well as vulgar.'

'It got me in the door, didn't it? Politeness got me nowhere,' Tabby traded, thinking of the many phone calls she had made in vain requests for an appointment. As for being called cheeky and vulgar, did she really care what some jumped-up, spoilt snob with loads of money thought about her? Yet her brain was already scolding her for her aggressive approach, telling her it was unwise. If she could get around the freeze front Acheron Dimitrakos wore to the world, he was in a position to help Amber while she was not. As far as Social Services were concerned, she could not be considered a suitable guardian for Amber because she was single, had no decent home and was virtually penniless.

'Start talking,' Ash urged, thrusting the door of his office shut.

'I need your help to keep Amber in my custody. I'm the only mother she's ever known and she's very attached to me. Social Services are planning to take her off me on Friday and place her in foster care with a view to having her adopted.'

'Isn't that the best plan in the circumstances?' Ash's lawyer, Stevos Vannou, interposed in a very reasonable voice as though it was an expected thing that she should be willing to surrender the child she loved. 'I seem to remember that you are single and living on benefits and that a child would be a considerable burden for you—'

Acheron had frozen the instant the phrase 'foster care' came his way but neither of his companions had noticed. It was a closely guarded secret that Ash, in spite of the fact his mother had been one of the richest Greek heiresses ever born, had once spent years of his life in foster care, shifted from home to home, family to family, enduring everything from genuine care to indifference to outright cruelty and abuse. And he had never, ever forgotten the experience.

'I haven't lived on benefits since Amber's mother, Sonia, passed away. I looked after Sonia until she died and that was why I couldn't work,' Tabby protested, and shot a glance brimming with offended pride at Acheron's still figure. 'Look, I'm not just some freeloader. A year ago Sonia and I owned our own business and it was thriving until Troy died and she fell ill. In the fallout, I lost everything as well. Amber is the most important thing in my world but, in spite of me being chosen as one of her guardians, there's no blood tie between Amber and me and that gives me very little real claim to her in law.'

'Why have you come to me?' Ash enquired drily.

Tabby rolled her eyes, helplessly inflamed by his attitude. 'Troy thought you were such a great guy—'

Ash tensed, telling himself that none of what she had told him was any of his business, yet the thought of an innocent baby going into foster care roused a riot of reactions inside him drawn from his own memories. 'But I never met Troy.'

'He did *try* to meet you because he said his mother, Olympia, used to work for your mother,' Tabby recounted.

Acheron suddenly frowned, straight black brows pleating as old memories stirred. Olympia Carolis, he recalled very well as having been one of his mother's carers. He had not appreciated when the guardianship issue had arisen that Troy was Olympia's son because he had only known her by her name before marriage, although if he stretched his memory to the limit he could vaguely recall that she had been expecting a child when she left his mother's employ. That child could only have been Troy.

'Troy was frantic to find a job here in London and you were his business idol,' Tabby told him curtly.

'His...*what*?' Ash repeated with derision.

'False flattery won't advance your cause,' Stevos Vannou declared, much more at home in the current meeting than he had been in the last, for the matter of the will would require considerable research of case law to handle.

'It wasn't false or flattery,' Tabby contradicted sharply, angry with the solicitor for taking that attitude and switching her attention back to Ash. 'It was the truth. Troy admired your business achievements very much. He even took the same business degree you did. That and the fact he saw you as head of his family explains why he put you down as a guardian in his will.'

'And there was I, innocent that I am, thinking it was

only because I was rich,' Acheron breathed with sardonic bite, his dark deep drawl vibrating down her spine.

'You really are a hateful, unfeeling creep!' Tabby slammed back at him tempestuously, fiery emotion ablaze in her violet eyes. 'Troy was a lovely man. Do you honestly think he realised that he was going to die at the age of twenty-four in a car accident? Or that his wife would suffer a stroke within hours of giving birth? Troy would never have taken a penny from anyone that he hadn't earned first.'

'Yet this lovely man left both his widow and child destitute,' Ash reminded her censoriously.

'He didn't have a job, and Sonia was earning enough money at the time through the business we owned. Neither of them could possibly have foreseen that both of them would be dead within a year of having that will drawn up.'

'But it was scarcely fair to name me as a guardian without prior discussion of the idea,' Acheron pointed out drily. 'The normal thing to do would have been to ask my permission first.'

Rigid with tension, Tabby made no comment. She recognised that he had a point but refused to acknowledge the direct hit.

'Perhaps you could tell us without further waste of time exactly what you imagine Mr Dimitrakos could do to help you?' Stevos Vannou sliced in, standing on the sidelines and thoroughly disconcerted by the sheer level of biting hostility erupting between his usually imperturbable employer and his visitor.

'I want to ask Mr Dimitrakos to support my wish to adopt Amber.'

'But is that a realistic goal, Miss Glover?' the lawyer countered immediately. 'You have no home, no money and no partner, and my own experience with Social Services and child-custody cases tells me that at the very least you need a stable lifestyle to be considered a suitable applicant to adopt.'

'What the heck does having or not having a partner have to do with it?' Tabby demanded defensively. 'This past year I've been far too busy to waste time looking for a man.'

'And with your approach it might have proved a considerable challenge,' Acheron interposed without hesitation.

Tabby opened and closed her lush mouth in angry disconcertion and took a seething step closer to the Greek billionaire. 'You accused me of having no manners? What about your own?' she snapped in outrage.

Studying the two adults before him squabbling and insulting each other much as his own teenaged children did, Stevos averted his attention from them both. 'Miss Glover? If you had had a partner it would certainly have made a big difference to your application. Raising a child today is a challenge and it is widely believed that *two* parents generally make that easier.'

'Well, unfortunately for me a partner isn't something I can dig up overnight!' Tabby exclaimed, wishing the wretched man would think of something other than picking holes in her suitability to adopt Amber. Didn't she have enough to worry about?

A germ of a wild idea leapt into Stevos's brain, and he skimmed his insightful gaze to Acheron and addressed him in Greek. 'You know, you could both help each other...'

Ash frowned. 'In what possible way?'

'She needs a stable home and partner to support her adoption application—you need a wife. With a little com-

promise on both sides and some serious legal negotiation, you could both achieve what you want and nobody
would ever need to know the truth.'

Acheron was always quick on the uptake but for a split
second he literally could not believe that Stevos had made
that speech, could even have *dared* to suggest such an
insane idea. He shot a disdainful glance at Tabby Glover
and all her many obvious deficiencies and his black brows
went skyward. 'You *have* to be out of your mind,' he told
his lawyer with incredulity. 'She's a foul-mouthed girl
from the back streets!'

'You've got the money to clean her up enough to pass
in public,' the older man replied drily. 'I'm talking about
a wife you *pay* to be your wife, not a normal wife. If you
get married, *all* your problems with regard to ownership
of the company go away—'

In brooding silence, Acheron focused on the one massive problem that would not go away in that scenario—
Tabby Glover. *Not wife material* screeched every one of
his sophisticated expectations, but he was also thinking
about what he had learned about Troy Valtinos and his
late mother, Olympia, and his conscience was bothering him on that score. 'I couldn't marry her. I don't like
her—'

'Do you *need* to like her?' Stevos enquired quietly.
'I shouldn't have thought that was a basic requirement
to meet the terms of a legal stipulation to protect your
company. You own many properties. I'm sure you could
put her in one of them and barely notice she was there.'

'Right at this moment the first thing on my agenda
has to be the child,' Acheron startled his lawyer by as-
serting. 'I want to check up on her. I have been remiss
in my responsibilities and too quick to dismiss them.'

'Look…' While Stevos was engaged in giving Ash an

alarmed look at that sudden uncharacteristic swerve of his into child-welfare territory, Tabby had folded her arms in frustration and she was glowering at the two men. 'If you two are going to keep on chatting in a foreign language and acting like I'm not here—'

'If only you were not,' Ash murmured silkily.

Tabby's hands balled into fists. 'I bet quite a few women have thumped you in your time!'

Shimmering eyes dark as sloes challenged her, his lean strong face slashing into a sudden smile of raw amusement. 'Not a one…'

Amber, Tabby reminded herself with painful impact, her heart clenching at the thought of the child she adored. She was here to ask for his help for Amber's sake, and Amber's needs were the most important consideration, not how objectionable she found the despicable man. His charismatic smile struck her like a deluge of icy water. He was incredibly, really quite breathtakingly, handsome and the fact that he found her amusing hurt. Of course, Tabby had never cherished many illusions about her desirability factor as a woman. Although she had always had a lot of male friends, she'd had very few boyfriends, and Sonia had once tactfully tried to hint that Tabby could be too sharp-tongued, too independent and too critical to appeal to the average male. Unfortunately, nobody had ever explained to Tabby how she could possibly have survived her challenging life without acquiring those seemingly unfeminine attributes.

'You want to meet the child?' Stevos stepped in quickly before war broke out again between his companions and wasted more time.

A sudden smile broke across Tabby's face like sunshine, and Acheron studied her intently, scanning her delicate features, realising that there could be an attrac-

tive female beneath the facade of bolshie belligerence.
He liked women feminine, really, *really* feminine. She
was crude and unkempt and the guardian of Olympia's
granddaughter, he reminded himself doggedly, striving
to concentrate on the most important element of the equation. And that was the child, *Amber*. He cursed the fact
that he had not known of the connection sooner, cursed
his own innate aversion to being tied down by anything
other than business. He had no relatives, no loving relationships, no responsibility outside his company and
that was how he liked his life. But not at the expense of
basic decency. And his recollection of Olympia, who had
frequently been kind and friendly to a boy everyone else
had viewed as pure trouble, remained one of the few *good*
memories Ash had of his childhood.

'Yes. I want to see the child as soon as possible,' Acheron confirmed.

Tabby tilted her head to one side, taken aback by his
change of heart. 'What changed your mind?'

'I should have personally checked into her circumstances when I was informed of the guardianship,' Acheron breathed grimly, angry with himself for once at the
elaborate and very protective support system around him
that ensured that he was never troubled by too much detail about anything that might take his mind off business.
'But I will take care of that oversight now and be warned,
Miss Glover, I will not support your application to adopt
the little girl unless I reach the conclusion that you *are* a
suitable carer. Thank you for your help, Stevos, but not
for that last suggestion you made...' Sardonic dark eyes
met the lawyer's frowning gaze. 'I'm afraid that idea belongs in fantasy land.'

CHAPTER TWO

'I COULD'VE DONE with some advance warning before you came to visit,' Tabby remarked thinly, after giving the uniformed chauffeur the address of the basement flat where she was currently staying, courtesy of her friend, Jack.

Jack, Sonia and Tabby had become fast friends and pseudo-siblings after passing their teenaged years in the same foster home.

Tabby eased slowly into the leather upholstered back seat of Acheron's unspeakably fancy limousine and studiously avoided staring starstruck at her surroundings but, dear heaven, it was a challenge not to stare at the built-in bar and entertainment centre. She had, however, enjoyed a mean moment of glorious one-upmanship when she sailed out of the front doors of the DT building with the doors held open by the same security guards who had, the hour before, manhandled her on the top floor.

'Obviously a warning would've been unwise. I need to see how you live without you putting on a special show for my benefit,' Acheron responded smoothly, flipping out a laptop onto the small table that emerged at the stab of a button from the division between front and back seats.

Tabby gritted her teeth at that frank admission. Any

kind of fake special show was not an option open to her
in the tiny bedsit that she was currently sharing with
Amber. It was purely thanks to Jack, who was a small-
time builder and property developer, that she still had
Amber with her and had not already been forced to
move into a hostel for the homeless and give up Sonia's
daughter. It hurt that her long-term friendship with Sonia
counted for nothing next to the remote blood tie Acheron
Dimitrakos had shared with Troy. What had they been?
Troy's gran had been a cousin of Acheron's mother, so
Acheron was what…a third cousin or something in rela-
tion to Amber? Yet Tabby had known and loved Sonia
since she was ten years old. They had met in the children's institution where they were both terrorised by the
older kids. Tabby, having grown up in a violent home,
had been much more used to defending herself than the
younger girl. Sonia, after all, had once been a loved child
in a decent family and tragically orphaned by the accident in which her parents died. In comparison, Tabby had
been forcibly removed by the authorities from an abu-
sive home and no longer knew whether her parents were
alive or dead. There had been a few supervised visits
with them after she was first taken away, many attempts
to rehabilitate her mother and father and cobble the family back together, but in reality her parents proved to be
more attached to their irresponsible lifestyle than they
had ever been to their child.

Acheron Dimitrakos worked steadily at his laptop,
making no effort to start up a conversation. Tabby compressed her generous mouth and studied him. She knew
he had already decided that she was a rubbish person
from the very bottom of the social pile. She knew he had
taken one look and made judgements based on her ap-

pearance...and, doubtless, her use of bad language, she conceded with a sneaking feeling of shame.

But then she doubted he knew what it felt like to be almost at the end of your tether. He was so...self-possessed, she decided resentfully, her violet gaze wandering over his bold bronzed profile, noting the slight curl in his thick black hair where it rested behind his ear and the extraordinary length of his dense inky-black eyelashes as he scrutinised the screen in front of him. Imagine a boyfriend with more impressive lashes than you have yourself, she ruminated, unimpressed, her soft mouth curling with disdain.

It annoyed her that he looked even more gorgeous in the flesh than he had in the magazine photographs. She had believed the photos must've been airbrushed to enhance his dark good looks but the evidence to the contrary was right before her. He had high aristocratic cheekbones, a perfectly straight nose and the wide, sensual mouth of a classic Greek statue. He was also extremely tall, broad-shouldered, narrow-hipped and long-legged—in fact, he was graced with every attractive male attribute possible.

Not a nice, caring person though, she reasoned staunchly, determined to concentrate on his flaws. Indeed, thinking of how he had outright refused to take any interest in Troy and Sonia's daughter, it was a challenge to understand why he should be suddenly bothering to come and see Amber now. She decided that she had made him feel guilty and that, after all, he *had* to have a conscience. Did that mean that he would support her application to adopt Amber? And even more importantly, would his opinion carry any weight with Social Services?

Acheron could not concentrate, which annoyed the hell out of him. Tabby Glover never sat still, and the constant movements of her slight small body on the seat beside him were an irritating distraction. He was too observant, he thought impatiently as he noted the bitten nails on her small hands, the shabbiness of her training shoes, the worn denim of jeans stretched taut over slender thighs, and he suppressed a sigh. He was out of his depth and although he had told Stevos to return to his office he was not enjoying the course he had set himself on. After all, what did he know about a young child's needs? Why did he feel guilty that he had already made up his mind to the hard fact that this young woman was not a fit sole guardian for a baby girl?

When the car came to a halt, Tabby slid out of the limo and bounced down the steps to stick her key in the front door of the basement flat. *Here goes,* she conceded nervously as she spread wide the door.

Ash froze one step inside, aghast at the indoor building site that comprised her accommodation. There was scaffolding, buckets and tools lying around, wires dangling everywhere, plasterboard walls. Tabby thrust open the first door to the left of the entrance.

Acheron followed her into a small room, packed with furniture and a table bearing a kettle and mini-oven and scattered with crumbs. Baby equipment littered almost every other surface. A teenage girl was seated on the bed with work files spread around her and when she saw Tabby she gathered up her files with a smile and stood up to leave. 'Amber's been great. She had a snack, enjoyed her bottle and she's been changed.'

'Thanks, Heather,' Tabby said quietly to the girl who lived in the apartment above. 'I appreciate your help.'

The child was sitting up in the cot wedged between the bed and the wall on one side. Acheron surveyed the child from a safe distance, noting the mop of black curls,

the big brown eyes and the instant dazzling smile that
rewarded Tabby's appearance.

'How's my darling girl?' Tabby asked, leaning over the
cot to scoop up the little girl and hug her tight. Chubby
arms wrapped round her throat while curious brown eyes
inspected Acheron over Tabby's shoulder.

'What age is she?' Ash enquired.

'You should know,' Tabby said drily. 'She's over six
months old.'

'Do the authorities know you're keeping her here?'

A flush of uneasy colour warmed Tabby's cheeks as
she sat down on the bed because Amber was getting
heavier by the day. 'No. I gave them Jack's address. He's
a friend and he bought this apartment to renovate and
sell on. He's allowing us to stay here out of the goodness
of his heart. He hasn't the space for us at his own place.'

'How can you live in such a squalid dwelling with a
young child and believe that you're doing the best you
can for her?' Acheron condemned.

'Well, for a start, it's not squalid!' Tabby flared defensively and hurriedly rose to set Amber back into her cot.
'It's clean. We have heating and light and there's a fully
functional bathroom through that door.' She pointed a
hand to the opposite wall, and the gesture fell down in
effectiveness because her arm shook and she hurriedly
lowered it again. Tears were suddenly stinging the back
of her eyes, and her head was starting to thump with the
onset of a stress headache. 'For the moment I'm just doing
the best I can but we're *managing*.'

'But you're not managing well enough,' Ash stated
curtly. 'You shouldn't be keeping a young child in accommodation like this.'

Her brow pulsing with the band of tension tightening
round it, Tabby lifted her hands to release the weight of

her hair from the ponytail. Acheron watched a torrent of long blonde hair fall down to her waist and finally saw something he liked about her appearance: blonde hair that was natural unless he was very much mistaken, for that pale mass had no dark roots or streaky highlights.

'I'm doing the very best I can,' Tabby countered firmly, wondering why he was staring at her, her self-conscious streak on override, her pride still hurting from the 'squalid' comment.

'And how are you supporting yourself?' Acheron asked with a curled lip.

'I'm still cleaning. I didn't lose all my clients when I had to close my business down, and those I kept I'm still working for. I take Amber with me to the jobs. Most of my clients are out at work anyway so her coming with me doesn't bother them,' she admitted grudgingly. 'Take a look at her. She's clean and well fed and happy. We're rarely apart.'

Ash assimilated the information with a grim twist of his expressive mouth. 'I'm sorry, but your best isn't good enough. Nothing I've seen here will convince me otherwise. You don't have a proper home for the child. You're clearly living on the poverty line—'

'Money isn't everything!' Tabby protested. 'I love her and she loves me.'

Ash watched the slender blonde lean over the cot rail to gently stroke the little girl's head and saw the answering sunny smile that the gesture evoked. No such love or tenderness had featured in his childhood experience, and he fully recognised the fact, but he was also bone-deep practical and not given to changing his mind mid-course. 'Love isn't enough on its own. If you had a supportive family to back you and a proper home to raise her in I might feel differently, but you on your own with her in this dismal room and dragging her out with you to cleaning jobs is *wrong*,' he pronounced with strong conviction. 'She could do better than this, she *should* have better than this and it is *her* needs and not your own that you should be weighing in the balance.'

'Are you saying that I'm selfish?' Tabby prompted in disbelief, because she had given up so much that was important to her to take care first of Sonia, after she had suffered her first stroke, and ultimately her baby daughter.

Beneath the shocked onslaught of eyes the colour of rain-washed amethysts, Acheron's stubborn jaw line clenched hard and his mouth compressed. 'Yes. You have obviously done the best you can and given her continuity of care since her mother's death but now it's time for you to step back and put her best interests ahead of your own personal feelings.'

The tears glistening in Tabby's eyes overflowed, marking silvery trails on her cheeks, and for the first time in years Acheron felt like a real bastard and yet he had only told the truth as he saw it. *I love her and she loves me.* Yes, he could see the strength of the bond before him but it couldn't cover up the cracks in the long-term struggle for survival he saw for them both. Olympia's grandchild deserved more. Yet how did he put a price on the love and then dismiss it as if it were worthless?

'What age are you?' he pressed.

'Twenty-five.'

'I should've dealt with this situation when it first came up,' Acheron acknowledged grimly, thinking that she was surely far too young and immature to take on such a burden and that he should have taken immediate action to resolve the situation the instant the guardianship issue arose. It was his fault that Tabby Glover had been left to struggle on with the child while becoming more and more dangerously attached to her charge.

'Not if it meant parting Amber and me sooner,' Tabby argued. 'Can't you understand how much I care about her? Her mother and I became best friends when we were kids, and I'll be able to share my memories of her parents with her when she's old enough to want that information. Surely there's something you could do to help?'

But on a personal level, Acheron didn't want to be involved. He always avoided emotional situations and responsibilities that fell outside company business, and it had been that very detachment that had first roused his late father's concern that his only son should have set himself on such a solitary path.

Tabby searched Acheron's handsome features, marvelling at his masculine perfection even as she appraised the glitter of his dark-as-jet eyes and the hard tension round his wide, sensual mouth. 'I'll do anything it takes to keep her…'

Acheron frowned, his brow furrowing. 'What's that supposed to mean?'

'What do you think? I'm desperate to keep Amber. If you have any suggestions on how I can be a better parent to her, I'm willing to listen and take advice,' Tabby extended with the new-found humility of fear.

'I thought you were offering me sex,' Acheron confided bluntly.

'*Seriously?*' Tabby gasped in shock at that misconception. 'Does that happen to you a lot? I mean…women… just offering?'

Acheron nodded cool confirmation.

Her violet eyes widened in astonishment and she lifted her head, pale blonde hair cascading in a silken tangle round her shoulders with the movement. In the space of a split second she travelled from *possibly* pretty to decidedly beautiful in Acheron's estimation, and desire kindled; a desire he neither wanted nor intended to act on. His body was stubborn, though, and the pulse of heaviness at his groin was utterly disobedient to his brain, throwing up outrageous images of her lying on his bed, that lovely swathe of hair spread over his chest, that lush mouth gainfully employed in pleasuring him. He gritted his perfect white teeth, suppressing the outrageous fantasy, furiously conscious of the child's innocent presence and his unprecedented loss of self-discipline.

'Women just offer themselves? No wonder you're so full of yourself,' Tabby remarked helplessly, aware of the tension in the atmosphere, but unsure of its source as she stared back at him. She liked looking at him, didn't know why or exactly what it was about those lean sculpted features that fascinated her so much. But as she collided with his stunning dark-as-midnight gaze, liquid warmth surged between her legs and her nipples tightened, a message even she couldn't ignore or deny. He attracted her. The filthy rich Greek with his dazzling good looks and hard-as-granite heart *attracted* her. How foolish and deceptive physical chemistry could be, she reflected ruefully, embarrassment colouring her pale cheeks.

I'll do anything it takes to keep her... And suddenly Acheron, rigid with the force of his self-control, was reasoning with a new and unfamiliar sense of freedom to think outside the box and he was thinking, Why not? Why the hell not? Possibly Stevos's bright idea had not been as off the wall as it had first seemed. He and this strange girl both wanted something from each other, and he could certainly ensure that Amber benefitted from the deal in every way, thereby satisfying his uneasy conscience where the child was concerned.

'There *is* a way you could keep Amber with you.' Ash dangled the bait straight away, as always impatient to plunge to the heart of the matter.

Tabby leant forward where she sat, wide violet eyes intent on him. *'How?'*

'We could apply as a couple to adopt her—'

Thoroughly disconcerted by that unexpected suggestion, Tabby blinked. 'As a couple?'

'With my backing it could be achieved but we would need to be married first,' Ash delivered smoothly, deciding there and then that he would not admit the truth that he would have a great deal riding on the arrangement as well. That acknowledgement would tip the power balance between them and he refused to take that unnecessary risk and find himself being blackmailed. The less she knew, the less power she would have.

Astonishment was stamped on her small oval face. *'Married?'*

'For the sake of the adoption application. I should think that the most traditional approach would have the likeliest and quickest chance of success.'

'Let me get this straight…you're saying you would be willing to marry me to help me get permission to adopt Amber?' Tabby breathed in frank disbelief.

Acheron dealt her a sardonic look. 'Naturally I'm not suggesting a proper marriage. I'm suggesting the legal ceremony and a joint application to adopt her. We would then only have to give the appearance that we are living below the same roof for as long as it takes to complete the proceedings.'

So, not a real marriage, a *fake* one, she mused, but even so she was still transfixed by the concept and the idea that he might be willing to go to such lengths to help her. 'But why would you do that for us? A couple of months ago, you simply dismissed the idea that you could have any obligation towards Amber.'

'I wasn't aware then that she was Olympia Carolis's grandchild—'

'Olympia...who?' Tabby queried blankly.

'Troy's mother. I only knew her by the name she had before she married. I knew her when I was a child because she worked for my mother and lived with us,' Acheron volunteered with pronounced reluctance. 'I lost all contact with that side of the family after my mother died. But I liked Olympia. She was a good woman.'

'Yet you don't have the slightest true interest in Amber,' Tabby commented with a frown of incomprehension. 'You haven't even tried to hold her.'

'I'm not accustomed to babies and I don't want to frighten her,' Acheron excused himself glibly and watched her process his polite lie. 'I should've taken a greater interest in the child when I was first informed that I was one of her guardians. Your situation would not have reached crisis point had I accepted that commitment and taken my share of the responsibility.'

His admission of fault soothed Tabby, who had not been prepared for that amount of candour from him. He had made a mistake and was man enough to acknowledge it, an attitude that she respected. He had also moved a step closer to the cot and Amber, always a friendly baby, was beaming up at him in clear expectation of being lifted. But his lean brown hands clenched into taut stillness by his side, and she recognised that if anyone was frightened it was not Amber, it was *him*. Of course, he was an only child, and she assumed he had had little contact with young children because his rigid inhibited stance close to the baby spoke loudly for him.

'So, you've changed your mind and you think I should adopt her?'

'Not quite that,' Ash declared levelly. 'If we go ahead with this, I will be on the spot to oversee Amber's welfare and if I'm satisfied that you're a capable mother, I will release her fully into your care after we divorce. Naturally I will also ensure that when we part you have a proper home to raise her in.'

In other words, she would be on probation as a parent for the duration of the fake marriage, which was not good news on her terms. But Acheron Dimitrakos had to *really* care about what happened to Amber to be willing to get so involved and make such a sacrifice as marrying a stranger for the child's benefit alone, she thought ruefully, suddenly ashamed of her prejudices about him.

He would be killing two birds with one stone, Ash decided with satisfaction, solving all his problems in one decisive act. He would choose a discreet location for the ceremony but at the same time, if anyone was to be expected to believe that they were a couple and the marriage genuine, she would have to undergo a major makeover first.

'I'll take you home with me now,' Acheron pronounced. 'Bring the baby…leave everything else. My staff will pack your possessions.'

'Are you joking? Walk out the door with a strange man and move in with him?' Tabby breathed in stark disbelief. 'Do I look that naive and trusting?'

Acheron studied her levelly. 'You only get one chance with me and, I warn you, I'm not a patient man. I can't leave you and the child living here like this and, if we decide to go ahead with the marriage and adoption plan, there are things to be done, forms to be filled in without further waste of time.'

Tabby leapt up. As he shifted his feet in their highly polished leather shoes and elevated a sleek black brow in expectation he emanated impatience in invisible sparks, filling the atmosphere with tension. He thought he was doing her a favour and that she ought to jump to attention and follow his instructions and, because that was true, she wasn't going to argue with him. In fact, just for once, she was going to keep her ready tongue glued to the roof of her mouth and play nice to keep him happy and willing to help. Yes, she would trust him, but common sense suggested that a male as rich and gorgeous as he was had many more tempting sexual outlets than a woman as ordinary as she was.

'OK…' Tabby stuffed nappies and bottles and a tub of formula milk into the worn baby bag, and threaded Amber's chubby arms into a jacket that was slightly too small before strapping her into the car seat that she had had no use for since she had had to sell her car.

Acheron was already on his phone to his PA, telling her to engage an emergency nanny because he had no plans to trail the baby out shopping with them. The deal was done, only the details had to be dealt with now and he was in his element.

Ash stayed on the phone for the first ten minutes of their journey, rapping out instructions, making arrangements, telling Stevos to make a start on the paperwork. For the first time in a week he felt he was back in control of his life and it felt good. He stole a reluctant glance at Tabby, engaged in keeping Amber occupied by pointing out things through the windows. The awareness that Tabby Glover was going to prove very useful to him compressed his hard mouth because he was convinced that she would be difficult.

'Where are you taking us?' she asked, still in something of a daze after that discussion about adoption and marriage. She was scarcely able to credit that her and Amber's luck had turned a magical corner because Acheron Dimitrakos bore not the slightest resemblance to a fairy godmother.

'Back to my apartment where we will drop off… Amber,' Acheron advanced warily.

'And who are you planning to drop her off with? Your staff? *That's* not going to happen,' Tabby began forcefully.

'I have organised a nanny, who will be waiting for us. We will then go shopping to buy you some clothes.'

'Amber doesn't need a nanny and I don't need clothes.'

Acheron treated her to a scornful dark appraisal that burned colour into her cheeks. 'You're hardly dressed suitably. If we're to put on a convincing act, you need clothes,' he contradicted.

Anger flared in her violet eyes and her head turned sharply. 'I *don't* need—'

'Just say the word and I'll return you both to your clean and comfy basement,' Acheron told her in a lethally quiet tone of warning.

Tabby sucked in a sudden deep breath and held it, recognising that she was trapped, something she never ever allowed herself to be because being trapped meant being vulnerable. But if she said no, refused to toe the line, she would lose Amber for good. There would be no coming back from that development because once Amber was removed from her care, she would be gone for all time.

Had Acheron Dimitrakos been right to censure her selfishness in wanting to keep Sonia's daughter as her own? It was a painful thought. She hated to think that he could know better about anything but she knew that

outsiders often saw more clearly than those directly involved. All she had to offer Amber was love, and he had
said love wasn't enough. But Tabby valued love much
more highly because she hadn't received it as a child
and had often longed for the warm sense of acceptance,
well-being and security that a loving parent could be-
stow. Only time would tell if Amber herself would agree
that Tabby had made the wisest decision on her behalf.

Amber hugged Tabby in the lift on the way up to
Acheron's apartment, the little girl clinging in reaction
to Tabby's increasing tension. Acheron stood poised in
the far corner of the mirrored compartment, a comfortable six feet three inches of solid masculine detachment.
Tabby studied him in growing frustration, noting the
aloof quality in his gaze, the forbidding cool of his lean,
strong face. He was so unemotional about everything that
he infuriated her. Here she was awash with conflicting
emotions, terrified she was doing the wrong thing, putting her feelings rather than Amber's needs first…and
whose fault was that? She had not doubted her ability
to be a good mother until Acheron Dimitrakos crossed
her path. Now she was facing the challenge of also sur-
rendering her pride and her independence to meet his
expectations.

'I don't think this is going to work,' she told him helplessly. 'We mix like oil and water.'

'A meeting of true minds is not required,' Ash im-
parted with sardonic bite. 'Stop arguing about every little
thing. That irritates me.'

'A nanny is not a little thing. Who is she?'

'A highly trained professional from a reputable source.
I would not put the child at risk.'

His intense dark eyes challenged her, and she looked
away, her cheeks burning, her mouth dry, her grip on

Amber still a little tighter than it needed to be. For a split second she felt as though Amber were the only sure element left in the world that he was tearing apart and threatening to rebuild. He intimidated her, a truth that made her squirm. Yet he was willing to help her keep Amber, she reminded herself doggedly, and that should be her bottom line. Whatever it took she should bite the bullet and focus on the end game, not how bad it might feel getting there.

'Won't the sort of marriage you suggested be illegal?' she heard herself ask him abruptly. 'You know, a marriage that's just a fake?'

'Why would it be illegal?' he countered with icy cool. 'What goes on within any marriage is private.'

'But our marriage would be an act of deception.'

'You're splitting hairs. No one would be harmed by the deception. The marriage would simply present us as a conventional couple keen to adopt.'

'You're hopelessly out of date. Lots of couples don't get married these days,' Tabby pointed out.

'In my family we always get married when it comes to child-rearing,' Acheron told her smoothly.

That's right, remind me that I'm not from the same world! Tabby thought furiously, a flush of antagonism warming her face as embarrassment threatened to swallow her alive. Her parents had not been married and had probably never even thought of getting married to regularise her birth.

Her gaze strayed inexorably back to him until she connected with smoky dark deep-set eyes that made her tummy lurch and leap and heat rise in her pelvis. There was just something about him, she thought furiously, dragging her attention from him as the lift doors whirred open and she hastily stepped out into a hallway, something shockingly sexy and dangerous that broke through her defences. She did not understand how he could act like an unfeeling block of superior ice and still have that effect on her.

CHAPTER THREE

THE NANNY, COMPLETE with a uniform that suggested she belonged to the very highest echelon of qualified nannies, awaited Acheron and Tabby in the spacious hall of Acheron's apartment and within minutes she had charmed Amber out of Tabby's arms and borne her off.

'Let's go,' Acheron urged impatiently. 'We have a lot to accomplish.'

'I don't like shopping,' Tabby breathed, literally cringing at the prospect of him paying for her clothes.

'Neither do I. In fact, usually the closest I get to shopping with a woman is giving her a credit card,' Acheron confided silkily. 'But I don't trust you to buy the right stuff.'

Mutinously silent as she slid back into the waiting limousine in the underground car park, Tabby shrugged a slight shoulder, determined not to battle with him when it was a battle she could not win. Even so, he could dress her up all he liked but it wouldn't change the person she truly was. No, she would be sensible and look on the clothing as a necessary prop for their masquerade, another move in what already felt more like a game than reality because in no realistic dimension did a girl like her marry a guy as rich and good-looking as him.

A personal shopper awaited them at Harrods where,

surprisingly enough, Acheron appeared to be in his element. Tabby did not attempt to impose her opinions and she hovered while Acheron pointed out what he liked and the correct size was lifted from the rail. She soon found herself in a changing cubicle with a heap of garments.

'Come out,' Ash instructed impatiently. 'I want to see you in the pink dress.'

Suppressing a groan, Tabby snaked into the classy little cocktail frock, reached down to flip off her socks and walked barefoot out of the cubicle.

Acheron frowned as she came to a halt and he strolled round her, staring at her slight figure in surprise. 'I didn't realise you were so tiny.'

Tabby gnawed at her lower lip, knowing she had skipped too many meals in recent months, painfully aware that she was too thin and that what delicate curves she had possessed had shrunk along with any excess body fat. 'I'm a lot stronger than I look,' she said defensively.

Acheron studied her doll-like dimensions with unabashed interest, his narrowed gaze running from her fragile shoulders down to her pale slender legs. He could've easily lifted her with one hand. He liked curves on a woman yet there was an aesthetically pleasing aspect to the pure delicacy of her build. Her breasts barely made an indent in the bodice of the dress and her hips made no imprint at all. Yet with that tousled mane of long blonde hair highlighting her pale oval face and bright violet eyes, she looked unusual and extraordinarily appealing. He wondered if he would crush her in bed and then squashed that crazy thought dead because sex would naturally not be featuring in their agreement. As she turned away, he froze, taken aback by the sight of the colourful rose tattoo marring the pale skin of her left forearm.

'That dress won't do,' Acheron told the assistant thinly. 'She needs a dress with sleeves to cover that.'

Gooseflesh crept over Tabby's exposed skin, and she clamped a hand over the skin marking she had forgotten about. Beneath her fingers she could feel the rougher skin of the scar tissue that the tattoo pretty much concealed from view, and her heart dropped to the pit of her stomach, remembered feelings of bitter pain and heartache gripping her in spite of the years that had passed since the wound was first inflicted. She had made the clear considered choice that she could live better with the tattoo than she could with that constant reminder of her wretched childhood catching her unawares every time she looked in the mirror. Of course, the skin ink wasn't perfect because the skin surface beneath it was far from perfect and the tattooist had warned her of the fact in advance. As it was, the rose, albeit a little blurred in its lines, had done the job it was designed to do, hiding the scar and providing a burial place for the bad memories. Only very rarely did Tabby think about it.

'How could you disfigure your body with that?' Acheron demanded in a driven undertone, his revulsion unhidden.

'It's of a good luck charm. I've had it for years,' Tabby told him unsteadily, her face pale and set.

The personal shopper was already approaching with a long-sleeved dress, and Tabby returned to the cubicle, her skin clammy now with the aftermath of shock—the shock of being forced back, however briefly, into her violent past. The rose was her lucky charm, which concealed the vivid reminder of what could happen when you loved someone unworthy of that trust. So, he didn't like tattoos; well, what was that to her? She put on the new dress, smoothed down the sleeves and, mustering her self-possession, she emerged again.

Acheron stared her up and down, his beautiful face curiously intent. Heat blossomed in her cheeks as he studied her with smouldering dark eyes, his tension palpable. Desire flickered low in her pelvis like kindling yearning for a spark, and she felt that craving shoot through every fibre of her body, from the dryness of her mouth to the swelling sensitivity of her nipples and the honeyed heat between her thighs. It made her feel light-headed and oddly intoxicated, and she blinked rapidly, severely disconcerted by the feelings.

'That will do,' he pronounced thickly.

She wanted to touch him so badly she had to clench her hands into fists to prevent herself from reaching out and making actual contact. She felt like a wasp being drawn to a honey trap and fiercely fought her reactions with every scrap of self-control left to her. Don't touch, *don't touch*, a little voice warned in the back of her head, but evidently he was listening to a different voice as he stalked closer and reached for her hands, pulling them into his, urging her closer, forcing her fingers to loosen within his grasp.

And Tabby looked up at him and froze, literally not daring to breathe. That close his eyes were no longer dark but a downright amazing and glorious swirl of honey, gold and caramel tones, enhanced by the spiky black lashes she envied. His fingers were feathering over hers with a gentleness she had not expected from so big and powerful a man and little tremors of response were filtering through her, undermining her self-control. She knew she wanted those expert hands on her body exploring much more secret places, and colour rose in her cheeks because she also knew she was out of her depth and drowning. In an abrupt movement, she wrenched her hands free and turned away, momentarily shutting her eyes in a gesture of angry self-loathing.

'Try on the rest of the clothes,' Acheron instructed coolly, not a flicker of lingering awareness in his dark deep voice.

Hot-faced, Tabby vanished back into the cubicle. Evidently he pressed all her buttons, and she had to stop letting him do that to her, had to stand firm. Of course he was sexy: he was a womaniser. He had insulted her with that crack about her tattoo and had then somehow switched that moment into something else by catching her hands in his and just looking at her. But she wasn't some impressionable little airhead vulnerable to the merest hint of interest from an attractive man, was she? Well, she *was* a virgin, she acknowledged grudgingly, as always stifling her unease about that glaring lack in her experience with men. After all she had not intentionally chosen to retain her virginity; it had just happened that way. No man had ever succeeded in making her want to get that close to him, and she had no plans to share a bed with someone simply to find out what it was like.

And then Acheron Dimitrakos had come along and turned everything she thought she knew on its head. For, although he attracted her, she didn't like him and didn't trust him either, so what did that say about her? That she had a reckless streak just like her long-lost and unlamented parents?

Tension seethed through Acheron. What the hell was the matter with him? He had been on the edge of crushing that soft, luscious mouth beneath his, close to wrecking the non-sexual relationship he envisaged between them. Impersonal would work the best and it shouldn't be that difficult, he reasoned impatiently, for they had nothing in common.

He watched her emerge again, clad in cropped wool trousers, high heels and a slinky little burgundy cashmere cardigan. She looked really good. She cleaned up incredibly well, he acknowledged grudgingly, gritting his teeth together as his gaze instinctively dropped to the sweet pouting swell of her small breasts beneath the clingy top.

He had done what he had to do, he reminded himself grimly. She was perfect for his purposes, for she had as much riding on the success of their arrangement as he had. Thankfully nothing in his life was going to change in the slightest: he had found the perfect wife, a non-wife...

He left Tabby alone with the shopper in the lingerie department and she chose the basics before heading for the children's department and choosing an entire new wardrobe for Amber, her heart singing at the prospect of seeing the little girl in new clothes that fitted her properly. The chauffeur saw to the stowing of her many bags in the capacious boot of the limousine, and she climbed in beside Acheron, who was talking on the phone in French. She recognised the language from lessons at school and raised her brows. So, that was at least *three* languages he spoke: Greek, English and now French. She refused to be impressed.

'We'll dine out tonight,' Acheron pronounced, putting the phone away.

'Why the heck would you want to do that?' Tabby demanded in dismay at the prospect.

'If we want to give the appearance of a normal couple, we need to be seen out together. Wear that dress.'

'Oh...' Tabby said nothing more while she wondered what social horrors dining out with him would entail.

She had never eaten out in a fancy restaurant, having always cravenly avoided such formal occasions, intimidated by the prospect of too much cutlery and superior serving staff, who would surely quickly spot that she was a takeaway girl at heart.

Two hours later, having showered and changed, Acheron opened the safe in his bedroom wall to remove a ring case he hadn't touched in years. The fabled emerald, which had reputedly once adorned a maharajah's crown, had belonged to his late mother and would do duty as an engagement ring. The very thought of putting the priceless jewel on Tabby's finger chilled Acheron's anti-commitment gene to the marrow, and he squared his broad shoulders, grateful that the engagement and the marriage that would follow would be one hundred per cent fake.

'Fine feathers make fine birds' had been one of her last foster mother's favourite sayings, Tabby recalled as she put on mascara, guiltily enjoying the fact that she had both the peace and the time to use cosmetics again. Make-up had been one of the first personal habits to fall by the wayside once she took on full-time care of Amber. But the nanny had been hired to work until eleven that night, leaving Amber free to dress up and go out like a lady of leisure. A *lady*? She grimaced at the word, doubting she could ever match that lofty description, and ran a brush through her freshly washed hair before grabbing the clutch that matched the shoes and leaving the room.

Acheron's apartment was vast, much bigger than she had expected. Tabby and Amber had been relegated to rooms at the very foot of the bedroom corridor, well away from the main reception areas as well as the principal bedroom suite, which seemed to be sited up a spiral staircase off the main hall. Acheron Dimitrakos lived like a king, she conceded with a shake of her head, wide-eyed at the opulence of the furnishings surrounding her and the fresh flowers blooming on every surface. They truly did come from different worlds. But the one trait they shared, she sensed, was an appreciation of hard slog and its rewards, so she hoped he would understand why she needed to continue to work.

'Put it on,' Acheron advised in the hall, planting an emerald ring unceremoniously into the palm of her hand.

Tabby frowned down at the gleaming jewel. 'What's it for?'

'Engagement ring...marriage?' Acheron groaned. 'Sometimes you're very slow on the uptake.'

Tabby rammed the beautiful ring down over her knuckle and squinted down at it, her colour high. 'I didn't know we were going for frills. I assumed you would choose more of a basic-package approach.'

'Since we'll be getting married pretty quickly and without a big splash our charade needs to look more convincing from the outset.'

'I'm already living with you and wearing clothes you bought for me,' she parried flatly. 'Isn't that enough of a show?'

'Many couples live together without marrying, many women have worn clothing I paid for,' Acheron derided. 'What we have has to look more serious.'

The restaurant was dimly lit and intimate and their table probably the best in the room. Certainly the attention that came their way from the staff was so constant that Tabby found it almost claustrophobic. Having studiously ignored her during the drive while talking on his phone, Acheron finally allowed himself the indulgence of looking at his bride-to-be. Her blonde mane tumbled round her shoulders framing a vivid and delicate little face dominated by violet eyes and a lush fuchsia-tinted mouth. He couldn't take his eyes off that mouth, a mouth modelled to make a man think of sin and sinning.

'How am I performing so far as your dress-up doll?' Tabby enquired mockingly to take her mind off the fact that she had still not established which knife and fork to use with the salad being brought to them.

'You answer back too much but you look amazing in the right clothes,' Acheron conceded, startling her with that compliment. 'So far I'm very satisfied with our bargain, and you can be assured that I will play my part.'

As he reached for one fork she reached for another and then changed course mid-movement, her gaze welded to his lean brown hands. *Just copy him*, her brain urged her.

'I've applied for a special licence. The legalities should be in place in time for the ceremony to be held on Thursday,' Acheron delivered. 'My lawyer is making all the arrangements and has contacted Social Services on our behalf with regard to our plans for Amber.'

'My word, he's a fast mover,' Tabby remarked breathlessly.

'You told me you didn't want the child to go into foster care,' he reminded her.

Her skin turned clammy at that daunting reminder of the unknown destination that would have awaited Amber had Tabby not gained his support. 'I don't but there are things we still haven't discussed. What am I supposed to do while we're pretending to be married?'

A winged ebony brow lifted. '*Do*? Nothing. You concentrate on being a mother and occasionally a wife. I will expect you to make a couple of appearances with me at public events. That is the sole commitment you have to make to me.'

'That's great because I want to start up my business again…in a small way,' Tabby admitted abruptly.

His handsome features clenched hard. 'No. That's out of the question. The child deserves a full-time mother.'

Tabby couldn't believe her ears. 'Most mothers work—'

'I will cover your financial requirements,' Acheron delivered with unquenchable cool. 'For the foreseeable future you will put the child's needs first and you will not work.'

Tabby gritted her teeth. 'I don't want to take your money.'

'Tough,' Acheron slotted in succinctly.

'You can't tell me what I can and can't do.'

'Can't I?'

Tabby's pulse had quickened until it felt as if it were beating in the foot of her throat, obstructing her ability to breathe and speak. Frustrated rage lay behind her choked silence as she stared across the table at him, her small face taut and pale. He was pulling strings as if she were a puppet. And wasn't she exactly that?

A chill settled over her rage, safely enclosing it. He was willing to help her to adopt Amber and she was stuck with his outdated idealistic attitude whether she liked it or not. Yes, she could walk away from him but if she did so she would also be walking away from the child she loved. And that, Tabby reflected hollowly, she could not do.

Amber had tugged at Tabby's heartstrings from the day she was born and Sonia was too weak, having suffered her first stroke within hours of the birth, even to hold her daughter. Consequently, for as long as Tabby needed Acheron's support she would have to conform to *his* expectations. Facing and accepting that ugly frightening truth had to be one of the most humbling experiences Tabby had ever known because it ran contrary to every tenet she had lived by since adulthood. The threat of no longer being in full charge of her life genuinely terrified Tabby.

'You seem to have lost your appetite,' Ash remarked, watching her move the food around her plate without lifting anything to her ripe pink mouth.

It was a steak cooked rare, not the way she liked it. But then she had coped with the menu being written in pretentious French simply by making the exact same menu choices as he had.

'You killed my appetite,' Tabby countered thinly.

A forbidding look flitted across his chiselled features. 'If restarting your business means that much to you, you should give up your desire to adopt a child, who will need much more of your time than you could give her as an independent businesswoman.'

Well, that certainly put his point of view across, Tabby conceded ruefully, sipping her water, ignoring the full wineglass beside it. She never touched alcohol, didn't trust the effect it might have on her, feared it might even awaken a craving she might find hard to control. She couldn't argue with Acheron Dimitrakos because setting up her business again *would* demand a great deal of her time. She compressed her lips, reasonably certain she could've coped without short-changing Amber but questioning for the first time whether or not that would have been fair to the child she loved. After all, she had personally never enjoyed the luxury of being a full-time mother and perhaps it would be more sensible to give that lifestyle a shot rather than dismissing it out of hand.

'Are we on the same page?' Acheron Dimitrakos asked impatiently over the cheese and crackers.

Mouth full at last of something she wanted to eat, Tabby nodded while trying not to imagine what it would feel like to be financially dependent on a man for the first time in her life.

As they emerged from the restaurant, Acheron banded an arm round her stiff spine, and she blinked in bewilderment at the daunting acknowledgement that they were literally surrounded by photographers. 'Smile,' he instructed her flatly.

And, hating it, she did as she was told.

'What was that all about?' she demanded once they were driving away.

'Public proof of our relationship,' Acheron supplied drily. 'There'll be an announcement of our engagement in *The Times* tomorrow.'

What relationship? Tabby thought with wry amusement. He said jump, she said how high? That was not a relationship, it was a dictatorship, but possibly he didn't know the difference.

The plaintive cry roused Acheron from a sound sleep. He listened for a while but the noise continued. After a moment, he rolled out of bed with a curse on his lips and reached the bedroom door, before groaning out loud and stalking back to rummage through a drawer and extract a pair of jeans. He hated having guests. He hated any interruption to his usual routine. But Tabby was a better option than a real wife, he reminded himself with satisfaction, and a good deal less likely to develop ambitious ideas about hanging on to her privileged position.

He pushed open the door of the nursery and saw the baby in the cot. It was kicking its arms and legs in furious activity, its little face screwed up as it loosed a wail that would have wakened the dead. Only, apparently, not her wannabe adoptive mother. Ash hovered by the cot, his wide, sensual mouth on a downward curve. The baby sat up in a flash and looked expectant, even lifted its arms as if she expected him to haul her to freedom. It looked far too lively for a baby supposed to be sleeping.

'No more crying,' Ash decreed firmly. 'I don't like crying.'

The baby's arms lowered, its rosebud mouth jutting out in a pout while its bright brown eyes studied him uncertainly.

'You see, crying gets you nowhere,' Ash explained helpfully.

Another heartbroken sob emanated from the baby. She looked incredibly sad and lonely, and Ash stifled a groan.

'Aren't you going to lift her? She needs comforting,' Tabby murmured from the doorway, studying the little tableau of inflexible male and needy baby. It was infuriating to register that she couldn't take her eyes off him when he was wearing only a pair of jeans. He had a six-pack that could have rivalled a top athlete's and his lean, muscular bronzed chest was state-of-the-art perfection, showcasing a male body that could have played a starring role in any female fantasy.

'Why would I lift her?' Ash enquired with a raised brow, flashing her a glance and noticing in that one brief look that she was wearing a pale nightdress that revealed more than it concealed of her tiny body while she stood with her back turned to the light in the corridor. He glimpsed delicate little pink nipples and a pale shadowy vee between her thighs, and his body reacted with instantaneous arousal.

'Because if you expect our adoption application to impress the powers-that-be, you need to be confident that you can handle Amber.'

'I will be perfectly confident if the situation demands that of me, but at this hour of the day it would be very unwise to remove her from the cot,' he declared. 'She's there for the whole night. It's two in the morning, in case you haven't noticed. Why raise her hopes by lifting her?'

Amber released another howl and, gripped by frustration, Tabby marched over to the cot, swept up the little girl and settled her without ceremony into Ash's arms. 'If she has a nightmare she needs comforting. She needs to know someone is there for her and a little cuddle usually soothes her.'

Amber was as shocked as Acheron to find herself in his arms. Wide brown eyes anxiously observed him. 'Cuddle?' Ash almost whispered the word in appalled disbelief. 'You actually expect me to cuddle her?'

CHAPTER FOUR

WITH A GASP of irritation, Tabby removed Amber from his awkward hold and pressed her close. 'Skin-to-skin contact is important,' she demonstrated, kissing Amber's hot brow.

'I'm not doing the kissing stuff either,' Acheron breathed witheringly.

'Then smooth her hair, rub her back, make her feel secure in other ways,' Tabby advised ruefully. 'Stop being so resistant to my suggestions.'

'And how do you suggest I do that? With a personality transplant?' Acheron derided. 'I'm no good with kids. I have no experience of that sort of affection.'

'It's never too late to learn,' Tabby told him with determination, settling Amber carefully back into his arms. 'Hold her closer, pet her. And please don't tell me you have no experience of petting women.'

'I don't pet them. I have sex with them. This is not an appropriate conversation to have around a child!' Acheron bit out in exasperation.

Picking up on his annoyance, Amber whimpered. He spread his fingers across her back in an uneasy rubbing motion.

'Bring her closer,' Tabby urged, approaching him to

tuck the baby into the curve of his shoulder. 'She's not going to bite.'

Acheron could never recall feeling quite so tense or uncomfortable. He knew what she wanted from him but he didn't want to do it. Then he thought of DT Industries, which would be one hundred per cent his only after the wedding, and he held the baby against him, deeming it a sacrifice worthy of such a result.

'And talk to her,' Tabby suggested.

'What about?' Acheron demanded with perfect seriousness, freezing as the baby nestled close of its own volition, disconcerted by the alien warmth and weight of her as she dug little hands into the flesh of his shoulder.

'Stocks and shares if you like. It doesn't matter at this age. It's the sound and tone of your voice that matters,' Tabby explained.

Acheron mumbled a Greek nursery rhyme.

'And if you walk around the room with her, it might make you feel more relaxed.'

Acheron gritted his teeth and started to tell the baby exactly what he thought of Tabby in Greek, careful to keep the antagonism out of his voice. Amber looked up at him with big trusting brown eyes, and he marvelled at her ability to award that amount of trust to a complete stranger. If the baby could try, he could as well even if it did stick in his throat to be listening to Tabby's instructions and following them. She maddened him, he acknowledged grimly, gently rubbing Amber's back as he talked. The baby slowly rested its head down on his shoulder.

'Give her to me,' Tabby murmured. 'She's going back to sleep.'

'And so ends lesson one,' Acheron mocked as she settled Amber back into the cot and covered her again.

Only it was not the child he was watching but Tabby. The pale grey silk glimmered in the dull light from the corridor, splaying across her thighs, outlining the plump little curves of her derriere as she bent over the cot rail, prominent nipples visible against the flimsy fabric as she straightened again.

Acheron was hard as a rock by the time he completed that far from fleeting appraisal. 'You might want to cover up more around me,' he commented. 'Or is this a come-on?'

Her violet eyes flew wide as she faltered at the doorway, and she flashed him an incredulous glance back over a narrow shoulder. 'Do you think you're irresistible or something?'

Acheron strode over to the doorway. 'You can't be that innocent. Men are fairly predictable when there is so much bare skin on display.'

'I am not on display,' Tabby countered furiously, crossing her arms defensively over her lightly clad length, sharply disconcerted by the idea that he could see her body beneath the nightie. 'When I came in I had no idea you would be in here.'

Acheron closed a hand around her wrist and tugged her into the corridor, shutting the door behind him. 'I like what I see,' he informed her softly.

Tabby stared up at him with fulminating force, noting the dark shadow of stubble outlining his stubborn jaw line and how that overnight growth enhanced his sheer masculinity. 'But I'm not offering myself.'

'No?' Acheron dipped his handsome head and nibbled at the corner of her inviting mouth, invading with his tongue as soon as she parted her succulent lips. Without further ado, he hauled her up against him, hands weaving across her slender back and then sliding up to glance over the taut peaks of her breasts in a caress that made her shiver.

That single kiss had unholy pulling power. Tabby bargained with herself to continue it. One second, just *one* second more to feel the hungry plunge of his tongue that raised a riot of damp heat low in her body and then his hands, dear heaven, his hands skimming, brushing the tender tips of her breasts before cupping her urgently sensitive flesh. 'No,' she told him shakily.

'No?' Wine-dark eyes glittered down at her, and her swollen mouth ran dry because she wanted another kiss, wanted the wildness she experienced beneath his skilled hands, wanted more with a ferocity that terrified her. Long fingers splayed to her spine, tipping her into revealing contact with the erection that his jeans could not conceal. 'We could have fun for an hour or two.'

'Do I strike you as that easy?' Tabby prompted tightly, outraged by the tone of his proposition. Did he think she was flattered by the idea of being his entertainment for a couple of hours? A quick and easy sexual convenience because there was no more appealing prospect available?

His stunning eyes narrowed. 'I don't make judgements like that about women. I'm not sexist. I enjoy sex. I'm sure you do as well.'

'You're wrong,' she began heatedly, thinking he was little different from the men who, having bought her a drink, had assumed that they were entitled to her body and could not comprehend her reluctance. Sex as a leisure-time pursuit was not her style.

'If you haven't enjoyed sex before then you've been with the wrong men,' Acheron assured her silkily, running a caressing finger along the ripe curve of her lower lip, and the breath feathered deliciously in her throat, a ripple of treacherous, unwelcome response quivering through her slender length.

'You're a class act in the persuasion stakes,' Tabby told him very drily, stepping back out of reach, fighting the unexpected chill of separation from the allure of his warm, vital body. 'But it's wasted on me—though I'm a virgin, I'm well aware that a man will tell you practically anything to get you into bed.'

'A...*virgin*?' Ash echoed in an astonished undertone, disbelief clenching his taut dark features. 'Seriously? Or is that a hook to pull me in deeper?'

Tabby slowly shook her head and then surrendered to laugh out loud. 'You are so suspicious of women it's not real. I don't want to pull you into anything. In fact, I think it would be a very bad idea for us to get that involved.'

'I wasn't thinking of involvement...I was thinking of sex,' Acheron traded smoothly. 'A simple exchange of pleasure.'

Tabby noted the way he even had to separate involvement from the act of sex and registered that he was positively phobic when it came to the concept of commitment. He did not want her to misunderstand what was on offer: a bodily exchange of pleasure, nothing more, no strings whatsoever. 'Goodnight,' she said gruffly, turning on her heel.

'A virgin...*seriously*?' Acheron breathed in her wake, the dark deep richness of his accented drawl vibrating through her in the stillness of the silent apartment.

Tabby turned her head slowly back to him. 'Seriously.'

Acheron frowned, dark brows drawing together, and stared at her, his eyes gleaming golden with curiosity and fascination in the overhead lights. 'But why?'

'I've never wanted to.' *Until now*, a little voice piped up in her brain, for that passionate kiss and the carnal caress of his well-shaped hands had roused more hunger in Tabby than she had ever felt in her life. A fierce physical hunger that she sensed could easily get out of hand.

'You wanted *me, hara mou...*' Acheron murmured with assurance as she walked away from him, blonde hair streaming down her back like a pale flowing river highlighting the curve of her bottom.

Tabby knew she should say nothing, but she couldn't resist the little devil inside herself that he provoked and she turned her head again, succumbing to temptation to murmur softly, 'But obviously...not enough.'

That crack might have affected some men like a challenge, Acheron mused broodingly as he strode back to his room for a cold shower, but he was not one of those men because logic had always ruled his libido. If he slept with her it would clearly get messy, and he hated messy relationships and didn't tolerate them for longer than it took to delete such women's numbers from his phone.

He reminded himself of the dire consequences of his last reckless encounter, and it was even worse that Tabby was still a virgin. He found that hard to credit but could not see any advantage in her telling such a lie. A woman who was still a virgin at twenty-five had to have *very* high expectations of her first lover for why else would she have waited so long? He would not be that man, would never fit that framework or meet the demands she would make. He had been warned and from now on he would keep his distance....

Tabby screened a yawn and settled Amber down on the rug at her feet. So far, it had been a very boring morning. Acheron's lawyer, Stevos, had arrived with a bundle of documents, which had been painstakingly filled in, and now he was engaged in explaining the pre-nuptial contract to her clause by painful clause. Naturally Acheron wanted to protect his wealth, and discussing the terms of divorce before they even got as far as the wedding would have been depressing had she been in love with him, but she wasn't in love with him and couldn't have cared less about his money.

'But I don't need anything like that amount of cash to live on after the divorce,' Tabby protested worriedly. 'I know how to live well on a small budget and even a quarter of that amount would be more than generous.'

'You're supposed to be out for all you can get,' Acheron chipped in helpfully from his restive stance by the window. 'Sign the contract and forget about it. Once you've lived in my world for a while, you'll find your tastes have changed and that you want more.'

Tabby slung him a look of resentment. 'I only want Amber out of this arrangement. I'm not going to turn into a greedy, grasping manipulator overnight either!'

'Mr Dimitrakos simply wants you and the child to enjoy a secure and comfortable future,' the lawyer interposed soothingly.

'No, Mr Dimitrakos wants to buy my loyalty and my loyalty is not for sale!' Tabby replied with spirit. 'I very much appreciate what he is doing to help me keep Amber in my life and the very last thing I will do is take advantage of his generosity in any way. Please accept that.'

'*Sign,*' Acheron slotted with raw impatience. 'This nonsense has taken up enough of my morning.'

'You mustn't forget to be present at the visit from the social worker this afternoon,' Stevos reminded him doggedly.

Stevos planted another document in front of Tabby when she had signed the first. 'It's a standard confidentiality agreement, which will prevent you from talking about the terms of your marriage to anyone outside this office.'

'That it's a big fat fake has to stay a secret,' Acheron interposed bluntly.

Suppressing a sigh, Tabby signed and then glanced up to watch Acheron as he talked to his lawyer in Greek. He was wearing a dark grey suit with a very subtle pinstripe and a purple shirt and he looked…absolutely amazing, as if he had stepped live out of a glossy magazine shoot. Sleek, sophisticated and breathtakingly handsome, he instantly commanded her gaze whenever he came within sight. There was no harm in looking at him and appreciating the view, she told herself ruefully. He was like a beautiful painting she could admire without needing to own, particularly as any woman with ideas of ownership where Acheron Dimitrakos was concerned was, in Tabby's opinion, in for a very rough ride.

They had shared the breakfast table in his dining room earlier that morning but the table was literally *all* they had shared. He had read his newspaper while she tended to Amber and munched toast, struggling to eat as quietly as a mouse in a cat's presence. It had proved neither sociable nor relaxed and she had already decided to eat her meals in the kitchen from now on.

'One of my assistants is going to take you shopping now for a wedding dress,' Acheron divulged as Tabby bent to lift Amber off the rug before she got her little hands on his shoelaces. 'And we will have to engage a nanny to take care of Amber when we're busy.'

Tabby straightened. 'I don't want a wedding dress… or a nanny.'

Scorching dark eyes assailed hers. 'Did I ask for your opinion?'

'No, but you're getting it, no extra charge.'

'A wedding dress is not negotiable.'

'Nothing's negotiable with you!'

Dark eyes flared sensual gold. 'If you were willing to try a little harder to please, you might be surprised,' he murmured huskily.

He was thinking about sex again: she *knew* it by the look in his eyes and the husky tone of his voice. Colour burned up hotly over her cheekbones as she dealt him a quelling glance.

'I'll be honest about this—I don't want to waste a wedding dress on a phony marriage. It just seems wrong,' Tabby admitted, lifting her chin. 'I want to save the white wedding dress for the day I do it for real.'

'Tough,' Acheron responded obstinately, moving closer. 'This may be a rush wedding but I want it to look as normal as possible and few women choose to get married without frills.'

Amber held out her arms to him and smiled.

'Cuddle her,' Tabby instructed, dumping the little girl into his startled arms. 'Practice makes perfect and, just as I have to look convincing at the wedding, you have to look convincing as an adoptive father-to-be this afternoon.'

Amber yanked at Acheron's silk tie with gusto and an appreciative grin suddenly slashed his mouth, shocking both his companions. 'Amber really doesn't give a damn about anything but attention and what amuses her in the moment.'

'A baby's needs are simple,' Tabby agreed wryly, striving not to react to that intensely charismatic smile of his, which made her want to smile back like a dream-struck idiot. Just looking at him, amusement falling from his features, she felt slightly light-headed and her tummy hollowed as if she were travelling downhill at breathtaking speed on a roller coaster. 'The nanny?'

'A necessity when you will have other calls on your time,' Acheron pronounced. 'Be practical.'

Tabby breathed in deep, reluctant to argue with him when the social services interview was to take place within a few hours. She took Amber back into her arms and strapped her into her buggy where the little girl screwed up her face and complained vehemently.

'She knows what she wants,' Acheron remarked. 'You will need to be firm as she gets older.'

'Obviously.'

'And you might find it a challenge to wear that wedding dress for real for some man when you already have a child in tow,' Acheron delivered with lethal cool. '*I* don't date single parents.'

'Tell me something that surprises me,' Tabby urged witheringly. 'You're too selfish, too concerned about protecting your own comfort level.'

'I just respect my limitations.'

'Nonsense. You can't stand the idea of having to consider someone else's needs before your own,' Tabby traded.

'So, what am I doing now in marrying you?' Acheron demanded curtly.

'You're righting the wrong you committed a couple of months ago when you refused to be Amber's guardian and no doubt that makes you feel so unselfish and perfect you think you're one hell of a guy!'

Listening to that exchange, Stevos was staring in shock at Tabby and her colour was high when she released the brake on the buggy and wheeled it out of the door.

Acheron's PA, Sharma, greeted her in the outer office and took her straight out to a limo for the shopping trip.

Tabby was surprised to be taken to an exclusive and very fashionable wedding boutique rather than a department store, but appreciated that with the time available it would be a challenge to come up with a sophisticated dress that fitted the bill. While Sharma played with Amber, Tabby tried on gowns, finally selecting the least fussy available and choosing the accessories suggested by the attentive proprietor. That achieved, she returned to Acheron's apartment and rang Jack to tell him that she was getting married and to invite him to the civil ceremony the following day.

'Is this a joke?' Jack asked.

'No. It is kind of sudden but I know exactly what I'm doing. Acheron wants to adopt Amber with me.'

'You've kept this very quiet. How long have you been seeing him for?' Jack enquired ruefully.

'A while. I didn't know it was going to turn serious or I'd have mentioned it sooner,' Tabby fibbed, wishing she could just have told the truth.

'It'll solve all your problems,' Jack pronounced with satisfaction. 'I've been really worried about you and Amber.'

Acheron turned up just in time for the interview with the social worker and swiftly proved a dab hand at twisting the truth, contriving to make it sound as if they had known each other far longer than they had. The older woman was so palpably impressed by Acheron and his incredible apartment that she asked few searching questions.

An hour later Tabby was feeding Amber and stealing bites from her own meal in the kitchen when Acheron appeared in the doorway, his expression thunderous. He swept up the highchair with Amber in it and turned on his heel.

'What on earth are you doing?' Tabby cried, racing after him.

Acheron set the chair down at one end of the dining table. 'We eat in here together. You do not eat in the kitchen like a member of my staff. That will not support the impression of a normal married couple.'

'I shouldn't think any of your staff could care less where we eat!' Tabby replied.

'But you need to be more cautious about appearances,' Acheron spelled out the warning grimly. 'Any one of my staff could sell a story to the tabloids and blow a massive hole in our pretence of being a couple.'

Tabby fell still. 'I never thought of that. Can't you trust your employees?'

'Most of them but there's always a rotten apple somewhere in the barrel,' Acheron answered with cynical cool.

Tabby nodded and returned to the kitchen to fetch her meal. He thought of every pitfall from every possible angle and it shook her that he had evidently already suffered that kind of betrayal from someone close to him. It was little wonder that he continually expected the worst from people, she reflected ruefully.

'Why were you eating in the kitchen?' he enquired as she settled at the table.

'I know you like your own space,' Tabby said quickly.

'You're not comfortable eating with me. I noticed that in the restaurant the first night,' Acheron commented, resting level dark eyes on her rising colour. 'You'll have to get over that.'

'Yes, but it was a strain that first night,' Tabby admitted, grudgingly opting for honesty. 'I couldn't read the menu because my French isn't up to it. I didn't even know which cutlery to use.'

A stab of remorse pierced Acheron. It had not even occurred to him that she might feel out of her depth at his favourite restaurant. 'Cutlery isn't important, *hara mou*—'

'Believe me, it *is* when you don't know which utensil to use.'

'In future, *ask*.' Acheron compressed his wide, sensual mouth, irritated that he had been so inconsiderate of the differences between them. 'I'm not…sensitive. I won't pick up on things like that unless you warn me. By the way, Sharma has engaged last night's nanny to work for us. I've also secured permission for us to take Amber abroad.'

'Abroad?' Tabby exclaimed. 'What are you talking about?'

'We're heading to Italy after the wedding. I have a house there. It will be easier to keep up the newly married act without an audience of friends and acquaintances looking on,' Acheron pointed out with irreproachable practicality.

Tabby woke early the next morning. Well, it was her wedding day even though it bore no resemblance to the very special event she had once dreamt the occasion would be. For a start, Sonia would not be there to play bridesmaid as the two women had always assumed she would, and momentarily Tabby's eyes stung with tears because sometimes the pain of losing her best friend felt like a wound that would never heal. She reminded herself that she still had Jack, but Jack was a man of few words and his girlfriend, Emma, was uneasy about his friendship with Tabby. As a result Tabby kept contact with Jack to the minimum. With a sigh, she rolled out of bed to go and tend to Amber and get dressed.

The nanny, Melinda, was in Amber's bedroom. Tabby had forgotten about the nanny, forgotten that she was no longer the only person available to care for the little girl, and Amber was already bathed, dressed and fed. A little pang of regret assailed Tabby because she had always enjoyed giving Amber her first peaceful feed of the day. But Sonia's daughter still greeted her with uninhibited love and affection, and Tabby buried her nose in the little girl's sweet-smelling hair and breathed deep, reminding herself why she was marrying Acheron and meeting his every demand. Amber was worth almost any sacrifice, she conceded feelingly.

The ceremony was to be held at an exclusive castle hotel, and Tabby was amazed at how much it had been possible to arrange at such speed. Then she reminded herself that Acheron's wealth would have ensured special attention and she scolded herself for being so naive.

Sharma had arranged for a hairstylist and a make-up artist to attend her at the apartment, and Tabby hoped that their professional skill would give her at least a hint of the glossy sophistication that Acheron's female companions usually exuded. As quick as she thought that, she wondered why his opinion should matter to her. Was it simply a matter of pride?

Sharma helped lace Tabby into her dress while the stylist adjusted the short flirty veil attached to the circlet of fresh flowers attached to Tabby's hair.

'With those flowers on your head you look like the Queen of Summer...' Sharma burbled enthusiastically. 'Mr Dimitrakos will be blown away.'

It dawned on Tabby for the first time that she was dealing with someone who thought she was about to attend a genuine wedding and she flushed with discomfiture, quite certain that the last thing Acheron would be was 'blown away'.

'And watching the boss go to so much trouble to get married in such a hurry is *so* romantic,' Sharma continued. 'I used to think he was so…er, cold, no offence intended…and then I saw him with the baby and realised how wrong I was. Of course fatherhood does change a man…'

And Tabby registered that Sharma had, not unnaturally, added two and two to make five in her assumption that Acheron was Amber's father. 'Actually, Amber is the daughter of my late best friend and Acheron's cousin,' she explained, deeming it wiser to put the other woman right on that score.

Grim-faced, Acheron paced while he awaited the arrival of the bridal car. He was very tense. It might be a fake wedding but with the arrival of his stepmother, Ianthe, and two of her adult children along with several good friends, it felt unnervingly real and he was already fed up with making polite conversation and pretending to be a happy bridegroom. Unhappily, a wedding without guests would not have been a very convincing affair, he reminded himself impatiently, and at least the woman whose attendance would have been least welcome had failed to show up. Stationed by the window of the function room adorned with flowers for the ceremony, he watched as a limousine embellished with white ribbons that fluttered in the breeze drew up at the hotel entrance.

Tabby stepped out in a sleek bell of rustling white fabric and petticoats, little shoulders bare, her veil and glorious streamers of golden-blonde hair blowing back from her oval face. Acheron's expressive mouth hardened even

more, a nerve pulling taut at the corner of his lips. She
looked as dainty and delicate as a doll and utterly ravish-
ing, he noted in exasperation, cursing his all-too-male
response to so feminine and alluring an image. Tabby
didn't just clean up well, in Stevos's parlance; she cleaned
up spectacular, Acheron conceded wryly, only absently
registering the emergence of the new nanny clutching
Amber, who was looking similarly festive in a candy-
pink dress and matching hairband.

Tabby was guided straight into the ceremony where
music was already playing. Her apprehensive glance
took in the sea of faces and then lodged on Acheron and
stayed there as if padlocked. *Whoosh!* She could feel all
her defences being sucked away by the pure power of
his compelling presence. He stared back at her, making no pretence of looking forward to the registrar, his
stunning dark eyes golden and bright as sunlight in his
lean face and so gorgeous he made something low in
her body clench tight like a fist. Knees a tad wobbly, she
walked down the short aisle between the seated guests
and stilled by his side, the words of the brief ceremony
washing over her while she frantically reminded herself that finding Acheron attractive was a one-way trip
to disaster and not to be risked lest it should somehow
threaten Amber's future as well.

He slid a ring onto her finger and she did the same for
him. Afterwards, he retained his grip on her hand, ignoring her attempt to tug gently free, and suddenly there
was a crowd of people round them murmuring congratulations, and introductions were being made.

His stepmother was a decorative blonde with a shrill
voice and she had a son and a daughter by her side, both
of whom seemed rather in awe of Acheron, which gave
Tabby the impression that he had never been a true part

of his father's family. Jack appeared with his girlfriend, Emma, and the other woman was friendlier than Tabby had ever seen her. Tabby chatted at length to Jack and turned only to find Acheron studying her, his handsome mouth compressed.

'Who was that?'

'Jack's an old friend and the only person I invited,' she proclaimed defensively.

'How much did you tell him?' Acheron enquired grimly.

'I told him nothing,' Tabby responded, wondering what his problem was. 'He thinks this is all for real.'

Drinks were being poured and toasts made by the time a tall, curvy brunette in a sapphire-blue suit swept into the room without warning.

Someone close to Tabby vented a groan. The brunette marched up to them like a woman on a mission and shot an outraged look at Acheron's stepmother, Ianthe. 'Mother, how could you take part in this insane charade when it goes against *my* interests?' she demanded loudly. 'I should have been the bride here today!'

'Let's not go there, Kasma,' her brother, Simeon, advised sheepishly. 'We're here to celebrate Ash's wedding, and I know you don't want to spoil the day by creating a scene.'

'Don't I?' Kasma struck an attitude, furious dark eyes glittering bright. She was a very beautiful woman with a great figure, a perfect face and a torrent of long dark hair, Tabby noted in a daze of agitation. 'Tell me, what has *she* got that I haven't, Acheron?' she demanded in a fierce tone of accusation.

Amber was starting to cry and Tabby took the opportunity to step out of the drama to join Melinda, the nanny, at the back of the room. After all, family squabbles and bitter ex-lovers were none of her business. Had Acheron had an affair with his stepsister? By the looks of it, it had been a rash move to utilise his charisma within the family circle, and she could understand why he had said on the first day that they met at his office that he had *no* family. His late father's family spoke to Acheron as politely as the strangers they so clearly were. Evidently he had never lived with them, which made her wonder who he *had* lived with when he was younger because Tabby was convinced she remembered his very famous mother's death being announced on television while she herself was still only a child.

Tabby took Amber into the baby-changing room, thinking that the histrionic Kasma would, with a little luck, be gone by the time she returned to sit down to a late and much-needed lunch.

But she was to have no such luck. No sooner had she finished undressing Amber than the door opened to frame Kasma's lush shape. 'Is that child Ash's?' she asked drily.

Tabby changed Amber, who was squirming like mad and craning her neck to look at the visitor. 'No.'

'I didn't think so,' Kasma said snidely. 'Ash has never been the daddy type.'

Exasperation kindling, Tabby straightened her shoulders and turned her head. 'Look, I don't know you and I'm busy here—'

'You know why Ash married you, don't you?' the brunette continued thinly. '*I* should have been Ash's bride. No one understands him as well as I do. Unfortunately for all three of us, he's too stubborn and proud to accept being forced to do what he should have done long ago.'

'I don't need to know what you're talking about,' Tabby told her uncomfortably. 'It's really none of my business.'

'How can you say that when by marrying Ash you're winning him a fortune?' Kasma demanded resentfully, her mother's vocal shrillness feeding into her sharp tone. 'According to the terms of his father's will if he stayed single until the end of the year he would lose half of *his* company to *my* family! And, of course, anyone who knows how Ash feels about his company would know that he would do virtually *anything* to protect it...even marry a totally unsuitable nobody from nowhere to maintain the status quo!'

CHAPTER FIVE

KASMA'S ACCUSATION RANG in Tabby's ears like a nasty echo during the flight to Italy. After the brunette's departure, lunch had proceeded quietly but Tabby had not had the advantage of a private moment in which to question Acheron. She had intended to raise the subject during the flight but Melinda was looking after Amber at the back of the cabin and she did not feel that she could speak freely.

Was it possible that Acheron had had a far more self-serving motive to marry than he had admitted? Tabby deemed it perfectly possible when she compared his refusal of all responsibility for Amber only months earlier with his sudden change of heart. Why on earth hadn't she been more suspicious of that rapid turnaround of his? He had to think she was as dumb as a rock, she thought painfully, feeling betrayed not only by his lack of honesty but also by her own gullibility. What terms had been included in his father's will? How could he possibly lose half of a company that belonged to him? And if Kasma's information was correct, why hadn't Acheron simply told Tabby the truth?

And the answer to that question could only be *power*, Tabby reflected with steadily mounting anger. As long as Tabby had believed that Acheron was doing her a favour for Amber's sake she had been willing to meet his every demand because she had been grateful to him, believing that he was making a big sacrifice even if theirs was only a fake marriage. But what if it wasn't like that at all? What if Acheron Dimitrakos had needed a conformable wife just as much as she needed the support and stability that would enable her to adopt Amber? That very much changed the picture and made them equals. But Acheron had never been prepared to treat Tabby as an equal. Acheron preferred to dictate and demand, not persuade and compromise. Well, those days were gone if Kasma had told her the truth…

'You're very quiet,' Acheron commented in the car driving them through the Tuscan countryside. She had changed out of her wedding gown before leaving London, and he had felt weirdly disappointed when he saw her wearing the violet dress he had personally chosen for her in London instead. The fabric and long sleeves were too heavy for a warmer climate and there was a flush of pink on her face in spite of the air conditioning. The colour, however, brought out the remarkable shade of her eyes and somehow accentuated the succulent fullness of her pink mouth.

Acheron breathed in slow and deep, dropped his gleaming gaze only for it to lodge on a slender knee and the soft pale skin beneath, which only made him wonder if her skin would feel as silky to the touch as it looked. He gritted his teeth, cursing his high-voltage libido. It had never once crossed his mind until now that, even with the options he had, a platonic relationship might still be a challenge, but evidently he was suffering from sexual frustration. Why else would he find her so appealing?

'I'm enjoying the views,' Tabby proclaimed stiltedly, so angry with him that she had to bite her lower lip before she started an argument while still trapped in the car with him. 'Where exactly are we going?'

'A villa in the hills. Like most of my properties it once belonged to my mother but I had it renovated last year.'

Despite her anger, curiosity stirred in Tabby. 'Your mother died when you were still quite young, didn't she?' she remarked.

His lean bronzed features clenched hard, dark golden eyes screening. 'Yes.'

The wall of reserve he used as a shield cast a forbidding shadow over his expressionless face. 'I lost my parents quite young too,' Tabby told him, rushing to fill the uneasy silence with an innate sensitivity towards his feelings that annoyed her. 'I went into foster care. That's where I met Jack and Amber's mum, Sonia.'

'I didn't realise you'd been in foster care,' Acheron breathed flatly, well aware she would not have had the escape route from that lifestyle that had eventually been granted by his inherited wealth.

'Well…' Tabby responded awkwardly, colliding with impenetrable midnight eyes heavily fringed by spiky black lashes and fighting a sensation of falling…and falling…and falling. 'They weren't the happiest years of my life but there were some good times. The last foster home I was in was the best and at least the three of us were together there.'

That appeared to be the end of that conversation as Acheron compressed his lips in grim silence while Tabby fought that light-headed sensation and struggled to focus on her anger. So, Acheron Dimitrakos was gorgeous and he kept on making her hormones sit up and take notice but he was also a skilled manipulator and deceiver and only a complete fool would forget the fact. In addition, it had not escaped her notice that he really wasn't interested in learning anything about her background and who she was as a person. But then had he ever seen her as a person in her own right? Or simply as someone he could easily use?

The car turned off the road and purred up a sloping driveway to the very large ochre-coloured stone building sprawling across the top of the hill. Tabby had to tense her lower lip to prevent her mouth from dropping open in comical awe because what he called a villa *she* would have called a palace. A fountain was playing a rainbow of sparkling water droplets down into a circular pool in the centre of a paved frontage already embellished with giant stone pots of glorious flowers. As she climbed out into the early evening sunshine, a flicker of movement from a shrubbery attracted her attention and a white peacock strutted out, unfurling his pristine feathers. The light caught his plumage as he unfurled it like a magnificent silver lace fan. The peacock posed, head high, one foot lifted, his confidence supreme in spite of his aloneness.

'You remind me of that bird,' Tabby muttered as the car carrying Amber and her nanny with the bodyguards drew up behind them.

Acheron raised an ebony brow enquiringly.

Embarrassed, Tabby shrugged. 'Never mind. Could we have a word in private?' she asked then.

'Of course,' he said without expression, but she didn't miss the frowning glance he shot in her direction as she moved to speak to Amber and her nanny. The little girl was fast asleep though, and a last feed and an early night were clearly what she most needed after a long and exhausting day.

The hall of the villa was breathtaking. Gleaming stretches of marble flooring ran below the arches that separated the reception areas. Tabby had never seen so many different shades of white utilised in a decor or anything so impractical for a household with a child in tow. Of course they would not be staying for long, she reminded herself, and Amber wasn't yet mobile so all the sharp-edged glass coffee tables and stylishly sited sculptural pieces on pedestals would scarcely endanger her.

'Very impressive,' she pronounced while Melinda followed the housekeeper up the wrought-iron and marble staircase.

'I have a few calls to make,' Acheron informed her and he was already swinging away, a tall, broad-shouldered male in a beautifully cut lightweight suit made of a fine fabric that gleamed in the light flooding through the windows.

'We have to talk…'

Over the years, far too many women had fired that same phrase at Acheron and had followed it with dramatic scenes and demands for more attention that he found abhorrent. His powerful frame tensed, his lean, strong face shuttering. 'Not now…later.'

'Yes…*now*,' Tabby emphasised without hesitation, violet eyes shimmering with anger, for she was not going to allow him to rudely brush her off as if she were the nobody from nowhere and of no account that Kasma had labelled her. If she toed his line and treated him like a superior being she would soon be thinking the same thing about herself.

'What is this about?' Acheron enquired coldly.

Tabby walked very deliberately out of the hall into the area furnished with incredibly opulent white sofas and slowly turned round, slim shoulders straight, chin lifted. 'Is it true that to retain ownership of your company your father's will required you to take a wife before the end of the year?'

His stubborn jaw line clenched. 'Where did you get that story from?' he asked grittily and then he released his breath with a measured hiss of comprehension. 'Kasma... *right*?'

'It's true, then,' Tabby gathered in furious disbelief. 'She told me the truth.'

'The terms of my father's will are nothing to do with you,' Acheron stated with chilling bite, his dark eyes deep and cold as the depths of the ocean.

But Tabby was in no mood to be intimidated. 'How dare you say that when getting married must've suited you every bit as much as it suited me? Didn't you think I deserved to know that?'

Acheron gritted his even white teeth together in a visible act of restraint. 'What difference can it possibly make to you?'

'I think it makes a *huge* difference!' Tabby slung back at him, violet eyes darkening with seething resentment. 'You made me feel as if you were doing me an enormous favour for Amber's benefit.'

'And wasn't I?' Acheron slotted in, utilising a tone that was not calculated to soothe wounded feelings.

'And you can stop being so rude right now!' Tabby launched at him, that derisive tone and superior appraisal of his lashing her like an offensive assault. 'Yes, Acheron, it *is* rude to interrupt and even more rude to look at me as if I'm some bug on the ground at your feet! I was completely honest with you but you, and no doubt your lawyer, deceived me.'

Eyes smouldering gold, Acheron was having trouble holding on to his temper. 'How you were deceived? I did exactly as I promised. I married you, I helped you to lodge an adoption application and I have ensured your future security. A lot of women would kill for one half of what I'm giving you!'

Her slender hands closed into irate fists. She wanted to pummel him as he stood there, the king of all he surveyed, cocooned from ordinary mortals and decent moral tenets by a level of wealth and success she could barely imagine. 'You are so arrogant, so hateful sometimes I want to hit you and I'm not a violent person!' Tabby hastened to declare in her own defence. 'Do you honestly not understand why I'm angry? I was frank with you. There were no lies, no pretences, no evasions. I believe I deserve the same respect from you.'

His wide, sensual mouth curled. 'This doesn't feel like respect.'

'Is this how you normally deal with an argument?'

'I don't have arguments with people,' Acheron responded levelly.

'Only because people probably spend all their time trying to please and flatter you, not because they always agree with you!' Tabby snapped back in vexation. 'For someone who appears very confrontational, you're actually avoiding the issue and refusing to respond to my natural annoyance.'

'I don't wish to prolong this argument, nor do I see anything natural about your annoyance,' Acheron admitted curtly. 'I don't make a habit of confiding in people. I'm a very private individual, and my father's will certainly falls into the confidential category.'

'I had the right to know that I didn't need to be grateful and submit to your every demand because you were getting even more out of this marriage than I was!' Tabby condemned, refusing to be sidetracked by a red herring like his reserve. 'You used my ignorance like a weapon against me!'

'The will was a matter of business and was of no conceivable interest to you,' Acheron stated in a raw undertone.

'Don't talk nonsense. Of course it was of interest to me that you had as much need to get married as I did!' she flashed back at him. 'It levels the playing field.'

'As far as I'm concerned, there *is* no playing field because this is not a game!' Acheron countered angrily. 'I married you and now that you're my wife, you're trying to take advantage of your position.'

Her violet eyes widened and she planted her tiny hands on her hips, just like a miniature fishwife getting ready to do battle, he decided, torn between grudging amusement and exasperation. 'Take advantage? How am I taking advantage? By standing up to you for once? By daring to state *my* side of the case?' she hissed back at him with simmering rancour.

Acheron strode forward, planted two hands over hers and hauled her up into the air before she could even guess his intention. He held her there, entrapped. 'You don't have a side of the case to argue, *moraki mou*—'

Enraged by his behaviour, Tabby glowered down at him. 'If you don't put me down, I'll kick you!' she launched at him furiously.

In response, Acheron banded her closely to his big powerful length, ensuring that her legs were as trapped as her hands. Dark golden eyes fringed by heavy black lashes held hers fast. 'There will be *no* kicking, *no* hitting, *no* bad language—'

'Says who?' Tabby bit out between gritted teeth.

'Your husband.' Acheron frowned as though that aspect had only just occurred to him and he was as much amused as irritated by the reality.

It was as if she were a firework and he had lit her

up inside. Rage blazed through Tabby. 'You are *not* my husband!'

Unholy amusement lit Acheron's eyes, whipping up the lighter tones she had noticed before and giving him an extraordinary appeal that made her mouth run dry and her tummy perform acrobatics. 'Then what am I?'

'A rat with a marriage certificate!' Tabby snapped at him informatively.

Acheron gave her a look of mock sympathy. '*Your* rat because you're stuck with me.'

'Put…me…down!' Tabby ground out fiercely. 'Or you'll regret it!'

'No, I much prefer this set-up to you shouting at me from across the room.'

'I was not shouting!'

'You were shouting,' Acheron repeated steadily. 'That is not how I conduct disputes.'

'I don't give a monkey's about how you like to conduct your disputes!' Tabby fired back.

It was those sparkling eyes, that incredibly succulent and inviting mouth of hers, Acheron mused abstractedly, conscious that she somehow hauled fiercely on every libidinous hormone he possessed and fired him up like a horny teenager. He didn't understand it, didn't care, didn't think he needed to, but without conscious volition he drew that tempting mouth up to his and crushed it under his, and the taste of her was as rich and fragrant and luscious as juicy strawberries on a summer day.

'No… No,' Tabby's dismayed objections, voiced as much to her wayward self as to him, were swallowed up by the hot, hungry pressure of his erotically charged mouth on hers.

Nobody had ever kissed Tabby as he did with all the passion of the volatile nature he kept under wraps, but which she sensed every time she was with him. He demanded and teased and the force of his sensual lips on hers followed by the invasive plunge of his tongue was unbelievably exciting and sexy.

He was very, *very* sexy, she acknowledged dimly, as if it was an excuse, and as he hoisted her higher to get a better grip on her slight body he let go of her hands and, instead of using them to get free of his hold, she balanced one on a broad shoulder and delved the fingers of the other into the springy, luxuriant depths of his black hair. With a guttural sound low in his throat he brought her down on something soft and yielding and then sealed her fast to the hard, driving length of his powerful frame.

And even as a faint current of alarm blipped somewhere in the back of Tabby's head she was aware of how much she loved feeling his strong, muscular body over and on hers. In fact, her every skin cell was leaping and bouncing with pent-up energy long before his fingers closed over the slight thrust of her achingly sensitive breast, and she strained up breathless and bound by a new tide of sensation. Indeed, desire had infiltrated her with such powerful effect that she scarcely knew what she was doing any more. Nothing had ever felt more necessary; nothing had ever felt more thrilling than the hot, hungry stimulation of his mouth and his hands. Spasms of excitement were quivering through her in a gathering storm. But then other sounds suddenly cancelled out those physical responses: a stifled gasp linked to the rattle of china and the sound of hastily receding footsteps.

'My goodness, what was that?' Tabby exclaimed, dragging her mouth from beneath his to find that she was lying on a sofa beneath him. *Beneath him*, her brain repeated, and her body went into panic mode when she collided with smouldering dark golden eyes and pushed at his shoulders, wriggling out from under his weight at frantic, feverish speed.

'Let's go to bed,' Acheron husked, closing long brown fingers over hers.

And it's just that simple and casual for him, she told herself angrily, furious that she had not contrived to resist him. She perched at the far end of the sofa, smoothing her tumbled blonde hair back from her brow, a slight tremor in her hands and her face so hot with mortification she could have boiled eggs on it. 'No, let's not…it would mess up things.'

'The bed would be more comfortable than the sofa,' Acheron declared single-mindedly.

'I'm not talking about *where*…I'm saying *no*, we're not going to do that!' Tabby slung back at him in frustration, wincing at the nagging bite of separation from his lean, hard body, fighting the ache of longing between her thighs with defiant determination. No way was she planning to be one more in a no doubt long line of easy women for Acheron, a mere female body to scratch an itch for a male unaccustomed to doing without sexual satisfaction.

Acheron sprawled back at the other end of the sofa, long powerful thighs spread so that she noticed, really couldn't help noticing, that that little tussle with her body had seriously aroused his. Her face burned even hotter and her tummy hollowed just looking at the prominent bulge at his pelvis, reactions to a physical craving she had never experienced before assailing her in an unwelcome wave.

All of a sudden and no thanks to Acheron for the lesson, she was realising why she was still a virgin. No other man had ever attracted her enough to make her drop her guard and yearn for sex. Sex, yes, that was all it would be, straightforward, unvarnished sex, not something a sensible woman would crave, and she was very sensible, wasn't she? *Wasn't she?* It really bothered her that even while thinking along those lines and carefully realigning her defences she was still fully engaged in appreciating the pure male beauty of Acheron's lean bronzed face and long, powerful body.

'You want me,' Acheron breathed a little raggedly. 'I want you.'

'Weird, isn't it…? I mean, we can't even be civil to each other,' Tabby pronounced shakily, still as out of breath as he was, recalling that wild entanglement and the fierce need he had sent powering through her and then suppressing the uncomfortable memory before standing up, smoothing down her dress with careful hands.

'Yet you burn me up, *hara mou*,' Acheron breathed huskily, springing upright with easy grace.

Tabby turned her head away. 'Let's not talk about that…you and me? It would be a very bad idea. We have as much in common as a cat and a dog. I'd like to see my room,' she completed, moving back with determination towards the hall.

'I'll show you. We've frightened off the staff,' Acheron volunteered with an unconcerned laugh. 'I think that noise was someone bringing us coffee and we were seen.'

'Yes, I can imagine what they saw,' Tabby cut in stiltedly, wishing he would drop the subject.

'Well, that's at least one person who will believe that we're genuine honeymooners,' Acheron replied nonchalantly, refusing to take the hint as he led the way up the marble staircase.

'But we're *not*,' she reminded him doggedly.

'You're not a very flexible personality, are you?'

'You'd roll me out like pastry if I was,' Tabby quipped. 'I'm still mad at you, Acheron. You took advantage of my ignorance.'

'I'm an alpha male, programmed at birth to take advantage,' Acheron pointed out with unapologetic cool. 'But you called me on it, which I wasn't expecting.'

He pushed open double doors at the end of the corridor and exposed a small hall containing two doors. 'That's my room.' He thrust open one door and then the second. 'And yours…'

Tabby worried at her full lower lip. 'Do we have to be so close?'

'I don't sleepwalk,' Acheron murmured silkily. 'But you're very welcome if you choose to visit.'

'I won't be doing that.' Tabby strolled in the big room, glancing into the en suite that led off and then into a dressing room to slide open a wardrobe, only to frown at the garments packed within. 'Didn't your last girlfriend take her clothes with her?'

'Those are yours. I ordered them,' Acheron explained. 'You'll need summer clothes here.'

Tabby spun back to study him with simmering violet eyes. 'I'm not a dress-up doll.'

'But you know that all I want to do is *undress* you, *moraki mou*.'

Tabby went pink again and compressed her lips.

'You blush like a bonfire,' Acheron remarked with sudden amusement as he strode off to make use of another door on the opposite side of the room that evidently led to his suite.

Tabby thought about turning the lock and then decided it would be petty, for surprisingly on that level she trusted him and had no fear that he might try to take what she was not prepared to offer. If she withstood his appeal, she was quite certain he would withstand hers and find some far more amusing and experienced quarry to pursue. Unfortunately, she didn't like the idea of him with another woman in the slightest and she told herself off for that because she knew she couldn't have it both ways. Either they were together or they were not; there was no halfway stage to explore.

Acheron stripped off for a cold shower. He was still ragingly erect and wondering when a woman had last turned him down. He couldn't remember, and the shock of Tabby's steely resolve still rankled. But it was a timely warning to steer clear, he reflected impatiently, his sensual mouth twisting as he stifled the urge to fantasise about having her tiny body wrapped round him while he satisfied them both. If she attached *that* much importance to sex, he definitely didn't want to get involved because sex meant no more to him than an appetite that required regular satisfaction.

Tabby rifled through the new wardrobe he had acquired for her without even mentioning his intent. She tugged out a long cotton dress that looked cool and, more importantly, covered up anything that she imagined a man might find tempting. If he kept his hands off her, she would keep her hands off him. She worried at her lower lip with her teeth. She had wanted to rip his clothes off him on that sofa, and the incredible strength of the hunger he had awakened still shocked her in retrospect. But nothing more was going to happen, *nothing*, she stressed inwardly with more force than cool. She could handle him, of course she could. He might be a very rich, very good-looking and very manipulative male but she had always had a good gut instinct about how best to look after herself.

Buoyed up by that knowledge, Tabby got changed, freshened up and went off to find out where the nursery had been set up.

CHAPTER SIX

'IT'S TIME YOU told me something about yourself,' Acheron declared, settling back into his seat and cradling his wineglass in one elegant hand.

Tabby was ill at ease. The grand dining room and the table festooned with flowers and fancy dishes for the first meal they were to share as a married couple made her feel like Cinderella arriving at the ball without a prince on hand to claim her. He had watched her watching him to see which cutlery to use, and the awareness had embarrassed her, making her wish that she had never confessed her ignorance. 'What sort of something?'

Acheron raised an ebony brow. 'Let's be basic—your background?'

He was so relaxed that he infuriated her, sheathed in tight faded denim jeans and a black shirt left undone at the throat. She had assumed he would dress up for dinner much as aristocrats seemed to do on television shows and, if she was honest, that was probably why she had picked the long dress. But instead of dressing up, Acheron had dressed *down* and, maddeningly, he still looked amazing, black hair curling a little from the shower, stubborn jaw line slightly rough with dark stubble, lustrous dark eyes pinned to her with uncompromising intensity and she couldn't read him, couldn't read him at all, hadn't a clue what he was thinking about.

'My background's not pretty,' she warned him.

He shrugged a shoulder in dismissal of that objection.

Tabby clenched her teeth and stiffened her backbone. 'I imagine my conception was an accident. My parents weren't married. My mother once told me they were going to give me up for adoption until they discovered that having a child meant they could get better housing and more benefits out of the welfare system. They were both druggies.'

Acheron no longer seemed quite so relaxed and he sat forward with a sudden frown. *'Addicts?'*

'I warned you that it wasn't pretty. Their drug of choice was whatever was cheapest and most easily available. They weren't parents in the normal sense of the word, and I don't think they were even that keen on each other because they had terrible fights. I was simply the child who lived with them,' Tabby proffered tightly. 'And I got in the way…frequently because children have needs and they didn't meet them.'

Acheron forced his shoulders back into the chair, his astonishment at what she had told him concealed by his impassive expression. He almost told her then and there in a revelation that would have been unprecedented for him that they had much more in common than a cat and a dog.

'Have you heard enough?' Tabby enquired hopefully.

'I want to hear it *all*,' Acheron contradicted levelly, slowly comprehending the base level of painful isolation and insecurity from which that chippy, aggressive manner of hers had undoubtedly been forged. Tabby had been forced at an early age to learn to fight for her survival, and that he understood.

'I was the kid in the wrong clothes at school...when they got me there, which wasn't very often. Then my father started to take me with him as a lookout when he burgled houses,' she confided flatly, hating every word she was telling him but somehow needing him to know that she could handle her troubled, crime-infested childhood and indeed had moved far beyond it. 'Social Services got involved when he was caught in the act and eventually, because I was missing so much school and my parents were incapable of looking after me properly, I was put into care.'

'As was I,' Acheron admitted gruffly. 'I was ten years old. What age were you?'

Tabby stared back at him wide-eyed. '*You*...were in care? But your parents must have been *so* wealthy.'

'Which doesn't necessarily mean that they were any more responsible than yours,' Acheron pointed out drily. 'Believe me, my mother's money didn't protect me, although it did protect *her* until the day she died from an overdose. Her lawyers rushed her out of the country before she could be prosecuted for neglecting me.'

'What about your father?' Tabby prompted sickly, still shaken and appalled that he, who seemed so very assured and rich and protected, could ever have lived within the care system as she had. All at once she felt guilty about the assumptions she had made.

'His marriage to my mother only lasted about five minutes. When she got bored with him she told him that the child she was expecting—*me*—was the child of her previous lover...and he believed her,' Acheron explained flatly. 'He couldn't have afforded to fight her for custody in any case. I met him for the first time when I was in my twenties. He came to see me in London because a relative of his had noticed how very alike we looked in a newspaper photograph.'

'So what did your mother do with you?' Tabby asked, sipping at her glass of water.

'Very little. The trust who controlled her millions paid for a squad of carers to look after her and keep her worst excesses out of the newspapers. She was addicted to drugs too,' Acheron divulged tautly. 'But once I was no longer a baby none of her staff had a direct mandate to look after me, and my mother was, all too frequently, high as a kite. So I was left to my own devices, which eventually attracted the attention of the authorities. I had no other relatives to take responsibility for me.'

Painfully aware of the grim memories shadowing his eyes and the sad knowledge that his father could not have been waiting in the wings to take charge of him, Tabby stretched her hand across the table without even thinking about it and rested it down on his, where his long, elegant fingers were braced on the tablecloth. 'I'm sorry.'

His arrogant dark head came up at a combative angle even as he lifted his hand to close it round hers, glancing down at their linked hands in virtual bewilderment as if he couldn't quite work out how that connection had happened. Dark colour crawled up to accentuate the high cheekbones that gave his face such strength and definition. 'Why would you be sorry? I imagine I got off lighter than you. I suspect you were physically mistreated…?'

Her oval face froze. 'Yes,' she almost whispered in confirmation.

'I only met with physical abuse *after* I entered the care system. I was an obnoxious little brat by then, semi-feral and may well have deserved what I got,' Acheron volunteered between gritted teeth.

'No child deserves pain,' Tabby argued.

'I endured two years of complete hell and innumerable different homes until my mother died and the trustees rescued me. I was sent off to boarding school for what remained of my childhood.'

Tabby's heart squeezed tight and her throat thickened at the awareness that just like her he had grown up knowing nothing of the love and security of a happy home and committed parents. She had been *so* wrong about him and it shamed her that she had been so biased purely because his late mother had been a famous Greek heiress. 'You never forget it…how powerless and lost you feel,' she framed unevenly.

Acheron looked across the table at her, his stunning dark golden eyes glittering. 'You leave it behind you, move on,' he told her squarely, suddenly releasing her hand.

'Yes, but it's always there somewhere in the back of your mind.' Starstruck even as she yanked her hand back, she collided with his eyes and the rare warmth of connection there and it made her feel not as if she was falling but instead flying high as a bird, breathless and thrilled.

'Not if you discipline yourself,' Acheron asserted smoothly.

'Tell me about your father's will,' Tabby urged, already dreading the return of the cold reserve that was beginning to clench his lean, darkly handsome features again.

'Some other time. We've raked over enough personal stuff for one evening…surely?' A sleek black emphatic brow lifted, the force of his will bearing down on her from the lambent glow of his beautiful lustrous dark eyes.

And Tabby, who was usually like a nail stuck to a magnet when in the grip of curiosity, quelled her desire to know more, conceding that, for a male as famously reticent as he was, he had been remarkably frank with her when he hadn't needed to be, for she knew of no stories referring to his dysfunctional upbringing that had ever appeared in the media. She swallowed back her questions and lifted a fork to attack the dessert that had been brought to the table.

'I'm crazy about meringue,' she confided. 'And this is perfectly cooked, crunchy on the outside, soft inside.'

A flashing smile crossed his wide, sensual mouth. 'A little like you, then? All fight on the surface and then all tender when it comes to another woman's child?'

In receipt of that rare smile, she felt her heart race. 'I only want Amber to have all the things I never had.'

'An admirable ambition. I've never had the desire to reproduce,' Acheron admitted, watching the tip of her tongue flick out to catch a tiny white crumb of meringue that could not possibly have tasted any sweeter than her lush mouth. Just like that he was hard as a rock again, imagining what else she might be able to do with her tongue, and the heavy pulse of mounting need at his groin was infuriating. It made him feel out of control and, because he despised that kind of weakness in any part of his life, he gritted his teeth and battled for restraint.

'I've never been the broody sort,' Tabby burbled, licking the fork before dipping it into the delicious dessert again, uncomfortably aware of the dark golden swoop of his gaze following her every move. 'But I was with Sonia when Amber was born and then I had to look after her the first few weeks until Sonia was strong enough after her stroke to leave hospital. I'm afraid that by that stage I was committed heart, soul and body to Amber...our attachment just happened and then Sonia had the second stroke and died immediately.' She paused, clashed with his caramel-shaded eyes and felt her mouth run dry. 'Please stop staring at me.'

'Then stop playing with the fork,' Acheron suggested huskily. 'Naturally I'm picturing you spread across the table as an infinitely more appealing main course than the one I've eaten.'

Surprised colour sprang into her face, and she dropped the fork with a clatter. 'Do you ever think of anything but sex?'

'And you're not thinking about it too?' Acheron derided thickly, studying her with burning intensity.

And the pink in her cheeks burned hotter than ever because he was perfectly correct. His raw masculine virility called to her on a visceral level. The table between them felt like a barrier she wanted to push out of the way. She wanted things she had never wanted before. She wanted to taste that intriguing little triangle of brown male skin visible below his throat, kiss a path along that stubborn jaw line, *touch*, explore. And even worse the mere thought of such experimentation made the blood race through her veins, her nipples tighten and push against her bodice while a liquid sensation of squirming warmth flowered between her thighs. *So, this is lust*, she told herself sharply. *Grow up and deal with it like a woman, not a frightened little girl.*

Acheron thrust back his chair and vaulted to his full commanding height of well over six feet. 'Come on…'

'No, sit down,' Tabby told him shakily, very much afraid that she knew exactly where he wanted her to go and even more afraid that she was ready to say yes, for never in her life had she ever felt anything as powerful as the primitive longing he awakened in her.

'Don't look at me like that and then try to tell me what to do, *hara mou*. It doesn't work,' Acheron advised, strolling round the table to move behind her and tug out the chair with her still seated in it.

'One of us has to try to be sensible,' Tabby protested in desperation.

Acheron bent down and scooped her out of the chair as if she were a child. *'Why?'* he queried thickly, his warm breath fanning her throat. 'We're not hurting anyone. We're both free agents. We can do as we like—'

'That's not how I live.'

'You've trapped yourself in a cage of irrational rules because that makes you feel safe,' Acheron countered, striding across the hall with her still cradled in his arms. 'But I can keep you safe too…'

Only he could still hurt her, just as easily as he could silence her arguments and sweep her literally off her feet, Tabby acknowledged feverishly even as her fingers reached up of their own accord to skate admiringly along the clean, hard line of his jaw. 'You don't make me feel safe.'

'But then you don't trust anyone,' Acheron countered with a swift downward glance at her anxious face. 'Neither do I. Even so, I *can* promise you that I won't lie to you.'

'Not much of a comfort when you could give tips to Machiavelli on how best to get your own way by nefarious means,' Tabby traded, provoking a surprised laugh from Acheron as he mounted the stairs. She knew decision time had come and gone and she wanted his mouth on hers so badly that it literally hurt even to think about it.

He lowered her to the carpet to open the first door, grabbed her hand as though he was afraid she would run off last minute and virtually dragged her into his bedroom. 'Now, I finally have you where I want you. Can you believe that this is our wedding night?'

'But it isn't…we're not really married.' Tabby leant back against his bedroom door, taut with tension because she was sincerely out of her comfort zone and could scarcely breathe for nerves. 'Let's not kid ourselves about that. Neither one of us ever had any plans to make this a proper marriage. I may be wearing a wedding ring but it's meaningless.'

Acheron didn't know a single woman of his acquaintance who would have reminded him of that fact at that precise moment, or who would have come to his bedroom without a carefully set agenda of ambitious and mercenary acquisition in mind. In the strangest possible way, Tabby was a breath of fresh air in his life, he reflected, uneasy with the thought.

'I know.' Like a hunter stalking a wary doe, Acheron approached and closed both of his hands over hers to pull her forward into his arms. 'But nothing that feels as exciting as this could possibly be meaningless,' he traded huskily.

'It's only hormones.'

'Says the woman who hasn't a clue what's going to be happening in that bed,' Acheron teased, feathering his mouth hungrily over the soft, silky contours of hers and making her shiver.

'Of course I know what happens…' But she still didn't quite know what she was doing there with him, breaking her rules of self-protection by letting him get that close, risking the vulnerability she always shunned. 'It's just sex,' she told him staunchly.

'It will be amazing sex,' Acheron predicted, skimming the straps down on her dress, pressing his hungry mouth to a slight-boned shoulder while pressing her close, letting her feel the hard-packed urgency in his lean body while reminding himself that he would have to go slow.

'I love your confidence,' Tabby whispered half under her breath.

'I thought it annoyed you.'

Tabby stretched up on tiptoe to link her arms round his neck and tug his handsome dark head down to her level. 'Shut up,' she told him helplessly, entrapped by dark eyes blazing like a banked golden fire across her face.

Acheron hoisted her off her feet and brought her down at the foot of the bed to flip off her shoes. 'I don't want to hurt you,' he admitted.

'If it hurts, it hurts,' Tabby said prosaically, determined not to surrender to apprehension because, with the single exception of her deep attachment to Amber, she had never felt as much as he made her feel either emotionally or physically. She supposed she was suffering from some kind of idiotic infatuation with him but assumed it would fade as time went on. 'Is this a one-time thing?' she asked him abruptly.

Engaged in slipping off her shoes, Acheron glanced back at her, amusement playing attractively about the wilful, passionate set of his mouth. 'You can't plan everything in advance, Tabby.'

'I do,' she told him tautly. 'I always need to know exactly where I am and what I'm doing.'

And his mouth claimed hers slow and deep and hungry and the tight knot of anxiety inside her unfurled because, in that moment, her senses locked to his, her body screaming with eagerness for more…more…more, and she couldn't stay focused the way she usually did. He unzipped the dress and extracted her from its folds with an ease and exactitude that briefly chilled her because she discovered she couldn't bear to think of him with the other lovers who must have honed his skills.

'What's wrong?' he prompted, more attuned to her than she had expected, instantly picking up on her renewed tension.

Perhaps she was, at heart, a terribly jealous, possessive person, she reasoned in mortification, troubled by
her thoughts and wondering how she could possibly know
what she was like when she had never enjoyed a deeper
relationship with a man. There she perched, shivering a
little in spite of the warmth of the room, suddenly conscious that she was clad only in bra and knickers and that
her body was far from perfect.

'Nothing's wrong,' she breathed while he continued
to study her troubled face with a frown. *'All right!'* she
exclaimed as if he had repeated the question. 'I was just
thinking that you're very smooth at stripping clothes off
a woman!'

And Acheron burst out laughing, revelling in that honesty, appreciating that she would simply say whatever she
thought without considering its impact and instead saying
only what he might want to hear. That quality was another rarity in his world. 'Thank you…I think,' he teased.

'And you're still wearing too many clothes,' Tabby
protested, all too aware of her own half-naked state as
she struggled not to recall that she had really tiny breasts
and was pretty skinny everywhere else where it was said
to matter to a man. After all, regardless of her deficiencies, he wanted her. That was a certainty that buoyed her
up as she watched dark golden eyes flare over her with
unashamed desire and appreciation.

He laughed and shed his shirt, kicked off his shoes
with the complete unselfconsciousness of a male who
had never been inhibited in a woman's presence or con-
strained by the fear that a woman might not admire what
he had to offer. Her throat ran dry as he unveiled the su-
perb expanse of his bronzed torso, exposing the lean,
ripped muscles of his six-pack. Poised there, black stubble
darkening his handsome jaw, eyes glinting, hair tousled

by her fingers with his jeans hanging low on his narrow hips as he unzipped them, he was as gorgeous as a tiger in his prime: glossy and strong and beautifully poised.

She tried and failed to swallow when she saw the tented effect of his boxers, the all too prominent evidence of his readiness outlined by the fine fabric. When his long, elegant hands began to sweep off that final garment she averted her attention and reached back awkwardly to unhook her bra, peeling it off before scrambling below the linen sheet to rip off her knickers in an effort to seem a little more in control than she was.

'I want you *so* much, *koukla mou*,' Acheron growled, yanking the sheet off her from the foot of the bed so that she sat up again, wide-eyed and thunderously aware of her nakedness. 'I also want to see you, *watch* you—'

'There's not a lot to see!' she gasped, her small body crowding back against the banked-up pillows.

Acheron locked a hand round one slender ankle and pulled her very gently down the bed. 'What I see is beautiful,' he breathed thickly, his hungry scrutiny skimming from the tangle of blonde curls at the apex of her thighs to the glorious hint of secret pink beneath and the mouth-watering swell of her breasts topped by prominent pale pink nipples. In one movement he was up on the bed by her side.

'I'm not.'

'Don't want to hear it!' he interrupted, long fingers fisting in the tumble of her golden hair to hold her still as he skated his mouth back and forth over her lips until they parted and his tongue speared inside, delving and exploring with a thoroughness that deprived her of breath and sanity. He could kiss, oh, yes, he could kiss, and then his fingers teased very gently at her straining nipples and he lowered his mouth there, catching a painfully sensitive peak between his lips and plucking it with a tugging intensity that made her nipple throb and arrowed heat straight down into her pelvis.

She trembled, and her spine arched as he pressed her flat on the mattress, dividing his attention now between the distended buds, suckling on her, flicking his tongue back and forth until the tingles of awareness rose like a tide to engulf her. She trembled, insanely aware of the gathering of heat and moisture between her thighs and the intolerable ache building there along with the desperate desire to be touched.

'You're very responsive,' Acheron purred, studying her with heavy-lidded eyes the colour of melted toffee set between the twin fringes of his black lashes. He skimmed a hand down her thigh, stroked her between her legs, and her hips shifted up in supplication. He possessed her swollen mouth again with carnal hunger before he sent a finger delving into her hot, damp heat.

A sound of helpless keening pleasure was wrenched from Tabby. All of a sudden everything she was feeling was centred in that one tormentingly sensitive area of her body. He settled his mouth to her throat and nuzzled a leisurely trail along the side of her neck, awakening nerve endings she had not known she possessed. What she could not understand was that in the space of minutes she had travelled from not being very sure of what she was doing to craving what he was offering with every straining sinew in her body.

'If at any stage you want me to stop, just say so, *koukla mou*,' Acheron husked.

'Wouldn't that be very difficult for you?' she whispered, her hand smoothing down over his muscled chest to discover the thrusting power of his erection.

'I'm not a teenager. I can control myself,' Acheron

growled, arching up into her hand as she traced the vel-vet-smooth hardness of his shaft while marvelling at the size of him. In that field, he had more than she had ex-pected, more width, more length, and she didn't want to think about how on earth he could make them fit as nature had intended. With a slight but perceptible shud-der of reaction he relocated her stroking fingers to his muscled abdomen and added, 'As long as you don't do too much of that.'

Satisfied that she could affect him as much as he af-fected her, Tabby lay back only to release a whimper of startled sound as he circled her clitoris with expert fin-gers, unerringly striking the exact spot and the exact pace that would drive her over the edge fastest. Her heart was racing when he shifted down the bed, slid between her thighs and employed his mouth there instead. She had known about that, of course she had known, and had never thought she could be that intimate with any man but the insane pleasure he gave her drove all such logic from her mind, and she gasped and writhed and cried out. Enthralled by an exquisite torture of sensation that built and built, her body leapt out of her control alto-gether and jerked spasmodically into an intense climax that left her weak.

In the aftermath, Acheron rose up over her, lean, dark features taut and flushed with hunger, and she could feel the wide, blunt tip of him at the heart of her, pushing, precisely stretching her inner sheath until a sudden sharp pain made her cry out in surprise, and he froze in place.

'Do you want me to stop?' Acheron prompted rag-gedly.

'No point now.' Tabby could see he was in no condi-tion to stop, could feel him hard and pulsing and alien in-side her. In any case, the pain of his invasion had already faded and the ache of hollow longing he had roused still lingered. She wrapped her arms round him, instinctively urging him on, fingers smoothing across the bronzed satin of his broad back.

'You're so tight,' he rasped, shifting with an athletic lift of his lean hips to surge into her again, deeper, further, harder in a technique that met every physical craving she hadn't known she had. 'I'm incredibly turned on.'

The flood of sensation returned as he withdrew and plunged back into her again, ensuring that she felt every inch of his penetration. The intensity of sensation shocked her and the powerful contracting bands in her pelvis turned her into a fizzing firework of wild excitement. He moved faster and she clung, riding out the electrifying storm of passion with a heart that seemed to be thumping in her eardrums. The explosion of raw pleasure that followed stunned her as the inner convulsions of her body clenched her every muscle tight as a fist. He vented a shuddering groan of completion while the waves of delight went on and on and on, coursing through her thoroughly fulfilled body.

In a dazed state of abstraction, Tabby lay in the tumbled bedding afterwards, watching Acheron stride across the room to retrieve something before vanishing into the bathroom, from which she soon heard the sound of running water. The instant their encounter had finished, the very moment he had attained release, he had rolled away from her and made no effort to touch her again. She was painfully aware of how much she would have liked him to hold her close in a caring, affectionate way that acknowledged their new intimacy and it disturbed her that she should feel so hurt by his withdrawal. After all, she wasn't looking for, or expecting, love or commitment, was she? No, she wasn't that naive.

She had slept with Acheron because for the very first time she had felt a fierce desire to experience that extra dimension with a man. But his swift departure from the bed had disappointed her, leaving her feeling ridiculously used and rejected. That was silly, she told herself firmly, because when it came to what they had just done he had not taken advantage of her in any way. Indeed, to some degree she was willing to acknowledge that *she* had taken advantage of *him* the moment she had estimated that he would undoubtedly possess the erotic skills that were most likely to ensure that she received pleasure from her first experience. That didn't, however, entitle him to forgiveness for disappointing her in the sensitive aftermath of sex.

Slithering out of bed, Tabby swiftly got dressed, finger-combing her tangled hair back off her damp brow before she approached the bathroom door.

A towel linked round his narrow bronzed hips, Acheron was in the act of stepping out of the shower cubicle.

'A-star for the sex, F for failure for the follow-up,' Tabby pronounced with scorn, mentally blocking out the lean, powerful vibrancy of his commanding presence. Yes, Acheron Dimitrakos was gorgeous but in her scheme of things that was unimportant in comparison to the way he treated her.

CHAPTER SEVEN

IN RECEIPT OF that attack, Acheron stiffened in astonishment and angled his arrogant dark head back, his black-as-jet eyes gleaming with angry incomprehension even as his attention lingered on how astonishingly lovely Tabby looked fresh from his bed with her long blonde hair in a waving, tousled mass round her shoulders, her small face warm with self-conscious colour and her ripe pink mouth still swollen from his kisses. Even as he fought to think clearly, his reaction to that view and those thoughts was instantaneous and very physical. 'What the hell are you talking about?'

'The instant you had your satisfaction you leapt out of bed and abandoned me as though I was suffering from some horrid contagious disease,' Tabby condemned. 'Not an experience I would be tempted to repeat—you made me feel like a whore!'

'That's melodramatic nonsense,' Acheron fielded with derision, willing back his increasing arousal with every fibre of his self-discipline.

'No, I don't think it is. You couldn't even bear to hold me close for thirty seconds,' Tabby reminded him doggedly. 'Well, I think it's sad that the only way you feel comfortable physically touching anyone is in a sexual way.'

Acheron cursed in Greek. 'You don't know me as well

as you think you do. But I warned you that I didn't do cuddling.'

'You think that excuses you?' Tabby asked with scornfully unimpressed eyes of violet blue dominating her flushed and furious face. 'It doesn't. It simply shows you up as selfish and inconsiderate, and I deserved better.'

'I don't fake affection for anyone just because it's the acceptable thing to do,' Acheron bit out between clenched teeth. 'And I have so little practice at it, I would feel foolish and uncomfortable!'

And that was the most strikingly truthful thing he had told her about himself to date, Tabby reckoned, stunned by the raw honesty of that irate reply. Indeed his admission of ignorance and discomfiture squeezed her heart like a clenched fist. Without even thinking about what she was doing, she closed the distance between them, deliberately invading his personal space to stretch her arms round his neck and look up at him.

'Practise on me,' she urged quietly. 'I practised on Amber. I wasn't a very touchy-feely person either before I got to hold her for the first time.'

Acheron swallowed hard, insanely aware that she was making a platonic approach and quite impervious to the reality that below the towel he was still ragingly erect. He didn't want to hug her as though she were his friend; he wanted to shag her senseless. But he knew that option wasn't in the ring at that moment and he closed his arms round her slowly and lifted her to the other side of the big bathroom. 'You shouldn't have got dressed again,' he scolded.

'I assumed we were done,' Tabby confided bluntly.

Acheron bent down and lifted the hem of her dress to take it off over her head. Totally disconcerted, Tabby froze there for a split second, her arms crossed defensively across her bare breasts. 'What are you doing?'

Acheron hooked a finger into her knickers and jerked them down, lifting her again into his arms to trail them off. 'I may have leapt out of bed but I *was* thinking about your comfort,' he breathed as he lowered her down into the warm embrace of the scented water filling the bath. 'Now lie back and relax.'

Thoroughly disconcerted, Tabby surveyed him in wonderment. 'You came in here and ran a bath for me?'

'I hurt you…I thought you'd be sore,' he breathed huskily as he lit the candles in the candelabra by the sink and doused the lights.

'It was just one of those things, not your fault.' But Tabby reddened and sank deeper into the soothingly warm water, resting her head weakly back on the cushioned padding on the rim. In truth she *was* sore, that part of her so tender she was now uncomfortably aware of her pelvic area. What a pair they were, she thought morosely. He couldn't do ordinary affection and she couldn't do sex.

There was a pop as Acheron released a cork from a champagne bottle and sent bubbling golden liquid down into a pair of goblets.

'Where did that come from? And the candles?' she pressed weakly.

'Honeymoon couple, wedding night? The staff had all the trimmings waiting in the bedroom… It would be a shame not to use them,' Acheron remarked, perching on the side of the bath to offer her a glass of champagne.

'No, thanks. I never drink,' she said stiltedly.

Acheron thrust the glass into her hand. 'Unless you have a drink problem, one glass isn't going to do any damage.'

Her small fingers tensed round the stem. 'No, I don't have a problem but my parents did.'

'That doesn't mean you have to avoid it altogether.'

'I always like to play it safe,' Tabby confided, taking a small sip of the champagne, tiny bubbles bursting below her nose and moistening her skin.

'I'm more of a risk-taker. I enjoy excitement,' Acheron traded wryly.

'I think I could've worked that out for myself.'

Acheron compressed his mouth, his eyes semi-concealed by his black lashes. 'I didn't stay in bed with you because I didn't want you to have unrealistic expectations of our relationship.'

She grasped what he meant immediately and wished she didn't, a tiny pang of hurt pinching somewhere down deep inside her. He didn't want her getting the idea that there was anything more complex between them than straightforward sex. 'I may be inexperienced but I'm not stupid,' Tabby told him with pride.

'And I'm not good with words if I gave you that impression,' Acheron acknowledged grimly. 'Tabby, I don't have conversations like this with women. I've never met a woman like you.'

'Are we *still* talking about me being a virgin?' Tabby asked in a small voice.

'I'm accustomed to women who know the score.'

'I know it too,' Tabby breathed, skimming a glance across his hard-edged profile, her chest tightening with a sense of constraint. 'I'm a very practical person.'

Acheron scanned her small, tight face, the set grip of her tiny hands over her raised knees as he read the valiant defensiveness she used as a screen and his stomach hollowed out at the prospect of hurting her. He had never felt that way around a woman before and he didn't like it at all. She might be fragile but she had made a choice, just as he had done, and they were both adults, he reminded himself impatiently as he straightened again.

At the same moment, Tabby sat up abruptly and set down the champagne flute, water sloshing noisily around her slight body. 'Oh, my goodness, what am I doing in here? I can't stay! The baby monitor is in my bedroom.'

'Melinda will take care of Amber's needs. Relax,' Acheron urged.

'Melinda can't be expected to work twenty-four hours a day. I told her I'd take care of Amber at night,' Tabby countered as she rolled onto her knees, concern for Amber overcoming her self-consciousness, and began to stand up. 'Pass me a towel—'

'No, you stay where you are,' Acheron instructed, his hand closing over her shoulder to press her back into the warm water again. 'I'll collect the monitor and check on Amber as well.'

Her violet eyes widened. '*You*...will?'

Acheron strode back into the bedroom to retrieve his jeans and wandered back to the doorway, dropping the towel with total unselfconsciousness to pull on the jeans. 'Why not? You've already shown me what to do with her if she's crying.'

'I wasn't expecting you to help,' Tabby commented. 'It's my job, not yours, after all.'

'Our arrangement isn't that clear cut. This is a joint venture when it comes to me requiring a wife and you requiring an adoptive father figure,' Acheron reminded her, turning on his heel.

Stiff with uncertainty, Tabby lay back in the warm water and sipped the champagne while still feeling thoroughly confused by Acheron's behaviour. She had got him wrong when she condemned him for abandoning her immediately after sex. But then, had the simple act of sex put him into a particularly good mood? Could a man be that basic? In consideration of her needs, he had run her a bath before he went for his shower. Now he was actually off to check on Amber for her as if the child was something more than the extra baggage she had assumed he deemed her to be. At the same time, however, he had also clearly felt the need to spell out the lowering message that the only thing between him and Tabby was sex. As if she didn't already know that!

Acheron was the ultimate womaniser, steering clear of involvement and commitment. And why shouldn't he? common sense asked. A young, handsome, wealthy male was in high demand in the world of women and had no need to settle on only one. In addition, Acheron had issues but then who didn't after such a childhood as they had both undergone? In remembrance, Tabby suppressed a shiver. He had probably learned just as she had that if you kept everyone at arm's length you didn't get hurt.

But Tabby had moved on from that self-protective stance when she first opened her heart to friendship with Sonia and then Amber and finally understood how much more warm and satisfying life could be with love and loyalty in it. She knew she had lost her business and her first home because she had chosen to personally care for Sonia and Amber but she had no regrets about the choices she had made.

Amber was now her sole responsibility, she recalled, while wondering what she was doing lying back in a luxury bathtub drinking champagne when the baby she loved might be in need of her. In an instant she had clambered dripping out of the bath and swathed herself in a big warm towel, hurriedly patting herself dry before reaching for her dress again. It was time to get back to the real world, she told herself urgently, and there was nothing 'real world' about lounging around lazily in Acheron's opulent bathroom.

Acheron groaned when he heard the baby crying through the monitor. The little plastic speaker was set on the dressing table and as he studied it he became aware that something had been written on the mirror.

'Go home, whore!' someone had printed with what looked like a red felt-tip pen.

Bemused, nerves still jumping at the sound of the baby crying, Acheron hesitated only a moment before striding into the bathroom to snatch up a towel, dampening it and walking back to wipe the mirror clean again before Tabby could see it. For a split second he paused, brooding over the disturbing awareness that only his household staff had access to the bedroom and that one of them clearly wasn't trustworthy. But why leave such a message for Tabby to find? he questioned furiously. She was his wife, his legal wife with every right to be in his house. Who would target Tabby? His handsome mouth down-curved: Kasma was the most likely suspect. Pure rage blazed in Acheron as he dug out his cell phone, called his head of security and brought him up to speed on the development. His temper uneven, he strode off to take care of the baby. She was only a baby, he told himself bracingly, of course he could handle one tiny baby without help.

Amber was sitting upright screaming at the top of her voice, her little face red as fire. Acheron hovered a few feet from the cot. 'Nothing's that bad,' he told Amber in what he hoped was a soothing tone.

Amber lifted up her arms expectantly.

'Do I need to come that close?' Acheron asked uneasily. 'I'm here. You're safe. I assure you that nothing bad is going to happen to you.'

Amber fixed bewildered brown eyes on him, tears

rolling down her crumpled face, and lifted her arms again in open demand.

Acheron released his breath on a slow measured hiss and moved closer. 'I'm no good at the cuddling stuff,' he warned her ruefully, reaching down to lift the child, who startled him by wrapping both arms tightly round his throat and hanging on as firmly to him as a monkey gripping a branch.

An exhausted sob sounded in his ear, and he splayed a big hand across the little girl's back and shifted his fingers in a vague circular motion aimed at soothing her fears. A vague shard of memory featuring a woman's face momentarily froze him where he stood. He didn't recall what age he had been but he had certainly been very small when the woman had come in the night to comfort him, rocking him in her arms and singing to him until he stopped crying. Had that woman been Olympia, Amber's late grandmother and his own mother's former carer? Who else could it have been? Only Olympia had ever shown him concern and treated him as if he was something other than a nuisance part of her well-paid job.

'I owe you,' he told Amber heavily and he rearranged her awkwardly in his arms and began to rock her, suppressing that rare memory of the past with the profound discomfort that such images always brought him. 'But even for you I can't sing.'

Amber startled him by smiling widely up at him, showing off her two front teeth, and he smiled back before he even knew what he was doing.

And that was how Tabby saw them when she came to a halt in the doorway: Acheron with a tousled black curl falling over his brow, his haunting dark eyes locked to Amber while the most glorious smile lifted his wide, sensual mouth. Barefoot and bare-chested, well-worn jeans hanging low on his lean hips, he looked both extravagantly handsome and unusually human at the same time. Her breath feathered in her throat and her mouth ran dry because that smile was pure sensual dynamite.

'Let me take her,' she proffered quietly. 'I'll put her back in bed.'

'We were managing fine,' Acheron announced, not without pride in the accomplishment as he settled Amber into Tabby's arms. 'Obviously she's not very choosy.'

'Well, you're wrong there. She can actually be quite choosy and can be difficult with some people,' Tabby admitted as she rested Amber down on the changing mat and deftly changed her before placing the child back into her cot, gently stroking her cheek when she grizzled. 'It's bedtime, sweetness. We don't play at bedtime.'

'I'll organise cover for the nights,' Acheron remarked as she joined him in the corridor.

'That's not necessary.'

'You can still go to her if you want but you can't be dragged out of bed *every* night,' he told her drily.

'I'm still the woman who wants to be her mother. It's my duty to be there for her,' Tabby reminded him gently. 'I don't want other people looking after her all the time.'

'Be reasonable.' Acheron paused outside the two doors that led into their separate bedrooms. 'Are you joining me for what remains of the night?'

The ease with which he asked the question disconcerted Tabby because she had assumed that once his lusty curiosity was satisfied she would no longer be of interest to him. His approach both pleased and annoyed her. 'I'm afraid if I did join you, there would have to be rules,' she murmured awkwardly, her hand closing on the handle of her own bedroom door.

'Rules?' Acheron repeated in wonderment. 'Is that your idea of a joke?'

'No, I rarely joke about serious stuff,' Tabby countered gently. 'If you want to hear the rules, ask me.'

'I don't do rules,' Acheron ground out between gritted teeth. 'Perhaps it has escaped your attention, but I'm not a misbehaving child!'

Tabby closed the door quietly in his face.

She had donned one of her slinky new nightdresses before the door opened again. She scrambled hastily below the top sheet and looked across the room enquiringly.

'What bloody rules?' Acheron slung at her, poised hands affixed to his lean hips, his hard-muscled abdomen prominent.

'One,' Tabby enumerated. 'Any relationship we have has to be exclusive and if you plan to stray you have to tell me and finish it decently. No secrets, no sneaking around on me.'

Acheron surveyed her with wild golden eyes of increasingly wrathful incredulity. 'I don't believe I'm hearing this!'

'*Two,*' Tabby continued unconcerned. 'You treat me with respect at all times. If I annoy you, we have it out but not around Amber.'

'You're absolutely out of your mind,' Acheron breathed with unsettling conviction while he studied her with seething, dark golden eyes. 'And I married you.'

'*Three,*' Tabby pronounced woodenly, although her colour was high and her hands clenched into fists by her side. 'I'm not a toy you can pick up and put down again whenever you feel like it. I'm not the entertainment when you're bored. If you treat me well, I will treat you equally well, but if you don't…well, all bets would be off then.'

'Na pas sto dialo!' Acheron murmured wrathfully. 'It means, go to hell, and take your precious rules with you!'

Tabby didn't breathe again until the door had snapped closed behind him and then she lay back in bed, her body feeling heavy as a stone dropped from a height, her tummy rolling like a boat on a storm-tossed sea. Well, that was one way of getting rid of Acheron without losing face, one way of ensuring he was forced to see her as an equal. What else could she have said? Sliding willy-nilly into a casual sexual affair with no boundaries was not her style and with a man as volatile as he was it would be a sure recipe for disaster. But now that the ultimate womanising, free-spirited man knew that she would make major demands, he would be careful to avoid her from now on.

And what sort of idiot was she to feel sad about that fact? She would get over her silly notions about him—of course she would, because there was really no other option open to her. He wanted one thing, she wanted another, so it was better to end it before it got messy and painful and humiliating. Better by far...

In the middle of the night, Acheron went for a cold shower. His erection wouldn't quit and he was still in an unholy rage. Rules, blasted rules. Was he suddenly back at school? Who did she think she was dealing with? Even more crucially, *what* did she think she was dealing with? Did she assume he had got into that bed and somehow signed up for the whole relationship charade? Trust a woman to take a concept as simple as sex and complicate it!

Even so, he was as furious with himself as he was with her. He had suspected that her naivety would lead to problems and he knew he should have listened to his misgivings. But just as the hot blood pulsing through his tense, aching body wouldn't stop, his desire for her had proved unrelenting. He'd had to know what she was like and he'd found out and, even worse, she had been amazing and no sooner had he stopped than he wanted to go again…and again…and again. His even white teeth clenched hard. That fast he was recalling the hot clenching of her tight little body around him, an explicit memory that did nothing to cool his overheated libido.

'So, who's the cutest little baby in the world?' Tabby chattered the next morning while Amber waved her spoon in the air, cheerfully responding to the warm, loving gush of Tabby's appreciation.

Acheron suppressed a groan and slung himself down into a chair by the dining table on the terrace. Baby talk at breakfast time, one more thing she had brought into his life that was not to his taste. First thing in the morning he liked sex and silence and since he had had neither he could not be expected to be in a good mood, he reasoned impatiently. The sight of Tabby in a little red strappy top and shorts that exposed far too much bare creamy skin for his delectation didn't help. Even a glimpse of the tattoo on her arm as she swivelled in her seat failed to switch off the ever-ready pulse at his groin.

Tabby tried to scan Acheron without being obvious about it, sending little flips of her eyes in his direction with her lashes quickly dropping again. He was *so* beautiful; it was surely a sin for a male to be so beautiful that she was challenged to stop staring at him. Even the awareness of the lingering tenderness between her legs couldn't dull her appreciation of that long, lean, powerful frame of his, gracefully draped in the chair like a work of art to be admired. The sunlight glittered over his black springy curls, and she wanted to run her fingers through his hair, stroke that stubborn jaw line set like granite until she awakened that wonderful smile again. Disconcerted by her treacherous thoughts, Tabby twisted her head away, resisting temptation.

Amber extended both arms in Acheron's direction and beamed at him. 'Not right now, *koukla mou*,' he murmured. 'Have your breakfast first.'

That he had acknowledged Amber's presence but not hers aggravated Tabby. Last night she had only been a body but this morning she was evidently invisible into the bargain. 'Good morning, Acheron,' she said curtly.

'*Kalimera, yineka mou*,' Ash murmured silkily, noting the fiery brightness of her extraordinary violet eyes as she settled her gaze on him. 'Did you sleep well?'

'Like a log,' Tabby lied, wondering why he brought out a mean streak in her that she had never known she had.

A maid poured his coffee, and the rich aroma flared her nostrils, inexplicably reminding her that Sonia had become preternaturally sensitive to certain smells when she first fell pregnant with Amber and an edge of panic suddenly sliced through Tabby's surface calm. 'Last night…' she prompted abruptly, waiting with a rapidly beating heart and hot cheeks for the maid to retreat. 'You *did* use protection, didn't you?'

Magnificently nonchalant in the face of that intimate question, Acheron widened lustrous, dark golden eyes in mocking amusement. 'You think I would be stupid enough to neglect such a precaution?'

'I think in the heat of the moment if you wanted something enough you would take risks,' Tabby admitted tautly.

Acheron lifted a winged ebony brow and cocked his handsome head in Amber's direction. 'Not if it meant risking the acquisition of one of those,' he declared. 'Passion doesn't rule me.'

'Or me,' she echoed half under her breath. As she leant forward to help Amber clear her plate, her breasts stirred beneath her tee with the movement, pushing her unbearably sensitive nipples against the fabric, and made her think that a bra would have been a better idea than going without. Particularly in Acheron's radius.

The same view was not wasted on Acheron either, who recalled the precise pout of her delicate flesh and his almost overpowering desire to eat her alive. While the smouldering silence at the table stretched, the nanny entered and removed Amber from her chair to bear her off for a bath.

Acheron dragged in a deep, cooling breath of the sunshine laden air, knowing that, for the sake of peace and better understanding, he had to challenge Tabby's misconceptions. 'Your rules?' he mused with a dismissive shrug of one broad shoulder. '*My* rules? I never ever get involved with clingy, needy women.'

Coming at her out of nowhere, that statement crashed down on Tabby like a brick dropped on glass and her head flew up, violet eyes wide. 'Are you calling me clingy and needy?'

'What do you think?'

Tabby sprang out of her chair, the feet of it slamming back noisily across the tiles underfoot as she stabbed her hands down on the table for support. Anger had gripped her in a stormy surge. 'How dare you? I've never been clingy or needy in my life with a man!'

'Yet your first move is to try and hedge me round with rules. You want reassurance and promises about a future that is unknown to both of us,' Acheron reasoned with cold precision. 'I don't own a crystal ball.'

'I don't like the way you operate!' Tabby vented fiercely.

'Yet you know nothing about me. For years I've been exclusive in my affairs and I don't move on without saying so when I lose interest,' Acheron declared lazily, rising upright to study her, his brilliant, dark eyes hard and glittering. 'It is offensive that you should condemn me for lies and infidelity on the basis of your assumptions about my character.'

'You're so smooth…I wouldn't trust a word that came out of your mouth!' Tabby hurled at him accusingly, refusing to acknowledge that he had a point.

'Now who's guilty of prejudice?' Acheron riposted with soft sibilance. 'What do you find most offensive about me? My public-school education, my wealth or my lifestyle?'

Ferocious resentment held Tabby rigid where she stood, her small face taut and flushed with indignation, but it was the soft pink fullness of her lush mouth that welded Acheron's attention there. 'What I find most offensive is your certainty that you know best about *everything*!'

'I do know that we are poles apart and that this arrangement will work most efficiently if we stick to the original agreement we made.'

Tabby's tummy flipped as though she had gone down in a lift too fast, sheer strain locking her every muscle into tautness. 'You should've kept your blasted hands off me!' she slammed back.

Acheron flashed her a grim appraisal from his stunning golden eyes, and his mouth twisted sardonically. 'Sadly, I *couldn't*…'

And with that final admission, Acheron strode back into the air-conditioned cool of the villa and left her alone to contemplate the truly fabulous view. The rolling green

Tuscan hills stretched out before her marked out in a colourful patchwork of woodland, olive groves and vine-
yards. She snatched in a deeply shaken breath, the hot
air scouring her lungs. He wanted them to return to the
sensible terms of their platonic agreement, which was
exactly what she had believed she wanted. Why, then,
when she had achieved her goal, did she feel as though
she had lost the battle? Indeed, instead of feeling relieved
and reassured by his logical approach to their differences,
she felt ridiculously hurt and abandoned…

CHAPTER EIGHT

TABBY ROLLED THE soft ball back to Amber where the child
sat below the dappled shade of an ancient spreading oak
tree. Amber rolled over and crawled to the edge of the
rug, a look of glee in her bright eyes as she scanned the
wide green expanse of freedom open before her.

Tabby marvelled at the speed with which the little
girl had learned to embrace independent movement. One
minute she had been rolling over and over again to explore further afield and the next she had perfected crawl-
ing. At just over seven months old she was a fairly early
developer but she had always been a physically strong
baby who met every developmental guideline in advance,
and Tabby wasn't really surprised that Amber had discovered how to get around without adult assistance ahead
of time. As she watched the little girl pulled a blade of
grass and stuck it in her mouth.

'No…no,' she was saying while retrieving the grass
when Melinda strolled up and offered to give her a break.

'Yes, and you're welcome,' Tabby confided ruefully.
'She's much more of a handful now, and I wouldn't mind
a little break to sunbathe and read.'

'We can manage that. I'm going to put her in the
buggy and take her for a walk,' the blonde nanny told
her smoothly. 'I just love it here.'

Tabby glanced at the younger woman, wondering why she found it such a challenge to like her and feeling rather guilty about the fact. After all, Melinda was great with Amber, a diligent worker and friendly. Perhaps it was the hungry little glances she often saw Melinda aiming at Acheron that had prevented Tabby from bonding more with the other young woman. It was not that she was jealous, Tabby reasoned uneasily, simply that she wasn't comfortable with a woman prepared to show that much interest in the married man who employed her. In any case, and to be fair to all parties concerned, Acheron had shown not the smallest awareness of Melinda's curvaceous blonde allure.

'Any idea when we'll be leaving here yet?' Melinda asked as she gathered up Amber's toys and stuffed them in a bag.

'Not yet, sorry…my husband hasn't decided how long we'll be staying,' Tabby replied, wryly impressed by the way that possessive label slid off her tongue. But that, she had learned, was the easiest way to refer to Acheron in front of the staff.

Yet he was as much a husband as a caged tiger in a zoo would be, she conceded unhappily, lifting her book and her sunglasses and heading for the cool courtyard in which the pool was situated. For the past week she had barely seen Acheron, who confined himself to his office most of the day and often half the night to work. Even when he was around his phone was always ringing and his single-minded focus on business was exactly what she should have expected from a goal-orientated alpha male.

Occasionally he would join her for a cup of coffee at breakfast time and he generally put in a rather silent appearance at the dinner table, eating quickly and then politely excusing himself. He was a cool and distant companion at those meals and there was never so much as a hint of sexual awareness in either his looks or his conversation. It was as though that wild bout of passion on their wedding night was the product of her imagination alone, but Tabby still found it a distinct challenge to revert to treating him like a stranger and that embarrassed her, denting her pride and her belief in her own strength and independence because no woman of character should continue to crave the attention of a man set on treating her like the wallpaper.

Yet amazingly, infuriatingly, Acheron was playing an entirely different ball game with Amber. Melinda swore that Acheron never passed the nursery door without coming in to talk to and play with her charge and Amber had already learned to make a beeline for Acheron whenever he was in her vicinity. In fact, when it came to Acheron, Amber took her welcome for granted. Maybe Acheron's ego was flattered by the amount of attention Amber gave him. Maybe he was even belatedly discovering that he actually liked and enjoyed the company of children? How could she possibly know what motivated his interest? Tabby had not got through a week of virtually sleepless nights without acknowledging that she knew very little at all about Acheron Dimitrakos. Her husband was a mystery to her in almost every conceivable way.

Acheron stood at the window and groaned at the sight of Tabby arranging her slim pale body on a lounger like an exhibition banquet for the starving. A purple bikini cupped her rounded little breasts and slender hips and every shift of her slim thighs drew his considerable attention. He shifted uneasily, struggling to rein back the heavy pulse of arousal that was making his nights so long and frustrating.

Although he had kept watch, as he told himself a protective husband should do, he had yet to see Tabby go topless to eradicate the risk of tan marks. He frowned, not wanting her to show that amount of naked flesh when there were always staff roaming the grounds. It was very strange, he acknowledged in bewilderment, that in spite of the fact he thought it was a very old-fashioned attitude, which he would not have admitted even under torture, he didn't like the idea of anyone but him seeing any part of Tabby bare. He thought that there was a very weird possessive streak in him somewhere and blamed it on the surprising fact that he had become his wife's first lover.

His wife, a label he had never thought he would use, he conceded hard-mouthed, his dark eyes hooded and unusually reflective. Had Tabby genuinely been his wife, however, she would have been in his bed throughout the long hot hours of the afternoon abandoning herself to the demands of his passion and losing herself in the release he would have given her. As his body hardened afresh under the onslaught of that X-rated imagery he cursed bitterly under his breath.

Regretfully, Tabby had all the flexibility of a steel girder: he could do the rules or he could do cold showers. There would be no halfway measures, no get-out clause with her. It would be all or nothing and he knew he *couldn't* do it, couldn't walk that line and change himself to suit when he knew there was no future in it. It wouldn't be fair to her. Yet right at that precise moment Tabby's rules had more pulling power than a ten-ton truck.

That evening, Tabby selected a drop-dead gorgeous blue dress from the closet. Over the past week she had worn a different outfit every day, reasoning that the clothes were there and there was little point wasting them. In any case it would be downright silly to choose to overheat in the jeans and tops that were virtually all she had left of her own clothes since her life first began to unravel after she had lost her own home. Back then she had had to surrender an awful lot of her possessions, whittling her collection of clothing and objects down until she retained only what mattered most and what she could carry.

She tossed the dress on the bed, put on her make-up and brushed her hair, not that how she looked mattered when Acheron was treating her as though she were someone's maiden aunt. But then Acheron *wasn't* the reason why she took the trouble to dress up, she reminded herself staunchly. She did it for her own self-esteem and the knowledge that behaving, at least on the outside, like a rich honeymoon bride was part of her role. Clothed, she eased her feet into perilously high heels and surveyed herself critically in the mirror, mouth momentarily drooping while she wished she were taller, curvier and more striking in appearance...like Kasma? The Kasma whom Acheron never, ever mentioned? But then what business was Kasma of hers? The fiery fury, ignited only a week before by the discovery that Acheron would benefit as much as she did from their marriage, had drained away. After all, she had married Acheron for only one reason: to become Amber's adoptive mother, and all she needed to focus on now was getting through their little charade of a marriage as smoothly and painlessly as possible. Worrying about anything else, *wanting* anything else was unnecessarily stressful and stupid.

Acheron was crossing the hall when Tabby reached the head of the marble staircase. Obeying instinct, she threw her head back and straightened her spine even as she felt perspiration break out across her skin. There he was, sleek, outrageously good-looking and sophisticated even when clad in jeans and an open-necked shirt. Her heart went bumpety-bumpety-bump like a clock wound up too tight, and she gripped the bannister with an agitated hand to start down the stairs. Unfortunately for her, her leading foot went down, however, not onto a step but disorientatingly into mid-air and she tipped forward with a shocked cry of fright, her hand slipping its light hold on the stair rail, her whole body twisting as she tried to halt her fall so that her hip struck the edge of a hard marble step and her ankle was turned beneath her.

'I've got you!' Acheron bit out as the world steadied again.

Mercifully Tabby registered that she was no longer falling but that pain was biting all the way from her hip down her leg…no, not her leg, her ankle. She adjusted as Acheron swept her up into his arms with too much enthusiasm and her leg swung none too gently and she couldn't bite back the cry of pain that was wrenched from her throat. 'My ankle…'

'*Thee mou*…you could've been killed falling on these stairs!' Acheron breathed with a rawness that took her aback, striding back down into the hall with his arms tautly linked round her slight body. He called out in Greek until one of his security staff came running and then he rapped out instructions.

Against her cheek she could feel the still-accelerated pounding of his heart and she wasn't surprised that he was still high on adrenalin because he must have moved faster than the speed of light to intercept her fall. She felt quite queasy at the realisation that but for his timely intervention she might have fallen all the way down the marble staircase and broken her neck or at the very least a limb or two. Relief that she had only wrenched her

ankle and bruised herself filtered slowly through her.
'I'm OK… Lucky you caught me in time.'

Acheron laid her down with exaggerated care on a
sofa and squatted athletically down to her level. 'Did you
feel anyone push you?' he asked, brilliant dark heavily
fringed eyes locked to her face.

She was astounded at the tenor of that question; her violet eyes rounded. 'Why would anyone push me down the
stairs?' she asked weakly. 'I lost my balance and tripped.'

Acheron frowned. 'Are you certain? I thought I saw
someone pass by you on the landing just before you fell.'

'I didn't see or hear anyone.' Her brows pleated and
her lashes screened her eyes, the heat of embarrassment
washing away her pallor because she knew exactly *why*
she had tripped but wild horses wouldn't have dragged
the confession from her. 'Yes, of course I'm certain.'

If she hadn't been so busy admiring Acheron and trying to pose like a silly teenager to look her very best for
his benefit, she would never have missed her step, Tabby
was reflecting in deep, squirming chagrin.

'I'm afraid I have to move you again…I'll try not to
hurt you,' Acheron told her, sliding his hands beneath
her prone length. 'But I have to get you into a car to get
you to a doctor.'

'For goodness' sake, I don't need a doctor!' Tabby exclaimed in growing embarrassment.

But over the next couple of hours while she was sub-
jected to every possible medical examination at the nearest hospital, she might as well have been talking to a wall
because Acheron refused to listen to a word she said. Furthermore, far from behaving like the cool, reserved male
she was accustomed to dealing with, Acheron was clearly
all wound up although why he was, she had no idea. He
paced the floor outside her examination cubicle, talked to

her through the curtain to check she was all right and not
in too much discomfort, insisted on an X-ray being done
while virtually ignoring the doctor who assured him that
she was suffering from nothing more serious than some
nasty bruising and a sprained ankle. Even more embarrassing, his security team spread out round them on full
systems alert as if awaiting an imminent rocket attack
on the casualty department.

'Ah...very much the adoring and anxious husband,'
the middle-aged doctor chuckled in his ignorance.

If only the man knew how wrong he was, Tabby
thought unhappily, feeling like a wretched nuisance and
a malingerer taking up valuable medical attention when
really there was nothing very much amiss with her.

If Tabby had died, it would have been *his* fault. Acheron
brooded on that thought darkly, rage and guilt slivering
through him in sickening waves and like nothing he had
ever felt before. But then he had never been responsible
for another life before and, though he would have liked
to have thought otherwise, he believed that his wife was
very much *his* responsibility. Naturally he was appalled
by the suspicion that someone who worked for him might
have attempted to hurt his wife. Having seen the rude
message left on her bedroom mirror, he was unimpressed
by her conviction that she had simply had an accident. In
the split second it had taken for Tabby to lose her balance
and topple she might not even have noticed that someone
had lightly pushed her or tripped her up.

He was even more frustrated that his security staff had
failed to come up with anything suspicious on any member of the villa staff. Acheron's mouth twisted. Unfortunately the Tuscan villa had rarely been used, hence the
renovation the previous year and the hire of employees

who were a new and unknown quantity and whose dependability would only be confirmed by the test of time. His lustrous eyes hardened and his stubborn mouth compressed into a tough line of determination. Tabby's safety was paramount and as he was very reluctant to frighten her with his suspicions. The wisest strategy would be to immediately vacate the villa and seek a more secure setting. That decision reached, Acheron gave the order, refusing to back down even when the chief of his security pointed out that such a move would entail rousing the baby from her bed as well. Regardless of the drawbacks of his plan, Acheron could hardly wait to get Tabby and the baby away from the Tuscan villa, which now, to his way of thinking, seemed a tainted place. He watched the doctor bandaging her swollen ankle, annoyance still gripping him that he had failed to prevent her from getting hurt.

'Sorry about all this.' Tabby sighed in the limo as they left the hospital.

'When you have an accident you don't need to apologise for it. How are you?' Acheron pressed.

'A bit battered and sore—nothing I won't quickly recover from,' Tabby responded with a smile. 'It'll certainly teach me to be more careful on stairs from now on.'

Acheron was quietly stunned. No woman of his acquaintance would have neglected to make a huge fuss over such an incident by exaggerating their injuries and demanding his sympathy and attention. Tabby, however, characteristically downplayed the episode and asked nothing of him, an acknowledgement that only increased his brooding discomfiture with the situation.

'Where on earth are we going?' Tabby enquired as he lifted her out of the limo and stowed her in the wheelchair already waiting for her use. 'Is this the airport?'

'Yes, we're flying to Sardinia,' Acheron said casually.

'Seriously? I mean, like *right now*?' Tabby stressed in disbelief. 'It's ten o'clock at night.'

'Amber and her nanny are already on board the helicopter, as is your luggage,' Acheron admitted.

There were many things Tabby could have said but she was fighting a dropped jaw and had already learned to think twice before she spoke her mind around Acheron. She clamped her lips firmly together and assumed that he was bored at the villa and that the evident appeal of a change of surroundings had persuaded him to act on impulse. Not only was he dragging Amber out of bed, but he was also forcing Tabby to travel when she was exhausted and in pain. Her lush mouth down-curved: he was being selfishly inconsiderate but she supposed that was normal behaviour for a male accustomed to thinking only of his own needs.

The helicopter was very noisy and Tabby, who hadn't eaten since lunchtime, was almost sick with hunger. She insisted on taking Amber from Melinda, though, and soothed the overtired baby herself. She was surprised when Acheron eased the drowsing child from her arms and settled her on his lap instead. Amber looked up at him, stuck her thumb back in her mouth and closed her eyes again, seemingly content with the exchange. Tabby must've dozed off at that point because she wakened confused by the bright light on her face and the jabs of pain from her ankle as Acheron carried her into a house.

'How do you feel?' he enquired again, stunning gaze sweeping her pale, taut face.

'I'll be fine—'

'Don't be a martyr—you look like death warmed over,' he countered impatiently. 'You're going straight to bed, *yineka mou*. I've organised food as well.'

A bed and a meal sounded very appealing to Tabby at
that moment. He mounted a staircase and a faint breeze
cooled her cheekbone. Her lashes swept up on a tall open
window framed by pale fluttering draperies just as Acheron laid her down on a ginormous bed and began to carefully ease the bedding from beneath her. It struck her
that for once he was being very kind and that set her
teeth on edge.

'Why are you being so nice to me all of a sudden?'
Tabby demanded abruptly.

That single question said so much that Acheron didn't
want to hear just then that he almost groaned his frustration aloud. Leave it to Tabby, he thought ruefully. Leave
it to Tabby to say what nobody else dared to say to Acheron
Dimitrakos. He breathed in slowly. 'You're hurt.'

'You don't do rules and I don't do pity,' Tabby told
him, tilting her chin in challenge.

'You're my wife.'

'Not really.'

'*Enough* my wife that I want to treat you like one,'
Acheron contradicted almost harshly.

Tabby screened eyes blank with incomprehension and
she was horribly tempted by an urge to slap him. He
should have come with a dictionary or some sort of instruction manual that explained how he worked because
once again she was all at sea as to what went on his complex and infuriating head.

'I want to make you feel better,' Acheron announced.

'No pity parties here, please.'

'I haven't behaved very well,' Acheron muttered in a
harsh driven undertone. 'I am trying to make amends.'

'Pity's pity,' Tabby told him, unmoved by that argument.

Acheron came down on the bed beside her. There was

something wild about the glitter in his seething golden eyes as he gently knotted one hand in the fall of her golden hair and closed his mouth hungrily over hers. He sent a jolt of such savage hunger rocketing through her that she froze in sheer fright.

'Does that feel like pity?' he growled.

Tabby made no comment because she could barely breathe. She wanted him to do it again and for longer and was only just able to keep her hands off that lean, powerful body so very close to hers for the first time in a week. One little touch and he made her feel like a sex addict ready to run scarily out of control. In sudden retreat, she dropped her head and then mercifully they were interrupted by the entrance of a woman carrying a tray.

'You need to eat,' Acheron told her unnecessarily.

With his assistance, Tabby leant back against the pillows and lifted the knife and fork. She literally didn't *dare* look at him again, couldn't trust herself that far, knew that she couldn't risk reliving that burning, driving sensation of sexual need in his presence. Hungry though she undoubtedly was, she had to force herself to eat because the sheer level of tension holding her taut was suppressing her appetite. She ate in silence while Acheron paced restively round the big room, constantly drawing her eyes until she remembered that she couldn't afford to look, and in fact had to blank him out to stay in control. And what did that say about her? Was she really that weak that she couldn't withstand him? This guy who had virtually ignored her for the past week? The same one who had slept with her and then backed off at supersonic speed? Shame engulfed her, increasing the exhaustion she had been fighting to contain.

The tray was removed from her lap. Her lashes

drooped, eyes so heavy she literally couldn't hold them open any longer.

'Get some sleep,' Acheron urged, and for once she was in the mood to obey.

Tabby awoke with a piercing need to go to the bathroom, eyes flickering open on darkness and a strong feeling of disorientation. She struggled to sit up and gasped in dismay at the pain that shot through her ankle while she stretched out a wildly flailing hand in search of a bedside light. Mercifully she found the switch attached to a hanging wire, and light illuminated the bedroom a scant second before the male lying on a sofa against the wall leapt upright.

'Ash?' she whispered in disbelief. 'What are you doing in here?'

Acheron was bare-chested and barefoot, low-slung denim jeans clinging to his lean hips. Her startled gaze clung to the muscled expanse of his magnificent bronzed torso and then flicked guiltily higher to take in the dark stubble masking his lower jaw and the unnerving intensity of eyes that glittered like black diamonds in the low light. 'I couldn't leave you in here alone.'

'Why not?' Tabby queried, her face hotter than fire as she forced herself to swivel her hips and shift her good leg off the edge of the bed. 'Why would you sleep on a sofa for my benefit?'

'What on earth are you trying to do?' Acheron demanded, striding across the room.

'I need the bathroom,' she breathed between gritted teeth, mortification rolling over her like a tidal wave.

'You are so stubborn, *koukla mou*. Right now, you need help and I didn't want to put a stranger in here with you,' he admitted impatiently, pushing the walking stick resting against the bedside cabinet into her hand and then slowly pulling her upright to take advantage of its support. 'Now go slow or you'll hurt yourself.'

But Tabby had already worked out that there was no way of moving her leg without her ankle hurting her and she simply clenched her teeth and got on with it, tears stinging her eyes as she hobbled clumsily towards the connecting door he had already opened for her benefit.

Acheron groaned something in Greek and carefully scooped her up into his arms to carry her into the bathroom and gently settle her down on the stool by the vanity unit. 'Pain's always worse in the middle of the night. You'll feel better tomorrow,' he predicted. 'Shout when you're ready to go back to bed.'

Reckoning that there would be two blue moons in the sky before she willingly asked for his help, Tabby studied her tousled reflection in the mirror in cringing horror. She was still wearing the make-up she had put on for dinner the night before and she had panda eyes, sleep creases on her cheek and hideously messy hair. How come he looked gorgeous in the middle of the night but she looked like the Bride of Dracula?

She glanced down and fingered the skimpy nightdress she now wore and swallowed back a groan. Acheron must've undressed her. So what? He had already seen her naked, she reminded herself doggedly, so he had seen nothing new and it was very silly to be embarrassed about it. Levering herself upright, she took care of necessities and then made use of the facilities to clean herself up as best she could. Feeling considerably fresher but pale and stiff with the amount of pain her every movement had made her suffer, Tabby hobbled back out of the bathroom.

Acheron was waiting to scoop her up and deposit her back on the bed.

'I still don't understand what you're doing here with me,' she said weakly, perspiration breaking out on her brow.

'There're only three bedrooms in the main house. I knew you wouldn't want Amber staying away from you in the staff quarters and Melinda needed the third room,' Acheron explained drily.

'There's *only* three bedrooms?' Tabby remarked in amazement. 'You really didn't plan this move very well, did you?'

Acheron dealt her a fulminating appraisal in seething silence. 'It's three in the morning…let's talk about it tomorrow.'

Tabby watched him move back towards the sofa and released her breath on a reluctant sigh. 'Oh, for goodness' sake, share the bed… It's as big as a football pitch. I'm sure we can manage to avoid each other.'

Acheron swung round, his surprise unfeigned, but he said nothing. He switched out the light, and she lay very still in the darkness, listening to the sound of his jeans coming off and trying very hard not to picture what he looked like without them. The sheet moved, the mattress depressed and she forced herself to relax. She was safe as houses with him, she told herself wryly. Acheron was powered by reason, not emotion, not passion. He knew they were a match made in hell.

It was dawn by the time Tabby woke again. Soreness and stiffness assailed her with her first involuntary movement, and she screwed up her face in silent complaint. She turned her head only for her breath to hitch at the sight of Acheron lying asleep only inches away from her. His hair, rumpled into ebony curls, stood out in stark contrast to the white pillow case, his black lashes luxuriant fans that rimmed his strong cheekbones, his wilful passionate mouth full and relaxed. She couldn't stop staring at him. The sheet was wrapped round his hips, the corrugated musculature of his bronzed chest and abdomen exposed as well as a long, powerful, hair-roughened thigh. The pure haunting beauty of his perfectly sculpted body grabbed her by the throat and shook her inside out while heat pooled in her pelvis. She wanted to touch him; she wanted to touch him so badly it hurt to be denied.

His lashes swept up and he stretched slowly and languorously, long, taut muscles defined like ropes below his smooth brown skin. '*Kalimera, yineka mou.*'

Tabby arched a brow. 'Which *means...?*'

'Good morning, wife of mine,' Acheron translated with rich amusement lightening his dark eyes.

'I'm not yours,' Tabby hissed back faster than a striking rattler.

A lean brown hand lifted and wound slowly and carefully into the tumbled fall of her blonde hair, his glittering dark golden eyes hot as boiling honey on her skin. 'How else would you describe yourself? You married me and then you accepted my body into yours. Don't you appreciate that that means that we legally consummated our union?'

Seized by chagrin and confusion, Tabby stiffened. 'I...I...'

He covered her mouth with his, lingering to nibble teasingly at her full lower lip before moving on to taste her with explosive eroticism. A chemical reaction took place inside her, her body jerking in response while within seconds a giant mushroom of heated hunger and longing surged up inside her, blowing her best intentions to hell. Helpless in the grip of that sensual offensive, she kissed him back and his tongue drove deep between her lips with a raw sexual charge that roared through her like a rocket attack.

'Ash?' she mumbled when he freed her long enough to breathe again.

He stared down at her with lancing impatience, every line of him rigid with tension. 'To hell with your rules,' he growled in a tone of decision, his broad chest vibrating against her swollen breasts. 'I only play by my own.'

Those words were still ringing in her ears when he slid his hands underneath her and lifted her slowly onto her side. 'What are you doing?' she gasped.

'I'm making what we both need possible,' Acheron rasped in her ear, his warm breath fanning her neck as he buried his mouth in the sensitive slope between neck and shoulder while his hands slid up from her waist to cup her achingly tender breasts. 'As you're in no condition to run away, shout loud if you want to say no.'

In stark disconcertion her violet eyes opened to their fullest extent and locked onto the sofa he had occupied the night before. She had invited him into the bed in the first place. Had he assumed her body was included in the offer? Or was he just as entrapped as she was by the chemistry between them? Naturally that latter interpretation pleased her more but, in the midst of her pondering, long fingers plucked at the straining peaks of her breasts and actual thought became too much of a challenge.

Acheron tasted the soft white skin of her throat and the sweet scent of her enclosed him, heightening his arousal to an almost unbearable extent. In need of release he pressed his throbbing erection against her bottom, and she gasped and leant back into him while he lifted her nightdress to caress the swollen bounty of her small, taut breasts, paying special attention to her plump pink nipples. 'I love your breasts,' he told her thickly. 'They fit perfectly into my hands, *moli mou.*'

Every tiny muscle straining as she trembled, Tabby looked down at the fingers, so dark against her paler skin, expertly caressing her. Sharp biting arrows of need were spearing down between her legs where her indescribably sensitive flesh was tingling. She shifted and a faint sound of discomfort was wrenched from her as she accidentally moved her ankle.

'Lie still,' Acheron urged. 'You don't need to do anything. Let me do all the work.'

Her desire was already so strong that she wanted to scream, wanted to tell him what to do and to do it quickly. The shock of the thought and a vision of his reaction cooled her teeming thoughts. But she hadn't known, hadn't ever dreamt that a kiss and a little intimate touching could send her temperature shooting from zero to overload and she knew that she was finally understanding the very basic reason why he had become her first lover. He burned her up like a lightning strike, awakened a craving that overwhelmed her defences.

His hand shimmied down over her thigh, flirting, teasing more intimate areas without delivering on the promise. She ached, she actually ached deep down inside where she felt hollow and desperate, her entire being locked to the playful passage of that provocative hand. Fingertips traced her hidden core, stroking nerve endings that were impossibly delicate. She dragged in a sustaining breath while he nibbled an enervating path down the side of her extended throat. 'In a minute I'm going to kill you,' she swore shakily.

'No, you're going to ask me to do it again.'

'You really don't suffer from low self-esteem,' she noted even more unevenly, her breath catching in her convulsing throat as a fingertip brushed her clitoris, and flame leapt through her entire core.

'Not between the sheets…no,' Acheron agreed silkily. 'You've been told you're wonderful?'

'Many times. I'm filthy rich. Telling me I'm rubbish in bed—even if it's true—wouldn't be profitable,' he advanced with cynical cool.

Consternation seized Tabby. 'That's *awful*—'

'Awful,' he mimicked, stroking the most sensitive spot on her whole body so that she jackknifed back against him with a startled yelp.

'I don't want your money,' Tabby exclaimed helplessly. 'I just want your body!'

A stark little silence fell, and she squeezed her eyes tight shut in horror. *I didn't say that, I couldn't possibly have said that!*

'I've got no objections to that goal,' Acheron husked, biting at her ear lobe with erotic intent, ostensibly undeterred by her claim. 'It's earthy and honest…why not?'

He touched her again and her mortification drowned in a sea of shivering response. She lay back against him, tiny muscles twitching, soothed by the heat and strength of him even as that amplified physical contact heightened her awareness. With immense delicacy he stroked the seam of her femininity and then slid inside where she was warm and wet and, oh, so needy. She quivered, pitched straight to a high of longing that she couldn't quell or even control. He sank a finger inside her, and she jerked and gasped as he plunged slowly in and out, raising her temperature to boiling point, making her squirm and shift, forgetting even the twinges of pain in her ankle.

'Hot, tight, ready,' Acheron growled hungrily in her ear as she arched back into his lean, hard body, instinctively seeking the fulfilment that only he could give while he angled away from her to don a condom. 'I've been fantasising about this for days.'

'*Days?*' she parroted in surprise as he lifted her un-damaged leg to spread her open for him.

'Every night since that first night, every day I saw you in that teeny tiny bikini, *glyka mou*,' Acheron con-fided, tilting her forward, long fingers tightening their hold on her slender thigh as he entered her with a groan of intense masculine satisfaction.

A muffled scream of pleasure was torn from Tabby's throat as her body was forced to adjust to his size, her inner channel stretching to the brink of insane pleasure.

'All right?' Acheron murmured thickly.

'Well, I wouldn't want you to answer your phone right now!' Tabby admitted shakily, her heart thundering, her blood racing, her whole body thrumming with sensation as he eased back and then slammed into her again, jolt-ing her with wicked pleasure.

'No boundaries!' he ground out forcefully. 'No bound-aries between us!'

She couldn't think, couldn't speak for the intensity of what he was making her feel. He tugged her head back and took her mouth with passionate, driving need and the taste and heat of him scorched her all the while the slow, sure thrust of his engorged shaft stimulated her senses to an unbearable peak of excitement. Her hips writhed. The pace quickened. The heat built. She was crying out, sobbing she knew not what when her wayward body fi-nally clamped down convulsively on him and she soared over the edge in a frenzied crescendo of release that took her by storm.

Ecstasy was still rippling through her weak body in small blissful waves when he wrapped his arms round her and kept her close.

'You're amazing,' he husked.

'You too,' she whispered, exhaustion pinning her to the bed.

'And we're going to do this over and over again,' Acheron decreed with lethally sexy assurance. 'No more cold showers, no more separate beds, no more posing in teeny tiny bikinis I can't rip off.'

'Sleepy,' she framed apologetically.

'Sleep…you're going to need all your energy,' he said.

CHAPTER NINE

WHEN TABBY WOKE for the fourth time in twelve hours, she was totally disorientated and she blinked in the strong sunlight flooding through the French windows. A split second later, she sat up and checked her watch to discover that it was mid-afternoon.

My goodness, she had slept half the day away! In guilty dismay, she clambered awkwardly out of bed, learning that Acheron had got it right when he had suggested she would feel better in the morning. Her hip still ached like the very devil but the pain in her ankle had become more bearable. Curious to see her surroundings, having arrived in complete darkness the night before, she limped over to the French windows with the aid of her stick and went out onto the sunlit balcony to stand at the rail.

A craggy cove stretched out below her, the towering rocks encircling a stretch of pure white sand lapped by a turquoise sea so clear she could see the ocean bottom. The lush tree-filled gardens ran right to the edge of the beach. It was absolutely idyllic and very beautiful but Tabby's attention was drawn straight to the couple standing together in the rippling surf. Amber's pram was parked in the shadow of the rocks and Melinda, clad in a minuscule red bikini that exaggerated her bountiful curves, was talking with apparent urgency to Acheron, whose lean, powerful body was sheathed only in trunks.

It was an unexpectedly intimate and disturbing sight, and Tabby couldn't take her eyes off the couple, jealousy spearing through her with an immediacy that appalled her. She jerked in dismay and snatched in a startled breath when Melinda rested a hand down on Acheron's arm. To his credit the contact only lasted for a second because he took an immediate step back from the forward blonde and with a brief final word strode back across the sand towards the house. Tabby hobbled back hurriedly indoors to get dressed, her brain struggling to encompass what she had seen at the same time as she accepted that, yet again, the very foundations of her relationship with the man she had married had been demolished and every-thing had changed.

Sexual desire had stimulated that change, she con-ceded, shame slivering through her. *No boundaries*, Acheron had proclaimed with passion and he was cer-tainly correct on that score: the rules she had tried to im-pose had been blown right out of the water along with her nonsensical belief that she could resist him. Even more pertinently, seeing Melinda touch Acheron had inflamed her with ferocious possessiveness and the sort of angry jealous feelings she had never before experienced. What did that say about her intelligence? What was she let-ting him do to her? Where were these violent conflicting emotions coming from? She was behaving like a love-sick idiot! Was that the problem? Had lust first sucked her in and then left her childishly infatuated with him?

Opening her as yet still packed cases, she extracted underwear and a long, loose sundress before stepping into the bathroom to freshen up. The whole process took her much longer than usual having to wash her hair in the sink, which was a challenge, and left the bathroom floor swimming by the time she had finished. When she finally emerged after mopping dry the floor, however, she felt more like herself with clean, tidy hair and a little make-up applied.

Acheron strolled into the bedroom and there Tabby was; captured in a patch of sunlight, long golden hair rippling down to softly frame her delicate features, her tiny body sylphlike in a pale blue dress that reflected her amazing eyes, which were currently pools of anxious troubled violet that evaded his. She was *so* open, *so* honest in her reactions, it literally shocked him. Nothing was concealed; nothing was hidden from him. His broad chest tightened as he expelled his breath and gritted his teeth. He could not begin to imagine how frighteningly vulnerable that lack of concealment and reserve made her. If he didn't act first, she was undoubtedly about to unleash a rash volley of accusations and questions about their renewed intimacy, which threatened to put them both right back where they had started after their car crash wedding night and her proclamation of her unnecessary rules.

'Tabby,' he murmured evenly, noting avidly that he could see the little points of her deliciously prominent nipples showing below the fine material of her dress as well as the slender outline of her shapely legs. An overpoweringly strong urge to claim her again assailed him.

'Ash,' she said breathlessly, studying his lean, darkly handsome features with a sinking heart because that fast she was out of breath and dizzy just looking at him. 'We need to talk.'

'No, we don't, *glyka mou*,' Acheron contradicted with stubborn assurance as he drew closer. 'Let's do this my way. We don't talk, we especially *don't* agonise over anything. It is what it is and we just enjoy it for as long as it lasts.'

He had snatched the confused words out of her mouth before she had even collected her thoughts enough to speak. She suspected that his solution was vintage Acheron in the field of relationships—say nothing, do nothing and the problem will go away. 'I wasn't about to agonise over anything,' she protested, swaying slightly because she found it hard to stand still for long and had to grip the walking stick in a tighter hold.

He closed hands round her forearms to steady her and slowly trailed his hands down to her waist. 'You can't help yourself.'

As she looked up at him, her lush full lips tingled and she was conscious of a sensation like prickling heat curling low in her pelvis. He angled his mouth down and kissed her with intoxicating urgency.

'Oh…' she said in breathless surprise at the development, her body humming into ready awareness with an enthusiasm that disconcerted her.

He lifted her dress slowly, brazen dark golden eyes locked to hers, daring her to object. Anticipation pierced her, sharp as a lance, liquid heat pooling between her thighs. His gaze not once leaving hers, he found her with his fingers, eased below her lace-edged panties and stroked and that fast she was hotter than the fires of hell, leaning up against him for support, making no objection when he gently lowered her back onto the bed. The stick fell forgotten on the floor.

'I only just got up,' she exclaimed, her surprise unconcealed.

'You should've waited here for me, *glyka mou*,' Acheron told her sibilantly.

'I can't believe you want me again already.' Tabby studied him with confused and wondering eyes.

'The instant I look at you I want you,' Acheron admitted in a slightly raw undertone because there was a lack of control and a weakness in such a truth that deeply disturbed him.

'Not the very first time you saw me,' she reminded him stubbornly.

'You swore at me…not your finest hour, *glyka mou*,' he mocked. 'Now that I know you, it wouldn't bother me at all or make me stop thinking that you're the hottest woman on the planet.'

Eyes wide with astonishment, Tabby was transfixed by that statement. 'You really mean that?'

'*You have to ask*? Here I am throwing you down on the bed to ravish and you have to ask how much I want you? I can't wait to get you horizontal and that's not OK,' Acheron groaned, yanking off her panties with scant ceremony and splaying her legs with a voracious hiss of all-male satisfaction, fully appreciating the pink glistening femininity he had exposed. 'No, don't spoil the view,' he censured when, hot-cheeked, she tried to scissor her thighs together again. 'I like to look and I *love* to appreciate.'

Tabby forced herself to remember that while he peeled off his trunks, revealing his long, thick erection. Heat rolled through her, moisture gathering at the heart of her along with a soul-deep yearning that should have terrified her. She realised that she was acting on instinct, not even pausing to think about what he had said, skipping the *agonising* as he had phrased it because what woman wished to be viewed in that light?

'*Thee mou*, hot, hot, hot,' Acheron rasped as he came down on top of her, punctuating every word with a passionate kiss and hands that traced every erogenous zone she possessed until her impatience steadily rose to match his.

Only then did he sink into her hard and fast, muttering something in Greek before he paused to press his lips to her brow. 'Am I hurting you?' he grated uneasily.

'Only if you stop,' she traded helplessly, her whole body clenching round him as possessively as her arms, hands smoothing over his satin-smooth back, clenching there, nails curving inward as he ground into her, and she cried out in helpless delight. Excitement rose in an unstoppable tide, and she lost the self she knew in it, living from one glorious moment of intense sensation to the next until the great gathering storm became too much to contain and the passion swept her off the heights down into the ecstatic rippling aftermath.

'Well, there wasn't much finesse about that,' Acheron remarked, cradling her up against him in a damp tangle of limbs. 'My apologies.'

'No need,' Tabby countered, pressing her mouth softly to his chest, revelling in the hot, musky smell of his skin and the closeness that he was embracing. 'It was another ten out of ten.'

'You're *grading* me now?' he demanded in obvious horror.

'If you drop down to a five or lower, I'll warn you,' Tabby teased, smiling because she felt amazingly light-hearted while she was studiously engaged in not agonising. The minute she forgot his maxim though the real world immediately flooded back and, assailed by those whirling doubts, insecurities and unanswered questions, she became tense again and marvelled that she had so easily suppressed what she had seen.

'I saw you with Melinda on the beach,' she told him

baldly, putting it right out there without holding back and judging her words and their effect.

Acheron's big powerful frame stiffened and he tilted her head back to study her troubled face. 'I'm bringing another nanny in to work with Melinda, who will eventually replace her. I've already made the arrangements. I don't want Amber upset by too sudden a change in staff,' he volunteered.

Tabby was wildly disconcerted by the announcement but relieved to know that Melinda would soon be moving on, while being impressed and touched that he had also been careful to consider Amber's need for consistent care. 'You're planning to sack Melinda?'

'She's on a temporary contract. We can let her go any time we like but I'd prefer to dispense with her services in the usual way. She knows a little too much about our marriage for my comfort.'

Frowning at that admission, Tabby prompted, 'What do you mean?'

'Melinda is clearly aware that we were using separate bedrooms at the villa. When we were on the beach she offered to share Amber's room so that I could take over hers,' Acheron explained grimly.

Wings of hot pink reddened Tabby's cheeks. Annoyance and embarrassment that their unconventional sleeping arrangements had evidently attracted the attention of the staff engulfed her. 'Perhaps she was planning to do a little wandering during the night once you were conveniently close. She *was* coming on to you, wasn't she?'

Lean, extravagantly handsome features impassive, stunning dark eyes screened, Acheron nodded. 'It happens.'

Tabby looked up at him, weak with relief that he had told her the truth without fanfare or fuss. 'Often?'

Acheron released a rueful chuckle at the innocence of that question. 'All the time. If I ignore it, it usually dies a natural death but Melinda doesn't take hints…possibly because she's already reached the conclusion that ours is not a normal marriage. She *could* take that information to the press, laying me open to a potential charge that I only married you to circumvent my father's will.'

Tabby grimaced. 'We'll have to work harder at being a more convincing couple. Share a room, spend time together, fake it up to behave more like a honeymoon couple is expected to behave.'

'But it doesn't have to be fake now,' Acheron pointed out with lazy assurance.

But in her heart she would know it *was* fake, Tabby reflected painfully. He gave her great sex but he wasn't offering to give her anything more. Maybe that was the only kind of giving he knew—short-term physical stuff with a built-in time limit, she conceded fairly, not wanting to judge him just because he was different. After all, was she any more evolved in the field of relationships? She wanted him *so* much, wanted his attention as much as Amber did, was willing to do whatever it took to hold that attention. But she was not willing to admit even to herself that he was also stirring up emotions that she was afraid she couldn't handle.

'Why did your father write a will that forced you to get married when you didn't want to?' Tabby asked quietly, knowing that that was the heart of the matter and the mystery that he had so far avoided explaining.

'In a nutshell? He wanted me to marry Kasma,' Acheron told her tersely, his beautiful mouth hardening. 'And I don't *ever* want to talk about that.'

With difficulty, Tabby swallowed an irritated comeback on that omission, knowing such a response would only reinforce his reserve and make him dig his stubborn heels in even harder. She could leave the thorny question of Kasma to one side for the moment and concentrate on other aspects. 'But surely your father knew how you felt? How close were the two of you?' Tabby persisted.

A tiny muscle pulled taut at the corner of his unsmiling jaw. 'I only met him in my late twenties,' he reminded her drily. 'I suppose it was more of a business relationship than most. His company was struggling. He asked me for advice. I went in to help and ended up taking over.'

'Didn't he resent that?'

'Not at all. He wasn't much of a businessman, more of a family man desperate to give his loved ones a secure future.'

'That was your stepmother and her children?'

Acheron compressed his lips. 'My father married her when her kids were very young and raised them as his own but I didn't meet them until about eighteen months before he died.'

'Why not?' Tabby asked in surprise.

'His family weren't relevant to me or to our relationship. They were strangers. There was no blood tie and I've never had a family, so I was very wary about getting involved in that side of his life. As things turned out, I was right to be wary and to have kept my distance for as long as I did,' he pronounced with dark finality.

A silence full of undertones enclosed them in the aftermath of that assurance, adding to Tabby's discomfiture. She was trying desperately to work out what his past relationship with his stepsister, Kasma, had entailed. Obviously there had been an affair that left the beautiful brunette with expectations that Acheron was not prepared to fulfil. Presumably the affair had ended badly with bitterness on both sides. Had some tragedy occurred? Had

Kasma fallen pregnant or some such thing? Mightn't that
explain why his late father had got such a bee in his bon-
net about Acheron marrying his stepdaughter? Certainly
the other woman had believed very strongly that she was
the only woman who should become Acheron's wife. Was
Kasma in love with him? Or was she more fixated on
his money and his status? But regardless of why Kasma
wanted Acheron, what did it matter when *he* didn't want
her? Tabby asked herself irritably, weary of suspicions
that were winding up her tension for no good reason. If
it was that simple though, why couldn't he just say so?

'I wish you didn't keep secrets. I wish you were more
frank and straightforward about things,' she admitted
before she could think better of it.

'You're so honest sometimes you terrify me, *glyka
mou*,' Acheron confided ruefully. 'And if this honeymoon
is going to work, we will each have to compromise our
most cherished ideals.'

Acheron peered down at the red-rose tattoo adorning
Tabby's slender arm with a frown and stroked a finger
gently across it. 'The skin underneath feels rough and
the design is already blurred. The tattooist must have
damaged your skin.'

Tabby gritted her teeth, relaxation abandoned as she
yanked her arm free of his light hold. 'Don't touch me
there.'

Lustrous dark golden eyes scrutinised her from below
inky-black lashes. 'Why not?'

'Are we about to have *another* one of those conversations in which you suggest that I go for laser treatment to
have it removed?' Tabby condemned, her small face taut
and pale as she decided it was time to tell him the truth,
which would surely conclude his interest in the subject.

'If you must know, I won't have it removed because it's covering up an ugly scar. In fact, the scar was there first. The tattooist did a marvellous job but he couldn't have made the ink design perfect when my skin was far from perfect to begin with.'

His lean dark features were frowning now. 'What sort of a scar?'

'Take it from me…you really don't want to know,' Tabby told him warningly, pulling away from him to scramble to her feet in the shade of the pine trees that overhung the pinkish pale sand. After checking that Amber still lay splayed out on her blanket in sleeping abandonment, her olive-skinned chubby limbs protruding starfish fashion from her white *broderie anglaise* play-suit, her rosebud mouth soft and relaxed, Tabby stalked on down the beach, a slight figure clad in shorts and a bikini top.

Acheron, she thought, her hands knotting into fists, her teeth grinding together in angry frustration. There were times she wanted to throw him into the sea from a great height. She had thought *she* was the nosy one but he didn't quit once he was on a trail either. Even worse, he was a domineering perfectionist. Although he wasn't planning to spend the rest of his life with her and Amber, he still wanted to persuade her that she should have the tattoo removed and he was as relentless as a steam roller running down a hill. At breakfast he had asked her if she would be happy for Amber to get something similar done, and Tabby had been betrayed into looking in dismay at Amber's smooth soft forearm and Acheron, being Acheron, had noticed that revealing appraisal.

'So, you *do* regret getting it done,' he had exclaimed with satisfaction.

Yes, Acheron had some infuriating traits, she acknowledged, but over the past month in Sardinia he had also been a highly entertaining companion, a very sexy lover and a patient and caring father figure for Amber. At that moment, Tabby couldn't begin to work out how an entire four weeks had flashed past faster than the speed of light. The first week had been a challenge while she was still hobbling round with a stick and pretty much sentenced to passing her time at the beach house. But once her ankle had healed, they had begun to go out and about.

Snapshots of special moments they had shared filled her memory with more comforting images. They had climbed the massive staircase to the Bastione terrace to see the amazing panoramic view of the rooftops of Calgiari. While she was still wheezing from the climb and overheated from the sun, he had told her that there was actually a lift but that he had assumed that she would enjoy the full tourist experience more. It had taken several cocktails and the cooling effect of the lovely breeze on the terrace before she had forgiven him, and if she was truthful her resistance had only truly melted when he slid long brown fingers into hers in the lift on the way down again.

They had made an evening visit to Castelsardo, a beautiful village dominated by a magical citadel all lit up at night, to enjoy live music in the piazza. Amber had adored all the noise and bustle going on around her and Acheron had enjoyed the baby's bright-eyed fascination.

The following night, however, they had sought out more adult fun, dancing until dawn at the Billionaire club where Tabby had felt distinctly overshadowed by the number of gorgeous women, sleek and deadly as sharks, cruising for a wealthy hook-up. That Ash had acted as if he only had eyes for her and had kissed her passionately on the dance floor had done much to lift her self-esteem.

Memory after memory was now tumbling inside Tabby's head. For forty-eight hours they had sailed a yacht round the national park of La Maddalena, a group of protected and largely uninhabited islands teeming with flora and wildlife. The last night they had skinny dipped in a deserted cove and made love until the sun went down. Exhausted, she had wakened to find Acheron barbecuing their evening meal, stunning dark golden eyes smiling lazily at her and making her heart somersault like a trapeze artist.

Of course, they had done all the usual things as well, like strolling round the famous boutiques on the Costa Smeralda, an activity or a lack of activity that Acheron was astounded to discover bored his bride to tears.

'But you *must* want me to buy you something,' he had protested. 'You *must* have seen something you liked. You do realise that the only thing I've bought you since we arrived is that bed linen?'

Tabby had seen the exquisite bed linen in an upmarket handicrafts shop and her childhood memories of being clumsy with a needle and thread had given her a true appreciation of the amount of skill involved in producing such beautiful embroidery. That had been a purchase to treasure, a gift she truly loved, and only later had it occurred to her that she would never see that winter-weight linen spread across a bed that she shared with Acheron and that it would inevitably adorn a bed she slept in alone. Once the summer was over, their marriage would be history.

But then while she had known they would be faking their honeymoon and had dutifully posed with him for a persistent paparazzo, who had followed them round Porto Cervo, she had not appreciated the lengths Acheron might go to in making their relationship look genuine from the inside and the outside. So, if occasionally she got a little confused and thought about him as if he *were* her real husband, who could blame her for making that mistake?

Or for falling madly and irrevocably in love with him during the process, she reasoned wretchedly. After all, no man had ever treated her as well as he did, no man had ever made her so happy either, and only he had ever made love to her several times a day, *every* day, as if she were indeed the hottest, sexiest woman on the planet. Naturally her emotions had got involved and she suppressed them as best she could, knowing that the last thing Acheron required from her was angst and a broken heart, which would make him feel guilty and uncomfortable.

It wasn't his fault she had fallen for him either. It certainly wasn't as though he had misled her with promises about the future. In fact, right from the outset she had known that there was no future for them. He had never made any bones about that. Once they had succeeded to legally adopt Amber, their supposed marriage would be left to wither and die. Tabby would make a new life with the little girl she loved while she assumed Acheron would return to his workaholic, womanising existence. Would she ever see him again after the divorce? As she confronted that bleak prospect an agonising shard of pain slivered through Tabby and left a deep anguished ache in its wake. Would Acheron want to retain even the most distant relationship with Amber? Or would he decide on a clean break and act as if Amber didn't exist?

Acheron crossed the beach, noting how Tabby's figure had rounded out once she was eating decent food, recalling with quiet satisfaction that she no longer bit her nails—small changes that he valued.

'How did you get the scar concealed by the tattoo?' he demanded obstinately, interrupting Tabby's reverie and shooting her back to the present by wrapping both arms round her from behind, carefully preventing her from storming off again. 'Were you involved in an accident?'

'No...it wasn't an accident,' Tabby admitted, past recollections making her skin turn suddenly cold and clammy in spite of the heat of the sun.

He was being supportive, she reminded herself doggedly, guilt biting into her former annoyance with him. When Amber had cried half the night because she was teething and her gums were sore, Acheron had been right there beside her, helping to distract the little girl and calm her down enough to sleep again. She had not expected supportiveness from Acheron but his interest in Amber was anything but half-hearted. When it came to childcare, he took the rough with the smooth, serenely accepting that children weren't always sunny and smiling.

The new nanny currently working with Melinda was called Teresa, a warm, chattering Italian woman whose main source of interest was her charge. Within a week the English nanny would be leaving to take up a permanent position with a family in London.

'Tabby...I asked you a question,' Acheron reminded her with deeply unwelcome persistence. 'You said you didn't get the scar in an accident, so—'

Dredged from the teeming tumult of her frantic attempt to think about just about anything other than the past he was trying to dig up, Tabby lifted her head high and looked out to sea. 'My mother burned me with a hot iron because I knocked over a carton of milk,' she confessed without any expression at all.

'*Thee mou...*' Acheron growled in stricken disbelief, spinning her round to look at her pale set face and the yawning hurt still lingering in her violet eyes.

'I was never allowed to be with either of my parents

unsupervised again after that,' she explained woodenly. 'My mother went to prison for burning me and I never saw either of them again.'

Bewildered by the great surge of ferocious anger welling up inside him, Acheron crushed her slight body to his, both arms wrapping tightly round her. For some reason he registered that he was feeling sick and his hands weren't quite steady, and in that instant some inexplicable deep need that disturbed him was making it impossible for him not to touch her. 'That must've been a relief.'

'No, it wasn't. I loved them. They weren't very lovable people but they were all I had,' Tabby admitted thickly, her dry throat scratching over the words as if she was reluctant to voice them. She had learned as a young child that loving gestures would be rejected but now more than anything in the world she wanted to wrap her arms round Acheron and take full advantage of the comfort he was clumsily trying to offer her, only that pattern of early rejection and knowledge of how abandonment felt kept her body rigid and uninviting in the circle of his arms.

'I understand that,' Acheron breathed in a raw driven undertone. 'I rarely saw my mother but I still idolised her—'

'What a pair we are!' Tabby sniffed, her tension suddenly giving way as tears stung her eyes and overflowed, her overloaded reaction to having had to explain and indeed relive what she never, ever talked about to anyone.

Acheron stared down at her tear-stained visage, pale below his bronzed skin, his strong facial bones forbiddingly set. 'I can't bear to think of you being hurt like that, *yineka mou*—'

'Don't…don't talk about it!' Tabby urged feverishly. 'I try never to think about it but every time I saw the scar in the mirror as a teenager, I remembered it, and sometimes people asked what had happened to me. That's why I got the tattoo…to cover it up, hide it.'

'Then wear that tattoo with pride. It's a survival badge,' Acheron informed her with hard satisfaction. 'I wish you'd explained weeks ago but I understand now why you didn't.'

'Oh, for goodness' sake, let's talk about something more cheerful!' Tabby pleaded. 'Tell me something about you. I mean, you must have *some* happy childhood memories of your mother?'

Acheron closed an arm round her slight shoulders to press her back across the beach towards Amber. 'The night before my first day at school she presented me with a fantastically expensive pen engraved with my name. Of course, I was only allowed to use a pencil in class but naturally that didn't occur to her. She was very fond of flamboyant gestures, always telling me that only the very best was good enough for a Dimitrakos—'

'Maybe that was how she was brought up,' Tabby suggested quietly. 'But you still haven't explained why that pen made you happy.'

'Because generally she ignored me but that particular week she was fresh out of rehab and engaged in turning over a new leaf and it was the one and only time she made me feel that I genuinely mattered to her. She even gave me a whole speech about education being the most important thing in my life…that from a woman who dropped out of school as a teenager and couldn't read anything more challenging than a magazine,' he told her wryly.

'Do you still have the pen?'

'I think it was stolen.' He sent her a rueful charismatic smile that tilted her heart inside her chest and interfered with her breathing. 'But at least I have that one perfect moment to remember her by.'

* * *

Acheron could not relax until he had commissioned a special piece of jewellery for Tabby's upcoming birthday, which surprisingly fell in the same week as his own. That achieved, he worried about having taken that much trouble over a gift. What was wrong with him? What sort of man went to such lengths for a wife he was planning to divorce? *Keep it cool*, a little voice chimed in the back of his uneasy mind. But it had proved impossible to play it cool when confronted with the harsh reality of Tabby's childhood experiences, which had had the unexpected effect of showing Acheron that he had a good deal less to be bitter about with regard to his own. His mother had been a neglectful, selfish and inadequate parent but even at her worst he had never doubted that she loved him. And possibly, but for the malicious machinations of a third party, his father might have learned to love and appreciate him as well…

The constant flow of such unfamiliar thoughts assailing him kept him quiet over dinner. Aware of Tabby's anxious gaze, he was maddened by the knowledge that he wasn't feeling like himself any more and that, even in the midst of that disorientating experience, withdrawing his attention from her could make him feel guilty. Never a fan of great inner debates, or even in the habit of staging them, he was exasperated and bewildered by the emotions Tabby constantly churned up inside him. *She was too intense*, too rich for his blood. He needed to take a step back, he decided abruptly; he needed some distance, and the instant he made that decision he felt better and back in control again.

'I have to go away on business for a couple of days,' Acheron volunteered as he strode out of the bathroom, a towel negligently wrapped round his lean, muscular body. His black hair tousled and damp, his lean, devastatingly handsome face clean-shaven, he looked amazing and Tabby's mouth ran dry before she could even process what he had said.

Realising that he was leaving her, Tabby went rigid and then scolded herself because he had done very little work in recent weeks and could hardly be expected to maintain that lifestyle indefinitely. No, she had been spoilt by his constant company and had to learn fast how to adapt to his absence. Was that why he had been so quiet and distant over dinner? Had he worried about her reaction? Well, it was time to show him that she was strong and not the complaining type.

'I'll miss you, but we'll be fine,' she responded lightly.

Acheron ground his teeth together, having expected her to object or even offer to travel with him. This was definitely a moment when he had believed she would cling and make him feel suffocated. He watched her clamber into bed, slender as a willow wand, the modest nightdress concealing the hot, secret places he loved, and lust kicked in so fast he felt dizzy with it. Lustrous dark eyes veiling, he discarded the towel, doused the lights and joined her. *Not tonight*, he thought grimly, as though he was fighting a battle; tonight he could get by without her.

Eyes sparkling in the moonlight, Tabby rolled over to Acheron's side of the bed and ran delicate fingers hungrily across a hair-roughened thigh while her hair trailed over his pelvis.

Acheron closed his eyes in despair. He could always lie back and think of Greece. If he said no like a frightened virgin, he would probably upset her, and there was no point doing that, was there? Why risk upsetting her? She found his swelling shaft with her mouth, and his hips shifted upward in helpless encouragement. It crossed his

mind that the divorce might upset her because she acted
as if she was fond of him, looked at him as if he was special, dived on him in bed if he didn't dive on her first,
never missed a chance to put her arms round him…al-
though strangely *not* this afternoon on the beach when he
had put his arms round her in an effort to offer sympathy
for what his thoughtless questions had made her cruelly
relive. A particularly strong wave of pleasure blanked
out the subsequent thought about *why* she might not have
responded, yet another thought he didn't want to have.
All that sentimental stuff, he thought grimly—he never
had been any good at that. He had probably been clumsy.

Afterwards, Acheron didn't hold her the way he usually did, and Tabby felt cold inside and abandoned. She
curled up on her side, hating him, loving him, wanting
him, fretting and reckoning that love was the worst torture in existence for a woman. There was no point always
wanting what he wouldn't give her, didn't even *want* to
give her, she reflected painfully. Their divorce was not
only written in the stars but also written into a pre-nuptial
contract from which there would be no escape.

And maybe he still had feelings for Kasma, whom he
would not discuss although she had on several occasions
worked the conversation helpfully round in that direction
to give him an easy opening. But trying to get Acheron
to talk about something he didn't want to talk about was
like trying to get blood out of a stone. In her experience
though, people only avoided topics that embarrassed or
troubled them, so his failed relationship with Kasma must
have gone deep indeed to leave behind such conspicuous
and quite uncharacteristic sensitivity…

The following morning, Tabby drifted out of sleep to
discover that Acheron had made an early departure and

without leaving even a note. She spent a quiet day with Amber and it was the next day before the silence from Acheron began to niggle at her. He didn't have to stay in touch when he was only planning to be away forty-eight hours, she conceded ruefully, and she was not so needy that she required him to check in with her every day. But as she lay in the bed that felt empty without him the day stretched before Tabby like a blank slate, shorn of anticipation, excitement and happiness.

Thoroughly exasperated with her mood, she went for a shower and got dressed in the bathroom, emerging to catch a glimpse of her reflection in the tall cheval mirror across the bedroom and wonder why she couldn't see it properly. As she automatically moved closer to see what was amiss with the mirror she realised that someone had written something on it, and she frowned at it in bewilderment.

He's using you! Tabby was gobsmacked. Why would anyone write that on their mirror for her to see? Clearly it was meant to be personal, and presumably Acheron was the 'he' being referred to. What on earth did it mean? Whatever, it really spooked her that someone had come into their bedroom while she was in the bathroom and left a message presumably intended to shock and insult her. After all, only someone in the house could have had access to their room and that knowledge made gooseflesh blossom on her exposed skin.

Without hesitation she lifted the house phone and asked to speak to Ash's security chief, Dmitri. Almost before she had finished speaking, Dmitri joined her in the room to see the mirror for himself. If his forbidding expression was anything to go by, he took the matter very seriously. Dmitri, however, was a man of few words and she left him to it and went downstairs for breakfast.

CHAPTER TEN

'CAN I ASK you where you're planning to go?' Melinda asked with a sunny smile, joining her at the breakfast table, which she never dared to do when Acheron was around.

'Into Porto Cervo to shop,' Tabby admitted. 'I'm looking for a birthday present.'

'There's some great jewellery boutiques...try the Piazzetta delle Chiacchere,' Melinda advised helpfully.

Tabby nodded, feeling guilty about how much she disliked the curvaceous blonde who would, by the end of the week, mercifully be gone from the household to take up her new appointment. Since Teresa's arrival and increasing involvement with Amber, Melinda seemed to spend a lot of time hovering unnecessarily and watching their comings and goings. Once, Tabby had even suspected that the blonde was eavesdropping on her and Acheron. No doubt the nanny had now registered that their detached marriage had developed into something closer. Or was that only her own wishful thinking at work? Tabby wondered heavily.

Acheron had been gone only one day and she felt bereft. That was a pretty poor show for a strong, independent woman, she conceded shamefacedly. She missed him so much, and her outlook wasn't improved by her recollection of his unusual behaviour on that last night they had spent together. He had been silent and moody, extraordinarily uninvolved when she had made love to him, saying nothing, doing nothing, in fact, acting like a right—

'Miss Barnes?' Dmitri appeared in the doorway. 'Could I have a word with you?'

'*Right* now?' Melinda prompted with a sparkling smile that seemed wasted on the granite-faced older man.

'Now would be a good time,' Dmitri responded evenly.

Tabby left Teresa in charge of Amber, having decided that dragging the little girl out to trail round the shops during the hottest part of the day would be unwise. The message was still on the mirror when she walked past into the bathroom to renew her lipstick and it made her shiver. *He's using you.* Well, as far as their marriage was concerned they were using each other, she told herself doggedly. Although things had changed drastically once they began sharing a bed in reality. Was Acheron only sleeping with her because that intimacy added to the illusion of their having a normal marriage? After all, if he was seen out by the paparazzi with another woman while he was supposed to be a happily married new husband, it wouldn't look good. So, was she being used on that basis? But how could she call it using when she was in love with him and wanted him to make love to her? Did that make her a silly lovelorn fool? Or was *she* taking equal advantage of *him*?

From the instant Dmitri phoned him and broke the news, Acheron hadn't been able to stay still or think with his usual logic. Gripped by insane impatience and mounting concern, he just wanted to get back to Sardinia and stand watch over Tabby and Amber. Unfortunately for him, getting a last-minute slot for the jet to take off in

Athens and jumping the queue took longer than he had envisaged. He cursed the fact that he had left them behind in the first place, cursed his conviction that he should protect Tabby at all costs from what Kasma might do next.

Why had he chosen to leave Tabby when he actually wanted to be with her? What did that say about him? That he couldn't recognise his own emotions and was prone to running away from what he couldn't understand? Feelings had never been so intense for him before and he had been torn between a kind of intoxication at the fire of them and a kind of panic at knowing he was out of control. He had never allowed that to happen to him before but he'd had no choice. He had jumped on the panic as an excuse and now he was paying the price. Thee mou, *if anything was to happen to them*, he brooded darkly, his fists clenching aggressively just as his pilot signalled him from across the VIP lounge that they were good to go.

'I really do believe that your husband would prefer you to stay in today,' Dmitri informed Tabby quietly.

Unfortunately, Tabby was in no mood to be grounded like a child and marvelled that Acheron could even think he could give out orders that way through Dmitri, particularly when he had taken off himself at such short notice. What was it? Why was he trying to keep her on the home front? Some sort of control issue on his part? And poor Dmitri was embarrassed to have to say such a thing to her; she could see it in the older man.

'I'm sorry but it's really important that I go out today,' she said levelly. 'I have something I have to buy.'

'Then I'll accompany you and I'll drive, Mrs Dimitrakos,' Dmitri responded with determination.

For the sake of peace, Tabby nodded agreement but knew she was going to have to have a discussion with

Acheron with regard to the intense security presence he maintained in their lives. Was it really necessary that they be guarded and watched over every place they went? Was there a genuine risk of their being robbed or kidnapped? Was there some kind of specific threat out against Acheron?

'You'll be very bored,' she warned Dmitri as she settled into the passenger seat of the SUV and watched another car full of security men follow them out of the entrance to the beach house with wry acceptance.

'It's not a problem. I'm used to going shopping with my wife,' Dmitri told her calmly. 'She can stare at one shop window for ten minutes before she's satisfied she's seen everything.'

Tabby knew she would be even more of a drag because she didn't even know what she was planning to buy and was hoping to be inspired by something she saw. What did you buy for the man who had everything? The massive monthly allowance he had awarded her, however, had piled up in her bank account and thanks to his generosity she had got to spend very little of it, so she had plenty to spend.

Dmitri following behind her, Tabby prowled through the exclusive boutiques and jewellery outlets. Acheron wasn't the sort of guy who wore jewellery. He wore a wedding ring and occasionally cuff links and that was all. But short of copping out by buying him another silk tie when he already had a rail of them, what was she to give him for his thirty-first birthday? Mulling over that thorny issue, she saw the pen. Actually *the* pen was the only possible description for a pen that bore a world-famous designer label. It would cost a fortune, she reckoned. But equally fast she recalled the pen his mother had bought him and decided that the cost was less important than what it meant, although why she was so keen to buy a significant gift for a man who couldn't even be bothered to phone her, she couldn't explain. Maybe it was the desolate thought that the pen might survive with him a lot longer than their marriage and act as a reminder of what they had once shared. Depressing, much? She scolded herself impatiently for her downbeat thoughts.

She bought the pen and arranged for it to be inscribed with his name and the date. She had to make use of the platinum credit card he had given her to make the purchase and, while trying to act as if she spent such sums all the time, she was secretly horrified at spending so much money and worried that Acheron would think she had gone mad. Pale and shaken after that sobering experience, she told Dmitri that she wanted to go for a coffee. He led the way to an outdoor café and insisted on choosing a seat a couple of tables away from her.

She had just bought the most expensive pen in the history of the world, she reflected guiltily, and when he saw the bill he might well freak out and regret telling her that her card had no upper limit. She was sipping her latte slowly, savouring the caffeine, when a shadow fell across her table.

Kasma settled her long elegant body down smoothly into the seat opposite. 'You've been so unavailable you've forced me into all this cloak and dagger stuff,' she complained.

Totally taken aback by the other woman's appearance, Tabby stared at the beautiful brunette with wide, questioning eyes. 'What on earth are you doing here?'

'You're here, Ash is here…where else would I be?' Kasma asked, rolling big dark eyes in apparent disbelief at the question. 'I refuse to believe that you're so stupid that you can't accept that Ash belongs with me.'

'Miss Philippides…' Dmitri broke into the conversation, standing straight and tall beside Kasma's chair. 'Please leave—'

Kasma slung him a defiant glance. 'We're in a public place and I can go where I please on this island. We're not in Greece now.'

'May I suggest then that *we* leave, Mrs Dimitrakos?' Dmitri continued, regarding Tabby expectantly.

Tabby breathed in deep. 'When I've finished my coffee,' she murmured, determined to hear what Kasma had to say since she sure as heck wasn't going to receive any information from Acheron.

Grim-faced, Dmitri retreated to an even closer table.

'I believe in getting straight down to business,' Kasma informed her. 'How much money do you want to walk out on this absurd marriage?'

Dumbstruck, Tabby stared at the older woman. 'You can't be serious.'

'Oh, I'm always serious when it comes to Ash. We belong together and he would have married me, *not* you, had my stepfather not foolishly tried to force the issue in his will,' Kasma contended confidently. 'You must know how proud Ash is.'

'Staying here, entering into this dialogue is a very bad idea, Mrs Dimitrakos,' Dmitri leant closer to spell out.

Kasma shot a vicious burst of Greek at the older man and the look on her face was downright scary. With the sudden suspicion that Dmitri's advice to retreat from the scene might well be the most sensible move, Tabby lifted her bag, settled some money on the table for the bill and stood up. Before she walked away, however, she had something to say. 'No matter how much money you offered me I wouldn't walk out on Acheron,' she murmured tautly. 'I love him.'

'Not as much as I love him, you bitch!' Kasma launched at her in a seething shout of fury that shook Tabby rigid.

Cupping her elbow firmly in his hand, Dmitri walked her away from the café at a fast pace. 'Kasma Philippides is a dangerously unstable woman. Your husband has a restraining order out against her on Greek soil and she's not allowed to approach him or make a nuisance of herself there. You can't talk to her. You can't reason with her. We've learned that the hard way.'

'Ash should've warned me. If he'd warned me, I would've walked away immediately,' Tabby protested defensively. 'I could see that she was obsessed with him at the wedding but I didn't understand how much of a problem she was in his life.'

'He wasn't expecting her to follow you here. He had no idea she was on the island. By the way, he's flying back as we speak.'

Relief swept Tabby. He would finally have to tell her the whole story. But he had had to take out a legal restraining order to keep Kasma at a distance? What had driven him to take his father's stepdaughter to court? That must have taken some nerve, particularly while his father was still alive. Had Kasma been acting like some sort of psycho stalker?

They were driving along the coast road when she noticed that Dmitri kept on looking worriedly in the driving mirror. Tabby glanced over her shoulder to notice the bright red sports car behind them. The driver had long dark hair just like Kasma's.

'She's following us,' Dmitri told her flatly. 'Make sure your belt is safely fastened. I may have to take evasive manoeuvres but I've already alerted the police.'

'Evasive manoeuvres?' Tabby gasped when there was

a sudden jolt at the rear of the car. 'She's trying to ram us? Is she crazy in that tiny little car?'

Dmitri didn't answer. His concentration was on the road because he had speeded up. Tabby's heart was beating very, very fast as she watched in the mirror as the red car tried to catch up with them again. They were zooming round corners so fast that Tabby felt dizzy and she was still watching Kasma's car when it veered across the road into the path of another car travelling the other way.

'Oh, my word, she's crashed…hit someone else!'

Dmitri jammed on the brakes and rammed into Reverse to turn and drive back. He leapt out of the SUV. The team from the other security car were already attending to the victims of the crash, carrying the passenger to the verge, the driver, still conscious, stumbling after them. The red sports car had hit a wall and demolished part of it. Tabby slowly climbed out, her tummy heaving as she approached the scene of frantic activity. Dmitri was talking fast on his phone as he approached her. 'Stay in the car, Mrs Dimitrakos. You don't need to see this. Miss Philippides is dead.'

'Dead?' Tabby was stunned, barely able to credit that the woman who had been speaking to her only minutes earlier could have lost her life.

'She wasn't wearing a belt—she was thrown from the car.'

'And the people who were in the other car?' Tabby asked.

'Very lucky to be alive. The passenger has a head wound and the driver has a leg injury.'

Tabby nodded and got back slowly into the SUV, feeling oddly distanced from everything happening around her. That sensation, which she only vaguely recognised as shock, was still lingering when she gave a brief state-

ment at the police station with a lawyer sitting in, volun-
teering information she couldn't understand in the local
language. That completed, she was stowed in a waiting
room with a cup of coffee until Acheron strode through
the door. He stalked across the room, emanating stormy
tension, and raised her out of her seat with two anxious
hands.

'You are all right? Dmitri swore you were unhurt but
I was afraid to believe him,' Acheron grated half under
his breath, his lean, darkly handsome features taut and
granite hard as he scanned her carefully from head to toe.

'Well, I was fine until you made me spill my coffee,'
she responded unevenly, setting the mug down and rubbing ineffectually at the splashes now adorning her pale
pink top. 'Are we free to leave?'

'Yes, I've made a statement. *Thee mou*,' Acheron murmured fiercely. 'Kasma had a knife in her bag!'

'A *knife*?' Tabby repeated in horror.

'But for Dmitri's presence she might have attacked
you!' Acheron lifted a not quite steady hand and raked
long brown fingers through his luxuriant black hair. 'I
was so scared when I heard she'd come here, I felt sick,'
he confided thickly.

'She's dead,' Tabby reminded him in an undertone.

Acheron released his pent-up breath and said heavily,
'Her brother, Simeon, is on his way to make the funeral
arrangements. He's a decent man. I hope you don't mind
but I've asked him to stay with us.'

'Of course, I don't mind. No matter what's happened,
your father's family deserve your consideration and respect.'

'Melinda's flying back to London,' Acheron volunteered.
'She was responsible for the messages on the mirror.'

'Messages…there was *more* than one?' Tabby queried in consternation.

Acheron told her about the message he had seen at the villa in Tuscany and how Dmitri had instantly worked out that Melinda had to be the perpetrator when the nanny did it a second time. Confronted that same morning after breakfast by Dmitri, Melinda had confessed that Kasma had approached her in London and had offered her a lot of money to leave the messages and to spy on Acheron while keeping Kasma up to date with information on where they were staying. It was Melinda who had warned Dmitri that Kasma was actually on the island, news that had alarmed Acheron into making an immediate return.

The fountain of questions concerning Kasma that had disturbed Tabby earlier in the day was, by that stage, returning fast, but the haunted look in Acheron's lustrous dark eyes and the bleak set of his bronzed face silenced her. He escorted her out to a car, and she slid in, appreciating the air-conditioned cool on her overheated skin.

'I have a lot to explain,' Acheron acknowledged flatly and then he closed his hand over hers.

In a reflexive movement, Tabby rejected the contact and folded her hands together on her lap. 'After the way you behaved that last night and the fact that you haven't been in touch since, I think holding hands would be a bit of a joke,' she said bluntly. 'You don't need to pretend things you don't feel to pacify or comfort me. As you noted, I'm unhurt. It's been a horrible day but I'll get over it without leaning on you.'

'Maybe I want you to lean on me.'

Tabby raised a brow, unimpressed by that unlikely suggestion. 'I'd prefer to fall over and pick myself up. I've been doing it all my life and I've managed just fine.'

Acheron compressed his wide, sensual mouth. 'I

should have explained about her weeks ago but the subject of Kasma rouses a lot of bad memories…and reactions,' he admitted with curt reluctance.

'Kasma's the reason you thought someone might have pushed me down the stairs at the villa,' Tabby grasped finally.

'Maybe she made me a little paranoid but she did destroy my relationship with my father before he died.'

'And that's why he wrote that crazy will,' Tabby guessed.

'I told you that I only met my father's family about eighteen months ago. I only agreed in the first place because it seemed to mean so much to him. What I didn't mention before is that the week before that dinner engagement took place at his home, I met Kasma *without* knowing I was meeting Kasma,' he told her grittily.

Tabby frowned. 'Without knowing it was her?' she echoed. 'How? I mean, *why*?'

'I doubt if I could *ever* adequately explain why from Kasma's point of view. She introduced herself to me as Ariadne. She certainly knew who I was,' he delivered with perceptible bitterness. 'I was in Paris on a stopover between flights and she was staying in the same hotel. I've never believed that was a coincidence. I believe I was set up. I was alone. I was bored. She targeted me and I fell for it…and you could not begin to understand how deeply I regret taking the bait.'

Tabby was studying him with confused eyes. 'The bait?'

'I had a tacky one-night stand with her,' Acheron ground out grudgingly, dark colour accentuating his spectacular cheekbones, his jaw line clenching hard on the admission. 'A couple of stolen hours from a busy schedule of work and travel. I'm being honest here—it meant nothing more to me. Although I treated her with respect I never pretended at any stage that I wanted to see her again.'

Tabby averted her eyes, reflecting that respectful treatment would not have compensated Kasma for his ultimate rejection, when presumably she had persuaded herself that she could expect a much keener and less fleeting response.

'She picked me up in the hotel restaurant. Afterwards she started acting as though she knew me really well. To be frank, it was a freaky experience and I made my excuses and returned to my own room.'

Tabby was swallowing hard at a level of honesty she had not expected to receive from him. 'But if she already knew who you were, why did she lie about her own identity?'

Acheron shrugged a broad shoulder. 'Obviously because I would never have touched her had I known she was my father's precious little girl.'

'His precious little girl?' Tabby queried.

'Her mother was widowed when Kasma was only a baby. My father raised Kasma from the age of three. She was the apple of his eye, his favourite child, and he couldn't see any fault in her,' Acheron advanced tautly, his lips compressing. 'When I walked into the family dinner the week after the hotel encounter I was appalled to realise that Kasma was my father's stepchild and furious that she had lied to me and put me in that position, but that wasn't all I had to worry about. Before I could even decide how to behave, she stood up and announced that she had been saving a little surprise for everyone. And that surprise—according to her—was that she and I were *dating*.'

'Oh, my word…' Tabby was as stunned as he must've been by that development. 'And that one…er…episode at the hotel was really the extent of your relationship with her?'

'It was, but not according to Kasma. She had a very fertile imagination and over the months that followed she began acting like a stalker, flying round the world, turning up wherever I was,' he explained, lines of strain bracketing his mouth as he recalled that period. 'She tried to force her way into my life while telling my father a pack of lies about me. She told him I'd cheated on her, she told him I'd got her pregnant and then she told him she'd had a miscarriage. He fell for every one of her tales and nothing I could say would persuade him that my relationship with his stepdaughter was a fantasy she had made up. And having made that first mistake by getting involved with her that night at the hotel, I felt I had brought the whole nightmare down on my own head.'

'I don't think so—'

'It was casual sex but there was nothing casual about it,' Acheron opined grimly. 'I went to bed with a woman who was a stranger and maybe I deserved what I got.'

'Not when she set out to deliberately deceive you and then tried to trap you into a relationship,' Tabby declared stoutly. 'I don't agree with the way you behaved with her but she was obviously a disturbed personality.'

'She assaulted a woman I spent time with last year, which was why I was so concerned about your safety and Amber's.'

'What did she do?'

'She forced her way into my apartment and punched the woman while ranting about how I belonged to her.' He grimaced at the recollection. 'My father begged me to use my influence and prevent it from going to court but I was at the end of my rope. Kasma was dangerous and she needed treatment but as long as her family turned a blind eye and I swallowed what she was dishing out, she was free to do as she liked. The court accepted that she was lying and had never had a relationship with me and therefore had no excuse whatsoever for attacking the woman in my apartment and calling it a domestic dispute.'

'Didn't that convince your father that you were telling him the truth?'

'No, Kasma managed to convince him that I must've bribed someone and she had been stitched up by me to protect my own reputation,' he proffered with unconcealed regret. 'The sole saving grace was that after that court case I was able to take out a restraining order against her and at least that kept her out of my hair while I was on Greek soil.'

Tabby slowly shook her head, which was reeling with his revelations. 'Why didn't you tell me about her? Why wouldn't you explain?'

His bold bronzed profile clenched hard. 'I was ashamed of the whole business and I didn't want to frighten you either. My wealth didn't protect me from the fact that Kasma could still get to me almost everywhere I went. You have no idea how powerless I felt when she even managed to gatecrash the wedding because I didn't want to make a scene with my father's family present,' he confessed grittily. 'I didn't want to publicise my problems with her while my father was still alive either. She caused him enough grief with her wild stories about how badly I'd treated her.'

'So why on earth did he want you to marry her?' Tabby queried, struggling to understand that angle.

'He believed she loved me and he genuinely thought I owed her a wedding ring. He blamed me for her increasingly hysterical outbursts and strange behaviour.'

'That was probably easier for him than dealing with

the real problem, which was *her*. He would've had more faith in you if he had ever had the chance to get to know you properly,' Tabby opined, resting a soothing hand down on his. 'Kasma had the advantage and he trusted her and that gave her the power to put you through an awful ordeal.'

'It's over now,' Acheron reminded her flatly. 'Her brother, Simeon, believed me and tried to persuade her to see a therapist. Perhaps if she had listened she might not have died today.'

'It's not your fault though,' Tabby countered steadily. 'You weren't capable of fixing whatever was broken in her.'

Acheron groaned out loud. 'It's so *not* sexy that you feel sorry for me now.'

'I don't feel sorry for you. I just think you've been put through the mill a bit,' Tabby paraphrased awkwardly. 'No wonder you don't like clingy, needy women after that experience.'

'I wouldn't mind if you clung occasionally,' Acheron admitted.

Tabby rolled her eyes at him. 'Stop being such a smoothie…it's wasted on me.'

'What do you mean?' Acheron asked harshly as the limo drew up outside the beach house.

'It's not necessary to charm me. We both had good reasons to get married and that's the only fulfilment either of us require from our agreement. You got a wife and, hopefully, I will eventually be able to adopt Amber,' Tabby spelt out as she slid out of the car and walked into the house.

'That's not how I feel,' Acheron informed her stubbornly.

'We're not twin souls and nor are we required to be,'

Tabby flipped back, walking through to the lounge, which stood with doors wide open to the terrace and the view of the cove, draperies fluttering softly in the slight breeze that never seemed to leave the coast. 'I think we're overdue a little plain speaking here.'

Outside, she leant up against the rail bordering the terrace and folded her arms in a defensive position. She knew what she needed to say. She was more than half-way to getting her heart broken by the stupid, danger-ous pretence that she was on a *real* honeymoon with a *real* husband! How had she let that happen? How had she let herself fall in love with a male who was simply doing what he had to do to give the appearance of being a newly married man?

'Meaning?' Acheron prompted, stilling in the door-way, six feet plus inches of stunning male beauty and charisma.

Tabby looked him over with carefully blank eyes. He was gorgeous; he had always been gorgeous from the crown of his slightly curly black head to the soles of his equally perfect feet. He focused sizzling dark golden eyes on her with interrogative intensity.

'Tabby?' he prompted afresh.

'Unlike you I call a spade a spade. I don't wrap it up.'

'I appreciate that about you…that what you say you mean,' he countered steadily.

Tabby threw her slight shoulders back, violet eyes wide and appealing. 'Look, let's just bring the whole charade to an end here and now,' she urged. 'Melinda was spying on us and she's gone. We've done all the newly happily married stuff for weeks and now surely we can both go back to normal?'

'Normal?'

Tabby was wondering what the matter with him was,

for it was not like him to take a back seat in any argument. Furthermore, he looked strained, having lost colour while his spectacular strong bone structure had set rigid below his bronzed skin. 'We were strangers with a legal agreement, Ash,' she reminded him painfully. 'We've met the terms, put on the show and now surely we can return to being ourselves again behind closed doors at least?'

'Is that what you want?' he pressed curtly, lean brown hands closing into fists by his side. 'Don't you think this is a decision best shelved for a less traumatic day?'

Tabby lifted her chin, her heart squeezing tight inside her chest, pain like a sharp little arrow twisting inside her because, of course, it was not what she wanted. She wanted him; she was in love with him but she had to protect herself, had to force herself to accept that what they had shared was only a pretence. 'No.'

'You want to go back to where we started out?' Acheron demanded starkly.

Tabby dropped her shoulders, her eyes veiling. 'No, I just want us to be honest and not faking anything.'

Acheron breathed in very slow and deep, dark golden eyes glittering like fireworks below the shield of his luxuriant black lashes. 'I *haven't* been faking anything…'

Tabby's dazed mind ran over all the romancing, the sexing, the hand-holding, the fun, and she blinked in bemusement. 'But *of course* you were faking.'

'It may have started out that way, but it ended up real, *yineka mou.*' Acheron surveyed her steadily but she knew he was putting up a front because he was really, really tense.

'How…*real*?' Tabby questioned, her heart thumping like mad.

Acheron lifted his arms and spread his hands in an oddly defenceless gesture. 'I fell in love with you…'

Tabby almost fell over in shock, her brain refusing to accept that he could have said that he loved her. 'I don't believe you. You're just scared that I'm about to walk out on our marriage agreement and you'll lose your company—but you don't *need* to be scared of that happening because I wouldn't do that to you. I'm still as determined to adopt Amber as I ever was, so I couldn't do that even if I wanted to,' she pointed out honestly.

'When I try to say, "I love you" for the first time in my life to a woman, you could at least listen to what I'm saying and stop talking a lot of rubbish!' Acheron shot back at her with scorching effect.

Tabby was struck dumb by that little speech. He was serious? He wasn't joking, faking, trying to manipulate her in some nefarious way? She stared back at him fixedly.

'And it was bloody hard to say too!' Acheron added in angry complaint at her response.

'I'm in shock,' Tabby mumbled shakily. 'I didn't think you had any feelings for me.'

'I tried very hard not to. I fought it every step of the way,' Acheron admitted ruefully. 'But in the end you got to me and you got to me so hard I ran away from it.'

'Ran away?' Tabby almost whispered in growing disbelief.

'I was feeling strange and that's why I took off on business…to give myself a little breathing space,' Acheron qualified tautly. 'But the minute I got away I realised I only wanted to come back and be with you.'

Tabby blinked slowly, struggling to react to that explanation when all her crazy head was full of was a single statement: that he loved her. *He loves me.* She tasted the idea, savoured it, very nearly careened across the terrace and flattened him to the tiles in gratitude, but mercifully retained enough restraint to stay where she was. 'You got cold feet, didn't you?' she guessed.

Acheron nodded. 'It was a little overwhelming when I realised what was wrong with me.'

Tabby moved closer. 'No, it wasn't anything wrong with you. It was a good thing, a wonderful thing…you love me. I love you.'

'If you feel the same way I do, why the hell are you putting me through this torture?' Acheron demanded rawly.

Tabby almost laughed, a sense of intoxication gripping her as she searched his darkly handsome features and the masculine bewilderment etched there. 'Talking about love is torture?'

Acheron rested his arms down on her slim shoulders and breathed, 'I thought once I said it, that would be that, but I was scared you wouldn't feel the same way and that you wanted it all to be fake.'

Tabby closed her arms round him and snuggled close. 'No, real is much better than fake. So, does this mean we're really and truly married?'

'Absolutely,' Acheron confirmed, and bent to lift her up into his arms. 'It also means we're going to be adoptive parents together because I sort of developed a fondness for Amber as well. Seems this love business is contagious…'

'Wow…' Tabby framed as he carried her upstairs to their bedroom and Teresa, with the baby in her arms, retreated back into the nursery with a warm smile. 'But how did it happen?'

Acheron arranged her on the bed with the care of a man setting up an art installation and stared down at her for what felt like ages. 'I think it started when I realised I was with a woman who was willing to sacrifice her home and her business to look after her sick best friend and child. I respect that level of loyalty and unselfishness. I respect what you were willing to do to retain custody of Amber even though I was pretty rough and crude about everything at the time. You stuck it out... you stood up to me...'

'And out of that came love?' Tabby whispered in shock.

'Out of those experiences came a woman I couldn't live without,' traded Acheron with a tender look in his lustrous dark eyes that she had never seen before. '*Thee mou*...if you had still wanted the fake marriage and the divorce I don't know what I would've done.'

'I don't want a divorce...I don't ever want to let go of you,' Tabby confided against his shirtfront.

'That desire is just about to come in very handy, *agape mou*,' Acheron murmured thickly, claiming her ripe mouth with his own, sending a thrill of heat and anticipation travelling through her relaxed body.

About an hour later, Acheron leapt naked out of bed to retrieve his trousers and dig into a pocket to produce a jewellers' box, which he pressed into her hand. 'I know it's not your birthday for another twenty-four hours but this is burning a hole in my pocket,' he admitted ruefully.

Tabby opened the box to find an unusual ring in the shape of a rose with a ruby at the centre.

'What do you think?' Acheron demanded anxiously. 'I wanted you to know that it was made in the image of your tattoo because it will always remind me what made you the special woman you are.'

'It's...gorgeous!' Tabby carolled as he removed his late mother's engagement ring from her wedding finger and replaced it with the new ring. The diamonds on the rose petals caught the sunlight and cast a rainbow of little sparkling reflections across the white bedding. 'But why on earth do you think I am so special when I'm so ordinary?'

'You're special because in spite of all the bad things that happened to you, you still have an open heart and a loving spirit. You love Amber, you love me—'

'So much,' Tabby emphasised feelingly as she smiled up at him. 'Although you might feel you love me a little less when you see what I spent on my credit card.'

'Never,' Acheron contradicted. 'You're the least extravagant person I know.'

'You might change your mind on that score,' she warned him, hoping he at least appreciated the gift of the pen on his birthday in three days' time.

'I love you,' he breathed softly, his attention locked on her smiling face.

He had fallen in love with her, he had genuinely fallen in love with her, Tabby savoured finally, and she allowed the happiness to well up inside her along with a sense of release from all anxiety. Somehow, by the most mysterious process of love known to mankind, two people who had loathed each other on sight because of their misconceptions had found love and formed a happy home and family and she was delirious with the joy of that miracle.

Tabby sucked in her tummy and studied the mirror. No, it was pointless: she was pregnant and there was no escaping that pregnant apple shape, no matter how well cut her maternity clothing was. With a wry smile at the foolishness of her vanity, Tabby went downstairs to check the last-minute arrangements for Amber's fourth birthday party.

The party was a catered affair, everything set up to entertain a whole posse of Amber's nursery-school friends.

There was a bouncy castle in the garden of their London town house, purchased after the birth of their first child, Andreus, who was already a rumbustious noisy toddler. Closely pursued by his nanny, Teresa, who had become as much a part of the family as the children, Andreus hurtled across the hall to throw his arms up to be lifted by his mother.

Tabby tried not to wince at the weight of her son, but, at eight months along in her second pregnancy, lifting a child who was already outstripping his peers in size was becoming quite a challenge. He hugged her tight, black curls like his father's silky against her throat, her own big blue eyes bright in his little smiling face. Sometimes, Tabby was still afraid that if she blinked her happy family life would disappear and she would discover she had been trapped in an inordinately convincing and wonderful daydream. And then she would look at Acheron and the children and she would be soothed by the closeness of their bonds.

Admittedly she would never have picked Acheron out as a keen father figure when she first met him, but exposure to Amber's charms had soon raised a desire in Acheron to have a child of his own. By the time the legalities of Amber's adoption had been settled and she had officially become their daughter, Tabby had been expecting Andreus. The little girl whom Tabby was currently carrying had been more of an accidental conception, thanks to a little spur-of-the-moment lovemaking on the beach in Sardinia where they had first found love, and which of all Acheron's properties they visited the most, although they had quickly extended the house to add on more bedroom capacity.

His father's widow, Ianthe, and her two surviving children had stayed with them there to attend Kasma's fu-

neral. It had been a sad and sobering occasion but it had
also done much to build a bridge between Ash and his father's former family. Ianthe had admitted to having been
seriously worried about her daughter's mental health but
Ash's late father, Angelos, had refused to face up to that
reality. Kasma's brother, Simeon, and his family also had
young children and the two couples had become close
friends since that last sad encounter.

The front door opened and Andreus scrambled down
from his mother's arms to hurl himself violently at Acheron, shouting, 'Dad!' at the top of his voice.

Tabby watched Acheron scoop his son up, and a warm
smile curved her generous mouth because she never loved
Acheron more than when she saw him with the children.
He was kind, affectionate and patient, all the things that
they had both so badly lacked when they were kids themselves. 'I thought you wouldn't make it back in time.'

'Where's the birthday girl?' Acheron enquired.

Amber came racing downstairs, a vivid little figure
clad in a flouncy new party dress, and flung herself at
her father with very little more circumspection than her
toddler brother. 'You're here!' she carolled. 'You're here
for my party.'

'Of course, I am,' Acheron said in the act of producing a present from behind his back, only to laugh as the
housekeeper opened the door to let Amber's best friend
and her mother enter and the two little girls went running
off together. 'So much for being flavour of the month
there!' he teased.

'But you're always my favourite flavour,' Tabby
rushed to assure him in an undertone before she went to
greet the arriving guests.

Acheron watched her acting hostess with quiet ad-
miration. *His* Tabby, the best and luckiest find he had

ever made, always warm, sunny and bright and still the
most loving creature he had ever met. It didn't surprise
him in the slightest that he loved her more with every
passing year.

* * * * *

MILLS & BOON

THE HEART OF ROMANCE

A ROMANCE FOR EVERY KIND OF READER

MODERN

Prepare to be swept off your feet by sophisticated, sexy and seductive heroes, in some of the world's most glamourous and romantic locations, where power and passion collide.
8 stories per month.

HISTORICAL

Escape with historical heroes from time gone by. Whether your passion is for wicked Regency Rakes, muscled Vikings or rugged Highlanders, awaken the romance of the past.
6 stories per month.

MEDICAL

Set your pulse racing with dedicated, delectable doctors in the high-pressure world of medicine, where emotions run high and passion, comfort and love are the best medicine.
6 stories per month.

True Love

Celebrate true love with tender stories of heartfelt romance, from the rush of falling in love to the joy a new baby can bring, and a focus on the emotional heart of a relationship.
8 stories per month.

Desire

Indulge in secrets and scandal, intense drama and plenty of sizzling hot action with powerful and passionate heroes who have it all: wealth, status, good looks…everything but the right woman.
6 stories per month.

HEROES

Experience all the excitement of a gripping thriller, with an intense romance at its heart. Resourceful, true-to-life women and strong, fearless men face danger and desire - a killer combination!
8 stories per month.

DARE

Sensual love stories featuring smart, sassy heroines you'd want as a best friend, and compelling intense heroes who are worthy of them.
4 stories per month.

To see which titles are coming soon, please visit

millsandboon.co.uk/nextmonth